Also by Alexandra Vasti

THE BELVOIR'S LIBRARY SERIES

Ne'er Duke Well

Earl Crush

Ladies in Hating

HALIFAX HELLIONS NOVELLAS

In Which Margo Halifax Earns Her Shocking Reputation

In Which Matilda Halifax Learns the Value of Restraint

In Which Winnie Halifax Is Utterly Ruined

Scandal of the Summer

ALEXANDRA VASTI

CORVUS

First published in trade paperback in the United States in 2026 by
St Martin's Publishing Group, an imprint of Pan Macmillan

First published in paperback in Great Britain in 2026 by Corvus,
an imprint of Atlantic Books Ltd.

10 9 8 7 6 5 4 3 2 1

A CIP catalogue record for this book is available from the British Library.

Paperback ISBN: 978 1 80546 650 5
E-book ISBN: 978 1 80546 651 2

Printed and bound by CPI Group (UK) Ltd, Croydon CR0 4YY

Corvus
An imprint of Atlantic Books Ltd
Ormond House
26–27 Boswell Street
London
WC1N 3JZ

www.atlantic-books.co.uk

Product safety EU representative: Authorised Rep Compliance Ltd., Ground Floor,
71 Lower Baggot Street, Dublin, D02 P593, Ireland. www.arccompliance.com

For Colleen Kelly, who provided truly heroic levels of emotional support throughout the writing, revising, and titling of this book. (I fear we will never top the brilliance of The Pirate Inside Me.*)*

And for Matt, who was victimized by hedges repeatedly as we drove all over Devon and Cornwall while I did research for this book. I'm sorry that, when I thought we were dying, my last words were, "Oh shit, the rental car!"

This novel includes references to past food insecurity, incarceration, parental death, and political and military conflict during the Napoleonic Wars. It also includes brief on-page gun violence.

Scandal of the Summer

Chapter 1

On the day Ruby Ballimore ruined her own life, she had ink stains on her gloves and was dressed like a sugared pineapple.

The dinner party had not been going well. The Marquess of Gravesmuir, having recently married off his eldest son to an American dry goods heiress, was trying very hard to pretend that he'd always had a great deal of money. There were an astonishing number of guests in the drawing room, and Ruby was—unfortunately—the only one who seemed to *glisten* in the candlelight.

She looked at the whirling ladies on the dance floor and then down at her frock. Her skirt was covered in tiny diamond-shaped flounces, each of which was Pomona green and featured a mirrored spangle that shot sparks of light in all directions. More green flounced up around her sleeves and neck in a design that had seemed quite regal in the illustrated plate but on Ruby looked rather a lot like tropical fronds.

The modiste on Albemarle Street had assured her that the

gown was the height of fashion, and Ruby suspected that it probably was. Somewhere.

Unfortunately, that somewhere did not seem to be the Gravesmuir town house.

Generally, Ruby had an excellent eye for color and balance. She'd been misled, she supposed, by her own unfortunate optimism as she'd looked down at the gilt-tipped fashion plate. The dress was bold but not outré. Eye-catching but still tasteful. Au courant but still somehow in conversation with classical design. *This* was the gown that would mark Ruby's conquest of society.

Finally. After four Seasons.

It did not seem to be working.

The dinner itself had not gone so badly. There had been eleven French courses to contend with, but Ruby had kept hold of herself during most of them. She'd lectured the industrialist on her left for a handful of minutes about the Egyptian greyhound design on the sideboard, but when she'd realized she was coming close to a discussion of cinerary urns, she'd managed to cut herself off. He'd looked only *slightly* green, and that might well have been a reflection off the purée de pois.

But the dancing had been a disaster. She'd thought the Earl of Kilmornay was asking her to dance—which he wasn't—and then she'd nearly trampled Isobel Crane in her haste to accept Kilmornay's non-request. Isobel, one of the few debutantes even shorter than Ruby, had been a trifle squashed, and so Ruby had stopped and attempted to help her restore her hairpiece.

The hairpiece had looked rather like a Greco-Roman swan sculpture, a fact that Ruby had been cheerfully relating to Isobel when she realized that Kilmornay was there, trying to secure Isobel for the waltz, and she, Ruby, was grasping Isobel's beaded swan pin with an enthusiasm that was preventing Isobel from escaping.

Also, her father had seen all of it.

False hope ought to be outlawed, Ruby thought, and morosely examined her gloves.

The ink thereupon had come from newsprint, now safely tucked in her reticule. She knew better than to read the newspaper with her gloves on, but she'd seen the headline from across the room—PRINCESS SERAFINA'S CORNWALL VISIT CANCELED!—and couldn't quite stop herself from crossing to the sideboard to pick it up.

It seemed distantly possible that an apparent interest in the news would help disguise the fact that no one thus far had asked Ruby to dance.

Moreover, if she familiarized herself with the princess's movements, she might have something to talk about with her father in the carriage on the way home. Her father, the Earl of Hangleton, was ambassador to the princess's home principality of Monfalcone, a tiny autonomous state just south of the kingdom of Lombardy-Venetia. The earl, currently on home leave in England, had been thrilled by the public's avidity for gossip about the mysterious and glamorous princess. He was delighted every time she appeared in the papers—and so Ruby was delighted by proxy.

Perhaps Ruby's familiarity with Serafina's schedule would demonstrate to her father that she was finally ready to assist him in his social duties, despite her dismal showing at the party.

Perhaps some particular knowledge of the princess would prove to her father that Ruby was *trying*.

She was so engrossed in the state of her gloves that she didn't at first register the sound of her name.

"There she is! Lady Ruby!"

She blinked. That was Gravesmuir's bluff voice, plummy and slightly overloud in the hubbub of the party. He was, indubitably, headed toward her, backed by a small crowd that—oh God—included Ruby's father.

She thrust her hands behind her back, though she feared her father had already noticed the state of her gloves. "Good evening . . . my lord?"

It sounded like a question—which, she supposed, it was. She would not have imagined that Gravesmuir could identify her.

"Lady Ruby," Gravesmuir said again. "I have it on good authority that you are something of an expert on Greco-Roman antiquities. Vases, masks. Things of that sort."

"Oh." Ruby tried not to gape. "Why, yes." Had her *father* told him that? Surely her father would have mentioned that her most recent academic paper had been on Egyptian masks, not Greco-Roman, though really she could be conversant on various classical styles . . .

But her father was not looking especially pleased. "Ruby does find ways to divert herself."

Ruby swallowed. Evidently someone else had spoken of her interests to Gravesmuir. *Not* her father. She tried to force her mouth to curve.

"Oh indeed!" Gravesmuir chuckled. "These modern young ladies and their accomplishments. Astonishing, how they have time for it all." He held out his elbow to Ruby. "Come, my dear. Take a look at my most recent acquisitions. See if you recognize them."

She winced a little, but her father was nodding at her. *Behave yourself tonight*, he'd told her in the carriage. *This is an important dinner for me, Ruby. I can't afford any blunders.*

Any of *her* blunders, he'd meant.

She did not want to let her father down. She took Gravesmuir's arm and pinned a smile to her face as the marquess led her around the circumference of the drawing room.

Inside a small sculpture gallery, more of the party guests milled and drank champagne. It was a lovely room, freshly decorated, still smelling faintly of varnish and sawdust. Gravesmuir had had octagonal columns installed to frame the chandeliers, and Ruby suspected that whoever had designed them had been inspired by the peristyle of the Temple of Theseus in Athens. A dozen midnight-blue draperies hung from a paler-blue ceiling, and each curtain framed a gleaming white statue centered upon a white marble plinth.

Ruby blinked.

"Well, my dear?" demanded Gravesmuir. "Tell me what you think of it." He smiled at her and then at the assembled company. "I had the whole gallery designed for these sculptures, you know. Can't let a treasure like this be hidden away in some dusty museum."

"A treasure?" Ruby repeated blankly.

"Why yes, of course. I had the marbles brought over from Monastiraki just last month. Safer here than there, I always say."

"From Monastiraki?" She couldn't seem to stop echoing his words as she stared at the sculptures, spiderwebbed with cracks and bright, bright white against the drapes.

"Indeed. Have you heard of it?" He chuckled. "Of course you have, with your hobby. Tell your father here he ought to take you there next time he's on the Continent. My friend who brought the statues over could no doubt fill you in on the region. A great man, Professor Quenby—an archaeologist—"

"I've been there," Ruby got out. "But your statues have not."

Gravesmuir stopped speaking, his face fixed in a half smile. "I beg your pardon?"

"These statues did not come from Greece."

Gravesmuir laughed again. Too loud. A flush rose on his cheeks like a slow cloud. "Of course they did. Quenby brought them over himself."

"He didn't," Ruby said. "No one did. They're fakes."

In all her four Seasons, Ruby had never before brought an entire room to a hush before. Something cold and terrible sank in her stomach like a stone.

"Ruby," her father said. He was trying to make it a joke, a scrap of amusement, but even the noted diplomat couldn't quite manage it. Her name in his mouth sounded like a warning.

Gravesmuir, meanwhile, had gone from red to white. "I paid a fortune in scaffolding—and the excavators—the firman—I assure you, child, the cost of the ship journey from Greece to Malta alone was—"

"These statues have never been to Greece," Ruby said. "They're all wrong. The color's off. There's no shading. There ought to be a crust on the marble—a patina. It shouldn't be *white* like that. And the—the stone isn't the right texture, it's cracked—"

"That's *enough*, Ruby," hissed her father.

"That's weathering," Gravesmuir said. "Thousands of years of—"

"That's not how stone weathers in Greece." Her voice sounded odd. Far away. Part of her was shouting, *Stop talking, Ruby!* But just as she had in the dining room, and in the middle of the ballroom, and a thousand other times in her too-blunt, too-enthusiastic life, she couldn't call the words to a halt. "These sculptures look more like Coade stone, only perhaps not properly fired. Devon clay, I'd say."

Gravesmuir seemed half strangled by his own ire. "And now we see why a little learning is a dangerous thing, don't we, my dear?" He turned back to the room at large. "Quenby? Come over here and tell Lady Ruby the story about bringing the statues through the Tyrrhenian Sea in a maelstrom. Sliding across the decks with ropes tied to the masts . . ."

His words trailed off.

At the side of the room, Ruby caught a glimpse of a well-built man of middle height—gray hair, stooped, spectacles—just as he slipped out the door.

A very peculiar feeling seemed to be rushing down her body, chilling the tips of her fingers, freezing her legs to the ground.

"Quenby?" Gravesmuir said again. "Did you hear me?"

There was no answer. The party had gone strangely still, the guests all frozen with their champagne glasses halfway to their mouths.

"Quenby!" Gravesmuir said again, a bit louder. And then, very suddenly: "Stop him! Stop him before he gets away!"

The room rushed back into sound and motion. Eyes—there were dozens of eyes on her, fans fluttering across faces, bodies swirling toward her and then away.

Fakes, did she say? Gravesmuir's marbles, yes—fakes—

Special dispensation from Parliament to acquire them, I heard— half his brand-new fortune—

Is he gone? That professor? Did someone stop him, for God's sake? Can't they catch him—

Ruby Ballimore—yes, Hangleton's elder daughter, the strange one—

Her father gripped her arm. His voice was low, whispered beneath the clamor of the crowd. "I'll have them call the carriage. Damn it, Ruby—do you understand what you've *done*?"

And, with a swell of horror, Ruby did.

Malcolm Archer flung himself onto the deck of his sloop. "Time to go," he gasped. "Quenby's dead."

Gerry and Lamentation, who'd been playing a hand of cards beneath the mast, leapt to their feet. Wall, who'd already been on his feet, put his hands on his substantial waist and glared at Archer. "What do you mean, 'Quenby's dead'?"

Archer swiped water out of his face. He'd dropped Quenby's spectacles in the mews behind Gravesmuir's town house and found a trough to dunk his head to rid himself of the hair powder, but he was still dripping despite the lengthy sprint back to the docks.

"Slain. Extinguished. Sent to his watery demise in a puddle of slime." Archer shrugged, ducked around Wall's bulk, and threw himself at the line that held the anchor.

"Tell me you at least got Gravesmuir's money," Wall said. His voice was pleading, but he too had begun to make the *Delphinium* ready.

Archer paused, one hand on the line.

"Don't," Wall groaned. "Don't say it."

"I got some of Gravesmuir's money."

"Don't *lie* either!"

Archer grimaced and went back to work on the anchor.

He hadn't got even half the money that he and Gravesmuir had agreed upon for the marbles. He supposed he shouldn't be surprised—the marquess had been perfectly willing to carve the friezes right off the bloody Acropolis. Archer shouldn't have supposed that that variety of thieving blackguard would be eager to pay the debts he owed, even to his dear friend, the now-departed Professor Quenby.

When Gravesmuir had invited Archer to his dinner party—well, invited Professor Quenby, who also happened to be a privateer-turned-confidence-artist named Malcolm Archer—it had seemed a fine opportunity to make another delicate play for the funds. Gravesmuir had wanted Quenby to show off, to brag about how difficult it had been to acquire the sculptures and how precious and important they were.

Archer had wanted his money.

He and Lamentation and Gerry and Wall and Eugénie down below—they *needed* the money.

So Archer had put on the Quenby disguise and prepared to make up another pack of lies about the marbles, which had actually come from a devious little sculptor in Dorset who apparently wasn't as tricky as she thought she was.

Archer was good at talking. The lies were always the easy part—easier than the Quenby costume or the sail from Cornwall to the London Docks.

Easier than keeping his crew together and fed, and making them believe that everything would be all right.

He'd been lying through his teeth and happy as a clam—though he still hadn't secured any coin from Gravesmuir—when he'd heard the little blond say that the sculptures were fakes.

For the briefest of moments, Archer had supposed he'd be able to talk his way out of the situation, spin shit-covered straw into golden thread and weave a dream out of it. The story about the sea crossing—Gravesmuir had always liked that one, and it had the benefit of springing from Archer's very real days under the rear admiral during the wars. He could tell that one, and Gravesmuir's guests would squeal and sigh and laugh, and everything would be fine.

He'd get his money. His crew would be safe. They would all go home together.

But then the girl had kept going. She'd been undeterred by Gravesmuir's growing outrage, by the other man's hissed order to keep quiet.

She knew what she was about. For all she looked like a confection—short, plump, pink-cheeked in her sparkling frock—she'd been grim and stubborn as she'd spoken. As ruthless as a knife.

Ten sentences. It had taken her all of ten sentences to demolish six months' investment and the security of Archer's precarious, half-built life.

Lamentation's curly blond head popped in front of Archer's face, where he'd been staring blindly at the water. "Captain? We can't set the sails until we know our heading."

Archer blinked back the desire to throw himself into the sea and instead made himself grin at his former bosun. *Everything's going to be fine, you see? Look at my smile and know I'll keep us safe.* "Home," he said.

Lamentation's gold brows came together. "Home?"

"Yes," Archer said. "Back to Pomeroy House."

He could come up with another plan. Another way to keep his people fed.

He had to.

Chapter 2

Sandwiched in between her two best friends at the British Museum, Ruby considered the soulless eyes of a stuffed golden-crested crane.

There was a three-foot radius of empty space around her. Complete social ruin came with one silver lining at least—it was certainly easier to talk.

"Ruby, dearest," Alice said delicately, "are you entirely certain you wish to be out and about?"

Ruby turned to face her friends. Lady Alice Eppington—only child of the disgraced Marquess of Rosthwaite—gazed back at her, dark-fringed cerulean eyes very soft. Tamsin Drake, by contrast, appeared barely able to smother her fury. Her freckled face was pink with outrage, which made an interesting aesthetic contrast with her cropped auburn hair.

Ruby's chest felt tight, and she reminded herself very firmly of her resolve. This was going to work. It was going to be *wonderful*.

"Yes," she said. "I'm certain. I've asked the two of you here because I have an idea. One we could not discuss in my drawing room.”

Unfortunately, Alice and Tamsin looked more dismayed at this pronouncement than Ruby might have wished.

“Do you?” Alice said. She sounded extremely polite. “Is this similar to the time you had us dress up as the Three Fates at the Yardsleys’ ball?”

Ruby hid a wince. That had not gone well. She’d taken the outfits rather far, and it had not been a masquerade.

“Not like that,” she said. “Much better than that.”

“Perhaps more like the time you staged a reenactment of the Battle of Thermopylae in Kensington Gardens?” Tamsin asked.

“Of course not, because that was for a paper I was writing, as you know perfectly well, and—”

There was a small commotion at the entrance to the avian exhibit, and Ruby felt her words die in her mouth. At the door stood a handful of familiar ladies, dressed in pale summer colors and delicate straw hats. Ruby knew each one; they’d all debuted the same year as herself and Alice.

At the sight of Ruby, Alice, and Tamsin, the ladies’ eyes widened. Their cheeks went pink and their gloved hands went to their mouths. And then, like a flock of birds, they all rushed as one in the opposite direction.

Ruby’s heart beat hard against her ribs.

Tamsin’s face went even redder. “This is absurd,” she snapped. “I don’t understand why everyone is acting as though Ruby pissed on Gravesmuir’s sculptures in the drawing room.”

“It’s not so bad,” Alice murmured. She was looking down at her gloves, and her dark curls had fallen across her brow. “It will be forgotten in time, Ruby. I’m certain it will.”

Ruby took a breath. For all her friends' reassurances, she knew precisely why her revelation in Gravesmuir's gallery had proven so disastrous. It was not just that Gravesmuir had been revealed as a gullible fool to the *ton*. The discovery of how thoroughly and expensively he had been hoodwinked had also drawn the attention of Gravesmuir's creditors—to whom, it turned out, Gravesmuir owed a very great deal of money.

The marquess could no longer shop on Regent Street or fence in his parlor. His social invitations had dried up. And Ruby's father, who had relied on Gravesmuir for political support, had lost one of his most important allies.

Tamsin was still shaking her head. "There's nothing to forget! *Ruby* didn't do anything wrong. She has a brain in her head, that's all. My God, don't tell anyone a woman is able to possess such a thing, or they'll start a petition to drain them out through our noses for the benefit of medical science."

As she always did, Ruby felt a surge of gratitude for Tamsin's bloodthirsty defense, for her stout rejection of their society's hypocrisies. Tamsin had courted scandal from her very first day in society. She gambled for money and wore her hair cropped; she was, as everyone knew perfectly well, a sapphist. Her parents, the Viscount and Viscountess Drake, had despaired of their unconventional eldest daughter, who never seemed touched by the censure heaped upon her.

But at this particular moment, Ruby's attention wasn't fixed upon Tamsin—nor was it fixed upon herself.

Ruby was thinking about Alice.

Alice—endlessly hopeful, impossibly kind—had brightened when she'd seen the women who'd once been their friends. And when they'd turned away, Alice had flinched.

Ruby's heart was still beating too hard. But for the first time in what seemed a very long parade of conversation and card parties and failures, Ruby knew the right thing to do.

"It doesn't matter," she said. "About them. About any of them. Let me tell you why I asked you to come."

She gestured with the reticule in her hands. It was the same one she'd brought with her to Gravesmuir's disastrous dinner party, gold-spangled to match her ill-fated pineapple gown.

It still had the folded newspaper inside. And for the thousandth time since Gravesmuir's dinner, Ruby pulled the paper out.

PRINCESS SERAFINA'S CORNWALL VISIT CANCELED!

Beneath the headline, some breathless journalist had related a lengthy description of Pomeroy House, the holiday home of the Monfalcone princess. Princess Serafina had not set foot in Cornwall since she'd acquired the estate two years ago in 1815, but the English public's ardent enthusiasm for the exquisite, fashionable, and extremely wealthy princess seemed to bring the mansion to public attention every time she was rumored to be visiting.

This time, the visit had been canceled due to some new outbreak of political discord in Monfalcone. Given the sheer number of royal siblings and cousins, infighting seemed to be the norm, rather than an anomaly—a situation that perhaps explained why the princess had not left the Continent in a decade.

"Pomeroy House," Ruby said as she brandished the paper in Tamsin and Alice's direction. "I think we should go there."

Tamsin and Alice did not appear instantly won over by the brilliance of the idea. In fact, they both seemed to be looking at Ruby as though she were back in the pineapple gown.

"You think we should go to Cornwall?" Alice said after a

moment. The expression of puzzlement on her face did not in any way detract from her extraordinary beauty. "Can I ask why?"

"Because," Ruby said, "London is not . . . is not . . ."

Is not working out. Is not going to work out. Is never going to be anything but the place where I am a disappointment.

"Is not hospitable," she said finally. "In Cornwall, we could do as we like. I can write my papers. Make art. Tamsin can play cards and read mathematics books and wear trousers. And Alice, you can be in *nature*. I'm certain Cornwall is home to all manner of butterflies you can catch or pin or . . . breed, is it?"

The vision had begun to fashion itself inside her head a week after Gravesmuir's dinner, when her father had left her alone—again—as he attempted to repair his social standing among the powerful and well-connected members of the peerage.

Ruby had been by herself at the table. Her sister Cassandra had very properly married a viscount two years earlier, and so when her father went out, Ruby dined alone. The footmen still set an elaborate table; there were five elegant courses, and for once, Ruby didn't feel up to pretending that there was a room full of people she was meant to impress.

She'd been tired of pretending that she could *ever* impress a room full of people. Tired of pretending that there was any way she could be like Cassandra: polite and soft-spoken and acceptable.

She'd brought a battered copy of Thomas Hope's *Household Furniture and Interior Decoration* with her to the table. And as she'd gazed into the familiar black-and-white etchings—at Hope's elegant, esoteric designs—she'd lost what remained of her good sense.

She'd dipped her finger into her wine, and, very carefully, painted the page of illustrated draperies red.

She'd glanced up.

Not one single footman acknowledged what she'd done.

She stuck her fork into the sorrel puree on her plate and then used it to shade in a pattern of stripes on Hope's engraving of a settee. And when the footmen brought out partridge with roasted carrots, and maraschino jellies, and coffee cream, she'd festooned each stark engraving with vibrant and deliciously scented color.

She'd felt a hot, burning kind of freedom as she'd painted the riot of hues into her very favorite book.

No one cared. She was ruined now. It no longer mattered that her enthusiasm and her absurdities and her intense passions were at odds with what society thought a proper lady ought to be. She could make something beautiful, something ephemeral, just because she wished it, and no one was there to laugh or tell her she was strange. Her father's grim, disappointed gaze was somewhere else—some distant house on Portman Square that she, Ruby, would never be invited to.

She'd imperiled her father's career. She'd proven to him that she could never be trusted to assist him, never be worthy of his respect as an equal.

And because of that, she didn't need to *try* any longer.

Ruby was sick to her soul of trying.

Now, inside the British Museum, she looked at the rows and rows of colorful birds from all across the globe, sitting frozen on their perches, decidedly and indubitably dead.

And then she looked at Tamsin and Alice. "I think we should go to Cornwall for the summer," she said. "And I think we should move into Pomeroy House."

Alice's black lashes were performing some very expressive

acrobatics. "Move into Pomeroy House? The princess's country estate? What would we do there?"

"Whatever we please," Ruby said. "That's the whole point. We can leave all this behind. We can forget about the Season, about all these people. We can live for ourselves."

"How?" Alice asked.

Ruby thought that was quite a bit more encouraging a question—but then, Alice was always the first to fall in line with one of Ruby's schemes. "The princess has never visited Pomeroy House, not once since she bought it. If we go there, we can tell the staff in residence that we are her ladies-in-waiting. They won't know any better."

"But the princess will know we are not," Alice protested.

"I don't think the princess is ever coming." She had not thus far. And if Ruby's father's recent interest in the machinations of the royal family was any indication, the political situation within Monfalcone was not likely to become more stable within the next few months.

Ruby hadn't quite sorted out all the details—such as how she would ever persuade her father to let her go—but together, she, Alice, and Tamsin could make the scheme work. She *knew* they could.

Each of them brought something critical to the task. Ruby had the ideas and the enthusiasm, and enough stubborn persistence to bring her plans to fruition. Too much stubbornness, perhaps: Had she been a trifle less determined, she might have realized that conquering society the way her sister Cassandra had was never going to happen.

Nor was pleasing her father.

But she shook that thought off. If they went to Cornwall, she no longer needed to worry about society or the Earl of Hangleton.

Tamsin, for her part, was the practical one. Tamsin had only to look at luggage and it packed itself; postilions rushed to do her bidding, and carriage traffic seemed to fall away in front of her steely blue gaze. And Alice—

Alice smoothed Tam and Ruby's rough edges. Everyone who met Alice adored her. If the house was full of Monfalcone royal stewards and servitors, Alice would have them all wrapped around her little finger in a heartbeat.

They had knowledge, and expertise, and a connection to the Monfalcone royal family by way of Ruby's father. They had money of their own to fund the trip; Ruby and Tam were both possessed of substantial inheritances, and Alice's father had never said no to her in his life.

And—it was exhilarating and a little painful to consider—they had some measure of freedom now. No one in London would mind terribly much if the three of them vanished for the rest of the Season.

Alice touched her fingers to the ribbon threaded through her black curls. "Ladies-in-waiting?" she repeated. "For the Princess Serafina?"

"Yes," Ruby said. "I can use my father's name and seal." Guilt flared at the thought of lying to the earl about her intentions, but she quashed it firmly. She *refused* to falter. The moment called for decisiveness, not for foolish regret. "He's the ambassador to Monfalcone. No one would question our right to be at Pomeroy House."

Alice's cheeks had gone pink, and her neat striped gloves were locked together somewhere at the level of her breastbone. "Don't ladies-in-waiting generally possess some sort of . . . skills?"

"We have plenty of skills. Tamsin's been running her aunt's home for years. I can manage the rooms, the art, the princess's wardrobe—pineapple debacle notwithstanding—"

Alice, who had not borne witness to the pineapple dress, blinked.

Ruby waved off the question on Alice's face. "You can do everything else, Alice. Etiquette, dancing, music, all the relevant languages. Even butterflies, if the princess is fond of those."

Before her father's disgrace, Alice had been the Diamond of the Season, the most popular and sparkling debutante of 1814. She'd been poised to marry a duke's heir—the gossip columns had already started to speculate about which modiste would be selected to fashion her wedding gown. And when her father had been accused of treason and only barely escaped a trial by his peers in the Lords, Alice had lost everything.

Everything except Ruby and Tamsin.

The pale column of Alice's throat bobbed as she swallowed. She was staring at the newspaper in Ruby's hands, and there was something bright and hopeful in her face. Though she would not admit it, Alice had chafed horribly these last years under the censure that had been heaped upon her and her father. "Do you really think we could do it? Leave London? Live in Cornwall together?"

Ruby directed a beseeching glance at Tamsin, who had not yet spoken. She too had her eyes fastened on the headline, and her freckled face looked very stern.

"Tam?" Ruby said cautiously.

"Yes," Tamsin said. Her hands made fists at her sides. "Yes. I think we should do it."

Ruby attempted not to gape. She had supposed that Tamsin—clever, pragmatic Tamsin—would be far harder to convince.

"It's a good idea, Ruby. Well—no, it's an outlandish idea that needs significant refining, but—yes. Let's go." Tamsin's dark blue eyes were fierce when she looked up and met Ruby's gaze. "I want to go."

"You—do?"

There was a hint of something strange on Tamsin's face. In some other woman, Ruby might have called it hesitation. "I have been thinking about leaving London myself lately."

"You *have*?"

"Mm. But I did not want to leave the two of you." Tamsin's wide mouth crimped at the corner. "Aunt Frankie is getting married, you see. To her childhood sweetheart. Who's finally persuaded her to move home."

Ruby had to pause to absorb this news. Tamsin's departure from her parents' home to live with her topsy-turvy aunt two years prior had been a profound relief to everyone involved. Tamsin organized Frankie's very existence, and in return, Frankie had given Tamsin a place to thrive.

Ruby's heart squeezed as she looked at Tamsin, tall and bold and perhaps not quite so certain as she always seemed.

"Frankie invited me to go with her," Tamsin went on. "Only—well, she'll be married, of course. And she doesn't—" Tamsin's voice wobbled, just a little, which made her scowl. "She won't need me now."

Alice put her hand on Tamsin's elbow. "Oh, dearest. She'll still need you. Nothing could possibly change that."

"I'm *happy* for her," Tamsin said fiercely.

Alice's eyes were as gentle as her grip on Tamsin's arm. "Of course you are."

"We know you are," Ruby agreed. "You can be happy for Frankie and worry about your own place in the world at the same time. That doesn't make you wrong, Tam, only human." But something Tamsin had said tickled the back of her mind. "Did you say . . . did you say that Frankie is moving *home*?"

Some of the tension seemed to drain away from Tamsin's face. One corner of her mouth quirked up, her expression growing more decided. "I did. Yes."

Alice looked between them. "What do you mean? Why does Tam suddenly look so smug?"

"Because the Drake family estate," Ruby said, "is also in Cornwall."

Tamsin nodded, crooked smile still fixed on her mouth. "Your father will never in a hundred years agree to let you go to Pomeroy House. I'm sorry, Ruby, but the man doesn't deserve a tenth of your devotion."

Ruby felt a clutch in her chest at Tamsin's words—her father wasn't *so* bad—but Tamsin wasn't done talking.

"But he *will* let you stay with Aunt Frankie. She's to be the Countess of Bridestowe now—your father will love that. I propose that you don't mention Pomeroy House to him at all. As far as your father need know, you're staying with Frankie and her new husband at the Bridestowe estate for the summer. Cornwall is far enough away that he'll never suspect anything's amiss."

Yes. That was the solution to the problem of Ruby's father. Trust Tamsin to come to it instantly.

The vision flashed in Ruby's mind again. The elegant mansion the papers had described. Cornwall, all fogged beaches and sea villages and stars. Nature for Alice; independence for Tamsin.

And for herself, freedom from judgment.

A summer. A single, golden summer, in which they could do as they wished, without expectation or disappointment. Without anyone telling them they were wrong simply for being themselves.

It was a good plan. An excellent, logical, *flawless* plan. Tamsin was a genius.

"We can do this," Ruby said. "We can take ourselves to Pomeroy House. We can live as we please there."

"As ladies-in-waiting for the princess," Alice murmured.

"But not truly waiting," Ruby said. She flexed her fingers at her sides, stretching them within her gloves. "I'm done waiting for my life to begin."

She was done looking for approval she was never going to find. She was altogether finished with trying to make herself into someone she could never be. She was Ruby Ballimore. She had a knowledge of antiquities, an eye for color, a passion for classical design. She had the two most loving, loyal friends in the entire world.

She had ruined her life.

And she was going to make a new one in Cornwall.

Chapter 3

There were sixteen casks of Rhenish wine in the Pomeroy House kitchen, which, frankly, was sixteen more than Archer had been expecting.

"For fuck's sake," he said, "how did you even carry them all?"

Lamentation had his arms crossed over his chest and an expression on his face that read, *criminally underappreciated*. "You said to bring the wine up from the cove after Oliphant's crew dropped it off. Which we did. From four o'clock in the morning until noon."

"It's not noon. It's ten."

Lamentation's scowl deepened. "Oh, I'm sorry, Cap. Gerry and I have only been at this thankless task for *six* hours and not eight. My mistake."

Gerry hadn't yet said anything, which was typical for Gerry.

Unfortunately, he looked vaguely wounded, which was less typical. Usually, in the presence of Lamentation, Gerry's face evinced nothing so much as besotted happiness.

"All right," Archer said. "All right. I'm sorry. Thank you for cleverly and uncomplainingly bringing the wine up from the cove. I don't—" He passed his hand over his face and shoved his hair out of his eyes. "I wasn't expecting casks, that's all. We'll have to figure out some way to transport them. Or decant them. Or something."

Smuggling had been a hell of a lot easier when he'd been transporting goods that weren't illegal. He'd had a real, actual bill of sale from Gravesmuir for the statues—along with plenty of Greek documents that Eugénie had forged—all of which had proven extremely useful every time they'd been stopped on the road between Dorset and London.

But in the two months since the Quenby scheme had dissolved, he'd been forced to pursue other avenues of financial gain. He'd taken charge of selling the illicit goods that Gill Oliphant's men brought in surreptitiously from the Continent, and then, under Oliphant's guidance, started to make Channel crossings with his own crew. In the preceding weeks, they'd smuggled French silk gloves sewn in the hems of their trousers and ostrich feathers in their shirtfronts. Last week, Archer had discovered that several bolt holes on the *Delphinium* could have their bolts replaced with cigars, with no obvious ill effects on his beloved tub's ponderous progress.

On one trip, every drum of wax had been cleaned out and filled with brandy instead, a stratagem that had proven shockingly effective. The brandy had tasted a trifle odd afterward, but Archer had convinced seven different tavern keepers that it was typical of a Gascon Armagnac.

Hiding the smuggled casks of wine would be considerably more difficult. Casks tended to look a great deal like casks, no matter how one attempted to disguise them.

"Should we leave them in here?" Lamentation looked only slightly mollified. "I would've asked you when we started bringing them in, but we couldn't find you."

Archer had been down in St. Petroc's, the tiny but bustling port village near Pomeroy House. He'd met up with Oliphant at the tavern to pay for the wine, and then spent the morning delicately ascertaining the tavern keeper's feelings about dodgily imported alcohol at excellent bargain prices while also trying not to let the grizzled old pirate drink him under the table.

In retrospect, he'd had the morning a lot easier than Gerry and Lamentation.

"The kitchen's fine for now," he said. "We're not anticipating guests."

The lack of guests—and his powerful need for funds—had made Archer's transformation from steward to smuggler rather easier.

Two years ago, he had become the Pomeroy House steward through the intervention of his former rear admiral, Jack Penney, with whom he still occasionally visited, even though Archer's naval career had smashed itself to bits like a hull meeting a rock.

Penney mixed with people like the Monfalcone royals now, ever since his elevation to baronet after the war. He'd mentioned the house to Archer because he and Archer had once spent five months patrolling the south coast of Cornwall. They'd reminisced over quite a lot of expensive brandy about furious chases on cliffs, and the time Archer had surprised a bull in a patch of gorse, and the enthusiastic vicar's widow who had taught Archer far more in one night than he would have supposed vicar's widows to know.

Penney had mentioned the empty house and the job opening, and Archer, warm with drink, had thought: *I could do that.* Why not? He'd captained a ship for five years—how different could a country mansion be?

It had been because of the brandy that Archer had asked Penney to put in a good word for him. He would not, normally, have asked it. Had he been cold sober, he would not have let the thought creep across his mind—that Penney owed him a favor.

But it had. And he'd asked. And Penney had done it, and Archer had intended, for at least four or five days, to do everything by the book.

His good intentions, as usual, hadn't lasted long.

The problem—then and now—had always been money. The Monfalcone royal family had hired him alone, and Archer, ever since the disastrous end of his naval career, came as part of a set. He had persuaded the royal family's majordomo that he needed to hire a groundskeeper too, but he'd been afraid to ask for further auxiliary staff. No one would benefit if the Monfalcone royal family suspected that he was embezzling the Pomeroy House budget.

Which, he supposed, he was. But it was for the very good cause of keeping his crew housed and fed.

They had a safe place to live in Pomeroy House. Free from the prying eyes of strangers, Gerry and Lamentation could love each other as they had back when all of them had been together on the *Swallow*.

All Archer had to do was make sure the money kept flowing.

And God. He was trying.

He turned back to Lamentation and Gerry. "Have you seen Eugénie? Perhaps a fake bill of sale can save us from eager excise officers." He rubbed his jaw, which had grown thick with whiskers since he'd given up the Quenby scheme. "If she can write us up some receipts that say we bought the casks in Wales, we can at least avoid the import tax."

Lamentation still looked skeptical. "Do they make wine in Wales?"

"Oh Jesus." Archer scratched his beard again. "I have no idea." He peered at Gerry, who shook his head.

"Don't look at me, Captain." Gerry spoke rarely, and when he did, his voice was a deep bass rumble. "I'm from Shropshire."

"It's awfully close," Archer said. "Do they make wine in Shropshire?"

"I think the Romans did."

Archer blew out a breath. "Oh good. Maybe we can have Eugénie write the papers in Latin."

"Does she speak Latin?"

"Not that I know of. But neither does your average English exciseman, so I collect we could get away with it. Where *is* Eugénie?"

At this direct inquiry, Lamentation began to look extremely innocent beneath his cherubic blond curls. "I understand Eugénie and Wall went down to the butcher."

Archer paused. "*Again*? That's thrice in three days. Is it for dinner or—"

He broke off. He'd heard . . . something . . . coming from the casks. A sound as of tapping.

Lamentation made a gesture somewhere between a wince and shrug. "I don't think it's for dinner, Cap. I think it's for the puppies."

Archer felt his teeth click closed, and he forced his jaw open with a creak. "What. Puppies."

The tapping sound, which had tapered off, started up again as if in response to Archer's ground-out inquiry. He crouched beside the barrels and shoved his hand into the shadowed gap between the staves and the cool kitchen wall.

He withdrew a small black puppy.

"No," he grated. As a protest, it lacked vigor, being drowned out by the sound of tiny canine squeaks. "How many times have I said it? No more dogs!"

Another damp black nose emerged from the shadows, and Archer very seriously considered weeping.

On the *Swallow*, Wall had been the ship's surgeon. But after he had left in the wake of Archer's disgrace, Wall had turned his skill from humans to his real passion: veterinary medicine.

At the time, it had seemed a most excellent idea. Archer had proposed a number of strategic moneymaking schemes that involved extracting exorbitant fees from ladies of leisure to attend their beloved pets. In practice, however, Wall had not found the time to travel to London and fleece aristocratic ladies of their coin, because he was too busy providing inexpensive veterinary care to every animal in the surrounding villages.

He and Eugénie—his wife and their crew's talented forger—had also proven quite competent at rearing orphaned puppies. There was, Archer felt, a veritable epidemic of puppies in Cornwall. Most of them now seemed to be living in his house.

He stuffed the puppy in the pocket of his trousers and reached into the shadowed gap behind the barrels, where his hand promptly encountered a second warm, squirming form, and then a third. Bloody *Christ*.

"Only three, I think," Lamentation said brightly.

"Three new ones," Gerry clarified. "On top of the five we already had."

Lamentation shot his beloved a hasty glance of betrayal.

Archer stuck the second puppy in his other pocket, where it wriggled and bit his thigh. He carefully extricated the third puppy, at which point he realized that he was out of pockets.

He considered wrapping it about his neck like a stole, and then decided not to, if only because Wall would have an apoplexy if he saw Archer doing any such thing.

"Outside," he said. "If we're going to feed and house every orphaned dog in Cornwall, we can at least keep them *outside*."

He was halfway to the rear exit, his right pocket nearly torn off by minuscule needle teeth, when he heard another unfamiliar sound.

Not tapping this time. More of a pounding, really.

At the front door.

"What the devil," he muttered and reversed course. Were Wall and Eugénie back so soon? And why were they *knocking*?

A brief vision of excise officers flashed through his mind, and he thought of the casks of smuggled Rhenish wine currently in plain sight in the Pomeroy House kitchens. He tucked the third puppy under his arm, ran his fingers through his hair, and recalled himself to his position.

He was the steward of Princess Serafina of Monfalcone. His position at Pomeroy House was entirely legal and sanctioned by the royal family. If British officers had descended upon the mansion, he would send them on their way on behalf of House di Sangro.

He tried to remember his few words of Italian and flung open the door.

Before him stood a trio of women. They were young, richly dressed, and apparently mid-argument. The tallest one had her fist upraised as if to continue pounding.

Barring some massive changes in the British military he'd not heard about, Archer felt fairly certain these were not excise officers.

He dropped his voice, made it smooth and mannered. "Good morning. Are you ladies in need of some assistance?"

The ladies stared blankly at him for a long moment.

Or—no. Perhaps they were staring at the puppy under his arm.

He smiled brilliantly at them and attempted to look as though small dogs were typical accoutrements for Cornish stewards. The projection of confidence, Archer had found, seemed to go a long way toward convincing people that he wasn't lying through his teeth.

Which he was. Usually.

Finally, the tallest of the ladies—reddish-brown cropped hair, her face scattered with freckles—cleared her throat. "Ah—perhaps. Is this . . . this *is* Pomeroy House?"

Archer tried not to let his surprise show on his face. He'd supposed these three—with their gowns and hats that probably cost more than his annual salary—were victims of some carriage accident. He'd not imagined they were at the estate on purpose.

"Yes," he said. "It is."

As if in punctuation, the puppy in his right pocket finally won her victory over the worn-out fabric. His pocket came free with a sound of tearing, and then he felt the slow drag of the puppy's nails as she slid down his leg and emerged at the level of his boot.

"Oh," said one of the ladies faintly. This one looked exquisitely fragile, with black hair and enormous blue-green eyes that Archer imagined had inspired flights of fancy from a whole legion of Byronic suitors. She glanced from the puppy to the inside of the house. "It's not quite how I pictured it."

Archer didn't have to turn around to know what she meant.

The front parlor was home to a vast array of veterinary supplies and also five more dogs.

His gaze fell to the final woman. She was considerably shorter than the other two, with buttery-yellow curls beneath a jauntily angled straw hat. Her cheeks were pink, and so was her frock, and her pointed chin lifted as she met his gaze straight on. She was . . .

Archer felt cold wash over him, freezing his legs, rooting him where he stood.

She was The Woman From The Party. The sparkling little confection who had revealed Archer's Quenby scheme, wrecked six months of his planning, and caused the chain of events that had led to sixteen casks of smuggled wine in his kitchen.

Oh, he thought. *Fuck me.*

It was due entirely to a lifetime of practice in lying that Archer managed to retain command of his face. He smiled wider even as his brain suggested, *Time to run away, you thrice-damned fool.*

Instead he said: "How may I assist you?"

The girl's chin went somehow higher. "I am Lady Ruby Ballimore," she said, "and these are my companions, Lady Alice Eppington and Miss Tamsin Drake. We are the Princess Serafina's ladies-in-waiting."

Archer's brain registered the words very slowly, as if they'd been poured through syrup.

The Princess Serafina's.

Ladies-in-waiting.

"I see," he choked out. "Welcome. Have you . . . come to view the estate?"

"After a fashion. The Monfalcone ambassador has asked us to reside here. Indefinitely."

Archer wondered if he was hallucinating.

This was, beyond all shadow of a doubt, the same woman. She had the same fussy white gloves on, with what must be far too many pearl buttons for one woman to manage. She looked precisely as he recalled her: sweet and vaguely edible, until one came to her eyes.

They were gray-blue. Confident. Penetrating. Her gaze seemed to fix him where he stood, and he had the strange sense that this woman could see right through all his layers of falsehoods and charm. All the way down to his guts and his bones and the blackened corners of his too-soft heart.

He had, he realized, lost control of his expression. When the puppy underneath his arm bit him straight through his shirt, he realized he had not moved or spoken in a very long time.

"Lovely," he croaked, and stepped back to let them in. "Welcome to Pomeroy House."

Chapter 4

Ruby was having trouble making sense of—

Well. Everything, really.

Pomeroy House—if this *was* Pomeroy House, which still seemed doubtful—was in shambles. Some of the rooms were empty of furnishings and smelled powerfully of vinegar and washing soap. Others seemed to have several rooms' worth of chairs and tables piled into them, every stick of which was carved with snarling fantastic beasts. The windows were almost impossible to see through, covered as they were with either thick fabric or a coating of sea spray, and Ruby could scarcely hear herself think over the enthusiastic welcome of a pack of bloodhounds.

The house looked *nothing* like the papers had described it, except for all the turrets and towers and its position on top of a cliff overlooking the sea.

And the man who had answered the door—

Ruby gritted her teeth and made herself look at him again.

He was of medium height, broad-shouldered, and powerfully

built. He wore no livery but rather a haphazard arrangement of braces, billowy trousers, and a threadbare coat. He had dark hair, a full beard, and eyes of a most piercing shade of blue.

He was, without a doubt, the handsomest man she'd ever seen.

He also had puppies in his pockets. Three, at least.

"I'll . . . take you ladies to your rooms," he said. He'd sounded a trifle hysterical a few moments ago, but he seemed to be recovering himself. "You didn't, ah, write ahead? To announce your arrival?"

"Erm," Ruby said. "No."

Alice shot Ruby a beleaguered look, which Ruby ignored. Alice—for whom discommoding another person was the most grievous offense imaginable—had wanted to write ahead. But Ruby had feared that her father would somehow get wind of their plans in the weeks it had taken to set everything into motion. When logical, practical Tamsin had sided with Ruby, the matter had been settled: They would forge the letter of introduction, supply their own funds, and show up without mentioning the scheme to anyone at all.

After all, Ruby had told herself, the mansion belonged to a princess. Surely they could occupy a few rooms without putting anyone to too much trouble.

As they passed through another parlor—this one holding inexplicable trays of catgut and needles and camphor in pots—Ruby was forced to revise her assumptions.

This was going to be a hell of a lot of trouble.

Two more men barreled around the corner and nearly collided with the extravagantly attractive and peculiarly dressed man—butler?—who'd answered the door.

"Cap," one of them said, "you have to—"

"Sir," the butler interrupted, in quite a louder and more stern voice than Ruby had heard him use thus far. "Please try to behave more sedately."

The two newcomers stumbled to a stop, and—

Good heavens. Alice stifled a gasp, and even Tamsin appeared slightly boggled.

These two were beautiful as well. One of the men—the one who had spoken—was delicate of build, with nearly white-blond curls framing an angular face. The other was tall, his flowing chestnut hair in a queue. His shirt was open nearly to the waist, which afforded Ruby a view of the human form that ought more properly to have been in an art book. Or a museum.

The butler turned to Ruby and bowed. "Allow me to present the staff of Pomeroy House to you, Lady Ballimore."

"Lady Ruby," she corrected absently. "I am unmarried. Did you say . . . the staff?"

"Indeed."

She blinked. "*All* the staff?" According to the papers—which were proving less reliable by the moment—Pomeroy House boasted twenty bedrooms, two kitchens, and a fully equipped stable on the grounds. Surely it couldn't be staffed by three men, no matter how blessed in appearance they might be.

The butler swallowed. And then a smile spread across his face—precisely as blinding and exquisite as the one he'd delivered outside. He drew himself up in a way that set off his breadth of shoulder, and an air of serenity seemed to overtake him. "No. Today is a feast day in this part of Cornwall. The rest of the staff have gone to church. To pray."

"A feast day?" Ruby narrowed her eyes. "What feast would that—"

"I am Malcolm Archer, Pomeroy House steward," the man continued, rather more rapidly. "And these are our footmen, Gerald and Lamentation."

At this introduction, the taller footman—the one with the ponytail and the chest—appeared to choke.

The angelic blond at his side blinked once and then nodded. "Ah. Yes. I am Lamentation. The footman. How may I serve your . . . feet?"

Ruby opened her mouth and then shut it again, quite unable to summon a response.

"Take these," Malcolm Archer said. He removed a puppy from beneath his coat and thrust it into Lamentation's hands. He plucked a second puppy from his trouser pocket, delivered that one as well, and then began, evidently, to look for the one that had emerged beside his scuffed boot.

Alice had rescued that one. She was holding it to her chest and murmuring into its tiny floppy ear.

"Put these back in the kitchen," Mr. Archer went on. "I'll take the ladies up to their chambers and meet you back down here expediently."

"To their . . . chambers?" Lamentation said faintly.

Mr. Archer's brilliant smile did not falter. "Indeed. I trust you ladies have luggage?"

Ruby nodded. "Outside. By the front door."

"Of course. Gerry can bring up your trunks after you're settled."

"Their *trunks*?" Lamentation echoed. "After they're *settled*?"

"Yes." Mr. Archer put out a hand toward Ruby and her friends. "These are Princess Serafina's ladies-in-waiting. And they will be residing here. At Pomeroy House."

Lamentation blinked several more times. "The princess's ladies-in-waiting? I . . . did not realize she had those."

She does now, Ruby thought, and tried not to look as guilty as she felt.

Mr. Archer, who no doubt had also been unaware of their existence—because they'd made up the job whole-cloth—didn't respond to the footman. Instead he directed the considerable force of his smile at Alice. "I'm sorry," he said, "about all the dogs. May I take that one from you?"

A look of alarm crossed Alice's face, and she clutched the puppy to her chest. "No! That is—" She modulated her voice. "No." A blush made its way up to her hairline. "If you don't mind, Mr. Archer, I should very much like to keep her."

The puppy seemed to have fastened her teeth around Alice's wrist, which did not deter Alice in the slightest.

Mr. Archer looked at Alice. He looked at the puppy. Then he glanced at Ruby, Tamsin, and the puppy-holding footmen. "Of course," he said. "Yes. Why not? Puppies for everyone. We have plenty to go around."

Ruby followed the little expansive gesture of his hand.

Her eyes narrowed. There was something peculiarly familiar about this Mr. Archer. Not his face, precisely, nor his name. But something about the arc of his shoulders—the sweep of his arm—

"Do I know you?" she asked, still staring at him. "Have we met?"

Lamentation and Gerry hastened out the door, puppies in arms and shirttails billowing in their wake.

In the light of the sun through the cracked window, a faint flush seemed to have settled around Malcolm Archer's throat. "No."

"Are you certain? Did you work in London before you came here? Perhaps my father—the Earl of Hangleton—"

His blush became more decided—carnation pink above and below his thick black beard. "Before I came here, I was a captain in His Majesty's Navy. We have not met."

"Were you on an engraving, then?" she pressed. "Some military recruitment poster? Or perhaps a parade? I am certain—"

"No," he said flatly. "I was not."

She blinked. Embarrassment hit her then, and she felt her face heat. She always did this: pushed too hard, spoke too much and out of turn.

This was meant to be her new life. She would not wreck it with her old ways.

"Let me take you to your rooms," he said, more gently this time. "This way."

Ruby clamped her mouth closed and let him lead them out of the parlor.

Perhaps she had been wrong. Perhaps she did not know him. She surely would have remembered that voice, rough and sweet as honeycomb.

They followed Captain Archer through a parade of blindingly clean and bizarrely furnished rooms. One held stacks of crates that reached to the ceiling; another boasted perhaps three dozen screens in rows that seemed to be hiding pots of winding green shrubbery and possibly more dogs. Everything smelled, still, of camphor.

After one set of steep stairs, he pointed them down a dark, narrow corridor. "There are three bedchambers here," he said. "I'll be sure to send the . . . the housekeeper to air out your rooms. After she returns from church. She may need some time to recover from her penance."

"Her penance," Ruby repeated. "From the feast day. At church."

"Cornish traditions, you know," he said vaguely, and shot them another smile. And then, before any of them could protest, he turned and fled back the way he'd come.

They stood in front of the doors in silence for several moments. Ruby looked from Tamsin to Alice to Captain Archer's retreating back. The corridor was dim, and unlike the rest of the house, it appeared not to have been used for some time. Possibly a century.

"Ruby," Tamsin said, "what the hell is going on?"

"*Shh*," Alice hissed. "He'll hear you!"

Captain Archer had peeled off as if his boots were afire, so Ruby suspected he probably wouldn't. Still, she plucked up her courage and pushed open the nearest door before she could talk herself out of facing whatever lurked therein. "Come on. Inside, both of you. And the dog."

The heavy door scraped against the floor as they entered, and Ruby was forced to revise her estimation of this wing's most recent use to three centuries ago at least. Every part of the room looked as though it had been plucked straight from Henry VIII's Hampton Court Palace. Half a dozen paintings leaned against a bed so monstrous it came with a stool for entering it. In contrast with the corridor's gloom, light poured into the chamber—because the draperies and bed hangings had been mostly devoured by moths.

"Good news," Tamsin said. "At least these windows have glass."

Ruby collapsed onto the bed. A plume of dust shot into the air.

"This is *insane*." Tamsin prowled around the perimeter of the room, nudging chewed-on velvet fabrics out of the way with the toe of her boot. "This can't be right. Are you certain this is Pomeroy House?"

"Relatively." They'd stopped at Bridestowe to visit Tamsin's Aunt Frankie, who'd sent them along to Pomeroy House in her private coach. "The coachman said it was. It's on a cliff at the edge of the sea. And it looks like the pictures, more or less."

"From the outside, maybe!" Tamsin made a wild sweep of her arm that nearly knocked over one of the leaning paintings. "*This* does not look like a princess's holiday home."

"The staff did say—"

"The staff," Tamsin repeated. "What staff? Did those fellows strike you as working servitors? Because I cannot say I was struck by their professionalism or"—she gestured again—"the results of their labors!"

Alice's soft voice broke in. "They didn't know we were coming, Tam. You can't blame them for not having the rooms prepared. It's our fault, really."

Tamsin stopped pacing to stare at Alice. "Are you just saying that because they were so beautiful to look at?"

"No," Alice protested.

Ruby brushed the dust on the counterpane, which served to transfer it to her skirts. "She's saying that because they gave her a dog."

"No," Alice said again, though she hugged the puppy closer to her chest. "It's only that they were very kind."

"Oh my God." Tamsin shoved her fingers into her hair. "It *is* because they gave you a dog."

"I suppose it was all of it together." Alice set her puppy on the ground and examined one of the paintings that Tamsin had nearly toppled. "They were awfully welcoming to a trio of unexpected"—she dropped her voice to a whisper—"faux ladies-in-waiting. And they *were* very attractive. Do you think there could be something especially salutary about the Cornish air?"

Tamsin groaned, leaned back against the wall, and slowly sank down to the ground.

Ruby wrapped her arms around her legs and put her chin on her knees. She looked out across the room and then to the nearest window, which might have afforded a view of the sea if she could see through the grimy glass.

There was something hard and cold in her chest, like a stone lodged in her breastbone.

How many times had she done this? Envisioned some fantastic scheme only to be confronted by a reality not half so shining and luminous?

Perhaps there was no way to reinvent herself. Perhaps—even here, in Cornwall, as far away as she could get from her past—she was still the same old Ruby Ballimore.

It felt hard to breathe. Difficult to swallow against the pressure in her throat.

"I think we should go back," Tam said. "Back to Bridestowe. For God's sake, what if this isn't the staff, and they've thrown the real servants into the sea?"

"I can't imagine that's the case," Alice said. "They seem very pleasant."

Tamsin shot her a perturbed look. "Alice, darling, I'm concerned by how easily you succumb to a handsome sea captain with a dog."

"To Alice's credit," Ruby managed to say, "the man has eight dogs. Eight times the persuasive power of a single canine."

Alice picked up her puppy again, which had piddled on the floor and was now engaged in a pitched battle with her boot laces. "He only has seven now. This one's mine. I'm not giving her back."

Tamsin made a faint despairing sound.

And Ruby found herself looking at Alice.

Alice was nuzzling the puppy's ear. Her face was pink and flecked with dirt and plaster; her boots were scuffed. She looked a thousand times more windblown and disheveled than Ruby had ever seen her in all their years of friendship in London.

And she looked *happy*.

It had been a long time since Ruby had seen her look so happy.

In the years since her father's disgrace, Alice had not asked Ruby or Tamsin for anything. She wanted to please—everyone, all the time. She never let her desires show on her face like this, lest her wanting prove an inconvenience. Lest she lose what little she had left to her that she loved.

But she had asked for the dog. And the captain had responded as though her request had been no hardship. As though it were in his nature to give.

Ruby bit her lip. She looked around the room: the moth-eaten drapes, the bare stone floor, the bizarre furniture and abundance of paintings.

She murmured, "Why not?"

Tamsin looked up from her position on the ground. There was dust on her face too, camouflaging the freckles on her cheeks. "What was that?"

"Why not?" Ruby said, louder this time. "Why not stay? What

does it matter to us if the house is peculiar? If it's scarcely staffed? What of it?"

"What do you—"

"Why should we mind?" She scrambled off the bed via the stool. "We're *here*. We've made it. They did not bar the door or send us back to London in disgrace." She hiked up the topmost layer of her skirts and used it to clean away the begrimed window, letting in more light. "We can stay for the summer, exactly as we planned. We don't need a palace or a cadre of servants. What we need is a place to be together."

Perhaps it was not precisely what she'd imagined. But that didn't mean she had to give up. The *house* didn't matter—only that they were together and happy, with freedom enough to fill their lungs with air.

She dropped her skirt. Light speared through the glass, illuminating Alice's flushed cheeks, glancing red off Tamsin's hair.

"We can fix it up," Alice said softly. She set the puppy back down and moved to the other window, scrubbing at it with her handkerchief.

"Yes!" Through the glass, Ruby could see the ocean and a tiny bird, white against the summer blue of the sky. "Why shouldn't we spend the summer restoring the house? We're the princess's ladies-in-waiting, and this is her home."

"We're not, actually," Tamsin said. "You do recall that pertinent fact?"

Ruby held out one of the moth-eaten drapes. The sunlight glanced through dozens of tiny holes, casting dappled shadows across the floor.

"That looks very pretty," Alice murmured.

It did. Somehow the pattern of light and dark looked like lacework: delicate and fine.

"God save me from the two of you and your imaginations," Tamsin said. But there was something lurking in her voice, a hint of weakening she couldn't quite suppress.

Ruby locked eyes with Tamsin and let her conviction show on her face. "We can make it beautiful here."

"It already is beautiful," Alice said. "It only needs a little shine."

Ruby bit her lip. "I think we should stay, Tam. I want to stay." *And Alice*, she wanted to say. *Look at Alice. Look how much easier it is for her to breathe.*

But Ruby didn't have to say it. Tamsin was already gazing at Alice, and by the expression on Tamsin's face, Ruby knew that she had noticed as well.

The puppy waddled over to Tamsin's place on the floor, and she put out her hand. The dog licked her palm, then, delicately, bit the tip of her ungloved finger.

Tamsin took a breath and looked up. Her dark blue eyes took in Ruby and Alice at once. "All right." Her mouth firmed; her freckled face went set and determined. "You win. We're staying."

Chapter 5

"This is a fucking disaster," Archer said.

It had been six hours since the ladies-in-waiting had arrived, and he had not yet regained his usual self-command.

He was panicked. He was panick*ing*. He'd *been* panicking, with increasing vigor and urgency, all afternoon.

"It's not that bad," Lamentation said. "We got the casks out of the house, at least."

Archer ran his hand through his hair, which reminded him that he needed to cut it. And shave. And find some new bloody clothes, if he was going to keep up appearances around three London ladies for a disturbingly nebulous period of time.

"It *is* that bad," Wall said. "I've never seen Archer pace like this. Not even when he got put off the *Swallow*."

Archer froze. He *had* been pacing; if there had been a rug on the floor of the kitchen, he would have worn a path in it by now. But—

Hell. Damn it. If Wall could see his disarray—if Wall was

bringing up Archer's disgrace on the *Swallow*, which they never spoke of, not even in extremity—then Archer needed to marshal some lies and give the situation a brilliant coating of gilt.

That was what he did. He made them believe they were safe.

He had to. Because he was the one, back in the navy, who had foundered them all on the rocks. And now he was the one who had to convince them they were not on the point of drowning.

He spun one of the kitchen chairs around, straddled it, and tried to force his jaw to unlock. "It's . . ." The words wouldn't come. Apparently *It's going to be fine* was a bridge too fucking far when he was confronted by The Woman From The Party in his own goddamned house. "It's not . . . ideal."

"I don't really understand what the problem is," said Eugénie. Her voice, lightly accented from her native Dominica, was soft but steely. "The girls brought loads of money with them. Gerry showed me the packet with the letter from the Monfalcone ambassador. Apparently he made budgetary allowances so that they might abide in the style to which they are accustomed. We can afford to feed them, Captain."

Archer had seen the money too: a fantastic sum, which only made him more concerned that the ladies-in-waiting meant to dwell in Pomeroy House for the rest of their natural lives.

"The Monfalcone ambassador is part of the problem," he said. "That girl—Lady Ruby Ballimore—is his daughter. If she writes to him and tells him something is amiss here at Pomeroy House, he'll tell the royal family. I'm under no illusions that House di Sangro has any loyalty to me personally. One word from the ambassador and we'll all be out on our arses."

"Then let's make certain nothing *is* amiss," Lamentation said.

"We can clean. Straighten. Maybe with all those guineas we can acquire a couple of villagers willing to work as chambermaids."

Archer shook his head. "We can't do that either. Because the royal family has only authorized the estate to be staffed by me and a groundskeeper. If Lady Ruby tells her father that it's fully staffed—if she tells the earl about all of you—we're equally fucked. None of you are supposed to be here."

When Archer had first been hired on, the Monfalcone royal majordomo had indicated that the princess had no immediate plans to visit Pomeroy House, despite plentiful rumor to the contrary. Archer had always assumed that if that changed—if the princess meant to descend upon the mansion in state—he would be afforded plenty of warning. Surely, he'd thought, the Monfalcone royals knew as well as he did that a mansion of this size could not be kept in perfect repair by a single steward.

Based on the day's events, perhaps they did not.

Eugénie's dark brows drew together, an elegant line above her perceptive gaze. "That makes no sense. If House di Sangro wanted the princess's ladies-in-waiting to live here, why would they not pay to fully staff the house?"

"I've no bloody idea. Maybe they're out of money and hiding it very cleverly." Archer knew plenty about that.

Wall got up from the table and moved to the stove, where he was boiling a bone he'd acquired from the butcher. Apparently the puppies had been orphaned too young; though they'd been weaned off milk, they were smaller than Wall preferred. According to a scientific text on sighthounds that Wall had ordered from a Swedish catalog, the puppies now required marrow jelly.

Wall decanted the reddish, slithery substance into a series of jars as he spoke. "There's also the problem of all the ill-gotten goods in the house."

"We moved the casks," Lamentation protested. "Gerry and I have spent the majority of our day moving casks to and from the cove, in point of fact."

"It's not just the wine," Archer said. "We've got all the left-over sculptures from Dorset in the stables, and those foul-smelling cigars, and about a thousand pairs of lace stockings in one of the tower bedrooms."

"And silks," added Gerry in his deep bass rumble. "Lots of silks coming next week, right, Cap?"

God. Archer had nearly forgotten the silks.

"Could you tell them you're a silk merchant?" Lamentation asked. "In addition to being a steward?"

Archer scratched at his beard. "I suppose I could try."

The greatest problem, though he had not said it aloud, was the fact that Lady Ruby Ballimore had seen him as Professor Quenby. And not just in passing—she had been the architect of Quenby's downfall. He'd not have supposed she would recognize him, without the hair powder and spectacles and stooping, except for those damned penetrating eyes. They'd been in the same room for roughly two minutes before she started demanding to know where she'd seen him before. If she realized he was the man who had sold the counterfeit statues to Gravesmuir, Archer would not just be out of a job at Pomeroy House—he'd be tossed in prison, probably. Or else transported. Or hanged.

But he couldn't tell his crew that. The very idea of letting them know how close they were to disaster made his skin feel too tight.

After his dismissal from the navy, Archer had found himself devoid of ship, career prospects, and any clear sense of his future.

But he'd not been left alone. Wall, Eugénie, Gerry, and Lamentation had stayed with him.

He *refused* to let them regret it. And so instead he would obfuscate and bluff and lie like his life depended on it—even, if necessary, to them.

He didn't need a perspicacious little blond to remind him that he was a scoundrel. He already knew.

Before Archer could finish racking his brain for some new scheme, he was interrupted by the soft sound of throat-clearing behind him. He spun about so fast he nearly knocked the chair over, which rather counteracted the impression of cool confidence he meant to convey.

In the door to the kitchen stood the ladies-in-waiting. Lady Ruby was at the forefront—she seemed, somehow, to be the leader of the trio—and she held a coal scuttle clutched to her chest. Her lavish frock, which had been fresh as new cream when she'd arrived on his doorstep, was now liberally streaked with grime, and her straw hat had vanished. Her face was even pinker than it had been that morning, and her lips were pursed, a state that did nothing at all to counteract her general impression of quivering edibility.

Archer smiled as though he'd never been so delighted to see anyone, which was perhaps the greatest lie his face had ever told.

"Good evening," he said. "How may I help you?"

Lady Ruby extended the empty scuttle, an action that revealed even more dirt upon her person. "Have you any coal?" She did not pause to let him answer, only continued to ramble. "We may not need it, of course, since it's July. But I thought it wise to acquire some, in case we do. Need it, I mean. I don't know how cold it will be in our chambers overnight." She wound down, her face having gone from pink to rather red.

They did, of course, have coal.

But as Archer regarded Lady Ruby, a new thought floated to the surface of his mind. What would happen if they didn't?

What if the conditions at Pomeroy House were inhospitable enough that the ladies-in-waiting simply . . . left?

They might complain to the Monfalcone ambassador, who might write to the royal family. But Archer suspected he could talk his way out of questions, if he had enough time and distance. He could probably pass their aspersions off as a misunderstanding, some misapprehension on the part of a trio of spoiled London ladies.

And they would be gone. There was no chance Lady Ruby Ballimore could identify Archer as Quenby if she weren't here to look him in the eye.

He might, if they scared the ladies off, lose this position.

But he would not lose his freedom. And he would not lose his crew.

Before Archer's embryonic plan could properly develop in his mind, Lamentation leapt up from the kitchen table.

"Of course," Lamentation said enthusiastically. "Of course we have coal. You needn't come all the way down here. We can bring some up to your rooms." He took the coal scuttle from Lady Ruby's arms, and she offered him a pleased smile.

Archer gazed at her. He recalled her from Gravesmuir's—recalled the ruthless clarity of her words. But she did not seem quite so ruthless now. She was pink and smiling, for God's sake. She was a sweet, innocent little debutante. While she was upstairs, she had changed her gloves into a pair that was even fussier, some delicate concoction of ribbon and lace.

He knew how to talk—even to pristine aristocrats' daughters.

He knew how to persuade people to do what he wanted and leave them feeling it had been their own notion all along.

Perhaps outfoxing Lady Ruby Ballimore would not be so very difficult.

Lamentation was cheerfully gesturing around the room with the coal scuttle, introducing Mr. Theophilus Wall—"our chef, *very* experienced"—and Mrs. Eugénie Wall, who was, evidently, Pomeroy House's secretary. Why Lamentation thought a mansion would need its own secretary, Archer could not begin to guess.

The tall freckled one—Miss Drake, Archer thought she was called—cast a suspicious glance at Wall. "The chef, is it? It certainly smells . . . pungent down here."

Lamentation opened his mouth again, presumably to bring up the puppies, but Archer clapped his hand on Lamentation's shoulder to silence him.

He smiled at the ladies-in-waiting. It was a real smile, now that he was sure of his plan, not the pasted-on grimace he'd managed that morning.

And then he did something he was good at.

He started to lie.

"Yes," he said warmly. "Mr. Wall is our chef. He's been with the Monfalcone royal family for nearly a decade. A personal favorite of the di Sangro princes and princesses. And in honor of your arrival, he's concocted one of his specialties."

All of his people were staring at him like he'd gone off his head, so he took Lady Ruby by the elbow and gently pivoted her away from the crew. "Lamentation. Gerry. Can you prepare plates for the ladies-in-waiting?"

Lamentation's face could probably have served as an illustration of the word *agog*. "Plates of the—"

"Yes," Archer said firmly. "The potage à la reine. Isn't that what you call it, Wall? The queen's favorite soup?"

Wall emitted a strangled sound.

"I think you will all find the yellow parlor most commodious," Archer told the ladies-in-waiting. He piloted Lady Ruby by the elbow back down the hallway, and the other two fell into place behind him.

"The yellow parlor?" Lady Ruby repeated. "Did we pass that one on the way in?"

He grinned as he directed her down a series of winding halls and corridors. By God, he was almost enjoying himself now. "Why, no. You didn't."

The house had been odd even before Archer had moved in, outfitted with strange and vaguely sinister furnishings. One of the chambers—the one he had in mind—had been forbidding enough that even the hounds had hesitated to enter.

"Here we are," he said brightly. He opened the door and gestured inside. "You may dine here."

Not a single one of them moved.

The room was not overlarge. It boasted a single small window, which permitted just enough sunlight to illuminate the walls and decorations.

Everything—every single thing in the room, so far as Archer could tell—was covered in a motif of lions. They twined rampant around chair legs and roamed across the upholstery. Toothy, roaring mouths inscribed the corbels, and the western wall held a tapestry that featured more lions, along with gazelles, giraffes, and a bloodcurdling display of viscera. Nearly everything was tipped in gilt, so that the general effect was one of golden carnivorous terror.

He smiled wider. And then he held out his hand, palm up. "The yellow parlor."

The dark-haired one—Lady Alice, the one who had taken the puppy—had her hand at her breastbone, as if to keep her heart from beating out of her chest. Miss Drake looked nearly as dismayed as Lamentation had when Archer had ordered him to serve marrow jelly as if it were a delicate French soup.

But Lady Ruby—

Bleeding, bloody, bollocking Christ, *why* was she so unpredictable?

She was smiling again, this time a delighted, astonished sort of smile, her gray-blue eyes shining like stars. She leapt across the threshold of the terrible room and started to run her fingers over the decorations on the walls.

"This is fascinating!" she exclaimed. "A whole boudoir dedicated to such a collection." Her fingers traced the lines of embroidery thread in the tapestry with such palpable tactile pleasure that Archer's skin prickled. "This imagery recalls to me the Herculaneum collection, and yet there is something reminiscent of Tentyris in the ornament of the aediculae. Do you know who designed this room?"

He kept his smile pasted on his face, though he wanted to scowl. Bloody *academics*. She was meant to be frightened of the room's leonine horrors, not prepared to write a monograph about them.

"I can't say that I do," he said. Another idea occurred to him, and he kept talking. "The Monfalcone representative in London knows everything there is to know about the history of Pomeroy House, however. You might put your questions to him directly." Perhaps if he could not frighten her off with architectural elements, he could send her bounding home in search of some greater expertise than his own.

But to his surprise, Lady Ruby paused in the act of stroking the tapestry. Her lips parted and she yanked her hand away and thrust it behind her back. Her expression of eager curiosity dimmed and then went out altogether, like an extinguished flame. "No," she said. "I don't think I will."

Before Archer could summon a reply, Gerry and Lamentation made their way into the room, bearing crystal and silver and an air of beleaguered discombobulation. They plopped the plates down on the glimmering lion table with a clatter—obviously neither of them had ever actually seen a footman—and Archer found himself ushering Lady Ruby into a chair.

Her skirts coasted over his shoes as she sat. Her mouth, which was pink and lush above her pointed chin, compressed just a trifle as she took in the slimy reddish substance on the plates.

Archer manfully held back a shudder. The marrow jelly was certainly edible—Wall wouldn't have prepared it if it wasn't—but the sight of it was . . .

Well. Wall had made it for the puppies, who were considerably less discerning about the appearance of their foodstuffs than your average London debutante.

He bent, just slightly, toward Lady Ruby. "The favorite of the Monfalcone queen," he murmured. "I hope you enjoy."

She tipped her head up to face him straight on, and he felt something catch in his brain, some scrape and spark as their gazes locked. It was those damned eyes of hers: clear and serious. She wasn't charmed, this woman—but neither was she afraid.

This close, he could make out her perfume, warm and moody and not too sweet. It reminded him of . . . of things that had no scent. Rich, soft velvet. Amber. The wooden hull of his own *Delphinium*, polished and gleaming in the sun.

His breath snagged in his chest.

And then her chin came up. Her fingers closed around the soup spoon that Lamentation had dropped beside her plate. And as he watched her dip the spoon into the marrow jelly, he thought of Gravesmuir's party. Pictured her there, with a sudden uneasy alarm.

She was stubborn, this woman. Determined. A great, galloping storm of public censure had not put her off her chosen course.

Perhaps this would not be as easy as he'd supposed.

"Thank you, Captain Archer," she said coolly. "I do intend to enjoy my time here."

And without taking her eyes from his, she dipped her spoon in the marrow jelly, smiled grimly at him, and took a bite.

Chapter 6

Twelve days later, Ruby peered into the depths of her teacup.

At the bottom—beneath a layer of strangely pinkish tea—rested a single whole walnut.

She looked up at Alice and Tamsin, arrayed around her in the Pomeroy House library. "It's getting worse," she said. "Do you think it's getting worse?"

Alice gazed down into the tea tray, which held a shriveled apricot, a pot of jam, and no visible flatware. "So many jellies," she murmured. "I've never seen so many jellies."

Tamsin was not attending to the horrors of the tea Gerry had brought them. At the moment, she was on her knees, sorting books into piles by subject and eating a chocolate biscuit she'd acquired down in St. Petroc's. She had changed into trousers on their second day and, when no one had turned a hair, had promptly shoved her frocks into the bottom of her trunk to molder.

"Another one on illnesses in dogs," she murmured. "That makes eleven."

"That's not *so* many," Alice said.

"Just on this shelf."

Alice blinked.

The three of them had decided to tackle the rooms in the house one by one. They'd begun with their own chambers out of necessity—Ruby's had been the only one with bed linens—but they'd quickly progressed to the large rooms on the lowest level of the mansion. If they *were* real ladies-in-waiting, Ruby had reasoned, they'd be tasked with readying the chambers that the princess was most likely to avail herself of whenever she did manage to visit.

The rooms, they'd quickly discovered, had been divided into either neat chambers used for bizarre and inexplicable purposes, or dust-ridden heaps that had been closed off entirely and abandoned to nature.

Over the last almost-fortnight, nature—and the Pomeroy House staff—had been forced to surrender to the combined efforts of Ruby, Alice, and Tamsin.

Tamsin had removed an entire collection of Ottoman Baroque chamber pots from a music room decorated in black marble and stars. Alice, it appeared, had discovered a heretofore unknown aggressive streak, judging by the way she had volunteered to beat the dust out of all the rolled-up rugs.

And Ruby—oh, it had been the greatest pleasure of her lifetime—had overseen the mansion's redecorating.

Pomeroy House wasn't terrible, not really. Unconventional, perhaps, but she liked unconventional—had always valued peculiar treasures and hidden eccentricities. She'd supervised the relocation of the immense Tudor furnishings to rooms more properly suited to their size. She'd lavished the dining table and chairs with furniture polish and had been delighted by the pattern of black roses and thorns her efforts had revealed. She'd carefully cleaned wall fabrics until they gleamed, and in the rooms that had grown faded with disuse, she'd found pigments and oils to retouch the once-colorful millwork.

And the staff had let them do it, with scarcely a word of protest. When she'd encountered Captain Malcolm Archer—which seemed to happen quite often, no matter where she was in the house, almost as though he were watching her—he hadn't batted an eye, even when he'd found her painting at the top of a ladder with her skirts knotted up around her knees.

He'd smiled extravagantly. He'd asked her how he could be of service. He'd answered every question she'd asked—about his relationship with the di Sangro family, about Pomeroy House's history—with a delightful torrent of words that, upon later reflection, did not seem to convey any real information.

The man's extraordinarily, *suspiciously* attractive and pleasant demeanor, however, had not distracted her from the bizarre happenings in the rest of the house.

Ruby dropped her cup untouched back into its saucer. "I really do think it seems to be getting worse."

Tamsin sat back on her heels. The pile of canine veterinary medicine texts wobbled precariously at her side. "How do you mean? I think we've done quite a lot in a short time, to be honest."

"Not our efforts. I mean"—Ruby gestured to the tea tray at Alice's feet—"everything else."

Alice looked down as well. "Last week, the tea tray at least came with a spoon."

"And a cake to deliver the jam to your mouth."

Tamsin shuddered. "I don't think that was cake. It tasted of celeriac. And clams."

"It's not just the food." Ruby turned to take in the rest of the library. "The peculiarities of the house seem to be mounting, somehow."

"It *was* odd," Alice mused, "when our bedclothes disappeared."

"That's exactly what I mean! Where could they have gone? And *why*, for heaven's sake?"

Tamsin chewed on her lower lip. "Overzealous laundering, perhaps?"

"Does this staff strike you as overzealous at any household task?"

"Well. No." Tamsin inclined her head. "You have me there."

"I think they are *making* it worse," Ruby said. "I'm almost certain there are more books in this library today than there were yesterday evening when we left. And the piles we made seem to have moved around in the night."

"If we're listing oddities," Alice murmured, "I can't quite grasp how that seagull got into the music room."

"Unless someone put it there!" Ruby exclaimed. "And *where* is this mythical housekeeper? I've never seen the woman, for all they keep saying she's just around the corner."

Tamsin's brows drew together as she pondered Ruby and Alice. "You are proposing that the Pomeroy House staff is engaged in some sort of machination to . . . magnify the house's defects?"

"I know it sounds like a flight of fancy, but—"

"No," Tamsin said. "Well, yes, rather ludicrous but also— strangely plausible?" She gestured to the leaning tower of veterinary books at her side, which exceeded the level of her head. "There's no way all of this happens by chance."

"But why would they do it?" Alice asked. "To what end?"

Ruby scavenged one of Tamsin's chocolate biscuits. "I have no idea. Surely they can't *enjoy* living in squalor and surviving on clam cakes."

"They're not ignoring their responsibilities and gadding about the village like absentee landlords," Tamsin said. "Because they're always *here*. I tried to make my way into one of the offices earlier, and their so-called secretary was already there, surrounded by papers and ink. She managed to remove me from the premises with the politest misdirection I've ever had the pleasure of being subjected to."

Ruby bit down on her chocolate biscuit and considered *misdirection*.

Perhaps half a dozen times now, she'd stumbled upon Captain Archer deep inside the labyrinthine corridors of Pomeroy House. She'd been looking for turpentine and lye the first instance, and then later some sort of plates or spoons for their bizarre breakfasts of courgette confit. In each encounter, he had rapidly covered his surprise with a brilliant smile. He'd cupped her elbow in his big callused hand and led her down corridors that she'd never seen before and had not intended to visit, and the fact that she *liked* the strange little rooms he showed her only made the whole thing more suspect.

He was too charming. The curled-up corners of his mouth screamed deceit and deception; every time he grinned fetchingly down at her, some black pirate flag began to wave in the back of her mind.

Was he trying to hide something from her?

Was he, for some inexplicable reason, trying to lead her in the opposite direction of a proper meal?

She picked up the teacup and gazed down at the walnut therein. "I think," she said, "I am going to search for some food."

Alice looked up, an expression of delight crossing her face at the prospect of spending time out-of-doors. Before her disgrace, she had been an enrolled member of the Aurelian Society, London's social group for entomology enthusiasts. "Do you mean down in St. Petroc's? For more biscuits? I wouldn't mind another ramble past the—"

"*Not* in St. Petroc's." Ruby brandished the cup. "In the house. Perhaps I can rescue some walnuts before they are pickled."

Tamsin cast a dubious glance in her direction.

"I shan't be long," Ruby said. "Wish me luck."

She took her leave of Tamsin and Alice and made her way in the direction of the kitchens. If the Pomeroy House staff was *not* dining on clam cakes and innumerable jams—if they had some alternative and more salutary food store of their own—perhaps she could work out where they were keeping the comestibles. As she strode down the corridor, it occurred to her that if the staff members were having their own, decidedly more palatable tea, she might be able to sneak around a corner and catch them in the act of stealth dining.

But then again—

She hesitated, chewing on her bottom lip. According to the papers—which, to be sure, had not proven especially reliable— there was meant to be a fantastically elaborate and plentiful wine cellar somewhere on the premises.

Could there be a secret store of food hidden there? And could Ruby simply pilfer some?

A direct assault on the staff was, perhaps, not a good idea. It seemed altogether too much like something the old Ruby would have done: as blunt and impolitic as she'd been back in London.

Three years ago, her sister Cassandra had debuted to general acclaim and fanfare. Cassandra was two years younger than Ruby, four inches taller, and possessed of the shy grace of a baby fawn.

Their mother had died when Cass was only five. Their father had been devastated and rudderless; he had never, as far as Ruby knew, considered marrying again. And so with no one else to fill the role, Ruby had stepped into the role of Cassandra's protector. Cass was compassionate, sweetly earnest—when she'd been presented in all her gentle beauty to the *ton*, Ruby had been determined to shield Cassandra from rakehells and fortune hunters.

She'd gone about it in her usual straightforward fashion. She could see that now—dash it, she'd been able to see it then too, only she had not known how to do it any differently. She had, on one memorable occasion, accused a little circle of Cassandra's admirers of rank avarice, only to later discover that the slight, elegant fellow in the back of the crowd was the grandson of a royal duke and also Cassandra's favorite.

Cassandra had turned scarlet. Another one of the debutantes, her arm linked with Cassandra's, had murmured, "Don't mind her, Cassie. She's only jealous that you have all the beaux and she has none at all."

Ruby had swallowed back the hot feeling lodged in her throat and fled for the library. And the duke's grandson had ceased calling on Cassandra.

No, she thought now. She should not confront the Pomeroy House staff directly. She was bound to say too much, too frankly. In all her well-intentioned forthrightness, she might somehow reveal that she, Alice, and Tamsin weren't meant to be in the house at all.

She reversed course, heading away from the kitchen, and found her way outside through one of the exterior doors. If there *was* a wine cellar—or a larder, or an ice house, or some other place for storing food—it would almost certainly be accessible to deliveries from the road.

The sun shone hot on her face as she prowled around the outside of the mansion in the direction of the kitchens. There were barrels of flowers everywhere out here—alliums and irises and delphiniums in a profusion of summer color. Ruby looked carefully for any apparent door that might lead to a larder or—

She froze mid-step.

Captain Malcolm Archer was standing beside the door to the kitchen.

And he was not wearing a shirt.

Ruby was a connoisseur of classical statuary. She had seen the Platonic ideal of the human form represented in paint and marble across continents, across centuries.

She had never, ever seen anything like Captain Malcolm Archer. His musculature flexed and leapt, all leashed power. His skin glistened with perspiration, gilded and wildly alive. His shoulders were just this side of too broad, and the tanned expanse of his chest was marked by flecked rope burns and old scars.

He was no statue. This was a body that was lived in, that had fought, that had forged its own way in a hostile world.

As she watched, Captain Archer picked up a bucket and upended it over his head. Cool, clear water spilled out, soaking his thick black hair and running in rivulets down his skin.

In the sun, the droplets sparkled, calling the eye to every place on his body they traversed. The sweep of his shoulders—the impossible ridges of his abdomen—the trail of black hair that clung to his belly and down, vanishing beneath the flimsy waistband of his—

Ruby suppressed the sound that wanted to emerge from her mouth, which she feared might have been *eek*. Her left foot, she realized, was still suspended in the air, so she returned it deliberately to the ground. And then, rather squeakily if she were honest with herself, she cleared her throat.

Captain Archer had to dash the water from his brow before he could see her. There was more rippling of muscles—Ruby *tried* not to gape, which was impossible—and then he opened his eyes and took her in.

And then—curse the man. He smiled. Dimples carved themselves into place on either side of his mouth.

"Lady Ruby," he murmured, "what a surprise. How may I assist you?"

She gazed at him in almost affronted astonishment. He had no shirt on, for heaven's sake, and still he smiled like that. Could the man truly be so comfortable in his own skin?

Ruby could not imagine such self-assurance. But then again, she'd also never imagined the human form in such glistening artistic perfection, so evidently her imagination had previously unperceived limits.

"Nothing," she squeaked—dash it, still squeaking?—and ducked around him, pressing her body to the mansion's granite wall. "Only . . . taking some exercise." She lifted her arms, then dropped them, and then wondered what in God's name she was doing. "The Cornish air is so salubrious!"

She was going to combust, she suspected, from the shocking

temperature of her cheeks and the ongoing force of Malcolm Archer's half-naked body.

Fortunately, before her incineration could properly begin, her hand found the door to the kitchen.

And then, to her surprise, Captain Archer's hand came to the door as well. Not to the handle—no, his palm was flat against the wooden surface, somewhere at the level of her head. He leaned in toward her.

Ruby's brain waved pirate flags and began to play a frantic, tuneful alarm.

"Shall we walk together?" he asked smoothly. "I can escort you down to St. Petroc's, if that's your aim."

"Oh—no. I'm finished, actually." She fumbled for the handle. "All done. Fully exercised."

He spoke more quickly. "Perhaps I can persuade you to walk with me down to the beach, then. There are some mineral formations that might interest you."

"No. No. I'm quite certain—"

"Lady Ruby, I—"

His hand closed over hers, but it was too late. She'd already got the door open, and with a quick wrench, she toppled into the warm, close Pomeroy House kitchen.

Arrayed around a low wooden table sat the four people who made up, as far as Ruby could tell, the rest of the staff at Pomeroy House.

The chef, Theophilus Wall, had his wife in his lap and four or five hounds at his feet. His broad arm was wrapped around Eugénie's waist, and his chin was pressed to the top of her head.

Gerry and Lamentation—Ruby had not yet learned their surnames, though she knew by now that Gerry was the silent one with the ponytail and Lamentation the effusive one with the blond ringlets—lounged in wooden armchairs, dice in hand and boots entangled on the ground.

A pot bubbled on the hob, and when the aroma struck her nose, Ruby felt her knees wobble.

Whatever was in that pot was, easily, the most delicious thing she had ever smelled.

"Ah," said Wall. He lifted his arm from Eugénie's waist, and she slowly slithered out of his grasp. "Cap. I see you've done bathing."

Lamentation dropped his dice, which bounced wildly across the table, and leapt to his feet. "Lady Ruby! What a . . . what a pleasant . . ." His eyes darted from Ruby to Captain Archer to the pot on the hob, and a look of guilty alarm passed across his face.

Ha! she thought triumphantly. She'd known it. They *were* keeping the real food for themselves. For some inexplicable reason, the Pomeroy House staff had this delicious supper in the kitchen, and they did not want Ruby, Alice, and Tamsin to know about it.

There was no way Ruby could bring herself to pilfer walnuts from the larder. Not now that she knew about the most ambrosial soup—stew?—in the entire world. Not when it was almost within her grasp.

Perhaps she could grab the pot and run. Perhaps she could—

"Lady Ruby was taking some exercise on the grounds," Captain Archer said from behind her. To her extreme relief, he'd put on a shirt while she'd been drooling over stew. "We happened to encounter each other outside."

"Entirely coincidental," she chirped. Somehow she'd moved farther from Captain Archer and closer to the stew. "My, that smells delicious!"

"Do you think so?" Captain Archer prowled nearer. "I'll tell the stable master you approve. It's mash for the horses."

Mash for the—

Surely not. There was no way she was literally slavering over a meal meant for equines. She hoped.

Captain Archer leaned in and smiled. His dimples flashed.

In response, Ruby narrowed her eyes. "Mash, is it? I visited the stables just a few days ago and did not notice any cattle."

"They must have been out with the grooms." He'd shaved regularly since the day of their arrival, but his whiskers grew quickly. She could see the black stubble on his jaw. "Taking deliveries. Carrying messages for House di Sangro. That sort of thing."

"I see." Ruby glanced down at the pot, which was full to the brim with tiny macaroni and fresh spring peas and cubes of bacon, all swimming in a creamy béchamel.

It was *not* mash. It looked like a pot filled with edible heaven, and she was not letting it go without a fight.

"If this is meant for the horses, perhaps I can deliver it myself." She looked up and met Captain Archer's brilliant blue eyes. "I do live to serve House di Sangro."

There. Let the man weasel his way out of that.

He made a little humming sound, which seemed to vibrate somewhere in her belly. "As do I—and that includes, of course, the princess's court ladies. I could not let you put yourself out. The grooms will take the mash when they settle the animals for the night."

"Ah," she said. "The grooms. To be sure. I should like to meet them, now that you mention it." She glanced over at the table and its two remaining empty chairs. "Why don't I wait upon their arrival?"

He drew even nearer. The sea-wind scent of him made her head spin, though perhaps that was an effect of her very gradual starvation over the previous twelve days. "Of course you should meet them. Perhaps tomorrow. They've gone all the way to Penzance today, and you might be waiting some hours."

She tried not to grind her teeth. He *was* a weasel, and a scoundrel besides. "I adore waiting," she said balefully, and plopped herself down into one of the spindly chairs.

She did *not* adore waiting. But she was not leaving this room without the macaroni.

"Ah," Archer said. "Certainly." He looked at the assembled staff, and whatever they read in his face made them all scramble to their feet. And then, lazily, like some great predatory cat, he lowered himself into the chair beside her and extended his booted feet. He put his hands behind his head. "I shall wait here with you until the grooms arrive."

His trousers were damp from his bath, and they clung to his thighs. Ruby looked resolutely away.

She knew what he was doing. She could see right through him. If he remained at her side, she could neither dive into the pot of macaroni nor steal it for Alice and Tamsin. He was smiling at her, the great smug lout.

Perhaps she could pretend a fondness for horse mash. How would he react if she stood up, crossed the room, and locked eyes with him while she slowly consumed an entire pot of food ostensibly for equines?

"While we wait," Archer said, "perhaps you can tell me more about Princess Serafina. I've never met her."

That was convenient, as neither had Ruby.

The room had emptied while they spoke, but before Ruby

could summon some half-remembered details about the princess, Lamentation caromed back. He gave the general impression of springs all over—his curls fluttered as he bounced up and down on his heels.

"Cap," he gasped, "we need you."

Archer looked from Lamentation to Ruby to the macaroni. "I wouldn't like to leave Lady Ruby alone."

Visions of bacon danced in her head. "Oh no," she said, "please. Do go on. Your footman needs assistance. I shall be fine here."

"I must insist—"

Lamentation cast an agonized glance at them both. "We *really* need you. Lady Ruby can return to her companions."

"Yes, of course." Ruby waved a hand at the door. "I'll follow just behind you. Don't mind me."

Archer cupped her elbow. "Perhaps Lady Ruby can come with us."

"That would not be wise," Lamentation said in a strangled voice.

Ruby plucked her elbow from Captain Archer's warm, callused grip. "Why not?"

"Because . . ." Lamentation looked helplessly around the room. "Because . . . we've been attacked."

"Attacked?" Archer echoed. His whole body tensed, even though Ruby was fairly certain he knew as well as she did that Lamentation was lying through his teeth.

"Yes!" Lamentation exclaimed. "Attacked. By the Scourge of St. Petroc's!"

Chapter 7

Archer sat at his desk and stared at Gerry and Lamentation. Both looked considerably more drooping and tragic than the bloodhounds at their feet.

"Tell me that it worked," he said. "Tell me they're finally leaving."

Gerry winced. "Ah," he rumbled. "No."

Archer tried not to grind his teeth. "Tell me that you did not fill this house with hundreds of green, malodorous beetles for *nothing*."

Five days ago, he'd been forced to abandon Lady Ruby to her own devices in the kitchen. She had, as he'd anticipated, promptly purloined Wall's favorite macaroni. Lamentation, meanwhile, had dragged Archer to the back of the house, where the makings of one of their schemes to rid the house of ladies-in-waiting had gone somewhat awry.

For over a week, Lamentation and Gerry—motivated, as usual, by Lamentation's penchant for brilliant ideas—had been gathering shield bugs, which they'd intended to loose in the ladies' bedchambers. Unfortunately, the shield bugs had broken free from their cardboard captivity and begun to flutter wildly about the room that Gerry and Lamentation shared.

It had taken hours to get the damned things back in the boxes, and Wall had been shouting about proper habitation and diet, and Archer was absolutely certain that a number of the creatures had slipped out through a gap beneath the door hinge. He kept finding the escapees in his coat and his trouser pockets and once, memorably, deep within one of his stockings.

Lamentation had promised Wall that they would release the remaining bugs into the ladies' rooms expediently, and Archer had spent the subsequent days hoping against hope for the sound of ladylike shrieks. Or packing. Or the departing footsteps of expensive slippers.

He had heard nothing of the sort.

"She liked them," Gerry said gloomily.

"Who did? Lady Ruby?" Archer sprang to his feet and started to pace. One of the bloodhounds bayed enthusiastically in response.

Of *course* she would like the beetles, damned devil creature that she was. She had certainly liked everything else he'd thrown at her.

He had thought this would not be difficult? It was bloody impossible. *She* was impossible—a little plum pudding of a woman who could out-scheme a hardened criminal. Somehow she'd turned the entire house upside down with her pigments and oils; he felt as though he spent three-quarters of each day attempting to anticipate her whereabouts and transport illegally acquired silks to new and more obscure hiding places. When they'd absconded with her bed linens, she'd had a fresh set procured in less than half a day. And when he'd put that damned seagull in the music room, she'd simply climbed a ladder, agile as a sailor on the ratlines, and chased it back outside with a fluttering lace glove.

He suspected if she had a mind for gambling, she could've coaxed fortunes out of half the rich sots in London with her air of sweetness and that twisty, ruthless brain. She—

"Not Lady Ruby," said Lamentation. "Lady Alice."

Archer halted. "Lady *Alice*? Are you certain?"

"I have managed to divine the differences between them, yes. Lady Alice. The black-haired one, who looks like she'd run screaming at the sight of a hole in her stocking. She squealed in delight when she found the beetles in her chamber, started talking in Latin, and then told the other girls all about how, in the South Seas, shield bugs come in enormous sizes and display a maternal instinct heretofore unknown in the kingdom. Or phylum. Or something."

"Also," Gerry put in, "she says they're not beetles. We got that bit wrong."

"They're not beetles," Archer repeated.

"No. No chewing mouthparts."

"No chewing—" Archer flung up his hands. "This is madness. Absolute, utter— 'No chewing mouthparts'? Are they ladies-in-waiting or natural philosophers?"

"I've never seen a lady-in-waiting," Lamentation said. "Perhaps this is typical."

"It is *not* typical."

Lamentation shook back his curls, and Archer saw a green bug flutter out from where it had been entrapped. One of the bloodhounds leapt eagerly to catch it.

Archer groaned, thrust his hands into his own hair, and then started to pace again.

"Cap," Lamentation said, "I know you said—"

"No."

"—not to bring this up except in the direst straits and—"

"*No*, Lamentation."

"—I hate to say this, but I think things have grown dire."

Gerry looked up from where he was using a handkerchief to polish the toe of his boot. "I agree. Never seen your eye twitch like that before, Cap. Not even at Grado."

Archer squeezed his eyes shut and then opened them again, which regrettably did not still the tiny tic. He elected to pretend it was not happening. "No. We are not bringing out the Scourge of St. Petroc's."

Lamentation settled his hands on his hips. "I don't see why not! I think it's a good idea."

"You think it's a good idea because you invented it. There is no Scourge of St. Petroc's."

Archer had never heard those words put together in that order until Lamentation had brought them out in front of Lady Ruby. Lamentation's powers of invention were, evidently, bolstered by bug-induced panic. And now that he'd planted the seeds for the creature's existence, Lamentation was inclined to take the scheme to its natural, outrageous culmination.

Lamentation was frowning lightly. "I am aware that the creature is not real. That's all the better. I've been saying it for days now, Cap: *We* can act the part of the Scourge. Clothe ourselves in sea wrack. Growl and moan outside their windows—"

"Their windows are about thirty feet in the air."

Lamentation was undeterred by this threat of physics. "Lurk

in the shadows and persuade them that the Scourge is here to devour their hearts. If we do it right, we take all the suspicion off Pomeroy House and put it on this mysterious foul beast."

Archer stifled another groan for fear of hurting Lamentation's feelings.

The trouble was, it was *not* a good idea. They had resolved not to imprison the ladies-in-waiting in the manor—despite Lamentation's enthusiastic suggestions to that effect—which meant that the trio visited the village regularly.

How was he to persuade them that there was a real and terrifying local legend known as the Scourge of St. Petroc's if none of the St. Petroc's residents had ever heard of such a thing?

Unfortunately, Archer was running out of good ideas. He had exhausted his own capacity for ingenuity with lions and marrow jelly and a bloody horde of insects. What would it take to frighten off these ladies-in-waiting if a *biblical plague* did not manage it?

"No," he said finally. "No foul beasts in the shadows. Not yet, in any case. Let me keep trying."

Frightening the ladies off had not worked thus far. But it still seemed possible that Archer could *talk* them into leaving. Somehow induce them to recall how lovely their lives were back in London and how much they missed their homes.

He cast a suspicious glance at Gerry and Lamentation as he left the office. Lamentation smiled angelically back, even as he whispered something to Gerry about sea lettuce.

Gerry, at least, would listen to Archer's orders. Gerry had been only eleven when he'd found himself on one of Archer's ships. He'd been narrow-shouldered and sullen then—afraid, Archer had thought, beneath his surly silence.

When he'd gone overboard with the iron ballast, no one had noticed but Archer.

It had been a hell of a leap and plunge to get the boy back onto the ship. Gerry hadn't thanked him, had glared furiously in the other direction, his arms across his chest and water dripping from his hair and into his mouth. He hadn't cried until later. Archer had found him curled up in the fo'c'sle, and when he'd sat down silently beside him, Gerry had flung himself wordlessly into Archer's arms.

He'd been Archer's ever since—would follow Archer straight into Hell.

Lamentation, on the other hand, was more likely to charge Satan with a saber out of the wrongheaded notion that he was protecting Archer from himself. When Archer had been sent down from the navy, Lamentation had been far more furious than the rest—would have happily thrown Admiral Penney in front of a cannon and been hanged for his efforts if it would have kept Archer on the *Swallow*.

Archer had to get these ladies-in-waiting out of the house before one of his crew did something catastrophic and wrongheaded and loyal.

But inside the library, he did not find the trio he'd expected— he found only Lady Ruby, standing on a stool and carefully repairing a crack in the wall with a silver mortar knife.

She hadn't heard him enter, so he took the opportunity to study her. He had contemplated her more than seemed strictly necessary this last fortnight—mostly how to expel her from the house—but in their typical interactions, he was generally scheming as rapidly as possible, trying his level best not to let her get the better of him. And when he was sparring with her, he could not properly take her in.

Now he could. Her blond fall of hair was pulled back off her face, and he could just make out her pointed chin, the round cheeks that gave her face the contours of a heart. He had no idea if her figure was in fashion in her circles—plump, buxom, soft about the jawline—

God above, he ought not think about her figure.

She was certainly in fashion to *him*.

He cleared his throat, and she jerked around to look at him. She colored pink, scrambled off the stool, and then glanced down in dismay as mortar fell in a gloomy plop onto the floor at her feet. Hastily, she drew the stool over the spill, winced, and then thrust the mortar knife behind her back.

She had cleverness and tenacity in spades, to be sure—but subtle, she was not.

"Captain Archer." Her voice was a trifle breathless. In her brief flurry of activity, her hair had burst free from whatever had held it back, spilling in a disheveled tangle down her neck and shoulders.

He strode farther into the room. "Lady Ruby. Your companions are out today?"

She stuck her fingers into her hair, which served to spread the mortar around a bit. "Lady Alice and Miss Drake are on an errand, yes."

"I wasn't aware that they'd gone." Perhaps they were arranging passage back to London. Archer could only hope. "What sort of errand?"

She gave him a distrustful glance from beneath the cover of her curly lashes. "One expressly requested by Princess Serafina."

That was a decidedly vague and suspicious answer, but he did not want her on her guard. He wanted to beguile her. Addle her, if possible. He wanted to remind her of the pampered ease she had enjoyed in London and convince her of how very much she wished to return home.

So instead of inquiring into the precise nature of the princess's request, he lowered himself onto the settee and tried to make himself look at ease and unthreatening. He caught a hint of that luxurious scent—amber and velvet and brandied fruit.

He gave her his best smile, a full helping of dimples. "This must be quite a change for you, Lady Ruby. Cornwall and Pomeroy House, I mean. Nothing at all like your life in London."

She shot him a dubious glance. "I suppose."

"Fewer parties." He cast about for some notion of how an earl's daughter filled her time. "Very little piquet. Or dancing."

For some reason, this made her frown harder. "To be sure. Not a quadrille to be had here. However shall I survive the loss?"

"You are not fond of dancing, then?"

Despite his leading example, she had not seated herself in one of the neighboring armchairs. Instead she glared down at him and said flatly: "No."

Good Christ, was there any other woman on Earth so unimpressed? He wanted to spin her into a waltz just to see what she would say. "You prefer classical art, is that right? There must be a great deal to see in London—galleries, collections—"

"Captain Archer," she said coolly, "what is it that you are about?"

He smiled harder at her and held back the desire to pinch the bridge of his nose. He'd never in his life been plagued by headaches until these exceptionally unlikely ladies-in-waiting had come to Pomeroy House. "Merely making conversation. About your life before you came here."

"Well." She crossed her arms across her chest. "Allow me to satisfy your curiosity. I recently finished my fourth Season, which places me very nearly on the shelf. I did not dance at parties because I was not invited to do so."

"Surely not," he protested.

But she had not finished. She seemed torn between lifting her chin defiantly and staring him down. "I have studied antiquities in Monastiraki and art in the Levant, and in the last three years, I have published four academic papers." Her chin won out. She jerked it up. "All of them anonymously, because my father would not have me shame him with my unladylike pursuits."

She had flushed hotter as she spoke, embarrassed and yet unrepentant. Archer suspected that if he glanced down, all the overflowing décolletage above her bodice would be pink as well.

He did not look. He'd never in his life so utterly flubbed a conversation with a woman, and he wasn't about to compound his errors by looking at her breasts.

He ran one hand through his hair and tried to regain some measure of composure, which had not seemed this difficult since he'd been taking heavy fire in the Adriatic. "It's obvious to me, Lady Ruby, that you and your companions are accomplished in any number of pursuits. The improvements you've made to the house in the past fortnight are remarkable."

She scowled. "Do not pour the butter boat on me. It will not work."

Yes, that had become increasingly apparent. Somehow she had him on his back foot again, except he was sitting, and she was standing above him, refusing to be charmed and smelling of heaven. She had the advantage of him in every possible way, and he had to rack his brain to recall what he'd come into the room to do.

To make her go, of course. That was what he ought to be about. If he wanted her to smile, it was only because it was part of his plan.

He took a stab in the dark, aiming for some memory she might be proud to relate. "How was it that the three of you came to be Princess Serafina's ladies-in-waiting?"

But that too, it seemed, was wrong. At his words, she bristled up, all plumpness and prickles, like a small angry hedgehog.

"I beg your pardon," she snapped. "Do you mean to suggest that we are not qualified?"

"No. Of course not. What have I said that could possibly be taken as a criticism—"

She spun away from him, and then back, advancing, and he had to scramble to his feet or else be trampled. "There is no one in England more suited to the position than Lady Alice and Miss Drake, I will have you know. Tamsin could plan a dinner party for the princess and all her retinue in half a day. Alice would fill this house with music if the pianoforte were not home to a pack of hounds."

The pianoforte was home to hounds? This was news to Archer.

"I assure you," he said, "I did not mean to question their skills. Or your own."

She took a step toward him, and his well-honed military instincts informed him that he was in deep water.

She was not charmed. And she was not poised to go. She was not stepping closer in order to share his space—she meant to invade it.

"It strikes me, Captain Archer," she said, low and firm, "that our association with House di Sangro is not half so unlikely as your own. Tell me, how did a naval captain come to be steward of the princess's holiday house?"

His presentiment of danger strengthened. "My former admiral put me up for the job," he said easily. It was true. Penney had. "I interviewed with House di Sangro's majordomo and was selected from a suite of qualified candidates."

"Were you?" she said softly. And then: "What's his name?"

"I—" He blinked. "What?"

"The royal family's majordomo." She no longer reminded him of a hedgehog—now she seemed as sharp-edged as her silver mortar knife. "What's his name? I seem to have forgotten."

Archer remembered the majordomo clearly. Signor Urbano Neri was a small bewigged fellow, with a bone-deep loyalty to House di Sangro that Archer had admired.

But he did not think Ruby needed to be reminded of the majordomo's name. She wanted to know if Archer knew it.

She did not trust that Archer was who he said he was.

And—hell. He ought not be surprised. When had he yet managed to deceive her?

"Signor Neri," he said finally, and then he caught her elbow in his hand to slip past her. He knew when he was out of his depth. He needed to retreat and regroup.

He had to get away before this devil of a woman uncovered something she wasn't meant to know.

He'd done the same perhaps a dozen times before—grasped her arm to lead her away from hidden silk gloves in a stack of crates or illicit French plums stashed in the larder. But this time, when he touched her skin, her lips parted on an indrawn breath. She had a tiny stripe of white mortar drying into dust on her cheek, and he had to stifle the desire to brush it away.

It occurred to Archer that, for the first time since he'd first seen her at Gravesmuir's town house, she was not wearing her fussy little gloves.

It occurred to him that he was imagining her bare hands on his skin.

When she spoke, her voice was the faintest bit unsteady. "And the rest? At dice with Tamsin, Lamentation said he served under you in the Royal Navy. How did he come to be a footman?"

Slowly, the import of her words registered in his mind. In his belly, which went sick and cold.

He dropped her elbow as though it had gone straight to molten iron in his hand. It was one thing for her to question his role in the house. He could manage her questions—at least, he *thought* he could manage them, though it was seeming less and less likely by the day.

But he did not dare let her turn those ruthless eyes upon his crew. He couldn't allow his people to come under suspicion. He would not let them get hurt.

"Lamentation was in service before he came aboard the ship," he lied smoothly, "to a countess."

"Was he? Which countess was that?"

Instead of answering, Archer stepped around her and moved toward the door.

As he did, he thought about Gerry and Lamentation in his office. He thought of sea wrack and lettuce. Of bugs and schemes. Of a little clear-eyed blond with a mortar knife and a tendency to ask far too many questions.

He thought of Professor Quenby.

And then he thought: *The hell with it.*

The hell with trying to cozen and cajole her. It was not working.

He felt as he had when facing a French warship with twice as many cannons as his own—reckless with fear and stubbornness. He looked at her mortar-daubed face and abandoned all caution and sense. "The truth is, Lady Ruby, I did not come to the library today to discuss House di Sangro at all. I came to warn you."

She paused. Blinked. "To warn me?"

"You mustn't leave the manor alone," he said. "Not without protection."

"I'm—sorry?"

He dropped his voice. In a tone of lethal earnestness, he said: "The Scourge of St. Petroc's has been sighted again. Along with the remains of its victims."

Her lashes flew up. She was still holding the mortar knife, now brandished at the level of her chest. "Its *victims?*"

"Oh yes. The bits left, of course. After it has devoured their hearts." He smiled at her: a wolf's smile, all teeth. "From what I hear in the village, it has a particular fondness for young ladies."

Chapter 8

There was almost certainly no such thing as the Scourge of St. Petroc's. Alice, who was Ruby's authority on all things nature, had never heard of it. When Ruby had related Captain Archer's story to her friends, Alice had immediately begun to take notes upon the creature's habitat and diet. ("The hearts of young ladies does seem awfully specific, don't you think?")

For her own part, Ruby didn't believe in the creature at all. The Scourge, thus far, had only been mentioned in moments of extremity on the part of both Captain Archer and his staff. Admittedly, she'd heard some mysterious scraping and moaning outside of her chamber the last two nights running, but the sound had stopped promptly upon her opening the door. When she'd got the candle lit, she had glimpsed angelic blond ringlets vanishing around the corner.

No. She was quite, quite positive that Lamentation had invented the sea monster, and Captain Archer had gleefully embroidered the details during their encounter in the library.

Except—

Well. She did not believe in the Scourge. And yet, as she crept into the larder at four o'clock in the morning, the shadows deep and the sound of growling still lurking in her memory, she felt the smallest, *tiniest* bit unsettled.

She gritted her teeth. There was nothing to be frightened of. Sea monsters didn't exist—only charming, suspicious sea captains with dreadful blue eyes and criminal dimples.

And besides, she had a plan to carry out. She was too busy to be afraid.

Four days ago, while she had been sparring with Captain Archer in the library, Alice and Tamsin had gone down to St. Petroc's for supplies. Though the food situation had improved ever since the macaroni incident—the staff seemed to have given up that particular gambit—Alice and Tam had felt it wise to procure biscuits and crackers and fresh fruit in case circumstances deteriorated once more.

They'd also acquired a host of supplies for the house's refurbishment: whitewash, paintbrushes, rich brocade fabric—and, because Tamsin was Tamsin, practical items like soap and stockings and candles. They'd paid in advance and asked the shopkeepers to deliver the unwieldy parcels directly to Pomeroy House that afternoon.

This excellent plan had been foiled somewhat by the fact that none of the items had ever arrived.

The parcels' disappearance was bizarre. Inexplicable. And, in light of the preceding month's other peculiarities, decidedly suspicious.

Ruby and Alice had ventured down to the village yesterday evening to verify that the items had indeed been delivered as they'd requested. After confirmation from a variety of bemused shop-keepers, Ruby had hatched a new plan: one that involved creeping surreptitiously around the house in the middle of the night, her dressing gown belted tight around her waist and her ears attuned to every sound.

If the Pomeroy House staff had intercepted the parcels for some baffling reason of their own, the items were no doubt hidden somewhere in the house.

And Ruby was going to find them.

She'd begun the search hours ago and had found nothing of note in the conservatory or the library. Her clandestine hunt had then taken her to the ice house—cold, empty of lady-in-waiting paraphernalia—and now to the underground larder beneath the kitchen. She was busy riffling through jarred jellies and finely milled flour, curls clinging damply to her neck, when she heard a sound from somewhere up above her head.

It was long and low and unearthly. A hiss—almost a rasp.

The hairs on the back of her neck rose. Had that been . . .

No, she thought. *Get hold of yourself, Ruby Ballimore.*

The Scourge of St. Petroc's was *not* real. And even if it was, it had no reason to spend its night creeping about six feet above her head, trapping her underground until her bones disintegrated to dust.

As she stood motionless beneath the rickety wooden staircase, the noise came again: a long, creaking, drawn-out scrape. And then, to her surprise, a mumbled curse.

She put fictional sea monsters firmly out of her mind. It was not the Scourge. It was a person—and the sound resembled not a terrifying monster stalking young ladies, but a heavy object being dragged across a freshly mopped kitchen floor.

Her heavy object, if Ruby did not miss her guess. And whoever was up there was on the point of spiriting it away.

She took the stairs two at a time and flung open the larder door.

In front of her, in a patch of moonlight, stood Captain Malcolm Archer. His booted foot was braced on a wooden crate, and his shirt hung open at the neck. He had, perhaps, been up all night: His jaw was thick with black stubble, and his mouth was set not in his characteristic smile, but in a grim slash of handsome concentration.

An expression that shifted, when he saw Ruby, to one of dismay.

"Ha!" she exclaimed. "I knew it!"

He blinked at her. "You . . . what?"

"I *knew* it. I knew you were up to something nefarious."

He glanced at the door and the dark expanse of the stairs behind her. "Did you just emerge from the larder in the middle of the night?"

"I— Well, yes, but that's not—"

He smiled at her, a long curl of wicked amusement. "Fancied a midnight snack, did you?"

Devil take the man, it was as if he couldn't help himself. She made herself scowl in the face of all that charm, despite the shivery sensation it set off inside her.

In truth, that smile only made him more suspicious. No one had ever flirted with Ruby like that without some ulterior motive.

"My whereabouts," she said distinctly, "are none of your concern."

He stepped closer, and she took a quick, shallow breath. Her eyes dropped helplessly from his mouth to the place where his shirt gaped open. His skin looked silvery-gold in the moonlight, his chest muscular and sprinkled with black hair.

"You are lady-in-waiting to my employer." His words scraped out, sweet and rough, and she could *feel* the warm proximity of his body. "And you are living in my house. Everything about you is my concern."

Oh God. Her stomach flipped at his words, his tone—but she refused to let him have the advantage. She gritted her teeth and removed her gaze from his throat so that she might glare at his wooden crate instead.

"I believe you have something that belongs to me," she said.

He followed the direction of her gaze to the crate. His expression went slightly bemused. "I don't think so."

"Do you not?" She set her hands on her hips. "Four days ago, Alice and Tamsin made a number of purchases in St. Petroc's, which were meant to be delivered to Pomeroy House."

He raised his brows. "And?"

Oh, he meant to play at innocence, did he? She frowned harder. "*And* while our parcels were purportedly delivered to the house, none of us have been able to locate them." She pointed at the crate so he could not pretend to misunderstand. "Until now."

"I think you are mistaken, Lady Ruby."

"I beg your pardon?" She took a little step closer to him as well. "Do you intend to suggest that we did not go down to the village? Or that our items have not gone missing? Because either way, I do not believe that—"

"No," he said. "I mean, I don't think what's in that crate is yours."

Goodness, she was awfully close to him now; she had to lift her chin to meet his eyes. "Forgive me *if* I seem unduly skeptical,

Captain Archer—but if that is *not* a crate of our stolen belongings, then why were you sneaking about with it in the middle of the night?"

His feet were braced wide, his chest a solid, sand-dotted expanse. His lashes fluttered briefly before he spoke. "I always move crates at night. This one in particular."

"You always move crates at night?" she repeated incredulously. "In the dark?"

"Of course. To avoid the . . ."

There was a brief silence.

"Yes?" she prompted.

"Dogs." He said it very definitely, and then he followed the word up with a blinding grin that—curse the man—made her knees feel weak. "It's bones. A whole crate full of bones from the butcher. Wall uses them in his potage à la reine."

"I don't believe you."

His breath hiccuped on a laugh. "I assure you, that potage was most assuredly made of—"

"*Not* about the soup." She lifted her chin a little higher. "Open the crate and show me."

"I can't. The scent of bones will attract the hounds. They'll wake the whole house with their clamor—you've heard them."

Good God, the way the man spun nonsense ought to be studied by natural philosophers. She scowled at him. "I'm willing to risk it."

He opened his mouth—no doubt to deliver more absurdities— and then stopped. His entire body went suddenly taut.

Ruby too froze, her gaze flying from Captain Archer to the wide kitchen window.

Something had moved out there in the dark. Some black, man-sized shadow had flitted across the glass.

Her skin went cold. Her whole body, in fact, felt as though she'd been plunged into ice.

That wasn't . . . Surely it couldn't be . . .

"What the devil," Archer muttered.

"Was that"—she had to pause to lick her lips—"one of your people?"

"No," he said flatly. "It wasn't."

He put his hand to her arm to hold her in place, and they both stood motionless, listening intently. In the ensuing silence, they heard a sound from outside—a small crack, like a twig snapping.

And then they saw the shadow flit once more across the window.

Archer pressed her behind him and then strode to the kitchen door in two long strides. "Stay here," he barked, abruptly naval and commanding. And then he vanished into the corridor.

She pondered this directive for half a moment. He was not *her* superior officer, was he?

No, she reasoned. He was not. She trailed him out into the hall.

He glanced back. "I thought I told you—" He broke off at another muffled sound from outside, almost inaudible. "Never mind," he growled. "Stay behind me."

He moved cautiously outdoors, and she followed, pressing herself to the exterior wall beside a barrel of blue delphiniums. The sky was slowly shifting from gray to pink; it was brighter here than it had been inside the kitchen. Archer's loose white shirt whipped slightly in the wind off the sea, rippling over his shoulders.

Ruby watched him, heart in her throat, as he eased himself around the corner of the house. As he—

Spun back.

Covered her body full-length with his own.

She gasped. The back of her head bumped the granite wall behind her, and his heated, solid body pressed into her chest.

"What—" she got out.

His mouth was at her ear. "Shh," he whispered. "There's someone out there. Don't move."

She held herself still as a stone, and so did he, his body crushed against hers.

Was it a trick? A lie? She couldn't make him out—couldn't think clearly beyond the roaring of the waves and the thunder of her own pulse. She sucked in silent gulps of air, her cheek pressed to Archer's bare chest. His breathing too was unsteady; each ragged exhalation ruffled her hair.

She couldn't say how long they stood like that. When she shifted, individual grains of sand from his chest scraped her skin: tiny pinpricks that flickered along her nerves. His hand tangled in the band of her dressing gown, holding her in place.

There was silence all around them. No more soft cracks or mysterious figures. Nothing but the throb of her own blood.

She felt . . . she felt . . .

She didn't know what she felt. Her blood was racing with terror and a sudden, dizzy awareness of his body against hers. Her skin felt hot, her thighs tight and loose at once. His thumb made a slow, slow arc at her waist, and she shivered.

When he pulled away, it felt like a loss.

As she watched, he stepped in front of her to peer around the corner and then strode off in the direction they'd heard the sounds. He moved easily, gracefully: a jungle cat, prowling about the edges of the cliff.

When he came back to her, his face was taut. "I think—whatever that was—it's gone."

Her mouth was still too dry to speak. To swallow. She licked her lips and watched as his gaze flickered, for the space of a heartbeat, down to her mouth.

And then he looked back up. His eyes were bright blue now that the sun was nearly up—fierce and deathly serious. "Tell me the truth. Was that one of your girls out there?"

"I—what?" Her voice wobbled, and she had to stop to clear her throat. "Of course not. Alice and Tam are in their beds asleep. I thought . . . it wasn't . . . one of the staff?"

He lifted his hand to rub at his stubble. "No."

Oh heavens, she felt exceedingly stupid saying this, but: "The Scourge, perhaps?"

"There is—" He broke off halfway through the syllable, staring down at her. A gust of sea wind snapped his shirt, baring more tanned skin.

"Yes," he said finally. "Of course. The Scourge. What else could it have been?"

She narrowed her eyes. His right hand was curled around the lip of the flower barrel, and his face had gone closed. He wasn't trying to charm. But he wasn't telling the truth either. She could read it in the careful blankness of his face.

They had seen *something* outside the window. She knew they had. And though she wanted to attribute Archer's actions to some ulterior motive, his urgency had seemed all too real.

"You don't know either, do you?" She moistened her lips again. "We are both in the dark."

His jaw tightened. "It was the Scourge." The edge of his hand brushed the delphiniums, and a few tiny blue flowers fluttered to the ground. "Go back inside, Lady Ruby. Keep your friends away from the village. As you can see, it's not safe to be out."

"But we—"

She broke off abruptly. His palm had come to rest, warm and heavy, on her waist, and the sensation shocked her out of speech. Her lips parted as she met his gaze.

"Quit skulking about the house," he said. He used the tie of her dressing gown to turn her around, back toward the kitchen door. "Especially at night."

She looked at him over her shoulder. "But our parcels—"

"I'll hunt down your missing items." His voice was low, and he looked her in the eye as he spoke—so earnest she could almost believe him. "I promise."

Chapter 9

It seemed possible that his crew had grown too good at smuggling.

Honestly, they'd only been at it for a handful of months. They did not have the excuse of a lifetime of piracy to explain their actions. Archer would have supposed that—upon finding several boxes of anonymous luxury items on their doorstep—Lamentation and Gerry would have at least *asked*.

But no. They'd leapt into action and secured the goods in a variety of obscure and ludicrous hiding places all over the house, most of which they couldn't entirely recall when interrogated. Only when Archer had confronted them after his encounter with Lady Ruby had they admitted that they'd thought the parcels were Archer's and thus needed to be promptly concealed.

Bloody Christ. It had taken him six days to track down all the items, which was approximately ten times as long as it had taken for Lamentation and Gerry to hide them in the first place.

To be fair—to himself—he'd not had an easy time of it. Every time he'd turned around, Lady Ruby seemed to be peering around a corner, or popping into whichever room he was in, or inventing an errand that involved nosing into every nook and cranny.

She was clever. Canny. She was the only person in the world who had ever seemed to see right through him, a fact that made him increasingly uneasy.

Had it been one of her ladies outside the window that night?

She had said it wasn't, and, somehow, he believed her. He recalled her blunt honesty from Gravesmuir's party. Even when it had not served her, she'd spoken the truth.

He shifted the last bulky, waxed-paper-wrapped parcel beneath his arm and headed downstairs.

If it had not been one of the ladies-in-waiting slinking furtively past the window, who could it have been?

There had been something—some anonymous figure—out there in the dark. He was certain of it. One minute he'd been attempting to hide a crate full of illicit Spanish oranges, and the next he'd been pressed full-length against Lady Ruby, trying desperately to shield her against what he'd believed beyond all shadow of a doubt to be an armed intruder.

He could've sworn that was what he'd seen. The flash of moonlight off steel—he knew that cold metallic gleam by heart.

But when he'd peeled himself away from her—all soft, ruffled temptation—he had found nothing at all. No trace of an intruder; no sign of danger. If there had been a stranger outside the house, the fellow had vanished into the cliffs.

Could it have been one of Gill Oliphant's men? Some rival smuggler, looking for contraband?

The Scourge, his brain helpfully suggested, a notion he quashed.

There was no Scourge, for God's sake. Lamentation had made it up.

When he arrived in the kitchen, he discovered most of the house's occupants arrayed around the wooden table. Tamsin appeared to have maneuvered Lamentation and Gerry into a game of cards, which she was winning handily. Ruby and Alice were seated together, their heads bent over a tray of sugared currants.

The food deprivation scheme had met its demise days ago. Wall was a pitifully soft touch—when he'd discovered how much the ladies-in-waiting had liked his macaroni, he'd folded immediately.

Archer set the parcel down and cleared his throat.

Ruby looked up.

All of them looked up, probably, but Archer couldn't say for certain.

God above, he was an atrocious fool. His eyes had gone straight for her face, and his mind had wheeled instantly back to that tense dawn: sea wind, and her unnameable scent, and his sudden, mad arousal as he'd shielded her against the wall. Each dip and curve of her body was engraved upon his mind—was right there before him every night when he closed his eyes.

A pair of black puppies tumbled drunkenly toward him, and he had to pretend to be very interested in picking them up and setting them on their feet. He cleared his throat again and handed one of the puppies to Lady Alice. "I believe this is yours."

She smiled winningly up at him from her chair. "Why, yes. Thank you."

He gestured to the paper-wrapped bundle, which he'd deposited just inside the door. "I've also located the last of your purchases."

"Have you?" said Tamsin dryly. "Strange, how they were all mislaid like that."

"Baffling," he agreed. "Perhaps the Scourge is to blame."

"Oh, indeed."

Ruby got to her feet and moved toward the door. Archer backed hastily away.

"Wait," she commanded.

He attempted to ignore her directive, but the remaining puppy seemed to be entangled in his bootlaces. He tried to dislodge her while also smiling innocently at Ruby. "So sorry. Can't stay. I have a prior engagement."

"Not right this minute you don't." She was already upon the parcel, her fingers searching out the paper seams. "I mean to ensure that all our purchases are accounted for. There were several items remaining we had yet to locate, and I require— Oh." She paused in the act of unfolding the waxed paper. "Alice, did you order this for me?"

Oh *hell*. Now Gerry and Lamentation were looking up as well, and the puppy was still fastened to the toe of his boot. He crouched down to try to pry her free and got a needlelike fang embedded in his finger for his trouble.

Alice glanced over at the item in Ruby's hand. "What is it?"

"A book. *The Polychromatic Ornament of Italy*. I've been longing to read it—however did you know?"

"I didn't." Alice's long black lashes fluttered. "Does it say where it came from? Perhaps it got mixed up in our things?"

Ruby riffled through the book's glossy pages. "It says . . . Kneebone's Circulating Library."

"That's in Penzance," Lamentation said, blithely unaware of the betrayal he was executing. "You ladies didn't go all that way, did you?"

"No, of course not," Alice said.

"You were in Penzance," Gerry rumbled. "Weren't you, Cap? Two weeks back?"

Archer stared at the recalcitrant, traitorous puppy and attempted to become invisible.

Ruby's brows drew together. She looked at the book in her hands. At the paper parcel she'd just unwrapped.

And then she looked at Archer.

He had not, evidently, succeeded in vanishing. He smiled weakly at her, and— Bloody hell. The puppy sank several more teeth into the tip of his finger, and he tried to pretend that was why his face felt hot.

"Do you know how this book got in here?" she asked.

"I've no idea." Through sheer will and iron fortitude, he managed to outmaneuver a dog the size of a turnip. He stood, deposited the creature into Alice's waiting arms, and then turned to the door.

Ruby was blocking his path of escape. The waxed paper had slipped to the floor, and she clutched the book to her chest. "You have no suspicion as to where it came from?"

"Not a one."

It had been an absurd notion. He had been in Penzance for the day with Oliphant, making plans for the next shipment of wine casks, which they meant to tie to the *Delphinium*'s stern and then drag underwater to avoid detection. Archer had taken a turn about the circulating library as he always did, his mind flickering helplessly back to his childhood and the room he'd shared with his mother, her hands tracing the crisp leaves of a new book.

When he'd seen the Italy volume, lying open on a shelf, he'd thought of Ruby instantly. It was brilliant. Vivid. Eye-catching and unapologetic. Like she was.

It was about classical art and decoration, which he knew well enough that she fancied. For some terrible reason that he refused to contemplate, he'd bought the thing before he could think better of it. He'd meant to slip the volume onto the Pomeroy House shelves and let her discover it on her own, but she and her ladies had scarcely left the library during the room's extended refurbishment. Hiding the book in the ladies' parcels had seemed a perfectly plausible alternative.

Only— Damn it to hell. He hadn't expected he'd *be there* when she opened it.

He blamed the situation entirely upon the dogs.

Ruby was still holding the colorful volume tight, as though someone might try to tear it from her hands. "Perhaps the book traversed the cliffs of Cornwall on its own, and then wrapped itself in my parcel."

"Maybe it was the Scourge," put in Lamentation brightly.

Alice perked up. "Is the creature known for its interest in milled paper?"

Archer attempted to sidle past Ruby in the threshold. She placed a hand on his arm, and—despite every one of his intentions—he went still. Her gloves were some filmy lace; he could see a single golden freckle above the knob of her wrist.

When she spoke, her voice was quiet. Her eyes were sweet and hopeful and earnest. "Did you procure this book for me?"

Archer tried to marshal a lie.

And for the first time in a very long time, he found he couldn't think of a single thing to say.

Of course not would hurt her feelings. *I just happened to see it in a shop* would admit his culpability.

I hope you like it would be both true and—God help him— downright catastrophic.

He mumbled something unintelligible, relocated Ruby's hand from his arm to her book, and shifted around her to make his escape.

At the table, Alice sighed dreamily. Tamsin groaned and put her head in her hands.

And Ruby kept her eyes on him. As he slipped past her, two of his fingers tangled—not quite on purpose, not quite by mistake—in one of the ribbons on her frock. The pale creamy length spooled out between them, a slow, silky glide.

He had to make himself let go.

Chapter 10

Plastered to the wall of an inn in St. Petroc's, half hidden in the shadows and clutching a bottle of sour wine, Ruby considered at what point her life had canted so abruptly into deceit and subterfuge.

Could it, perhaps, have been when she'd decided to forge a letter from her father and pretend to be a lady-in-waiting to a princess?

No, she decided. That wasn't it.

Her life had taken a sharp left turn on the day she'd first met Captain Malcolm Archer.

It had been four days since she'd unwrapped the book on Italian architecture. Four days since he'd . . .

Had he given her the book? She did not know. Her body went hot and flushed and unsettled every time she considered the notion.

Was it some new misdirection? Some bizarre sideways sort of charm?

She forced herself to recall the many ways he'd tried to coax and flatter her. He was a rake. A liar. He was, she had begun to suspect, some sort of pirate king who'd taken over Pomeroy House and had disposed of its proper staff, though hopefully not through means of outright murder.

She could not trust him. But she—

Oh, heaven help her. She wanted to. Some part of her—some small, foolish, *absurd* part—wanted to believe that he'd bought the book to please her. Because he'd known she would wish to have it.

It was dreadful. A nightmare. She refused to admit his duplicitous charm might be working.

Under no circumstances, she'd told herself, *are you to let Captain Archer get the better of you.*

She'd persuaded Tamsin and Alice to walk with her down to St. Petroc's despite Captain Archer's warnings. She'd made vague reference to the acquisition of more candles, but in truth, she meant to find out what the villagers knew about the Scourge and, beyond that, the true nature of the staff of Pomeroy House.

They'd been in the village for roughly a quarter of an hour when Ruby had seen Captain Archer duck into a bustling public house. With a hissed word to Tamsin and Alice, she'd followed him. She'd watched his familiar broad-shouldered form sweep right up the stairs and into the connected inn, and had promptly ordered her friends to stay in the pub, collect whatever gossip they could find, and wait for her to return.

Alice had blinked. "Do you mean to confront him again?"

"No! No. I'm going to follow silently. Watch from the shadows. Unravel whatever scheme he is currently about."

Tamsin's auburn brows had looked very skeptical. "Do you think he might be . . . enjoying a mug of ale from the pub?"

"He's gone upstairs to plot," Ruby said firmly. "I know it."

Alice had snatched a three-quarters-full wine bottle from an abandoned table and thrust it into Ruby's hands. "Here," she'd said. "Take this. In case you need to explain why you're wandering the halls. You can say you're delivering this to a patron."

Ruby suspected Alice had a grandiose notion of the level of service offered by this establishment, but she nodded and clutched the bottle to her chest as she headed up the stairs. As she strode down the corridor, she listened hard for Captain Archer and whatever "nefarious purposes" sounded like. She took a rather rash sip of wine from the bottle and shuddered.

Perhaps Captain Archer had come upstairs to meet with a fellow pirate. Or to do away with more unsuspecting servants. Perhaps he'd come to craft a life-sized model of the Scourge of St. Petroc's and set it in her bedchamber. Perhaps all of his machinations were an elaborate facade to hide the fact that he was wanted by the Crown for a lifetime of unsavory crimes.

At the corridor's final door, Ruby stopped abruptly.

She'd heard something. She was certain of it—a sort of long, drawn-out squeak. She squeezed close to the door and pressed her ear against the rough surface.

Yes—there it was again. Another squeak, and another, almost rhythmic. And then she heard a familiar low voice emit a strangled oath.

Her jaw dropped, and she clapped her free hand over her mouth.

It seemed she had found Captain Archer. And his activities were not so much nefarious as—

The rhythmic squeaking started up again.

Oh God. Sweet merciful heavens. Her face was on fire and her ear was still pressed to the door.

Had he really taken himself off to the inn in the middle of the day for a liaison? Had that choked-out oath been the sound of *pleasure*? Was that what a man sounded like when he was in the throes of passion?

And why, why, *why* had her stomach dropped at the sound?

This had not been a good idea. She was perfectly willing to confront Captain Archer over his schemes and his falsehoods. She was *not* prepared to confront him with his trousers off and in the middle of—the middle of—

Ruby spun hastily away from the door, which turned out to be another critical error of judgment. As she whirled, the wine bottle—unbalanced and still mostly full—slipped from her hand and launched itself full bore at the doorjamb.

Her heart flipped over in her chest as she felt the bottle slide free from her grasp. As she watched in horror, it hit the wooden frame with a hearty *thwack*. She flailed, caught it before it crashed to the floorboards, and held back a little whimper of dismay as vinegary wine sloshed over her glove.

And then, before she could move or think, the chamber door came open.

"Lady Ruby?" Captain Archer demanded. His tone was all incredulity, and his shirt was open at the neck again, baring half a foot of glistening chest. His hair and face were flecked with white plaster dust.

She met his glacial blue eyes and said feebly: "No?"

He looked up and down the corridor, then caught her by the arm and began to drag her inside the chamber.

Ruby dug in her heels, and more wine sloshed across her forearm and Captain Archer's sleeve. "No," she said again, "truly, Captain Archer, please permit me to leave you to your privacy."

"To my privacy?" he said incredulously, and then she was inside the room, the door flung shut behind her. "If you meant to leave me alone, then why in God's name did you track me down and . . ."

He trailed off.

Ruby had slammed her eyes closed the moment she'd crossed the threshold, but curiosity overcame her at his extended silence. She cracked open her right eye.

He was glaring at her. His arms were folded across his chest, which caused his pectoral muscles to leap into sharp relief. There was no naked paramour in the room with them, which was something of a relief. On the other hand, the room was covered from end to end with various linens, chunks of fallen plaster, and an extraordinary amount of rope.

Honestly. *Rope.* It wasn't even dark out.

"What are you doing here?" he said finally. "Do not prevaricate. I warned you not to leave Pomeroy House."

"You said it was not safe," she allowed. "But we brought a pistol. And Vanessa."

He looked baffled and outraged beneath his plaster dust. "Who the devil is Vanessa?"

"Alice's puppy."

"Oh well, if you've a puppy then—" He broke off, his eyes narrowing. "*What* are you looking at?"

"Nothing!" she said, which was a lie. She'd been staring at the open window and wondering if it was large enough for a recently postcoital adult to exit from.

"Is something about to leap through that window and attack me?"

"No!" She paused. "I hope not. I was wondering if— Ah. If that's where your companion departed from. The window, I mean."

"My *companion*?" he repeated. He looked her up and down. "Are you *drunk*?"

"I beg your pardon," Ruby said frostily and then realized she had gestured to the window with the wine bottle.

"Foxed. Fuddled. Three sheets to the wind."

"Of course not. I was downstairs with Alice and Tamsin and the puppy, and then I was . . . upstairs. Coincidentally."

"I can't believe this," he said. "You're positively soaked."

"I most certainly am not. And you ought not cast stones, Captain Archer. Shouldn't you be attending to your duties at the manor? Not . . . not . . ."

"Not what?" His eyes gleamed with suppressed mirth. "Don't leave me in suspense."

"Whatever it was that you were doing!" Her mind kept providing remarkably vivid illustrations, most of which had been inspired by a book called *Aristotle's Masterpiece* that Ruby had borrowed from Belvoir's Library last year and that had not, it turned out, been about Aristotle.

"I am trying," Archer said, "to hang these four hammocks for Mrs. Enys."

Ruby blinked. Surely the second, third, and fourth hammocks were superfluous. "Mrs. Enys?"

"Floss Enys," he clarified. "The innkeeper, ever since her husband died. She has four sons and only the one spare bedroom during the high season. She can't squeeze four beds in here, and the boys have grown too tall to share, so I told her I could try affixing hammocks to the beams. It's how we slept on—my ship."

Four hammocks. For a widow's four growing sons.

"Oh, for heaven's sake," Ruby said. "You must be joking."

She'd spent the last four days building a thorough case against him in her mind—ever since she'd looked at his handsome face and flushed cheeks and *known* he'd bought the book for her.

He was a rake. A pirate. A liar.

A rakish lying pirate who had, apparently, come all the way down to St. Petroc's to help a widowed mother of four.

Her heart performed some acrobatics in her chest, which she did not appreciate. It had absolutely no right to involve itself in her feelings about Captain Archer, who was a dreadful flirt and expert dissembler and—God help her—loyal and inventive and kind.

No. *No.* This was a disaster.

"Well," she said, "best of luck with your ropes." She gestured with the wine bottle again. Goodness, the scent emanating from it was certainly pungent. "I'll be going now."

He did the thing again with his arms and his chest. Ruby forced herself to look at his plaster-dusted hair instead.

"Absolutely not."

"No?" She raised her brows. "Do you mean to tie me up?"

Astonishingly, his throat went pink at her words. "I told you. It's dangerous to be alone. *Especially* here in St. Petroc's. I will escort you home."

"I have Alice and Tamsin—"

He yanked open the door and thrust her back out into the corridor. "I'll escort all three of you, then. You should not be in the village at all."

"I don't know how else you expect me to acquire beeswax tapers for the candelabra, Captain Archer. I assure you, they do not come buzzing in on tiny bee-drawn carts. May I remind you that I am not a prisoner at Pomeroy House?"

"You ought to be," he muttered.

He marched her down the stairs with his hand still wrapped around her upper arm. His palm was callused; his grip felt warm and rough and strong. Tiny shivers of arousal raced along her skin, and she tried very hard to ignore everything about her current situation. Including Captain Archer.

They were confronted at the bottom of the stairs by a tall handsome woman in a ruthlessly clean apron.

She put her hands on her hips and glared at Archer and Ruby both. "Caught her red-handed, did you?"

Ruby blinked. Was "her" . . . *her*?

Archer removed his grip from her person—she quashed the part of herself that wanted to sigh a little at the loss—only to sling an arm companionably about her shoulders. "Something wrong, Floss?" he said easily.

"To be sure there is. *This* one"—she gestured at Ruby, who had no idea what she'd done wrong—"has run off with my best wine and hasn't paid for it."

Ruby glanced down at the bottle, and the sticky red stains on her glove. Surely "best" could not be right. "I beg your pardon," she began. "My companions—"

"I ejected them ten minutes ago. I don't allow dogs in my establishment. They drank nothing and paid for nothing and it was only when I went to clear the table that I noticed the wine gone and no coin left."

"Oh," Ruby said, "well—let me—" She fumbled for her reticule, at which point it occurred to her that Tamsin had taken charge of the financial aspect of their visit to St. Petroc's and she, Ruby, had no money with her at all. "Ah"—she swallowed—"if you'll give me a bit of time to—"

"To what?" demanded Floss Enys. "Run off, and with half

my wine on your frock and the other half on Captain Archer's shirtfront?"

Ruby felt herself wilt. Patrons were starting to look up; she thought she heard someone laugh behind his hand.

She felt a familiar hot rush of embarrassment, and she *refused* to look up at Captain Archer. She'd told him weeks ago that she was a failed debutante, but that was altogether different from standing beside him as he watched her blunder.

"I— Perhaps I could work the debt off in the kitchen," she said. "I am quite good at scrubbing. Captain Archer can vouch for that."

When he jostled her closer, she did not see it coming. She felt the hard press of his chest as he tucked her more firmly beneath his arm, and she could hear in his voice that he was smiling. "She's a dab hand at cleaning," he confirmed. "You can take her at her word. Used to be a barmaid in Nether Bishop, our Ruby."

Mrs. Enys was still scowling, but she had softened under the force of Captain Malcolm Archer. "At her word, is it? Is that as reliable as yours, fancy lad?"

"Come now," he said cheerfully. "When have I ever let you down, Floss?"

Mrs. Enys pursed her lips. "Does that mean you've finished your preposterous project upstairs?"

"Not yet. I scoured the hammocks last night and laid them out, and I'll be back later on to hang them. I'll have William and George and Sidney and Alfie in their own beds before the sun goes down tonight. I swear it." He produced a coin and flipped it through the air toward Mrs. Enys. "For the wine. She doesn't need to scrub."

Ruby felt herself flush from head to toe.

Mrs. Enys caught the coin out of the air, and at his words,

her mouth crooked up. "Keeping her hands as pretty as your face, love?"

"As pretty as yours, maybe."

When Ruby looked up, she saw that he was grinning at Mrs. Enys, all dimples and ease. Her skin burned hotter.

He had . . .

Oh God. He had *rescued* her. He had directed the force of his considerable personality at Mrs. Enys to save Ruby from a contretemps of her own making.

He had no reason to do it. She had accused him of all manner of deceit and duplicity; she had tracked him down here and confronted him in what might well have been *flagrante delicto*. And still, despite it all, he'd come to her aid.

No one, so far as she could recall, had ever rescued her in her life. She felt feverish and prickly: shame and gratitude and resentment all tangled inside her. Captain Archer's fresh salt scent seemed to have fuddled her brain.

"I beg your pardon," she got out. "Thank you for the wine, Mrs. Enys."

Mrs. Enys waved her off. "Get on with you, then. Before I change my mind and put you to work."

The dismissal was clear, but Ruby found herself hesitating. She forced herself to recollect that she was no dewy-eyed miss, easily swayed by a comely ship's captain who laughed and paid for her wine and smelled of the sea.

She had entered this inn for a reason. She tried to recall it.

"Tell me," she said, before she could lose her nerve, "have you heard of any new sightings these last days?"

Mrs. Enys's brows rose. "Sightings?"

"Yes," Ruby said. "Of the Scourge of St. Petroc's."

Archer's arm around her shoulders went from *cozy familiarity* to *iron bar*. He spun her about, pointing her toward the door. "Time to be off!" he said. "I'll be back later, Flossie."

Ruby tried to look back to ascertain Mrs. Enys's response and caught Captain Archer as he mouthed some words over her head.

Drunk as a lord, she thought it might have been.

She hopped a little, trying to catch his gaze. "What did you say?"

He grinned down at her, his face all unrepentant dimples and plaster dust. "Nothing, my darling little barmaid. Come now. Let me take you home and I'll fetch you another bottle of wine."

She stopped dead, and he hauled her back into motion, the implacable strength of his arm keeping her on her feet. "If you call me 'darling' again I shall—"

"Farewell!" he called over his shoulder to Mrs. Enys, drowning out Ruby's protest.

"You are a scoundrel," she muttered into his shirt as he dragged her down the street. "A rogue and a liar. I don't believe a word you've ever said to me."

For just a moment, his steps faltered.

Ruby looked up.

"That's probably wise," he said. For the space of a heartbeat, he looked almost pained. But then his summer-blue eyes fell back to her, and they crinkled at the corners as he smiled. "Though if we're cataloging crimes, pet, *you're* the one who stole the wine. Not me."

And then—horrid, *horrid* man—he winked.

Chapter 11

Archer shoved the final barrel deep into the shadows of the cliffside cave with a grunt.

It was heading to dusk, and he was covered in sweat and sand. It had taken him a solid two hours to move the smuggled casks into a larger cave, where he could first decant the Rhenish wine and then begin the process of selling, profiting, and enthusiastically hoping not to get arrested. Wall had offered to come with him, but Archer had refused.

He wanted to think.

More properly—yes, he could admit it, at least in the privacy of his own mind—he wanted to brood. The cove was an excellent place for brooding.

He'd hustled Lady Ruby out of the inn before she could do any significant damage. He'd reiterated his warnings about slavering beasts who ate crucial bodily organs, but even as he'd said it, he'd known it was hopeless.

The Scourge story had not worked, and neither had the bugs

or the food or any of their other schemes. They'd made no discernible progress in ridding the house of three ladies-in-waiting, and worse, *far* worse—

He liked Lady Ruby Ballimore. A lot.

He liked sparring with her. He was astonished by the changes she'd wrought in the mansion and impressed despite himself by her persistence. He admired her loyalty and her eyes and all that stubborn, heart-wrenching bravura, and he dreamed—God help him, he couldn't seem to *stop* dreaming—about the way she'd felt pressed against his body.

It was a bad stroke. The precise opposite of what he ought to feel. He was not meant to enjoy every moment he spent in her company, and he should not, *should not* hope that she was enjoying it too.

When Benji Woon had laughed behind his hand in the inn's public room, Ruby had supposed it directed at her. Archer had thought so for a moment as well—he'd seen Ruby flinch, and his gaze had snapped to Benji.

Benji hadn't been laughing at Ruby. He'd been laughing at Floss's tiny, angry kitten, fleeing through the front door with a pigeon twice her size. But in that moment—in a bright, blazing, impossible-to-ignore revelation—it had occurred to Archer that if someone had laughed at Ruby, he would've killed them on the spot.

That did not seem to bode well.

He puffed out a breath and shoved his hair out of his face, an action that left a smear of sand on his cheek. The sand in the cove was dazzling at dusk, Archer had always thought—all flecks of glitter and rippling lines left by the waves.

Golden. Exquisite. Somehow both soft and sharp at once.

Impossible to be free of, once you'd touched it.

Archer ground his teeth and headed toward the water's edge to fling himself into the ocean and thereby rid himself of the metaphor. But before he could finish peeling his shirt over his head, he heard a familiar squeaky throat-clearing behind him.

He let go of his shirt and spun about. Lady Ruby stood, tucked behind a shelf of rock, not ten feet from the cave in which he'd hidden sixteen casks of wine. Her chin was up, her eyes fixed on the streaked pink clouds, and her expression so innocent that he almost expected her to begin to whistle.

She was absurd. And he more so, because his heart had leapt in his chest at the sight of her.

"Oh," she said brightly, as if only just noticing him. "Captain Archer. Fancy seeing you on the beach."

"A coincidence, I'm sure," he muttered, and prowled toward her. He needed to distract her—needed to keep those damned penetrating eyes directed away from the cave at the foot of the cliff. "Did Lamentation send you down here?"

She locked her hands together, her gloved fingers intertwined. "Erm . . . no."

"How did you find this cove, then?"

"Well," she said. The faux innocence on her face was slowly evaporating as her cheeks pinked. "If you must know, I followed you."

"You followed me?" he demanded. Bloody *hell*. Had she been watching as he'd moved the wine? Surely not—he knew her well enough to think she would not have remained silent as he blithely committed crimes in front of her nose.

She looked even more guilty now. "Your trail, rather."

He squinted at her. The light was low, but—yes, her frock did appear to be covered in sand and bits of pink thrift and white campion. "You followed my *trail*?" He kept on echoing her words, but only because she was such a fantastic enigma. Was she some kind of tracker of wild game, in addition to her expertise in Greek statuary and home decorating? Had she crawled along the footpath looking for signs of where his boots had trod?

No doubt she had. There was no sense in continuing to be shocked by anything she came out with. If she took wing and flew to the top of the cliff, he would have to simply accept it as another talent she'd kept hidden away.

She was quite red now and yes, in fact, her flush *did* go all the way down to the tops of her breasts, visible above her low-cut bodice.

He cursed himself for noticing.

"In the interest of honesty," she said, "I will admit that it took me several tries to locate you."

He was close enough now to put his hand to her elbow, and so he did. He plastered a smile on his face as he gripped her arm, though at this point any effort at charm was mostly reflex. "Lady Ruby, you continue to astonish me. Have you any interest in showing me how you managed such a feat?"

She widened her stride so that he could not spin her away from the cave's entrance. "As a matter of fact," she said, "no."

Of course. Of course she did not. "Then might I escort you—"

"No," she said again. "I have come down here, Captain Archer, for the express purpose of determining what brings you to the beach so often."

Bleeding, bloody hell. She could not find these damned casks. He would do whatever it took. Anything.

He turned his desire to wince into a brighter, more enthusiastic smile. "'Often' must be an exaggeration—"

"Twelve times," she said crisply, "in the four weeks since we arrived at Pomeroy House. I can't think what one would call that frequency other than 'often.'"

"You pay remarkable attention to my person, Lady Ruby," he got out. Only force of habit kept the words from emerging through gritted teeth.

But to his surprise, her flush, which had just begun to fade, flared back again, hot and pink. Her gaze fell to the open neck of his shirt. To where his chest was bared beneath her gaze.

Archer realized he was still holding on to her, nothing but rough sand between his fingers and her skin.

He had not meant to suggest that she had some licentious interest in him. But his blood heated beneath the slow drag of her eyes—more gray than blue in the gathering dark.

Perhaps he *had* meant to suggest it. Perhaps some part of him had known that beneath the ruthless scrape of her gaze was something hotter, more intent.

That when he was looking at Ruby, she was looking back. Even when she did not mean to.

"I attend to you merely to ascertain the various scopes and shapes of your deceptions," she said. But her voice had lost some of its mortar-knife edge—gone blurred, just a bit, beneath the sound of the sea.

He stepped closer. Her eyes traced a path from his throat up to his face, and the flush on her skin deepened beneath the red glow of sunset. Her lips parted.

She was not susceptible to his charm. But he remembered the way she'd gasped, almost silently, when he'd touched her skin in the library. He remembered the way her gaze had caught and dragged on his shoulders when she'd found him outside the kitchen.

He thought, with a hot throb of guilt and lust, that she might be susceptible to *this*.

He could distract her this way. If he moved even closer, he might keep her eyes away from the cave.

"The truth is," he said, low and soft, "I am very fond of swimming."

Ruby moistened her lips. This time her gaze did not drop. "You do not appear particularly damp."

"I had not yet begun." His mouth curled up. His pulse had risen. He felt the way he'd felt in every naval engagement—as if he must plunge forward or die. "I can show you, if you like."

"I am familiar with the notion of sea bathing."

"I am certain you are," he murmured. He took one of her hands in his and set his fingers to her pretty, fussy glove. He could smell the sea, the honeyed scent of campion crushed against her skirts. Her own velvety warmth.

Slowly, slowly, he slipped one pearl button free. Another.

"I could take you to my favorite pool," he said. He watched her eyes, her mouth. Her throat. "Show you how deep the water goes. How it feels, cool and lapping over your skin."

She didn't say anything. She did not move, except for the way her chest rose and fell.

He unfastened the final button and slid the glove from her hand. He let himself enjoy the slow luxurious glide—because it was an act, because he needed this to seem real.

Her breath hitched.

"I'd close my eyes while you bathed," he said. His voice

sounded thick to his own ears. "Or else swim with you. If you wished it."

He'd found her other glove. He pushed against the cool smooth surface of the first pearl button. Slid it through the buttonhole. Let his thumb press against the pulse at her wrist, which galloped as quickly and unevenly as his own.

"Tell me," he murmured. "Say you want me to take you there."

She moistened her lips again, and her mouth moved into the shape of a word, which Archer thought—hoped beyond all reason—would be *yes*.

Both of her gloves were off now. His fingers tangled with hers, then slid up her forearm. He could feel the shape of her. The warmth. The tiny surrender of soft flesh.

His blood beat hot. Longing throbbed like a pulse beneath his skin.

It was at this point that Archer realized he'd lost the plot. Somewhere between when he'd begun talking and when he'd ended, his mind had unfolded a vision of cool water and damp skin and bare voluptuous limbs, a pale flurry in the dark. He'd meant to distract her with his words, with his nearness—and now he was the one flushed, heated, imagining—

Things he ought not imagine. Things he'd spent the last four weeks dreaming of, restless and fevered. Things he had resolved each morning to forget.

"You," she said finally—not *yes*—"ought to attend to your duties at Pomeroy House. Not spend your afternoons sea bathing."

He dropped her arm and stepped back, almost stunned by the depth of his disappointment. The air between them was a cold shock—a plunge into the sea.

He'd thought to fluster her with his proximity, with his

questions, with his wits. But now he was the one on his back foot. Affected. Painfully, suddenly aroused.

He'd done all this to unsettle her, hadn't he?

Or had he merely wanted to feel her skin beneath his hands?

Hurt and confusion made his tongue run wild. "I ought to? And what of you, Ruby Ballimore, lady-in-waiting to the Princess Serafina? Is your relentless attention to my activities a royal decree or merely a way to pass the time?"

She jerked her chin up. "I don't see how that's any of your—"

"Tell me, Lady Ruby, how exactly does the princess transmit her royal orders? Because I notice you've received no correspondence at the manor at all since you arrived."

She tried to step backward, but the dark face of the cliff was at her back. "I beg your pardon. Do you mean to suggest—"

She broke off, but she did not need to finish. He knew what she was thinking, could see it written all over her transparent heart-shaped face.

Did he mean to suggest that she had invented her position? That she was not, in fact, the princess's lady-in-waiting?

That she was as much a fraud as he was?

He'd met court ladies once, at a dinner party with Admiral Penney; they'd been delicate and highborn, and they'd not appeared to lift anything heavier than their forks. They had neither discoursed on Greek statuary nor joyfully exclaimed over bugs. They had not brandished mortar knives and carefully, painstakingly restored a thousand spiderwebbed cracks. They had not polished windows until they gleamed.

He did not know what exactly he suspected. But he knew—in his bones and his brain and his soft, stubborn heart—that there was more to Ruby Ballimore than she let on.

"We receive our correspondence in St. Petroc's," she said finally.

"Do you? Could you show me your letters from the princess, if I asked?"

Her mouth tightened. Her chin came up. "Is this an interrogation, Captain Archer?"

He had never been able to resist playing with fire. Not as a privateer. Not as Quenby. And not now, face-to-face with Lady Ruby Ballimore.

"If I meant to interrogate you," he said, "I'd already have the truth from your lips."

"The truth?" she echoed. "Tell me, Captain Archer, what are you trying to prove?"

Her eyes were cool and gray. Unmoved. Unpersuaded. Able, as always, to see right through the layer of charm and obfuscation that had never—*never*—failed him before.

What was he trying to prove?

Everything. All his life, he'd been trying.

"*Astra inclinant*," he said quietly, "*sed non obligant.*"

Her lips parted. The words seemed to still her. Nothing moved except the pulse that fluttered at her throat and the waves that lapped the beach behind them, closer and closer to where they stood as the tide crept in.

He could see in her face that she recognized the words: the motto of House di Sangro.

The fact that she knew it proved nothing about her, not really. Nothing about her relationship with the Monfalcone royals. But still—she knew what he'd said.

The stars incline us, but they do not bind us.

Archer could remember the rough planks of the room he'd

shared with his mother as a boy, the ice he'd skimmed off her cup in the mornings before he let her drink. He'd believed, even then, that he could hazard his way into a different world. That he could tear off the future he wanted—with his teeth, if he had to.

He had done it. For a time, he had done it, and then everything had gone away, and now he was back where he'd started—scrabbling and clawing and desperate not to let anyone know the truth of what he was.

Ruby's voice, when she spoke, was soft. "I have always felt bound by what I was born to. Until I came here."

It had grown dark. Her skin was shell-pale in the moonlight. There was a foot of space between them, and he wanted to close that distance with a yearning that felt like desperation. He wanted to put his mouth to hers, find all that sweet, raw courage, and drink it down until he was sick with it.

He could not. It was madness to invite further intercourse between them—to let her slip past his defenses and discover evidence of his crimes.

If she found his cave—if she recognized him as Quenby—it was not only his own life that would fracture. It was all their lives—his and Wall's and Eugénie's and Gerry's and Lamentation's.

And still—still—he looked at her and *wanted*.

"We are none of us bound," he said.

He believed it to be true. He had to believe that he could be more than what he'd been: a thief, a convict, a disgrace.

His crew needed him to be more. And if he had to lie and cheat to keep them fed, well—someday he could make it up to them. Someday, perhaps, he would be safe enough to change.

He tightened his fingers around the glove he still held. Broke her gaze as he stepped back. "It's dark," he said. "The tide's coming in."

Her lashes fluttered as she glanced down to where the waves had met his boots. If she remained, the sea would cut her off from the rocky path she'd used to follow him down to the cove.

"Go back before you're trapped down here," he said.

She did. Her skirts brushed the sand as she turned—away from the cave that held the casks. Away from him.

Go back, he thought, *before you get hurt.*

Chapter 12

"Ruby."

Ruby rolled over and pressed her face into her pillow, shutting out sound and light in a pile of down.

"Ruuuuu-beeeee."

She batted a hand in the direction of the voice—it was Tamsin, crisp and vigorous and far too alert—and tried to sink back into the dark heat of her dream. The cove. The sand. Captain Malcolm Archer, gleaming in the sunset, the roar of the ocean, his hand on her waist, her heart beating like a drum as he set his mouth to her—

"Ruby. Wake up."

She groaned into the pillow. She did not wish to wake. She had a vague sense that her dream—hot and blurred and pleasurable—would give way to a reality that she did not particularly wish to recollect.

"Do you think she might be ill?" That was Alice's sweet, worried voice. "She seems fevered and she's making a dreadful sound."

Ruby flopped over, her eyes still clamped closed. "I'm fine. I'm perfectly well. I only . . . fancied a lie-in."

"It's eleven o'clock in the morning!" Tamsin sounded scandalized.

That made sense. Ruby had not been able to sleep until dawn, what with the way she kept tossing and turning and alternately quashing her memory of her encounter with Archer in the cove and fantasizing wildly about what would have happened had it continued.

She had an excellent imagination, on top of what she'd read about in *Aristotle's Masterpiece*. In her mind, Archer had . . .

No. She *refused* to dwell upon it for a second day running. He was an irrepressible flirt, and she a foolish wallflower. He'd only murmured hot words and removed her gloves to throw her off her course. He'd had no intention of kissing her or caressing her or hiking up her skirts and—

She squeezed her eyes shut harder. "Perhaps I *am* fevered," she muttered. In her *brain*.

"Sit up," said Tamsin ruthlessly. "Open your eyes."

"We've brought tea," Alice said, "and bacon too. I stole it out of the pan myself while the household was distracted." She sounded a trifle smug at this minor crime.

Ruby opened her eyes, shoved herself into a seated position, and accepted a cup and saucer from Alice. The plate was empty; Vanessa, in the corner, appeared to be gnawing on the bacon.

The windows in the chamber sparkled now, and someone— probably Tamsin—had thrust aside the filmy drapes Ruby had hung. Sun poured into the small room. Ruby had whitewashed the walls one evening when she'd been unable to sleep, and then had picked out the elaborate white scrollwork in a deep blue-gray paint, the color of the sea at dusk. The floor was covered in a fanciful blue-and-white unicorn rug she'd found in one of the lower parlors, and more lacy fabric swathed the four-poster bed. She'd cleaned the bedding with hot water and lye and a rough brush she'd turned up in the stables, and—

The room looked beautiful now. She'd known it would.

It had occurred to her, these last weeks, that she loved it here at Pomeroy House. Loved the immense cliffside manor with its oddities and its dogs. Loved her own freedom, and the sense that she knew how to set things right.

She loved matching her wits with Captain Archer's.

She'd told herself her treks across the cliffs and down to the beach were for the purposes of investigation—for determining what he was truly about when he was not attending his duties at Pomeroy House.

The truth, she feared, was simpler. She wanted to see him.

"We've been waiting for you to rise for half the morning," Tamsin said. "We have news."

Ruby looked up. "News?"

"Tam has made a discovery," Alice said. "She's been sneaking about."

Tamsin patted Alice's hand. "You helped, dearest. And Vanessa." She fixed her gaze back on Ruby, who was attempting to restore her brain to its usual functioning with a hearty application of warmish tea. "You know that I've been trying to get into the captain's office ever since we arrived."

"I am aware of that, yes. It's always either locked or occupied by Eugénie."

Tamsin seemed to be trying and failing to suppress a grin. "Well. Captain Archer is nowhere to be found this morning, and so I thought I'd mount another attempt."

Ruby did not wonder where Archer was. She *did not*.

"Eugénie was in there as usual, attending to her secretarial duties," Tamsin went on, "but Alice and Vanessa happened to discover a small family of stoats living in one of the upper chambers."

"Vanessa discovered them," Alice said modestly. "I merely accompanied her."

"And then all the dogs somehow became involved. There was quite a lot of noise and baying—really, Ruby, I am astonished that this did not wake you—and Eugénie and I sprinted for the staircase to find out what the devil was going on." Tamsin's eyes gleamed. "But then, while she was distracted, I doubled back and found myself alone with all of Captain Archer's papers."

Ruby felt an odd sensation in her belly. She knew that Captain Archer was lying about something. Though he was clearly familiar with the Monfalcone royal family—his declarations in the library and the cove had determined that much—there was still a great deal about the man and his staff that did not make sense.

And yet . . .

Some part of her shrank back from the idea of Tamsin riffling through his ledgers and records. She did not want to hurt him, somehow. Even if what endangered him was simple truth.

But she bit her lip and thrust back the notion. He would be fine. *She* was the one who stood to lose everything if the truth of her circumstances came out.

"And?" she prompted. "What did you discover?"

"Quite a lot," Tamsin said. "He *is* the steward of Pomeroy House. There were years of letters from Signor Neri attesting to Captain Archer's employment."

An absurd wave of relief swamped Ruby, and she had to take another sip of tea to recover herself.

"But as far as I can tell, most of the rest of the staff are *not*. Employed here, I mean. There's a budget—a modest budget—for a steward and a groundskeeper. Nothing for footmen or a cook or a secretary. Gerry and Lamentation and Wall and Eugénie—if those are their real names—" Tamsin hesitated, then forged on. "They're not meant to be here, Ruby. They're frauds. Fakes. They're no more employed by House di Sangro than we are. And if I do not miss my guess, they are funding their continued residence with a side of casual smuggling."

Ruby's brain called up the vivid image of Archer in the cove—a play of light and shadow, a chiaroscuro portrait in the fading light. The sand on his angular cheekbone, the heat of his gaze. The easy line of his mouth gone deathly serious.

Astra inclinant, sed non obligant.

The stars incline us, but they do not bind us.

"I know," Ruby murmured. "I already knew."

Somehow, she had. In the library, he had answered her queries smoothly until the moment her questions had shifted from *his* role in the house to Lamentation's. Only then had he lost control of the encounter and launched into his outrageous tale of the Scourge.

She could recall with vivid clarity the moment in the kitchen when Lamentation had mentioned an attack and Archer had gone instantly, ferociously alert. She remembered how he'd covered her with his body outside the kitchen at dawn, and the way he'd rescued her, without thought or hesitation, at the inn.

He could not hide his nature. His first thought—the first instinctive leap of his body—was to protect. To keep the people around him safe.

If he was lying, he was doing it for his staff. Not for himself.

She looked up. Tamsin had her arms crossed over her chest.

"You already knew?" she said. "Are you telling me that I nearly had an apoplexy when I thought someone had discovered me in the office—it was a bat, if you're wondering, not a person—and you *already knew* what I was in there risking my life over?"

Ruby couldn't help herself. She laughed. "Had you died of a bat-induced apoplexy, please know we would have left that out of your eulogy."

Tamsin scowled.

"Ruby's right," Alice said. "Your eulogy will be filled with only the most dignified of encomia. You can trust us."

Ruby smothered another laugh and relented. "I didn't know that exactly, no. It's only . . ." She hesitated, trying to put her feelings into words. "I knew that Lamentation and the others had been with Captain Archer for a very long time. And I knew that whatever deception the captain was about, it involved keeping his people safe."

Tamsin gave her a long, considering look. "I see."

Ruby felt herself blush, just a little, beneath the acuteness of Tamsin's gaze.

Alice, meanwhile, had begun to fuss with the lace on her frock. "Do you . . ." She paused, her dark lashes veiling her eyes, and then looked up again. "Do you suppose we ought to tell someone what we've discovered? The Monfalcone royal family? Or perhaps your father?"

"Absolutely not," Ruby said.

She paused. The words had launched themselves from her mouth before she'd even thought to formulate them. Her father . . .

Her father would want to hear what they had learned. She knew he would—even if it meant revealing her presence at Pomeroy House.

But if he knew the truth, her father would oust the false staff and thereby prove his usefulness to the Monfalcone royals. He was proud of his position of influence with the di Sangro family; if he had the opportunity to further cement his status, he would take it.

Her father would never let Captain Archer and his people stay.

She glanced at Tamsin, and her heart fluttered with relief. Tamsin too was shaking her head.

"No," Tamsin said. "Not a chance."

Alice sighed and sat down on the chintz chair that Ruby had personally carted up a flight of stairs. "Oh, I'm *so* glad. I would have gone along, had you two insisted upon it. But it would have been wrong, I think, to throw them out of their home." She looked up, a little hesitantly. "Even if they aren't properly supposed to be here."

"Dear heart," Tamsin said, "you do not always need to appease us, you know. You are allowed to have opinions of your own."

"I do have my own opinions," Alice protested. "In fact, I think smuggling is a perfectly reasonable career in the face of the same rapacious oligarchy that has put into place the Corn Laws."

Ruby blinked. She had not known Alice felt so decidedly about free trade.

"But there's nothing wrong with following your lead," Alice went on. "With trusting my dearest and cleverest friends to make the right decisions."

"I *am* very good at leading," Tamsin said, and Alice laughed.

On the bed, her teacup balanced on her knees, Ruby didn't quite laugh with her.

Alice favored harmony. She had always moved easily through the world; the fact that the world had turned its back on her seemed a great betrayal of fate. Alice was meant to be charming and lively and cosseted—she was not meant to be an outcast like Ruby.

But—it was true, now that Tamsin pointed it out. Alice was only too willing to sacrifice her own desires if by doing so she might keep the peace. If smothering her own wishes made other people happy.

And had Ruby not done the same?

Before she'd turned nineteen and made her debut, she had traveled all over the Continent with her father and her sister. She could recall so many days with sun-soaked clarity: Cass on the steps of the Tower of the Winds, her bonnet strings fluttering behind her head; their father, pleased and content in the morning, his tray full of black coffee and crisp pastry with rose-petal jam. The three of them together and happy, and she, Ruby, trying to keep them that way.

How much of her life had been devoted to just that delicate balance? How long had she spent trying to fulfill her father's desires for her and for Cassandra?

If she told her father about Archer and his false staff, the earl would be pleased. Proud of her. She *knew* he would. And if she did not tell him—if she let Archer and his crew remain—her father would see it as a betrayal.

The notion was horribly uncomfortable, digging at her ribs like stays knotted too tight. She wished she did not care about his approval. She would have liked for defiance to be easy—for her long-held need for her father's approbation to vanish like smoke.

It hadn't. She still hated to displease him.

But dash it, she could be uncomfortable if she had to be. She could weather her father's scorn, if that was what it took to do the right thing.

Tamsin was chewing aimlessly at one of her thumbnails. "I don't think we should reveal their secrets," she said. "I like them. And their silly pack of dogs. But"—she dropped her thumb and looked at Ruby—"they don't know you won't reveal them."

Ruby felt her brows draw together. "What do you mean?"

"Blackmail," Tamsin said succinctly. "I think you should blackmail Captain Archer."

"I beg your pardon?"

Tamsin's freckled face had taken on a distressingly piratical cast. "Locate him, tell him what we've discovered, and then threaten to reveal what you know to your father, unless . . ." Her mouth quirked. "Unless he agrees to keep our presence here a secret from House di Sangro."

"Then he would know for certain we're not supposed to be here," Alice protested. "There is no way to blackmail him without revealing our own fraudulent purposes here."

"Alice, darling, I have a strong inkling he already suspects."

Ruby hesitated.

She thought of Archer's face in the cove, the charged push-and-pull of their strange dance. The way honesty crept in like starlight around the fractures in his charm.

Astra inclinant, sed non obligant.

"I'm not going to blackmail him," she said finally. "I have a better idea."

Chapter 13

Archer had his hand in his pocket—where he kept her absurd little pearl-buttoned glove—when Ruby appeared at the mouth of the cove.

He'd known she was coming. Bloody *known* it. He'd spent the entire morning and afternoon peering over his shoulder whilst also receiving and then frantically hiding colorful French silks. Honestly, he'd suspected she'd come sooner—had been rehearsing various explanations and deceptions for when she invariably found him out.

He almost wanted her to catch him. Part of him—a stupid part, the part that had stuck her glove in his pocket each morning for three days running—wanted to tell her the truth.

But when she finally appeared, she was flushed and disheveled, her pretty beribboned frock sandy and windblown. Her hand was in a fist at her breastbone, and her eyes were huge and terrorized.

His whole body shot to alertness. "Ruby? What is it?"

"Captain Archer!" She barely got the words out past her uneven breaths. "Thank goodness I've found you."

It didn't seem wildly surprising, considering he was about forty feet from where she'd discovered him three days earlier. "What's wrong?"

"The Scourge," she gasped. "It's here!"

Archer stared at her in frank astonishment. The Scourge? What in the bloody, bleeding—

"The *what?*" he demanded. Surely he had misheard.

"The Scourge," she said again. "It's here—just past this cove. It was after me. Hunted me. I scarcely managed to get away!"

"What?"

He was typically more adept at talking, but then again, under typical circumstances, invented monsters did not come to life and stalk ladies-in-waiting on the beach.

She caught his hand and dragged him down the sand. "I'll show you."

He yanked at her hand to stop her. If there was something after her—not the Scourge, for God's sake, because Lamentation had invented it, but *something*—surely she need not run directly at it.

Though, on the other hand, of course she would. She seemed to have a knack for hurling herself directly into trouble instead of fleeing it.

She freed her fingers from his grasp, then broke into a run. She tossed him a glance over her shoulder—a quick blue challenge. "Come on! Before it gets away."

Shouldn't she *want* it to get away? Did she mean for him to subdue whatever it was with his bare hands?

"Wait," he hissed. "Slow down."

She ignored him and darted around an algae-covered cliff face, her slippers leaving hasty footprints as she ran. The tide was coming in again; Archer's boots shifted in the damp sand.

He ducked around the corner and nearly knocked her over. She'd stopped to look out at the beach, and all of his body collided with all of hers: softness and heat and trailing, tangled ribbons.

He caught her waist to steady them both and then, hastily, thrust her behind him.

"There it is," she whispered, her gaze fixed on the sea. "The Scourge of St. Petroc's. In the flesh."

He followed her gaze, searching for the thing—the monster—that had frightened her.

He froze, looking out at the water's edge.

The Scourge of St. Petroc's, it appeared, was a seal. An enormous, scarred, spotted bull seal, for some baffling reason nowhere near the colony that lived on the other side of St. Petroc's. He was making his way ponderously out into the ocean, but he stopped at Ruby and Archer's approach. As they watched, the seal lifted his head and emitted a long, high-pitched, bone-chilling moan.

Archer froze in horrified anticipation. Did seals . . . charge?

To Archer's relief, the seal dropped his head and resumed his trek into the ocean.

And behind Archer, Ruby giggled.

He spun to face her. "What the devil—"

"I'm sorry," she said—she did not look sorry in the slightest— "but your *face*." She clapped a gloved hand over her mouth, but more laughter broke out around the edges.

"You ungovernable little—" He caught her waist and dragged her backward into a small hollow in the cliff's face. She tried to dig in her heels, and one of her slippers fell off, sticking in the sand. "You knew there was no Scourge."

Her face was tipped up to his, all amusement. Somehow her fingers had locked around his upper arms. "I knew," she said. "I've always known."

He tucked her into the hollow, her back against the damp rough shelf of stone. "Why would you—"

"It was a mad notion, I know." Her laughter was still there, in her voice, in the peach-tender curve of her mouth. "I kept running into that fellow when I was trying to find your hiding place on the beach. And it struck me that if there *was* a rumored legend about a monstrous sea beast, he was probably the cause." Her eyes were bluer than he'd ever seen them, and her hands were still on his biceps. "He did not truly hunt me. I was joking about that bit."

"God," he muttered. "Lunatic. Witch. You wouldn't laugh like that if I'd met the damned thing on the field of battle and been eaten for my trouble."

"You needn't worry." Her eyes sparkled. "I was prepared to hold you back by any means necessary."

He crowded closer to her—damned impossible woman, she deserved crowding, deserved to be knocked off her feet and unsettled. "You don't think I would've won?"

"Against a fifty-stone bull seal? To be honest—no."

"I can't think what I've done to deserve such little faith. Did you note the part where I put my body between you and the mysterious Scourge?"

Her eyes were on him—on his face. "I noted it," she said.

Her voice had gone soft. All of her was soft—soft and unbearably close. Without his strictly intending it, his hands found hers, and he tugged at the fingers of her gloves.

But she closed her hand to stop him before he reached her skin.

"I brought you down here," she said quietly, "because I wished to be alone with you. I wanted to tell you that I know, Archer."

He looked at her—her clear, encompassing gaze—and felt a cold wash of fear.

He tried to make his voice light. "About the Scourge? You've proven that well enough."

"Not just the Scourge. I know everything."

As always, he felt exposed by her. Vulnerable. He didn't know what she thought she knew. "'Everything' seems a high bar," he murmured. "Even for you."

"I know that you truly are the steward of Pomeroy House," she said, "though you use it as a cover for your smuggling operation. And I know that the rest of the house's staff is . . . not. Not staff. Not meant to be there. They're yours, aren't they? Your people. Your crew."

His heart clenched, and if he hadn't been holding her hands, he might have stumbled backward.

His crew. She knew about his crew.

An agonized tangle of emotions tightened his throat, cutting him off from speech. Relief—some part of it was relief, that he no longer had to lie and dissemble, that he could stop trying to skip out from the purview of her damned relentless eyes.

But more potent than his relief by far was his fear. Fear that she might use her knowledge against them all, that she would put an end to their living as quickly as she'd eviscerated the Quenby scheme—and as ruthlessly.

And Quenby. Bloody hell. Surely she'd not put that together as well?

Perhaps she had. She wasn't done talking. Her voice was low

and desperately, painfully earnest. "I brought you down here because I wanted to tell you that it doesn't matter to me—to any of us—how you came to be here. We're not going to reveal your secrets to House di Sangro or my . . . my father."

His chest hurt. Her words seemed to have hit him directly in his solar plexus, as solid as cannon fire, and he couldn't sort out how to respond.

She knew about his smuggling, and she knew about his crew, and it seemed to him that she held their future in her small gloved hand. Four months ago, he had stood at the side of a room and *watched* her put his carefully crafted scheme to the flames. And now she was asking for his trust—asking him to believe that she would not do it again.

It doesn't matter to me how you came to be here, she'd said.

Somehow, he wanted to believe that she meant it. He wanted to believe that it did not matter where he had come from, but only that he was here, on the beach, with her.

Slowly, her gaze dipped to where their hands were entangled, and she closed her fingers around his. Gently, as though she thought he might flee.

And then she looked up. "Tam and Alice and I are no more meant to be here than your crew. We are *not* ladies-in-waiting to Princess Serafina. It is a scheme of my own devising because I wished for freedom. For a different life."

His heart beat hard against his ribs. Surprise rocked him, bright and sharp as an electric shock.

She moistened her lips. "If you asked for our letters from the Princess Serafina," she said, "I could not give them to you. No one knows we are here. Not even my father."

He stood motionless, off-balance, staggered by the percussive force of her words. Not by the revelation of her scheme—that much did not startle him—but by the way she had given the information up.

If you asked for our letters, I could not give them to you.

If he wrote to Signor Neri, he could have her evicted from the house. If he told her father, her dream of a different life would vanish like so much smoke.

What mad impulse had led her to trust him this way? Through what insane store of courage and fortitude could she put her faith in him so utterly?

"Ruby," he got out. His voice was hoarse, and he found that he was gripping her hand.

"I don't want you to be afraid," she said. "That's why I'm telling you all of this. We won't use the truth against you. We will not harm your crew."

He had to force his jaw to loosen. Had to push the words out, all grit and rasp. "You think I'm not afraid of you?"

She blinked. Her lips parted. "I'm—sorry?"

"You terrify me." He put his free hand to her cheek. His thumb just touched the corner of her mouth. "You and your damned honesty. Your stupid, reckless courage."

Her chin came up. Blood rushed to her cheeks, warm beneath his hand. "I did not come down here to be insulted."

"I'm not insulting you." He reached down to pull off her gloves, first one and then the other, and she let him bare her warm, amber-scented skin. "I'm telling you the truth. I'm afraid of your damned gloves. Your interfering ways. Your eyes, all big and blue and stubborn as hell."

"My eyes," she snapped, "are not blue. *Your* eyes are blue. Honestly, if this is the best you can do, I find—"

"I know what color your eyes are," he said. "I've spent half my life in love with the goddamned sea. I recognize it when I see it."

He let go of her hand, but only to tangle his fingers in the ribbon at her waist.

Some idiocy, this was, to try to hold her to him. Not to let her go.

"A thousand different shades," he murmured. "Cool and warm and glorious and wild. I've thought from the first that your eyes were as dangerous as the ocean." This was perilous ground, he knew it was, and he could not make himself stop. "Gray when you're being clever. When you're seeing too much."

She was staring at him. Her every indrawn breath brought their bodies closer, her breasts almost touching his chest.

"But blue now," he said. "Like the sky reflecting off the ocean when you're three months at sea and you've forgotten the feel of land beneath your feet. A blue that pierces down to the heart of you. So blue you forget how to breathe."

She licked her lips, and Jesus, it was hell to hold himself apart from her. Nearly impossible to keep from pressing her back against the rock.

"Don't—lie," she said finally. "Not now. Not about this."

"You know I'm not lying." He brought one hand to cup the back of her head. His knuckles scraped the stone behind her. "You know I mean every word. You are a goddamned strike of lightning, Ruby Ballimore, and you scare me witless. Wordless. Out of my mind."

Her fingers—bare now—slipped up his shoulder and found the back of his neck. Her touch was warm and light, and he was fevered. Dizzy with temptation.

"You've never been wordless a day in your life," she whispered.

And— Oh, the hell with it. The hell with all of it.

He tightened his grip on her waist. Pushed her back against the rock with his body. And kissed her.

Ruby felt everything.

Cool wet sand beneath her bare foot. His palm cradling the back of her head. The rough slab of stone behind her, and the press of his body, hard and heated, into hers.

His kiss was delicate, probing—at odds with the powerful grip he had on her body. He tasted of salt, of sea air, and she wanted him. Wanted more.

His tongue touched the corner of her mouth, and her belly turned over. She shoved her fingers into the soft weight of his hair and parted her lips beneath his. A hot throb pulsed through her body. Her nerves felt sensitized, every movement of his mouth sparking tension in her limbs, knotting desire deep within her.

She wanted to tell him to put his tongue in her mouth. She wanted to take whatever he wished to give.

Instead he pulled back. Opened up space between their bodies. He looked flushed—a little wild. His throat was pink.

His fingers were still locked in the ribbon at her waist.

"Ruby," he gritted out. "I can't—"

"Oh no," she said. "Absolutely not."

He paused. "What?"

"Don't you dare. This is the most exciting thing that's ever happened to me. Don't you even *dream* of ruining it."

He stared at her—it was offensive to the mortal world, she thought, that he should still be so handsome while also thunderstruck and befuddled. And then, very slowly, his long, wicked mouth curled up. His dimples made tiny shadows in the fading light.

His smile was awful. Terrible. She fancied it *so* much.

She curled her fingers into his hair and dragged his mouth back down toward hers.

He came willingly. He made a hot, rough little sound into her mouth, and it worked like a spark to tinder, catching, flaring, curling up through her whole body.

His mouth was harder now, fiercer, more delicious. She pushed up into him, her breasts crushed against his chest and her mouth open to his. Her skin felt tight; all her body seemed taut and aching.

He licked at her lips. Sucked. His hand behind her head had gone from careful cradle to eager demand, pulling her into him. His fingers at her waist spread wider and his thumb brushed the bottom edge of her breast.

She caught her breath. Thought: *Yes.*

He broke their kiss, but only to move his mouth to her neck. "I want you," he muttered. "I want *this*. I've goddamned dreamed of this." With each word, his lips brushed her skin.

She shivered and gave herself up to the surge of her need.

"I want it too," she said. She stroked the back of his neck, the soft weight of his hair, then dipped her hands down to his shoulders. He was muscled there, and right now rigid with tension. Holding himself in check.

She liked that too. She felt drunk on the notion that he desired her; that he had to hold himself back from what he might wish to do.

She touched his back, then slid her hand down his side. He groaned and pressed close to her, and she felt the rigid length of his erection against her belly. He licked her ear, and she gasped. Sensation pierced her, a hot current that landed between her thighs.

"I shouldn't," he muttered, and then put the lie to his own

words by sliding his hand up, the tiniest movement, to frame her breast. He closed his teeth over her earlobe.

"Don't—stop on my account," she managed.

He broke the grip of his teeth to laugh, breathless and ragged, and cup her more fully, taking the weight of her breast into his palm. "All of this is on your account. Everything."

Somehow it was more heady even than the thick weight of his arousal.

He desired her, yes. And she made him laugh.

He came back up to her mouth and kissed her again, harder. The back of her head bumped the rock, and he swore against her lips, and she didn't care. Her mind—normally a busy, racing thing—had gone fogged, wine-soaked, blurred beneath the sweet throb of his mouth on hers.

She tried to wrap a leg around him to pull him closer, but her skirts felt cold and heavy. She realized vaguely that the tide had come in; the water was up to her knees and her skirts were sodden.

She didn't care. It felt right—the ocean tugging at her balance, Malcolm holding her still.

When he pulled back, it was only to press his forehead against hers. He was breathing hard—they both were. His fingers slipped into the spaces between her ribs and held there.

"God," he said thickly. "Oh hell. The tide . . . We can't . . ."

He broke off and found her eyes with his. He breathed a helpless laugh, as if to say: *I told you. Wordless.*

She looked down at the water at the level of her knees, rapidly filling the cove as they stood against the rock. And then she looked back up at him. "I believe," she said, "we may be cut off from the house."

His mouth curved up. "I hope you know how to swim."

"Don't be dramatic," she said. "We can wade, surely."

He was still smiling. His eyes were pure sapphire in the fading light, and there was something almost dazed about his expression. Some dazzled shape to his piratical mouth.

A lightning strike, he'd called her. And somewhere in herself—in some deep and unknown place—she found she almost could believe it.

"Wade," he agreed. And then he dimpled at her, quick and devastating. "I'll race you."

Chapter 14

Archer was still holding Ruby's hand when they reached the front door of Pomeroy House. He ought to have dropped it. He should have let her go—oh hell, an hour ago in the cove. Weeks ago.

But he couldn't. He didn't want to. He was glad that, despite his very best attempts, she had not left Pomeroy House.

He couldn't make himself regret their kiss. In his memory, it was all sunset colors: the slow flush of desire like a red-hot tide inside his body, the peach-and-pink shades of Ruby's mouth and skin. It had been a struggle at times to overcome his smile in order to fit his mouth to hers. Never, in all his life, could he remember a kiss that had made him so bloody happy.

I want it too, she'd said, and because it was Ruby, he knew it was the truth. She would not dissemble, would not pretend or flatter to get what she wanted.

She wanted him. She knew the truth, and still she wanted him.

Although—the thought came to him with a sudden uneasiness—perhaps she had not uncovered the Quenby scheme.

She had not mentioned it. Surely she would not have left it out if she had known.

But his unease refused to unfold into something more powerful. They were at the door, and her hand was in his, and when she looked up at him, she was smiling. Bedraggled and barefoot and soaked to her skin, sand in her hair and on the curve of her ear. And still, she was grinning, pleased with him and with herself.

How many times had she smiled like that at him? Once? Twice? It wasn't enough. He thought he could never have enough.

She appeared to ponder the state of his clothing—heavy with water and sand—and then her own, which was possibly worse. "Do you think we ought to sneak in the back?"

"Possibly. Though I understand your ladies have wheedled their way into dining with my crew in the kitchen most nights."

Her lips quirked in tacit acknowledgment, and it occurred to Archer that it had been some minutes—a month, perhaps—since he'd removed his gaze from her mouth. "They have," she said, sounding far too smug for a woman garbed mostly in sand. "And I suspect it's suppertime. The front, then."

Archer set his hand to the door, pushing slowly to prevent the escape of a pack of rogue hounds. He scarcely had the door open, however, before he heard a small but decided clamor emanating from some nearby room.

He paused and looked down at Ruby. "Shall we try the back?"

"Perhaps," she said, "but was that not—"

Lamentation burst around the corner, Gerry and Tamsin at his heels. He spotted Archer and Ruby at the door, and his mouth tightened into a sickly smile. "Cap," he croaked. "Thank goodness you're back."

"Is everything all right?" Archer asked. He was through the door now, and he'd let Ruby's hand slip from his before anyone saw. It felt far bigger a loss than it ought to have; he wanted to catch her around the shoulders and drag her up against his body. He wanted to tangle his hand back in her wilted ribbons; he did not wish to let her go.

"It's fine," Lamentation said, still with that peculiar expression pinned to his mouth. "Everything's just as it ought to be here at Pomeroy House. Don't you think so, Estate Steward Captain Archer?"

This speech alarmed Archer extremely. "Ah," he said, "yes?"

Tamsin pushed ahead of Lamentation. "Pull yourselves together," she whispered. "They're here."

Ruby glanced from Lamentation to her friend and shoved helplessly at the damp, sandy mass of her hair. "Who's here? What are you talking about?"

Tamsin's wild-eyed gaze took in Ruby and Archer together, and then the wet trail they'd left behind them on the marble. "Oh God. *Now* is when you—" She broke off, flinging her hands in the air. "Never mind. Just . . . hide. Both of you should hide. *Not* together."

"I don't understand what I'm hiding from—"

Ruby's whispered words cut off abruptly as Alice's voice floated in from the corridor. Alice sounded inhumanly calm, her voice lilting and polite.

She sounded, Archer realized with a sense of rising horror, as if she were talking to a stranger. In their house.

"Right this way," Alice's disembodied voice said sweetly. "Allow me to show you into the blue parlor. We've only just finished outfitting it."

"Tamsin," Ruby hissed, "who is Alice talking to?"

But before Tamsin could reply, there was a crash from the blue parlor. And then a clamor of raucous barking, followed by a pitchy wobble from Alice, not quite indecorous enough to be called a squeak. "Oh! I had forgotten about the hounds in here. They're— Oh! Oh goodness. If you could perhaps call her back, I would be most grateful. Oh—oh dear . . ."

Alice's trailing words were drowned out by the sound of a reedy voice—an accent somewhere between French and Italian, oh hell, oh *shit*—wailing: "Zenobia! Zenobia, vieni qui!"

And then a small, springy gray dog bounded into the room and launched herself six feet in the air, directly at Gerry's chest.

Helplessly, Gerry caught her.

The dog—Zenobia, Archer presumed—was an outrageous-looking creature, all spindly legs and narrow face and absurd bat ears. She wore a thin bejeweled collar around her arched neck, and she was digging aggressively in Gerry's shirtfront with her snout and her paws.

Zenobia was an Italian greyhound, if Archer did not miss his guess.

And Archer was—quite spectacularly—fucked.

Before he could move or speak, a short, spare man barreled around the corner. His velvet frock coat was bottle green and spotless, though his wig and spectacles were possessed of a slightly drunken tilt.

He was, indubitably, Signor Urbano Neri. The majordomo to the princess of Monfalcone.

"Zenobia," he moaned, "scendi!"

Zenobia did not come down. Instead, she nestled more snugly

into Gerry's arms and sent the signore a look that could most accurately be described as smug.

Archer's limited Italian could not quite follow the series of salty imprecations that followed, but they seemed to be directed toward the dog's character, lineage, and obstreperous conduct on the sea journey from Monfalcone to Cornwall.

Gerry looked pitifully from Archer to the signore as Zenobia began to lick his chest.

Archer swallowed very hard. And then he put on his most blinding smile—perhaps it would distract from the sand liberally coating his entire body—and strode forward. "Signor Neri—" His voice cracked, and he had to swallow again. Dear God, he wanted to cover his eyes and sprint in the opposite direction. "What a pleasure to welcome you to Pomeroy House. And the . . . princess?"

It came out a question. Archer looked to the threshold through which Alice had emerged—sans Monfalcone princess—and tried to project an air of confidence, rather than the sense of doom he actually felt.

"The princess is not here," Neri said.

Archer's head went light with relief. "What a shame," he got out. "And here we were so eager to welcome her. Perhaps in time. How might I best serve you in her stead?"

Neri was still not looking at him, only aiming an expression of dark betrayal at Gerry and the dog as he straightened his wig. "I have come to make the house ready for Her Highness."

"Ah." Archer's voice cracked again. "She is coming soon, then?"

"She follows in a fortnight," Neri said, "in an armed ship for her protection. She has commanded me to precede her and to make comfortable her dog."

"A fortnight," Archer repeated. "To make comfortable her dog."

Neri adjusted his spectacles and looked sourly at Gerry. "I have tried everything. Everything! But the beast does not wish to be made comfortable by me." He turned back to Archer. "You have received my correspondence? You have prepared the canine chamber?"

"The . . ." Archer could not think how to respond. The correspondence? The *canine chamber*? "If you have sent advance notice, Signor Neri, I fear it went astray. But we can certainly—ah—make ready. Make . . . something . . . ready."

Neri glanced around at the house. The front parlor was in relatively good repair, thanks to Ruby and her companions, but the hounds in the blue parlor were still barking raucously as Wall attempted, in a muffled voice, to quiet them. "This house does not appear ready."

Archer swallowed. His throat was very tight, but he kept on smiling, like a puppet with a single painted-on expression. "To be sure. We have recently been in the process of some renovations to the lower chambers." He thought of the piles of smuggled rugs in the upper tower, and the lace stockings in the stables, and—oh God—the absolute masses of extremely illicit and brightly colored silk in six separate wardrobes spread out across the house. "Perhaps you might tour the grounds while we air out your chamber."

If Archer were very lucky, perhaps Signor Neri would fall off a cliff.

"Just so," Neri said, and then he paused. His gaze traveled over the assembled company, from Alice behind him to Tamsin and Lamentation and Ruby and then to the place where canine sounds still echoed. "You are . . . hosting guests? At the princess's home?"

Archer's belly pitched. Disaster loomed.

But he could do this—surely he could do this. He could invent some tale, allow the story to embroider itself as it passed his lips. This was what he did: talked and talked and somehow made people believe him.

But Ruby spoke first.

Her bare hands locked together beneath her breastbone. Her hair was honey-dark from seawater, curling up in wild sandy tangles as it dried. All the distracting pink had faded from her cheeks; she was pale, eyes dark, lips pressed into a line.

"Signor Neri." Her voice wobbled. "These gentlemen are the staff of Pomeroy House. And I am . . ." She licked at her lips, then tried again. "My father is . . ."

For the space of a moment, Archer thought she too meant to dissemble. To convince Neri that she was where she ought to be.

But her eyes had gone huge and tragic, and she swiped at the salt on her cheekbone before she spoke. "My father is the Earl of Hangleton, ambassador to Monfalcone. I am . . . not acquainted with the princess. I am only visiting."

Only then did it dawn on Archer what was happening. Damned plainspoken impossible woman—she meant to tell the truth.

He wanted to shake her. He wanted to clap his hand across her mouth. Just like that, she was going to give herself up. Abandon her dream of independence when she'd only now begun to live it.

Why would she do it? Did she fear that Signor Neri might report her presence to her father?

But no. She had spoken first—had chosen to reveal herself to

Neri. The signore would not have known her if she had not admitted her identity.

Archer looked at the ivory heart of her face. Her mouth. Her storm-tossed eyes, all raw courage and tenacity.

If she was afraid, he realized, it was not for herself. It was for him.

These gentlemen are the staff of Pomeroy House, she'd said. The first thing—the very first words out of her mouth had been meant to protect his crew. She was poised to get herself sent home to take suspicion off *him*.

And even as he realized what she'd intended, he also knew that he could not let her do it.

"Hangleton sent the ladies from London at my request," Archer heard himself say. "His daughter and two of her companions."

There was a moment of startled silence and Archer tried very hard to think what to say next.

Ruby's lips parted. "I—"

"No, no," Archer cut in. "Please, my lady, allow me." He did not under any circumstances mean to let her keep talking. "Lady Ruby Ballimore, may I present to you Signor Urbano Neri, majordomo of House di Sangro?" He turned back to Neri. "Or—I beg your pardon, signore. Perhaps you have already been introduced to her ladyship?"

Neri squinted through his spectacles at Ruby, who did not look especially like anyone's ladyship in her current state. "Hangleton's *daughter*?"

"The . . . elder," she said faintly. "Yes."

Archer let the lies spool out from his lips. "I asked for the ambassador's assistance in the renovation of the house. And he, knowing his daughter's exceptional taste and talent, sent her to Cornwall. She has been the one to select the drapings and the wall coverings and—and—"

Here his imagination stumbled. He could not say rugs. Or silks. Or, God forbid, wine.

But Ruby had marshaled her forces. "All the ornamentation," she said through white lips. "The entablatures and pediments are done in the Erecthean style. I thought it would appeal to the princess."

"There, do you see?" By God, he almost wanted to cheer. "The Erecthean style. Naturally." Neri still looked incredulous, so Archer lowered his voice and said confidentially, "Lady Ruby is known as something of a genius in certain circles. Hangleton does not like to boast."

Neri blinked. And Ruby went pink to her hairline.

"It's unfortunate that we have not finished the project in time for your arrival, signore," Archer continued, "but we shall carry on undeterred. I don't doubt that with Lady Ruby's excellent guidance, we can have the lower floors at least prepared within the week."

Neri appeared mostly mollified, and his gaze went to Gerry again. "Your man will take over? With the dog?"

Gerry offered a pained sort of smile. "Most assuredly."

"I will help," Alice said. She'd crept closer and, as she spoke, she reached out to gently stroke Zenobia's enormous ear.

Zenobia responded to the soft entreaty with a low growl. Alice blinked and withdrew her hand.

Archer's smile widened as he looked at Neri. "Fortuitous, isn't it, that ladies of the princess's own age and standing should be here in time for her arrival. Why, it's almost as if—"

He glanced at Ruby, who was flushed and warm and edible, exactly as he most liked.

God above, he couldn't help himself.

"It's almost as if they are her ladies-in-waiting," he said cheerfully.

And then he winked.

She was staring back at him. Her face was flecked with salt and sand, and her ribbons hung in a tangled mass at her waist. She looked flustered and disheveled and—

Well. There was some bit of hope written on her face, flaring back to life like an ember, and Archer felt at once terrified and hideously pleased to have engendered it.

Tamsin stepped forward. "It is a pleasure to make your acquaintance, Signor Neri. I am Miss Tamsin Drake, daughter of Leopold, Lord Drake, and niece to the Countess of Bridestowe." She paused as if to let the grandiosity of her rank distract from the sight of her trousers. "Perhaps you will allow me to escort you down to St. Petroc's while the maid prepares your chamber."

Neri attempted to protest, but Tamsin overrode him.

"There is a very fine public house. Excellent wine. And"— she had linked her arm with his and was now leading him to the door—"not a single dog to be found there."

"It has been a very long journey," Neri said. "By ship. By carriage. And . . . you say there are no dogs?"

She had marched him almost fully outside as he spoke, but she tossed a harried glance back over her shoulder, mouthing a hasty sentence before she disappeared from sight.

"What was that?" Lamentation asked. "What did she say?"

Archer too had been unable to make out Tamsin's words.

But Ruby had. Her fingers fisted and then released, and she

moistened her lips before she spoke. "She says . . . we should pre-pare. In case my father decides to come to Pomeroy House as well."

Alice, who'd been once again rebuffed by Zenobia, turned abruptly. "Oh, Ruby! Do you think he will?"

"I . . . don't know," Ruby said. She swallowed. "If Signor Neri writes—and tells him that the princess is coming—I think he might. I know he has long wished to meet her."

Her father. The Earl of Hangleton. Here at Pomeroy House.

The notion struck Archer like a blow. Hangleton had been at Gravesmuir's dinner party. Hangleton might know him as Quenby.

His eyes flew to Lamentation. To Gerry, who was still cradling Zenobia.

"Cap?" Lamentation said. "What's wrong?"

"Nothing," Archer lied. "Go . . . fetch the silks, will you? Put them in your chamber, if they'll fit."

Lamentation offered him a hasty smile and a slapdash salute, and Archer's stomach twisted.

He was still lying to them. He didn't know how to stop it.

What had he done? What events had he set into motion, here in the parlor with his easy deceptions? *He* had told Neri that he kept up a correspondence with Hangleton. His lies might bring Hangleton's attention to Pomeroy House.

Archer had rescued Ruby's dream. But in so doing, he had also thrown his own crew squarely in the path of disaster.

It felt like the *Swallow* all over again—every turn tangling him further in the net of his conflicted loyalties, every twist tightening the rope about his neck. There was no right play—no words that might spin him free.

In the parlor—in the cove—he had not thought of anything

but Ruby. His whole world had been Cornwall, and the beach, the soft curve of Ruby's cheek and the deeper curve of her mouth. There had been no past to haunt him nor impossible future— only the present as he held her to him, as he drowned himself happily in the bright horizon of her laugh.

For so much of his life, he had lived in the present moment. Dodging fancy gents in the streets after he'd fleeced them of their coin. Charging ships twice the size of his *Swallow* but half her speed.

Even when he'd sat beside his mother in her bed, a handful of flowers balanced on her palm, he'd known it would not last forever.

But not anymore. He had his crew now. There would be no easy vanishing, no quick departure if he failed them.

And Ruby—

Ah God. She was no dalliance. No temporary madness. She was not a woman for whom affairs came and went like candied fruit, bits of sweetness to be cast aside and forgotten. She took things seriously; she took them to heart.

Already—already he was letting her down, and she did not even know it. She did not even know that he was Quenby.

"I'll clear the chambers," he said roughly. He could not quite look at her. He couldn't look at any of them. "I'll have it done before Neri comes back."

Chapter 15

Ruby balanced several boxes of live bugs—beetles?—in her hands and tried very hard not to drop them as she pushed her way into the disused stables.

They had spent the twenty-four hours since Signor Neri's arrival in a flurry of activity. Alice and Tamsin had taken turns entertaining the signore on jaunts across the Cornish cliffsides while everyone else raced around Pomeroy House and tried to make it presentable. Ruby had painted and carted furniture, and Archer and Lamentation had darted about locking doors to rooms that held various illicit items. Wall had transitioned fully into the role of French chef, and Eugénie had been charged with the creation of a luxurious suite for Zenobia as far away as was possible from Vanessa, toward whom Zenobia had developed a powerful antipathy.

Gerry had not been able to participate. If he left Zenobia's side, she howled until he returned. If anyone else dared to approach— even Lamentation—she growled low in her throat and showed her tiny, pearl-white teeth.

By the morning, Ruby had turned to an enthusiastic decoration of the remaining bedchambers, including Tamsin's and Alice's. Alice had consented to have the beetles relocated to the stables, so long as Ruby had promised that Alice could attend to their habitation regularly.

She'd just settled the creatures into an abandoned stall—she hoped that they got on; if they ate one another Alice would be crushed—when she heard a noisy splintering and then a muttered curse. She peeked out around the corner of her stall, though of course she already knew who it was. She recognized his voice.

Archer held an immense wooden crate, which he'd evidently knocked into a beam as he'd entered. The bottom of it had broken open, and out of it had spilled an extraordinary cache of white lace stockings, which he was hastily stuffing back into the upended container. His jaw was sharp and clean-shaven, and his dark hair tumbled over his eyes, obscuring all that piercing blue.

She had scarcely spoken to him since Neri's arrival.

Since their kiss, rather. Since she'd told him everything she knew—revealed her own secrets—and then plunged, reckless and falling, into his embrace.

She cleared her throat, and he looked up, and oh, she felt like a soap bubble, thin and floating. Her heart was in her throat as she looked at him, and worse—

Far worse. She feared her heart was in her eyes.

He'd run with her back to the house, and when she'd fallen behind, he'd laughed and pretended to gloat in his victory, and then bent to fiddle with his shoe and feigned shock when she outstripped him.

He'd held her hand.

And when she had been poised to give up the Pomeroy House

scheme—when she had been certain that everything had come to an end, the last brilliant vestige of her dream stamped out—he had not let it happen. He had lied absurdly, madly, and somehow brought her wishes into being. He had transformed the fabric of the world so that she might remain here, with him.

A lightning strike.

Could it be so?

But she knew herself—knew her tendency to embroider and dream. She held herself back and tried to make her voice light. "Those are fetching. I'm surprised you could spare them from your wardrobe."

He blinked at her and then looked down at the stockings. The corner of his mouth tipped up. "I hear white is quite out this Season. Lady Alice says I'll be barred from Almack's if I turn up in stockings any color other than heliotrope."

"Well. Alice would know. To the bonfire with these, then?"

"Oh, undoubtedly. Kindling, all."

He was still smiling at her, but something in it was . . . not right. She could not have said what, precisely—he was still dimpled, still soft-eyed. But there was an edge of falseness to it, a lightness that she sensed he did not truly feel.

She wobbled, just a trifle, as she spoke. "They're French? These stockings?"

Smuggled, she meant.

She was not certain if she ought to ask. Things had shifted between them after her revelations on the beach, and then again with Neri's appearance. They were on the same side now, their forces joined to prepare for the princess's arrival. No longer at odds.

And yet she feared saying too much, as she so often did. Perhaps she was meant to pretend, even now, not to know.

He looked down at the crate again, then brushed a bit of straw from where it clung to the topmost scrap of lace. "Not really. These are from Wales. We purchase them wholesale, then cart them to London and pass them off as illicit French ones. Turns a shocking profit."

"You . . ." She hesitated, but her curiosity won out. "You don't actually smuggle things, then?"

He sighed shortly. "Believe me. We smuggle plenty. It's an even race between the things I oughtn't have in the house and the things I merely lie about instead."

She opened her mouth, helpless to hold back her questions, but his mouth twisted down, and he cut her off.

"Ruby." His jaw tightened, a tiny pulse obvious in the hollow of his cheek. "Lady Ruby. We did not have a chance to speak last night. I've been hoping to draw you aside."

"Oh," she said, and even though her instincts were shouting that something was wrong, hope still broke loose inside her, buoyant and irrepressible.

He'd wanted to get her alone. Her brain spun out a brief fantasy before she could stop it—his big hands on her waist again, her back against the rough wood of the stall—

"You will have to tell your father you're here," he said.

Her heart pitched at the words.

He blew out a breath. "I'm afraid I've made that unavoidable with my deception. The next time Neri writes to your father, the signore will be sure to mention encountering you at Pomeroy House. You cannot hope to keep your whereabouts secret from your father now."

"Oh," she said again.

It occurred to Ruby then that she had closed the distance

between them, edged nearer to his warm, solid form somewhere in between their remarks. She took a very small step back and hoped he would not notice. Cursed herself for her foolish, ebullient hope.

"I suppose you're right," she said. "Tam and I talked it over yesterday—she's going to do her best to persuade Neri to bring Princess Serafina to London, rather than inviting my father here. Alice has offered to accompany the princess on the journey. But still—" She swallowed. "It's possible that Neri will mention me to my father. Perhaps if my father inquires, I can say that we stopped by to visit the manor on a brief sojourn from the Bridestowe estate."

That seemed plausible. The earl would probably believe it.

"I don't expect my father to ask too many questions of Neri," she added. "At least—not about me."

She said it casually—she thought she did—but Archer's jaw ticked again.

She barreled onward. "In my letter, I'll be certain to mention that you have everything well in hand here. I shan't mention your crew, of course. I won't—"

"Ruby," he said, and then seemed to grind his teeth. "*Lady* Ruby."

She quashed everything inside her. Ruthlessly stamped out any wild imaginings at the sound of her name in his mouth. "Yes?"

"I'm—sorry." He was still tight-lipped, stiff, uncomfortable. "I should not have importuned you on the beach."

She drew back, shocked into speech despite herself. "You did not . . . you did not *importune* me."

"I did."

"Of course you did not. How on earth could you think—" She knew she should stop talking, that she was poised to reveal too much. But as usual she could not stop her own reckless words. "How could you possibly believe that I did not share in your enthusiasm?"

"I importuned you," he said again. His shoulders were tight, and he was not looking at her, his dark lashes shielding his eyes. "I took advantage. I should not have done so."

With considerable effort, she strangled another protest.

She'd practically begged him to continue on. Her fingers had been in his hair, her mouth open beneath his. *Don't stop on my account*, she'd said, as blunt and plain as day. He could not believe her indifferent. It was impossible.

Was this meant to be some sop to her dignity? Some misguided attempt to allow her to salvage her pride—to pretend she had not wished for his embrace?

He was still looking down—at his shoes, perhaps. At the crate of stockings at his feet. "It won't happen again."

It was easy to make sense of his words, to fit them into place in the story of her life. Of course he did not wish to kiss her again. She had dreamed herself once more into an impossible flight of fancy, as she so often did. And yet . . .

She'd never felt so right in her own skin as she had with him.

Astonishing, how much it hurt to have this new hope dashed: that this man might somehow want her exactly as she was.

Her nose burned. She plucked at a piece of straw on her glove. "You needn't apologize. I had no expectations of you."

"No," he said flatly. "Of course you did not."

The bit of straw had become entangled, somehow, in her glove's lace trim. She wanted to yank at it. She wanted to tear it free. "I'll compose a letter to my father. I am . . . I have made a great deal of progress in the house. It will be as ready for the princess's arrival as I can make it."

Ruby had thought, when she'd first entered society and been such a miserable failure, that she need only try harder. If she read *The Tatler* instead of *The Times*, dressed in camelopard and wore her sleeves puffed, eventually she would take. She would be invited to dance; she would have a houseful of callers. Society would deem her acceptable. And so would her father.

But it had not worked. There had been no effort great enough to effect that sort of transformation.

And here at Pomeroy House—as she'd painted and cleaned, as she'd bantered with Archer and kissed him in the cove and tried to protect his crew—she'd begun to think that perhaps she need not change herself after all. Perhaps she, Ruby Ballimore, was already enough.

But. Well.

It seemed she'd been wrong.

"I have to go." She looked down at the ground, away from the straw that still clung to her gloves. Away from Archer. "I will let you know when I hear from my father."

Chapter 16

Archer did not intentionally seek her out again.

In fact, he did his best to avoid her, telling himself it was for her benefit, knowing he meant it for his own. It was not quite bearable to look at her—her face so transparent, like the finest new glazing, a thin shell of crystalline glass.

He'd hurt her feelings. He had known it was inevitable the moment he'd realized what his lie to Neri meant. He'd—

Hell. Some part of him had known he would hurt her from the moment he'd tugged off her pearl-buttoned glove. From the moment she'd stepped inside Pomeroy House.

But she would forget her hurt, and him. She would go home to London—perhaps her father would fetch her, despite what she thought—and return to her right world. Hang curtains and talk of statues and upend someone else's life for a change. Worm her stubborn, impossible, interfering way into someone else's heart.

He had hurt her. He'd known he would. And so he turned around when he saw her in a room and made excuses to be outside when she was in. He carted boxes down to the cove, and took Signor Neri to the public house, and tried, with little success, to separate Zenobia from Gerry.

When he found Ruby in the north tower—at the top of 197 individual stairs, with a crate of fake Greek statues in his arms—it was entirely by accident. A misfortune so great he went briefly lightheaded.

He'd nudged open the door with his toe. His arms were otherwise occupied with the statues, which he still vaguely hoped to sell someday, ideally to someone with fewer knowledgeable dinner guests than the Marquess of Gravesmuir.

He hadn't been expecting her. There was no reason for her to be there—the tower room was used for nothing besides storage, and the journey up the stairs was protracted.

But she'd found a different use for the room, it seemed. She was painting. Not canvas—of course not, she was too busy with practical things just now—but rather a trio of decorative screens a head taller than she was.

Archer was fairly certain that, two weeks prior, the same screens had been located in the music room and had functioned as trellises for a variety of intrusive plant species. But now they were soft, dreamy seascapes, pale and luminous with Ruby's delicate brushstrokes.

The tower had large windows, and the glass opened onto the sea. The room was half drowned in liquid gold from the setting sun. Everything smelled of walnut oil and turpentine, and Ruby was—

She was—

She had stripped out of her pretty flounced frock and hung it on a peg on the wall. In its stead, she'd wrapped herself in some sort of . . . of hellborn painting smock. It was made of a stiff, heavy fabric, splotched with blue and white. It tied at the front—a deep vee that revealed a stupefying display of Ruby's paint-spattered bosom.

Her tongue peeked out at the corner of her mouth as she concentrated on her work. Her skin was pink from the sun and slightly damp with sweat. She had a streak of blue paint in her hair, and one on her cheek, and he could nearly see her areolae, for Christ's sake, if he looked hard enough, which he most certainly was.

Dear God. *She* was the Scourge of St. Petroc's.

He needed to sit down. There was a battered chaise longue in the corner, but in his current state of extremity the floor seemed preferable to furniture. When he let his eyes linger on the chaise, his mind instantly furnished a vision of—

He dropped the crate, which crashed notably, and Ruby looked up with a start.

"Oh! Captain Archer." She did not adjust the Torture Smock, possibly because she had no idea what she looked like, or else because she was a demon sent from Hell to make Archer pay for his sins.

God grant him mercy. He was paying.

"Ruby." He cleared his throat. "*Lady* Ruby."

She looked curiously at him, nosy hellion that she was, and then down at the ground. "You've brought . . . something? All the way up here?"

Oh Jesus, the statues. He shoved the crate as hard as he could with his boot, into the corner where the sunlight did not reach. "Nothing. Empty crate. Getting it out of the way."

She looked at the crate, which had groaned its way across the floor as he'd shoved it. "Empty?"

"Mm."

"Is it . . . made of lead?"

"Lead-lined walnut." His mouth wanted to curve up at the expression on her face, and—because he could not stop it—he let himself smile at her. "A new device—all the crack in Cornish crate-making."

She laughed, and he felt so damned smug he added it to his catalog of sins.

But then she sobered. "Do you need this room? To prepare the house for the princess? I can leave you to your privacy."

"No," he said quickly. "You needn't go. *I* can go."

"You don't have to." She plucked up her brushes and some small jars of pigment and oils, shoving them haphazardly into a wooden box. "I'm done anyway. If you'll only give me a moment to clean up—"

"Ruby."

He'd barely touched her, only brushed his fingers against her upper arm. But she froze anyway, her eyes on him, her mouth clamped down tight.

"I'm sorry," he heard himself say.

He had not meant to say it. It was . . .

Hell and damnation. It was not a good apology. He was sorry for the expression on her face, sorry he'd had a hand in putting it there. But he was not sorry for what he'd done.

He did not regret the fact that he'd pushed her away in the stables. He'd had to do it. Her father might come; her father might know him as Quenby. There was no possible future that allowed him to put his mouth on hers again, and smile while he did it.

And at the same time, he could not bring himself to wish he had not kissed her. He *wasn't* sorry for it, not even a little bit.

Every time he closed his eyes, the world was all sunset and Ruby Ballimore, and there was no part of him that wished it had not happened. He wouldn't give up the memory. Not for a fortune of gold.

"I assure you, there's nothing to apologize for." She said it so brightly her voice cracked.

The sound made Archer's throat hurt. He wanted to hold fast to her arm. He wanted to kiss her again, hard enough to wipe away the memory of what he'd said.

"The house seems ready," he told her, instead of whatever madness was in his mind. "Everything looks in order. I could not have imagined it would come together so quickly nor so well."

"I'm glad." She looked down, then back up, and then said, all in a rush, "I had thought to go to Bridestowe. Soon. Now. Before the princess arrives."

"Go?"

She waved a hand. "Alice and Tamsin are the ones who ought to stay to receive the princess. They possess the skills to be her ladies-in-waiting. I've finished. My contribution is at an end."

Some revolt had started up in his body, in his fingers that couldn't quite let go of her arm, in his feet that had brought him closer without his realizing it.

He said: "You're giving up, then?"

"I'm not giving up." Her voice was a touch too loud in the quiet room. "I am accepting the reality of my circumstances, Captain Archer. I am perfectly cognizant of my strengths, and I do not need the appearance of Her Royal Highness to remind me that the social graces are not among them."

He remembered the way she'd flinched in the tavern when she'd heard Benji laugh. The way she'd assumed it directed at her.

The story she'd flung at him in frustration in the library. *I recently finished my fourth Season, which places me very nearly on the shelf. I did not dance at parties because I was not invited to do so.*

"Ruby—"

But before he could say anything more, she jerked her chin up. "Alice and Tamsin will do perfectly well for the princess. Better, in truth, if I am not around to make a mull of things."

"You don't make a mull of things."

She did not let him go on, only barreled forward, stubborn and bright and lying through her teeth. "I will no doubt prefer to reside at Bridestowe anyway, rather than blunder about trying to pose as a court lady. Alice and Tamsin will know better than I what to say to the princess when she arrives. They'll know"—here she stumbled, just a bit, on her words—"how to act."

"Ruby." His thumb just stroked her sun-warm skin. "You don't have to go. Not on the princess's account—nor mine."

It was absurd. Stupid. He had spent weeks trying to persuade her to go, and now that she was poised to do it . . .

Bloody hell. He could not stand to watch her flee. He couldn't stand to see her look this way, foolish and stubborn and heartbroken and brave.

But she wrenched her arm out of his grasp. "That's easy for you to say. Has there ever been anyone in your entire life that you could not charm?"

"Of course. A little blond scourge with terrifying eyes."

She looked up, looked him full in the face. Her gaze—storm gray, sheened with tears—pinned him in place. "You have no idea what it's like."

"I don't know what you mean."

She breathed a laugh, a pained, bitter thing he did not recognize.

"Of course not. You can't possibly imagine what it's like to walk into a room and be greeted by derision. To be reminded—constantly, daily—that the way you exist in the world is *wrong*."

"Ruby—"

"When I wrote my first paper—when it was accepted by the Royal Archaeological Society—do you know what I did?" Her lips pressed hard together, as if to hold the memory back. But she lifted her chin and kept going. "I laid the journal beside my father's plate at the breakfast table. I had woken early, you see, to have it waiting for him when he came down. I thought—I truly thought—that he would be proud of me."

Archer didn't know how the story ended, but he hated it already. Hated the bruised tenor of her voice.

"He did not look at the journal," she said quietly. "Only nudged it aside. Finally I plucked up the nerve to show him. *That's you?* he said. And then, *Thank God you've only used initials, Ruby. What a nightmare for me if this got out.*"

Archer's chest hurt. He wanted to run the earl through. Wanted Hangleton on the other side of a cannon.

"I published the next three under a false name," she said, "to protect his reputation. His career. But I still . . . told him about them. I still—I kept hoping—" She broke off to wipe furiously at her face. "I don't understand what's wrong with me that I can't stop *hoping*. Even this—even coming here—I thought things would be different. I thought *I* would be different. And I'm not."

"Ruby," he murmured.

"I would change, if I could," she said, low and fierce. "I've been trying. If I could, I would be as sweet and pleasing as my sister, Cassandra. But I can't. I don't"—her voice cracked again—

"want to wait here for the princess to arrive, only to discover once again that I am not suited for the role."

"Ruby." He set his hands to her shoulders. She was soft beneath the heavy smock; the blue paint on her cheek had run in a faint trail down to the corner of her mouth. "You don't need to be anyone other than who you are."

Her lips twisted down. She said wryly, "Pretty words, Captain Archer. But I have not found them to be true."

"You don't." He shook her, just a little. He wanted her to listen. He wanted to push the words into her skin. "You don't have to make yourself small just to—" He thought of Gravesmuir's dinner party, the marquess's angry face. Her father, whispering furiously into her ear. "Just to please a pack of fools who cannot recognize what's right in front of their eyes."

If men like that sought to silence her, it was only because she was more earnest and clever than they had any hope to be. For all their words of superiority, the only thing wanting was in themselves.

Ruby didn't say anything back, only looked him full in the face. Sharp-edged and defiant. Disbelieving.

So he pushed closer. Slid one hand down to her waist and the other up to cup her cheek. Her skin was warm and paint-streaked, and touching her *hurt*, like a clenched fist of want in his belly. "There's not one thing about you I would change."

Her throat bobbed as she swallowed. "Pretty words."

Goddamn it, she was the most obstinate—the most difficult—

He yanked her up against him. "I'm not trying to flatter you," he snapped. "You know I'm not."

Her lips parted, as if to argue.

Archer kissed her instead. He plunged madly into it, leapt

toward the dark ocean of her, and let gravity and desire pull him down. He was angry and resentful and fevered with want, and oh hell, it was relief and torment in one to feel her. To press himself into the lush shape of her body, feel against his chest the stiff smock and the crush of her breasts beneath it.

She was still with shock at first, and then—

She came up on tiptoe and shoved her fingers into his hair. Her mouth opened beneath his, and she kissed him back, hungrily.

His brain went blurred. He could feel his heartbeat in his cock. He wanted and wanted and *wanted*—

Half desperately, he pulled back. He was breathing hard, his whole body alight with yearning.

"Nothing," he said, and his voice was as rough and hot as his need for her. As barely checked. "There is *nothing* about you I would wish to be different. No possible way you could be more desirable to me. If I wanted you any more, Ruby Ballimore, I'd die of it."

Her lips were wet. Peach-ripe. Her smock clung heroically to the very tips of her breasts. "I thought you said this would not happen again."

He had one lock of her hair between his fingers. He'd wound it around his thumb as he'd kissed her.

He bent his head again and let his mouth hover just above hers. Breathed in turpentine and oil, and beneath it the amber scent of her skin. "Ah, pet," he muttered. "I lied."

Chapter 17

This time, she kissed him first. She pulled his head down, brought their mouths together in a clumsy clash, and parted her lips to let him taste her.

Archer shuddered at the sensation of her mouth beneath his, at the eagerness of her sweet curvy body pushing up and into his own. She made a hungry sound at the back of her throat when his tongue came into her mouth, and so he put his hand to her lower back and dragged her closer.

He wanted to make her sound that way again. The knowledge of her desire aroused him further, faster—his cock throbbed as he found her neck with his mouth, the edge of her smock with his thumb.

"Do you believe me now?" he murmured. He swept his thumb along the smock's stiff seam, tracing the inside curve of her breast. Her skin was damp from perspiration and oil paint, and touching her—even with the side of his thumb—felt like an electrical shock. A charged pulse that flickered through his body.

He grazed her neck with his teeth, just the tiniest bit, to see if she would whimper or moan.

But she did neither. Instead she pulled at his hair, bringing his mouth back toward hers. "I am not quite convinced," she gasped. "But do feel free to keep trying."

And so he was smiling, again, as he kissed her.

She was as thorough in this as she was at everything else. She kissed him slowly: tasted the corner of his mouth, pressed her tongue against his in a slick glide. It made him think of—other things. Other hot, erotic slides.

Pleasure skimmed along the surface of his skin, tightened to a knot in his belly. He relished the tension between the slow luxury of their kiss and the rising ache in his body. Holding himself in check was sweet, unholy torture.

Her hands slipped cautiously around to find the hem of his shirt, and then—beneath it—his bare back. He groaned into her mouth at the sensation, and she broke away to scrutinize his face.

"You like that," she said. She sounded satisfied—a scholar come to a conclusion after examining the evidence.

"What do I like? When you touch me?"

"Yes. And the other. The kissing. The—licking."

God help him, he would rather die than laugh now. "I don't suspect there's anything you could do to my person that I wouldn't like."

She tried to put her hands on her hips, but she seemed to have become somewhat entangled in his shirt. "I doubt that."

"I don't."

"What if I slapped your face? What if I stabbed you with a bayonet?"

This time he did laugh, because she'd meant for him to. "Have you got a bayonet under your skirt I don't know about? Don't tell me if you do. I'm keen to be surprised."

"I have the Elgin Marbles under here, actually. I was in the midst of smuggling them back to Athens when you stumbled in here with your crate."

He'd lifted his hand to wipe at the blue paint on the side of her cheek, but at her words, he slowed. His thumb brushed hesitantly across her skin, a hairbreadth from settling in the corner of her mouth.

God. His crate. The statues. The bloody Quenby scheme.

He was still lying to her. Every moment that he stood in front of her and pretended to be no more than Captain Malcolm Archer, he was lying.

But the very notion of telling her the whole truth seemed a betrayal of his crew. He had endangered them enough—had already tempted fate by pretending a connection to Hangleton that he did not truly possess.

He was still touching her cheek, paralyzed by indecision, when she turned her head and brought her mouth to his thumb. She let her lips—soft and plush and devastating—graze his skin. And then, slowly, as if concentrating fiercely, she licked a hot stripe up the pad of his thumb.

Bloody *hell*. His cock surged, a rigid throb against her body. He had to stifle a groan.

"Did you like that?" Her lips moved against his skin.

"You could say that," he ground out. "I think I saw stars."

Slowly, her lips parted, and slowly he watched himself press his thumb into her mouth, close and wet and scalding hot, and he thought he might die.

Don't, he told himself, and groaned at the catastrophic pleasure of her mouth.

He ought not continue to pursue her. He should turn around and leave this room, and he should not—should *not*—slip her smock off her shoulders and spend the next eight or ten hours relishing her breasts.

She sucked hard, and he had a brief, blistering terror that he might spend in his trousers without even touching his cock.

And then, to his mingled relief and agony, she stopped. She pulled her mouth free—holy God, his thumb was wet and slippery, and so were her lips.

"What about that?" she said, a little shyly. "More stars?"

He couldn't say anything back. He felt as though his heart might stop.

Bleeding, bloody hell. He couldn't reject her. He could not leave her now—she would think he did not want her. He would wreck all that delicate unfolding confidence, the slow revelation of her own seductive power.

And so he didn't. Instead of stepping back, of walking away, Archer slid his slick thumb down the front of her throat. He traced a path down between her breasts, and then over, hooking beneath the edge of her smock. He gave in to the desire to pull it aside—to glimpse the petal pink of her areola before he put his mouth to her ear. "Not stars," he said roughly. "Galaxies."

She turned her face to his, and, helplessly, he kissed her again.

This was for her. That was what he told himself as he licked into her mouth, as he unlaced her stays. As he took the heavy weight of her breasts into his palms and felt his breath catch in his chest. This was for *her*.

Evidently some vestigial bit of honor still lingered at the back of his brain, because as he tasted his way down the valley between her breasts, he thought, *Ah yes, Cap. Positively selfless.*

But mostly he thought of how goddamned luscious she was, the sweet give of her flesh beneath his mouth like ripe fruit. She gasped as his tongue slid across one nipple, and he stopped to look at her.

She was flushed and paint-spattered; her hair was curling up around her face in sweat-damp ringlets, tangled where it hit her bare shoulders. Her eyes were glassy, and her bare breasts were a bounty, a goddamned paradise, some stupefying leap past any other erotic sight he'd ever encountered in his life.

He had to force himself to swallow. To loosen his grip on her waist. "All right?" he said thickly. "For me to touch you here?" His thumb moved along the bottom curve of her right breast as if in demonstration, without his quite intending it.

She shivered. "Yes," she said. Her voice was quiet. Fiercely determined. "Yes. I want you to go on touching me. And I want to touch you as well."

Ah God, he had to press his face into her neck to stop himself from groaning aloud. He wanted that too. He wanted to take her palm and press it against his cock, wanted it so much his whole body felt like a knot drawn tight.

He licked at her neck again, then the inner curve of one breast. She tasted like salt and walnut oil from her paints, and she squirmed restlessly beneath him as he worked his way closer and closer to her nipple. Her deft fingers found the edge of his shirt again.

He circled her nipple with his tongue, then rolled it lightly, so lightly. She made a choked sound, and her body jerked.

His mind felt blurred, his senses going dark and close. His

world shrank down to Ruby, and her taste, and the small sounds of her pleasure. He moved his fingers to her wet nipple, teasing her, listening to the sounds she made to see what made her gasp again, and louder.

"Malcolm," she said, and the sound of his Christian name was a strange gauzy pleasure that shifted through his body like light in water. "I—I want—"

He dropped his mouth to her other nipple and kept his mind resolutely off the hem of her chemise and his proximity to everything beneath. "Believe me, darling. You have no idea how much I want to give you what you want." His knee had slipped between her legs—he did not know when he'd done it—and he could feel her clench her thighs. His delicate torture grew rougher, messier. He couldn't help himself. "I'm trying to be a gentleman."

"Is that what this is called?" Her voice was somewhere between a gasp and a laugh. "I was wondering."

He was unbearably aroused. The temptation to stroke his own cock was anguish and pleasure at the same time, almost impossible to resist.

He pulled back, just a bit, and grappled for control.

But—bloody hell, looking at her like this did not do him any favors. She looked dazzled, pleasure-drunk, hungry for more. She looked like every erotic fantasy he'd ever had, multiplied by a thousand and then spattered lightly all over with blue paint.

"Come here," he said, a little unevenly. "On the stool. Let me clean you up."

She blinked hazily at him until her vision cleared, and then she looked down at herself. Her smock dangled at her elbows, her chemise beneath nearly transparent. Her stays were on the floor, and he kicked those aside too, just in case she had any idea of putting her clothes back on.

She went even pinker than she had already been. "You don't have to—"

"I want to," he said. "Trust me."

Her lips parted as she looked up at him. The room was growing darker in the fading light, and so too were her eyes—a deep velvety gray-blue now. "I do, you know," she murmured. "Trust you."

Oh God, things she said sometimes. He felt as though she'd stabbed him in the heart. "On the stool," he said roughly, and picked up the little jar of oil she used to mix into her pigments. "Is this walnut oil?"

"Yes. Are you— Oh!"

He'd pulled his shirt over his head. Her eyes went wide. Her thick curly lashes fluttered, and she stood stock-still, roughly six inches in front of the battered wooden stool. He almost laughed at the expression on her face.

Instead of laughing—which ought to be impossible, given his rampant erection—he poured oil onto the corner of his sleeve and then drew closer to her, nudging her down to sitting and stepping between her legs. Then he brought the sleeve of his shirt to her cheek and slowly wiped away the traces of blue.

Her breath hitched. Her eyes flicked along his body: his shoulders and his chest and then his abdomen, precisely at the level of her mouth.

She licked her lips, a quick flash of pink tongue, and then set her hand to the waistband of his trousers. Her fingers coasted over his abdominal muscles, which leapt at her touch, his whole body coming to desperate attention.

"Hold still," he said. "You've paint all over you."

She didn't move, but he set his left hand over hers anyway, then slowly moved the oil-damp fabric over her upper arm. Her collarbone. Then down the slope of her breast. Her chest rose and fell, and he could see the quick beat of her pulse.

He dropped the shirt, poured a bit more oil into his palm, and then coated his thumb. He made a slow, slick circle around her wide pink areolae, first one and then the other. She parted her lips as if to speak, and then left them that way, almost panting. Her fingers dipped down inside the waistband of his trousers, and she clutched hard at the fabric, pulling him nearer.

He swallowed. That tight clasp, so close to the agonizing throb of his cock—

But no. He put the thought right out of his mind. She *trusted* him. He would not seduce her—not even if, right now, she seemed to want him to.

Instead, he rubbed his thumbs across her nipples, all slippery glide now, and she groaned and pressed her knees into his thighs, twisting restlessly on the wooden stool. The legs of the stool rocked, and she gripped him harder to steady herself. The base of her thumb brushed his cock, and—

Hell. He was going to Hell, or else already there.

How had he got himself to this place? He did not want to dishonor her; bloody hell, he would not use her for his own pleasure, not even if resisting killed him.

And yet he could not leave her like this—clearly aching, so obviously in need.

He set his mouth to her neck and his palm to her upper thigh.

She jerked in surprise at his touch, and then her knees—which had been digging hard into his legs—went loose. Splayed apart, all soft whimper and invitation.

His reservations—his last pitiful scruples—slid helplessly away. His hand slipped beneath her chemise, and he sucked at her skin as he stroked her inner thigh. He felt the sweet sting of her nails on his back, and he found that his grip had gone rough. Almost bruising.

So had his mouth at her throat. He wanted, as he never had in his entire life, to leave a mark where his mouth had been.

He wanted her to see it there. He wanted—God help him—for everyone to see it. To see that he'd used his teeth, and that she had tipped her head and begged for more.

But though the notion was heady—dizzying—it was not just arousal that beat hard in his body. It was yearning too. He wanted something that would last beyond the night. He wanted this night not just in his memory but inked on her skin. He wanted to tattoo it in his heart; he did not want any part of it to slip away from him.

He knelt between her thighs. He shoved up her chemise—Jesus God, his hands felt clumsy, not quite in control. He looked up at her then—fixed his gaze on her face, flushed in the last embers of the day.

He picked up the jar again and watched her face as he trickled oil over her sex. Her eyes—always so clear, so ruthless—looked glassy, her pupils wide. She whimpered at the sensation and then, when he let himself touch her, she made a different sound, heated and frantic.

Her hips lifted, chasing the sensation, and he clamped one hand over her thigh to hold her still. He circled her clitoris, lightly, watching her face, judging her reaction. She was almost panting; her breasts trembled, her nipples slick and glistening, and he—

Oh fuck, he wanted to put his fingers inside her so badly. He wanted to feel her wet heat, the clench of her channel as she came. He wanted to drag her down off the stool, spread her legs, and lower her onto his cock.

But her toes were flexing and pointing, her thighs trembling, and he kept up his rhythm, steady and unhesitating, and she was slippery and hot and exquisite beneath his fingers, and the throaty, desperate whine at the back of her throat turned into something fractured as she came, as her hips arched up, as her thighs shook.

Only the grip of his hand kept her on the stool throughout the rough waves of her orgasm. He thought, dazedly, that he could come too, like this, between her legs, with his mouth inches from her sex.

Oh God, he thought. *Ruby.*

And when she opened her eyes to look down at him, he realized he'd said it aloud.

He took an unsteady breath, his eyes locked with hers. And then he came shakily to his feet. He had to get out of the tower. He had to get himself as far away from her as possible before he lost whatever thread of his sanity remained.

He had to—*had to*—close himself in his chamber and get his hand around his cock.

But she stopped him. Her fingers brushed his stomach, and her eyes held his. "Wait," she whispered. "Don't go yet."

She set her hand to the buttons of his fall, and he froze as she tugged at the fabric, as her fingers played along the stiff length of his erection.

"Ruby," he said hoarsely, and he did not know if he meant to beg her to stop or plead with her to go on.

She glanced down, a heavy fan of golden lashes, and then

back up. "The oil," she said. Her voice was still a little ragged. "I thought I could use the oil to touch you too."

Jesus Christ. He thought she might never stop surprising him.

His mouth was so dry he almost couldn't swallow. He could feel his heart beating in his cock, and he suspected she could too, even through his smallclothes.

"If you'd like that," she added softly. Her mouth tipped up, and God, he relished the tiny seductive tilt of her mouth, her obvious awareness of her own power over him. "Would you like that?"

"So much it might kill me."

She bent to fetch the oil, her lips passing so close to his cock that he could feel her breath. His hips jerked, and he tried to get himself in hand, tried to master his baser desires, *tried* to make himself leave—

"Let's find out," she murmured, and then slid one delicate fingertip down his length.

He gave in.

He wasn't leaving the tower. He wasn't leaving her side.

"It's—" His voice went choked as she poured the oil in her palm, then slid her palm around him. "There's nothing—I won't like. Touch me however you wish. But—oh fuck—I'm going to spend in your hand. It's going to—my seed—"

Bloody *fuck*, he couldn't string words together. His vision was going black. Her hand was so slippery, and she had no sense of rhythm or finesse, stroking his bollocks, sliding up and around and over—

"R-Ruby," he got out, and oh Jesus it had only been about twelve seconds and he was about to spend in her hand. He tried to hold back, trembled in the earthy tension of restraint and relief together.

"Malcolm," she whispered back, and her fingers closed tight

around him, and then he did come, hard, gasping, messy and end-less, pleasure on pleasure on pleasure.

He wasn't leaving.

The thought revolved in his head, a sweet resonance, his sole certainty. He thought it again as he pulled her down atop him on the chaise; again as he wrapped his arms around her warm, soft body; again as he nestled his chin into her hair.

He wasn't goddamned leaving her. Not ever.

Chapter 18

Ruby supposed it could have been awkward. She knew awkward—knew sidelong glances and hot embarrassment rising to her skin—and the morning after ought to have been ripe for such a feeling, as she crept down the tower stairs with her chemise sticking to her legs and blue paint all over Archer's irremediably pigment-streaked shirt.

It ought to have been awkward. But she could not stop laughing to feel it.

His hand was on her waist, holding hard to the ribbons there, and their legs kept knocking into one another. There were 197 steps to descend, and she supposed he couldn't pause to kiss or touch her on *every* one, but he certainly seemed to be trying.

He wanted her. It was perhaps a sign of her weakness that the very notion of her own desirability could bring her such pleasure, but—well. She was weak, then. She liked this sweet-tongued, true-hearted, wicked piratical man so terribly much, and she wanted him to fancy her too.

As they crept down the stairs, she felt almost lightheaded with happiness. The princess was coming, and the house was nearly ready. Ruby had painted and patched and carted furniture and put earth in pots and somehow, the peculiar old house was almost beautiful now.

Somehow, it seemed to her that they had made it that way— she and Archer together.

For however long it lasted—however long she might be able to remain here at Pomeroy House—they were on the same side.

At her own corridor, she hesitated. They had stayed all night in the tower room, tangled together on the chaise. The sun was just now rising, and Tamsin and Alice were sure to be asleep in their chambers, here in this very hall. "Do you suppose I should try to hide?" She glanced down at herself—whisker-scraped along her breasts, glistening with oil in spots, and heaven only knew the state of her *hair*—and then back up at him. "I'm afraid I look . . ."

"Guilty as sin?" He was laughing too, his dimples softening the impossible angle of his jaw. "Edible? Do you know, the first time I saw you sparkling all over, I thought you looked like a comfit. Come on, stand behind me. We'll creep down the corridor and if someone peeks her head out of her room, it'll look as though I'm walking by myself."

"Oh, to be sure. Whilst your petticoats flap around your ankles. No one will suspect a thing."

He winked lasciviously at her. "I suppose you'd best remove your petticoats, pet. For the purposes of disguise."

"Is this your offer of assistance?"

He nudged her back against the wall, fitting his body to hers. "Anytime," he said fervently. "Day or night."

His mouth was at her neck. Her voice came out breathless. "Your purposes are so often nefarious."

"Mm. My motives always ulterior."

The string of tiny nips and bites he had delivered to her throat seemed to have touched off sparks inside her body, and her attempt at further repartee emerged, unfortunately, as a melting sort of whimper.

"God," he mumbled, "I could—"

Any further interesting revelations of what he could do—hopefully to her person—were interrupted by the resounding slam of a door.

And then the distinctive and furious barking of an Italian greyhound.

And then a scream.

He lifted his head, cast her a single, startled glance, and then dropped her ribbons and sprinted toward the stairs. "Stay put," he ordered.

Honestly, she could not fathom why he thought his barked commands would work upon her. She picked up her skirts and chased after him.

They made it all the way to the front door of Pomeroy House before they ascertained the cause of the commotion. Lamentation, Gerry, Wall, Eugénie, Tamsin, Alice, Signor Neri, and four or five dogs were crowded in clumps in the parlor, which resounded with barking and shouting in at least two recognizable languages. Vanessa cowered in the corner, as far as possible from Zenobia, who was growling furiously from her position in the arms of a small, sodden, exceptionally bedraggled woman. The woman's black hair hung in wet, sandy clumps all the way down to her waist. Her lips were white and her teeth appeared to be bared and lightly chattering.

She looked irate. And freezing.

"What the devil's going on?" Archer demanded as he skidded into the room. "What was that screaming?"

"I am so sorry," Alice said, sounding choked. "That was me. Vanessa got free when Zenobia raced by, and—"

The tiny angry woman drew herself up.

And with a dawning sense of horror, Ruby recognized her.

"What is this?" the woman demanded. "Why is Zenobia loose among these other canines?" She clutched the snarling greyhound closer. "What have you people done to her?"

"What have *we* done?" exclaimed Lamentation. "What has she done to us, you might as well ask. I've lost two fingertips and a *boot* trying to feed her cuts of lamb. I've—"

"I beg your pardon," the woman said frostily. "Who are you, to speak of Zenobia so?"

"Oh, I'm nobody. I'm just the footman to a bloody Italian royal dog! Who are y—" Lamentation's speech cut off abruptly, like a bird colliding with a pane of glass.

Revelation, it appeared, had reached him too.

The woman stood ramrod straight. She looked very much the way she did in all the newspaper engravings, except covered head to toe in water and sand. "I am Serafina Fiammetta Paxe Maria," she said, "of House di Sangro. Princess of Monfalcone."

"Oh," Lamentation said weakly. He swallowed. "Welcome home."

It was at this point that the clamor they had interrupted broke out again. Neri leapt forward, his handkerchief raised as if to brush the sand from the princess's royal personage. Zenobia growled, and Vanessa, with a tail-down whimper, fled the scene, Alice and the bloodhounds hot on her heels.

And Princess Serafina surveyed them all, pale and bedraggled and icily furious. "Who," she demanded, "are all of you people in my house?"

Once, when Ruby was twenty and Cassandra eighteen, the Earl of Hangleton had entertained the prime minister for dinner. He did not usually have guests at home, not since his wife had died. Ruby had been painfully thrilled and anxious at the notion that she might play the role of hostess, and even her father's stern warning—*Don't embarrass me, Ruby, not tonight*—had not cooled her enthusiasm.

At dinner, Cassandra had been the picture of calm, decorous politesse, and Ruby had been too—grimly determined to do everything, *everything* right.

And then, as she'd watched, the candelabrum behind Liverpool's head had somehow lit the drapes on fire.

Liverpool, a stern, fair-haired Tory in his middle forties, had not seen the flames. No one had except Ruby, who'd looked desperately from her sister to her father to the liveried footmen and watched a very slow-moving catastrophe happen right in front of her eyes.

That was how she felt as she watched the Princess Serafina take over Pomeroy House.

The princess had waved off Neri's handkerchief. She had fixed her gaze upon Tamsin's freckled face instead, flung out a commanding hand, and said: "You will find for me a bath. And a dressing gown."

Tamsin—daughter of the 6th Viscount Drake and niece to the Countess of Bridestowe—had gone rather pink and smothered at that. But she had done what she was told.

Only once she was bathed and wrapped in Ruby's own robe did the princess consent to explain why she was here at Pomeroy House several days early, alone and half drowned.

"Assassination," she said acidly. "A poor attempt at one."

She sat erect on the high bed in the chamber that Ruby had painstakingly outfitted for her these last weeks, her knees tucked beneath her. The fresh flush on her olive skin and her damp hair made a startling contrast with the aristocratic authority on her face and the perfect set of her shoulders.

The words hung in the air. Even the dogs had gone hushed, sensitive to the sudden crackle of tension in the room.

Ruby stared.

Had the woman said . . . "assassination"?

It appeared she had. Neri had found himself a place on the ground near the princess's feet, and at her words, he found his handkerchief again. This time he dabbed at his own brow. "Ah, sua maestá," he whispered. "Not Verdura? Not again?"

"Sí," she said coolly. "Verdura."

And then she explained.

She had been, it seemed, visiting a cousin in Sardinia and had set out from there by ship to meet Signor Neri at the holiday house in Cornwall. She had been three-quarters of the way through the ship journey when her schooner had been set upon by what she had at first taken to be pirates.

The first mate—her own man, a servant of House di Sangro—had hustled her into a dinghy and begun the slow process of rowing them to shore. But to her astonishment, three of the pirates had left the schooner and given chase.

"I was the target," she said. The words were flat. If Ruby had not seen the way her hands trembled on Zenobia's diamond-studded collar, she might have thought the princess emotionless. "The men were not after the ship. They were after me. They meant to see me dead."

She had plunged from the dinghy into the water, and the mate had charged the pursuing pirates, brandishing his pistols. He had led them away from her—had let her slip away unscathed.

"House di Sangro will not forget," she said. Her voice sounded like acid-etched glass, but her hands on Zenobia's collar shook harder. "His family will be rewarded for the service he rendered me."

"Maestá," Neri said. He looked sick. "How did you make it to shore?"

She lifted her chin, and if Ruby had not known she was royalty, the self-possessed gesture alone would have revealed it. "I swam," she said. "All night. And when I was close enough to the cliffs, I recognized the silhouette of my own house."

Ruby's heart lurched. She could imagine it all—the violence, the angry noise of steel and gunpowder, the cold seawater and heavy weight of a sodden gown. The princess's feet had been bare, and the walk up the cliffs was steep and cragged. She could imagine the princess's terror, the stark relief at the sight of Pomeroy House, turreted and looming at the top of the cliffs.

But Serafina did not look terrified now. She looked angry and cold with it, down to her bones. "My cousin the duke," she said, "has long plotted to remove me from the line of succession. His attempts on my life grow increasingly bold. Verdura is the reason I departed for Cornwall in the first place."

There was another brief clamor as the assembled company demanded answers, explanations, but Ruby didn't hear it. She knew the Duca di Verdura—knew *of* him, at least. As ambassador to Monfalcone, her father had been in contact with Verdura on numerous occasions; the royal duke frequently traveled to England to represent the Monfalcone nation's interests. Once, like Liverpool, Verdura had dined at their house.

"This was not his first attack," Princess Serafina said. "But it was certainly the closest he has come to success." Her jaw tightened, sharp as a stiletto, and she looked out at the company assembled in her chamber. "Someone has schemed with him. Someone who knew my ship, the time and date of my travel. Someone who, perhaps, waited here in Cornwall and reported to the duke when I was meant to arrive."

Ruby felt a sharp shock go through her as the import of the princess's words registered. Serafina believed that one of *them* was a traitor—had played a role in this attempted assassination.

The dark shadow she and Malcolm had seen outside the kitchen window—could it have been someone looking for the princess in her home? Perhaps even preparing for this very attack?

Very likely it had been. And yet even if she told Princess Serafina what they'd seen, she did not know if the woman would trust her. The very fact of their presence in the house, Ruby realized, was desperately suspicious. None of them was meant to be here—no one except for Malcolm. His crew's presence in the house would never stand up to any sort of scrutiny. And neither would—

Ruby's skin went cold. Her gaze flew to Alice, who had shrunk back into the shadows.

Betrayal. Treason.

It had been an accusation of treason, never proven, that had brought down Alice's father. That had destroyed Alice's life. If the princess's suspicion were to fall on one of them, it would turn, first and quickest, to Alice.

"Let me make myself clear," Princess Serafina said. "If one of you has put my people in harm's way, there will be no end to the devastation I will wreak upon you and your house. I will have justice by my own hand. I will flay your skin from your body. I will—"

"We didn't," Ruby heard herself say.

The princess's black-marble gaze swung to her.

Ruby swallowed. She remembered the fire, slowly creeping up the drapes behind the prime minister's chair. She remembered this too: the frantic, tearing knowledge that disaster loomed and that to stop it meant her own ruin.

She had leapt out of her seat and flung herself at the fire anyway. She could never have done anything differently.

"We didn't scheme with Verdura. Lady Alice and Miss Drake—they don't even know who that is. But . . . I do."

Serafina's gaze sharpened.

Ruby hurried on. "I know him because my father is Lord Hangleton, ambassador to Monfalcone. And he—I—" She broke off, hesitating on the words, then forced them out. "I can get in touch with my father. I can tell him everything that's happened here. He will help you."

"Ruby," Alice said softly.

Ruby shook her head.

Her father had been furious with her, that day with Liverpool in the dining room. The dinner had dissolved into chaos, and the wall coverings had smelled of smoke for months until she'd ordered replacements from the milliner. After that, she'd vowed to make herself smaller, more polite, to speak nothing but pleasantries, to repeat only whatever she heard Cassandra say first. She'd done it for months until her father seemed to forget his ire.

But it was not in her nature to be silent. Not when something needed to be fixed. The princess needed their help, and Alice and Archer needed her protection, and perhaps—

It seemed to her that here, in this moment, she could do some good. She *refused* to let herself be daunted by the cost.

"I can write to my father," she said. "He will be able to investigate Verdura. He has the connections, the political acumen—he can determine with whom Verdura might have schemed."

She left the rest unspoken: that to write to her father about the princess would be to reveal to him the fact that she, Ruby, was here at Pomeroy House.

If she told her father the truth, he would make her leave.

She had gone to Cornwall because she wished for a life of independence. She had wanted to make her own choices, free from the constraints of society and the disappointment of her father.

And here she was: choosing.

Despite her effort to keep her gaze on the princess, Ruby found her eyes flickering to Malcolm. Did he understand what she was about?

She thought he did. He was watching her, all tension in his angular jaw, his eyes blue and wrenching. And if some part of her wanted to dissemble—wanted to disclaim any connection to her father, wanted to stay right here and pretend she could live like this, with him, as happy as she'd been the previous night in the tower—she couldn't do it.

She had the power to protect him, and his crew, and Alice. And she would use it.

She looked back to the princess. "We can hide you here, keep your survival a secret until we hear back from my father." Her voice dropped, vibrating with all her earnest hope. "I know you do not know me. But we have lived here in your home for weeks, and we have taken care of it as best we can. We have not schemed to put you in danger, Your Highness. We will not let you down."

And then, to her surprise, Neri nodded. "I have looked into their papers, maestá, and their correspondence. Nothing has come in or out from Verdura. I have seen nothing that would suggest a plot."

It was Tamsin who spoke up then, her dark blue eyes fixed on Neri. "That's why you came to Pomeroy House unannounced, isn't it? Not to make the house ready for a royal dog—but to ensure it was safe here for the princess."

Neri gave Tamsin an unreadable glance through his spectacles.

"Do not be absurd," the princess said sharply. "Zenobia is most discriminating in her tastes. Of course my Neri was here for her."

Neri turned back to the princess. "They have been good to Zenobia these last days, maestá," he said. "And not only because she belongs to you. But because they are good to all the dogs."

Princess Serafina inclined her head in acknowledgment, then looked away from her majordomo and out at the rest of the room. The silence stretched as she eyed them each in turn: as she weighed and measured them. Her gaze lingered on Ruby, on Archer, on Tamsin.

"I do not trust a single person on this island," she said finally. Ruby's heart sank.

But the princess was not finished. "Except you, Neri. If you say that they have not schemed with Verdura, I will take you at your word." She looked back at Ruby and gave a single nod. "I will permit you to hide me here—only for now. Until we receive word from the ambassador."

Chapter 19

Archer managed not to flee until all of it was over: Ruby off to her own chamber with her friends, the princess satisfied, Neri armed with assurances and delicacies for his maestá and her dog.

He made himself wait for calm waters. For reefed sails and no wind. Then he left. He took himself out the back door, stripped off his paint-smeared shirt, and poured cold water over his head, the scent of the ocean drowning out walnut oil and Ruby's amber warmth, which still lingered somewhere on his skin.

He'd watched her, there in the parlor, with a sense of impending doom. She'd put her chin up and plunged forward like a sailor at battle, all honor and stubborn bravura. She would give herself up—give up her dream, if it meant saving the princess's life.

And she didn't see—

Ah God. It was his own fault, every part and parcel of it. He'd lied to her from the first. He'd made it impossible for her to know the import of what she'd done.

We will not let you down, she'd said, and he'd felt the words crack the air like cannon blasts.

He brushed water out of his eyes and tossed back his hair, crumpled his shirt in a ball, and spun toward the—

He froze in his attempt to make his way down to the beach.

Ruby was in his path. She'd changed out of her pretty ruffled thing and into a different pretty ruffled thing—she always looked so goddamned edible, so unbearably, torturously delicious. Her mouth was very pink and her eyes were very blue, and he could see the handful of bruises he'd left on her neck, for Christ's sake, marching in a line of ferocious desire from her poppy-orange be-ribboned bodice all the way up to her perfect, delectable ear.

"I beg your pardon," he said, and moved to go around her. "I'm—I didn't—"

Bloody Christ, the woman made him forget how to talk.

"I'm for the cove," he managed to say. "I mean to look for the remains of the princess's dinghy, if I can find it. Or anything else that's somewhere it should not be."

His casks were hidden. And his silks, and his sculptures, and his illicit goddamned stockings. He wasn't worried about the prin-cess discovering his smuggled goods—not really.

And still, fear was a weight in his belly—an anxious tension tangled up with his feelings for Ruby, with his guilt, with his pain-ful unchecked desire.

"I'll come with you." She fell into step beside him on the path, and her hand twitched toward his, and then fell back.

Uncertain. She was still uncertain of herself, of how she would be received if she made an overture toward him. And why wouldn't she be? They had made each other no promises. He could not offer her anything beyond this patch of space and time—vivid and fleeting as the sunset.

It was, he supposed, already over.

His chest hurt. He kicked a rock on the path hard enough to send it exploding into a nearby clump of gorse. "There's no need."

"No," she said slowly, "but I thought perhaps we could talk. About—the princess. About—"

"You ought to stay here at the house." He was still striding along, and she was keeping up with him, a little flouncy confection made of steel and willpower. "It'll be safer with everyone around."

"Surely it will be safe on the beach," she said doubtfully. "It is a beach. We can see someone coming from nearly any direction."

"There are caves and cliffs and—" He broke off, glowering at her bare fingers. In her haste, she'd forgotten her gloves. "Never mind. Fine. Come then, if you like."

She walked beside him in silence for a time—he'd scarcely ever known her to keep silent, and certainly not for a whole quarter hour—and her mouth only twitched once, when he launched another pebble off the side of the cliff.

"You said you wanted to talk," he said finally when they were nearly down to the cove. "And you're not."

"Not—what?"

"Not talking. Not—"

He didn't know what the hell he was saying—of course she wasn't talking, he was acting like a sulky polecat, she was no doubt terrified—but he didn't explain himself. She didn't let him finish.

"What," she said crisply, "in the world is the matter with you?"

Ah. Not terrified, then. Of course she was not. When had she ever been what he expected?

"Nothing is wrong with me," he snapped, in a startling display of maturity and good sense.

"I don't believe you. You are scowling, for heaven's sake. Brooding. I've never seen your face make that expression before. Are you hungry? Do you require some sustenance? Is that the explanation for your mood?"

There was certainly *something* he wanted to devour—

He whirled toward her. "This," he said wildly. "All of this. It's not going to work. It's a goddamned natural disaster."

We will not let you down.

Fucking hell. Of course he would let her down. There was no good outcome here, no chance for success—no way to protect his crew and have Ruby and untangle the plot against the princess. Her father would learn the truth; Archer would lose his position and his crew. He could no longer keep pretending that he could be everything, juggle a dozen balls and never let one drop. He could no longer let his people believe that they were safe, because they weren't, not anymore.

A thousand decisions in his past, one after another after another, had made all of that impossible.

"What do you mean?" she asked. Her eyes looked like smoked glass in the sunshine reflected off the sea.

"This plan. Your scheme to have your father investigate while we hide the princess."

She flushed a little and straightened the ribbon at her waist. "I do not think it bound to fail. My father is knowledgeable and well connected. He—"

"I don't mean that it's going to fail. Of course it won't. Your father will find out everything."

She shook her head. "I don't understand what you're trying to—"

"I am Quenby." His voice came out low and furious. "That is what your father will find out. I was Quenby, and I am a confidence artist and a smuggler and a goddamned professional liar, and your father *saw* me at Gravesmuir's dinner, and so did you."

It felt like relief and ruination at the same time. He wanted to cup her face in his palm. Tangle his fingers in her ribbons and beg her to pretend she hadn't heard.

He didn't.

"I'm a bastard," he said. "A spinner of tales and a peddler of horse shit. If your father pulls the wrong thread in his investigation of Verdura, the fabric of our lives here at Pomeroy House will unravel. And I cannot"—he had to force the words out past the tight knot of his jaw—"I will not ask you not to write to him. I won't make you lie on my behalf. Not to your father. Not for me."

Her pointed chin tipped up, her mouth firm, her eyes cool. "I know," she said. "I already knew that you were Quenby."

"You . . ." He stared at her. "You—what?"

"I suspected it the very first day. I recognized you, do you not recall? I knew for certain in the inn when you had plaster dust all in your hair, and even if I hadn't sorted it out on my own, you told me yourself."

"I never said a single thing—"

"This morning," she said. "On the stairs. You said the first time you saw me, I was sparkling all over. You remembered me from Gravesmuir's dinner party." She touched his arm, and the brush of her fingers made his head spin. "I've known this whole time."

He tried to make sense of what she was saying. The breeze off the sea was cool on his skin, and he could hear the birds as they cried and wheeled above the waves.

Ruby knew. She'd known all along.

She'd known he was Quenby when she'd pulled his mouth down to hers in the cove. When she'd slept, velvet-soft and vulnerable, all night in his arms.

She'd known when she'd spoken to the princess.

We will not let you down.

"I knew," she said. "My father—" She paused for the briefest moment on an unsteady breath. Her mouth crimped a little as she wrestled down the tiny hesitation. "He will not recognize you. I will not reveal your secret identity, and he will not suspect it. You are Captain Malcolm Archer and *only* Captain Malcolm Archer when it comes to my father."

His chest hurt. "I don't think—"

"No," she said, "it *will* work. I'll make it work. I will burnish your reputation and praise your stalwart protection of the princess. I will make certain that my father sees you as nothing less than a hero."

"Ah God," he said, and he couldn't help himself. He put his hand to her cheek and brushed back the tangled buttery curls that the wind had pushed across her mouth. "Ruby."

"I can protect you," she said stoutly, "and the princess. I can manage it. I can *do* this."

"Oh, pet," he said, and bloody Christ, she was so radiant in the light that she hurt his eyes to look at. So bright he thought he might weep. "It won't work. It's not"—she'd opened her mouth to speak, and he forestalled her—"it's not you. You could do anything you set your mind to, of that I have no doubt. But I'm not—" His throat wanted to close. He didn't want to say what had to come next. "I'm not Captain Archer. I'm no more a naval captain than you are."

Her lips parted beneath the seeking touch of his hand. "You're—what?"

"I used to be. I—"

Oh Jesus, he was going to tell her everything, wasn't he? He was going to open his mouth and pour out every scrap of his stupid, stupid heart.

"Come here," he said instead. "Come with me."

He took her by the hand and drew her down the path—not all the way down to the beach, not this time, but to a cave, half disguised by brush. And then he brought her inside.

"What is this?" Her voice was curious, wondering—trusting.

He found he could scarcely bear it. "A tunnel. I learned of it from Gill Oliphant, a free trader who lives in St. Petroc's, when we first came here. When I was looking for some way to feed and house my crew."

He'd brought her a dozen paces inside now, far enough that the roof of the tunnel had begun to dip, and he had to bend his head. They were sheltered from the wind, and from the light too, and it was easier to say the words now that she was shadowed. Now that he could not make out the blue-gray scalpel of her gaze.

He raised his hand, meaning to put it to her waist, but he could not do it. He couldn't touch her and tell her what he needed to say. He placed his palm against the cool, moist surface of the stone instead and felt his body tilt toward her, a satellite in her orbit, a plant turning to the sun.

"I used to be a captain," he said again. "And before that, a privateer. I talked my way into command when I was far too young and stupid to know any better, and I did it because the money was good and because—"

His voice cracked, and he froze, trying to hold himself together, trying to keep inside the old grief that threatened to break the surface of his skin.

"Tell me," Ruby said gently, and she did not touch him, and he was glad. He did not think he could've withstood the soft press of her hand.

"We were almost in the workhouse." The ice on his mother's cup, the gnawing pit of hunger in his belly—the memories felt inches away, as though he could reach out and touch them, separated by the thinnest scrim of glass. "My mother and me. I was a bastard, and she had no husband, and she was sick. Brave as hell, and tooth-grindingly tough, and—sick."

She had always been sick. She'd been a maid when he was a boy, and he could still remember the scent of furniture polish, the books her mistress had let her borrow, the pages too clean for his fingers to touch. But she'd lost that place and then the next—lost position after position because sometimes she woke glassy-eyed and fevered, because sometimes she could not bend to clean the grate.

He had not realized the precarity of their lives, not at first. She had made it seem an adventure—an endless chance to explore new homes, to see how well they could mend their clothes, to stuff her shoes with rags and make them fit on his own too-small feet. She had been playful and clever, and everything he loved about the world had come from her.

He felt the condensation on the tunnel's stone wall, damp

and cold beneath his fingers. "I was six or so when I realized I could lie. When I realized that no matter what I said, I could smile and people would believe me. I brought her home stale bread and spring bulbs I filched from a churchyard, and books. She loved stories." He remembered her hands—red and swollen, hot to the touch where they covered his on the fine cloth-covered boards. "I told her that someone had given them to me, when the truth was I pretended I was an errand boy and stole them straight off the shelves. I couldn't—tell her. I couldn't tell her any of it, and when I was twelve years old, I got caught."

He clenched his jaw to hold back—

He scarcely knew what he wanted to hold back. All the memories. All the painful, precious arc of his childhood: blue delphiniums in the black earth, and a small square room, and his mother's hands on the fresh-cut pages of a book. "I was—in jail. When she died. She didn't even know where I had gone."

"Malcolm," Ruby whispered. She reached up: he sensed the movement more than saw it in the tunnel's dim light.

He took her hand and pressed it against the stone, locking his fingers between hers.

"I was . . . lost after that. I scarcely knew—" He cleared his throat. "I joined the first ship that would have me, and I worked my way up through recklessness and hunger and big, foolish talk that I was too stupid not to believe in myself. And then I met Jack Penney and everything changed."

Penney had not been admiral, not yet. That had come later: the mad charges into battle, the scream of shattered wood and cannon shot, the hot scent of tar. The death and fear and victory, again and again and somehow again.

"He was the making of me. He vouched for me, despite my prison sentence, though he had no reason to do so. He taught me to speak like a gentleman, to turn my rough twaddle into perfect gilded company talk. He told me he would make me an officer, if only I followed his lead, and I did. I would have followed him straight off a cliff. And then—"

He laughed roughly. He could smell the amber scent of Ruby's skin, and a ghost of wind blew her hair against his lips. "And then I did."

Her hand twitched beneath his. "What do you mean?"

"We were in the Mediterranean Fleet. He was on the flag-ship, the *Victorious*. I captained the *Swallow*. We were raiding the coast—he had taken down half a convoy himself before he called for our aid. It was raining. He—" Archer swallowed. His throat was dry, and the stone was wet beneath his hands, and his ears still rang, sometimes, with screaming. The way they were doing now. "We collided. We lost seventeen men. Penney—he didn't see us. It was dark, we were straight on ahead of his bow, and the rain—"

It had been raining so hard.

"He hit your ship?" Ruby said. "With his own?"

"We collided," Archer said again, although that had not been what he'd reported. That had not been the phrase he'd used aloud. "I was discharged. Stripped of my rank and pension. I cannot call myself a captain, not really. Not any longer. Not when it counts."

Penney hadn't even seen it happen. He'd argued with the sail-ing master—they'd both been belowdecks, in Penney's cabin, and they shouldn't have been, not in that weather, not with a bosun untried and the fleet converging. The *Swallow* had been so much smaller than the *Victorious*; the wrench of wood and cold slap of water that had torn Archer's ship in half had barely rocked the flagship.

Ruby's voice caught hold of him in the dark. Brought him back. "I don't understand. If Admiral Penney hit your ship, why did you—"

"I did what I was good at," Archer said. His voice cracked again. "I lied. I said it was my fault. My error. My carelessness."

He could feel Ruby's body, her chest rising and falling, the warmth of her like succor, like the dream of home.

She was shaking her head. "I don't understand. Why would you do that?"

"I couldn't let them court-martial the admiral. The fleet needed him more than it needed me. But I . . . my crew, they—" He ran his thumb against Ruby's palm, soft, gentle, aching. "They knew it hadn't been my fault. They refused to stay in the fleet. They would not let me go. They were—stupid. Loyal. Idiots."

"And he allowed it?" Ruby asked. She sounded appalled. "Penney ordered you to lie for him? He made you take the fall?"

"He did not make me. I chose it."

In the years since he'd lost the *Swallow*, he'd almost convinced himself that the disaster *had* been his fault. He'd told the story a dozen times, again and again, to all the officers and government men who'd interviewed him when he'd made his stunned and hollow journey back to England. He'd said it so often, he'd almost come to believe it.

He could not have chosen anything else. When he closed his eyes, he still saw Penney's face, white with agony, his hair damp from rain and blood. Counting the bodies in the water, anguished, disbelieving. And sorry—so sorry for his mistake.

"I don't understand," Ruby said again.

Archer licked his lips. "The fleet couldn't go on without him. The war, the men—everyone needed him. *I* needed him. I needed him to be the man at the wheel, and I . . ." He hesitated, searching for the words. "I owed everything to him. This was my chance to pay him back. But Ruby—"

His thumb crept from her palm down to her wrist, lodged against the quick throb of her pulse. "Penney got me this position. Secretly. Through his connections to House di Sangro. If your father investigates who might have betrayed the princess—if he looks too closely at the staff and our pasts—he will find me as I am. Not a captain, but a discharged officer, sent down in dishonor. Even Penney could not speak up for me publicly after I lost the *Swallow*. Not again."

She freed her hand from his grasp, but only so that she could reach up and touch his cheek. And—Christ, he was a besotted fool.

He relished it.

"Penney could have spoken up for you," she said stubbornly. "He should have told the truth. He was wrong to let you—"

"He was *right*." Archer had heard the same argument even then from his crew. Lamentation more than any of them had been heartbroken and furious—and, in the end, determined to keep them all together. "Penney had to remain. He knew what his leadership meant to the fleet."

The admiral had meant everything to Archer: safety and confidence and the security he'd lost when he was twelve. A way out of the maze of grief and fear.

"He did not have to do what he did for me," Archer said hoarsely. "I was nothing before he came into my life, before he took me under his protection. And after the navy—after the *Swallow*—I only went back to what I was before."

"You weren't nothing," Ruby said. Her fingers shifted—his jaw, his throat. In the dark, her thumb brushed his mouth. "You were never *nothing*, Malcolm."

"I've never done an honest day's work in my life."

"You were a boy. A hungry child who loved his mother. You did what anyone would have done—"

"I didn't." He gritted his teeth against the desire to press into her, to feel the small solid weight of her body, the press of her bones, the uncompromising rhythm of her heart.

He had taken all his fear—all his want and hurt, all of his uncertainty—and pressed it tight into a ball, then shoved it deep down in his belly and smiled.

Smiled so his mother would not know he was afraid. Smiled when that first crew had known him for a foolish, brainless boy— smiled and charmed them anyway.

"I lied," he said. "I haven't stopped lying. I've stolen and smuggled and run from my past, and now it's caught up with me, and I can't hide from it any longer."

He could not dissemble, not anymore. Not even if he wished to.

He ached to hold Ruby's face in both his hands. He wanted to pretend this moment was a lifetime and a lifetime was infinite. He wanted to dream that she was his and tell himself it was no dream.

He didn't want to let her go.

"Your father will find out the truth," he said, "when you write to him. He'll find out who I truly am."

There could be no more than this: a handful of stolen moments, seawater swirling around them in the cove, blue paint on Ruby's cheek. Her dear, brave, plainspoken loyalty, and her heart as big as the ocean. For a minute—for one brief, glorious moment— he'd had all of it.

He supposed he ought to be used, by now, to letting things go. He supposed it ought not hurt so much.

She jerked her chin up. Her hands dropped from his face to his shoulders, and then his bare back, and then the top edge of his trousers, which she clutched in her fists. "And what of it?"

"I don't know—"

"No," she snapped. "He'll find out who you really are? Let him."

He didn't mean to do it. He tried to resist. But still, when he spoke, he found that his hands were at her ribs, his palms spanning flesh and bone. "What do you mean?"

"You are decent. Self-sacrificing. Loyal and hardworking and kind."

He almost laughed, so ludicrous did it seem. "Ah, pet."

"You *are*. Your crew came with you because they care for you, and because you deserve it. You held them together through sheer force of will. You found them a house. You built four hammocks for four boys because you could and because it was the right thing to do."

"Ruby." He could feel the ribbons at her waist, the seam of her bodice and, above it, the steep curve of her breast. In the dark, his face had come close to hers. He could almost taste the shape of her mouth. "Don't. There's no good that can come of this."

"I see you," she murmured. "I've always seen you."

He felt run through, laid open. Cleaved by the ruthless clarity of her gaze.

She had. God grant him mercy. She had.

"I'm not a good man," he said roughly.

He meant it. He wanted her to know the truth of his past, to be frightened of the consequences of honesty. He wanted her to tell him to go.

And—God. He wanted to have her right here in the dark. If they had only days or weeks to be together, he wanted them all with a hot selfish greed. He wanted to breathe the air from her lungs, let himself drown in the gluttony of his desire.

He spread his fingers. His thumb grazed the underside of her breast.

Her breath caught, and at the sound, Archer's body surged beneath the furious check of his control.

Slowly, she dragged her nails up his back, and he shuddered at the touch, at the lush closeness of her body.

"Prove it," she whispered. Her voice was low; her breath fluttered against his chest.

He fisted his hand in her skirt. His heart beat out a pained tattoo: *I want you; I want you; I can't.*

"Show me," she murmured. "Do your worst. I want to know what sort of villain you are, Malcolm Archer."

"Yours," he said hoarsely.

And then he went down on his knees and showed her.

Chapter 20

It was close inside the apothecary shop: hot, still, the summer air thick with lavender and sweet potent cordials. Ruby had already unfastened the top two buttons at her throat; as she passed by the small square window, she unfastened two more, and then gave in and pulled off her gloves.

Tamsin, Alice, and Princess Serafina had gone ahead to the village, an errand that Ruby suspected was going poorly. The fashionable princess evidently did not enjoy Tamsin's attempts to disguise her in ill-fitting bonnets or frocks; she'd taken to snarling anytime Tamsin got too close.

Everyone else in the shop was busy with their purchases. The apothecary had gone out, his assistant was harried in the corner, and no one was watching Ruby. At the window, she leaned forward, pressed her palm to the glass, and sighed out her relief. Cool, blessedly cool and—

She looked out the window and her sigh transformed into a hastily stifled gasp.

There, in the shade behind the shop, stood Archer.

Or—leaned, rather. He lounged against the thick-mortared brick, his feet crossed at the ankles, his shirt dangling open at the neck, his eyes blue and hungry.

He saw her notice him. His mouth tipped up, and then he tilted his head, a slow invitation, all languor and syrup.

Come here to me.

Her skin went hotter—a flush of warmth, a flip in her belly. Shards of memories, all fractured by pleasure: his mouth on her skin, his fingers pressed deep inside her, the hot bite of his teeth high on her thigh.

Come here to me, Ruby Ballimore, he'd whispered to her in the dark, the night after the princess had arrived. The moon had been out, and he'd already pleasured her once that day, and she hadn't cared, not a whit, that someone might see when she'd made her way to his chamber. She desired him; she ached for him. She wanted to show him how much.

Let me take care of you, pet. Let me.

And he had—and *she* had too—touched and whispered and mapped each flex of his jaw, the hard ridges of his abdomen, the coarse sound of his cry as he spent himself in her fingers or— once—in her mouth. In the twelve days since the princess had arrived at Pomeroy House, they had found their way to each other in pockets of shadow, in brief unnoticed gaps, and once, a long, slow night of wanting, cresting, wanting again.

Soon they would have an answer from her father. Soon they would be parted.

But not yet. She could have this now. And if, sometimes, pleasure felt like danger—like the anticipation of a knife stroke—she forced her mind away from the pain to come.

She was out the door into the back alley before she could think, and then his hands were on her shoulders and his lips were on hers.

"Thought you'd never look out that window," he muttered against her mouth. "God, you taste good. Sweet."

She stood on her toes, gripped his shirt in her fists, and held him close. "Have you been waiting for me?"

"Following you, more like." He pressed his mouth to her neck, her collarbone, the skin revealed just above her breasts. "Saw you—in the confectionery—ah God, let me undo a few more buttons, darling, and I promise I'll make it worth your while."

Her head fell back against the brick. "Anyone could pass."

"Keep the watch for me," he murmured. "Please."

She whimpered as his mouth did something wicked to her ear. His fingers played at the gape of her bodice, dipping into the hot damp valley between her breasts—but he did not move to unfasten her frock further.

She knew he wouldn't, unless she gave him leave.

In some ways, she was the hungrier, the more reckless. She wanted to lie with him—she throbbed with it, an empty clenching ache between her legs. She had not realized, at first, that the string of tiny bruises on her neck had come from his mouth—not until she watched him do the same to the pale skin of her lower belly.

She wanted him to mark her. She wanted him awfully, irrevocably; she wanted to feel his body a part of hers, take him deep into her own fierce need.

But he held back. *We can't,* he'd said, when she'd tried to press herself against his thick length that night in his chamber. *Sweetheart— oh God, Ruby—you've no idea how much I want to. Only we can't— hazard the risk.*

He was right.

She could stand it. She told herself she could stand it—this temporary madness, the brief luminous pleasure of knowing herself wanted, the stars that burst behind her eyelids when he pleasured her with his mouth and hands.

Temporary. But for now, hers to relish. Hers to take.

"I'll keep the watch," she said into his hair. But she closed her eyes instead and let herself savor the rough vibration of his lust-drunk groan.

"Thank Christ." He flicked her next few buttons and yanked hard at her chemise. "Saw you in the sweet shop when I passed. Don't know what you were eating—something sticky, I collect, by the way you sucked your fingers after. Haven't had a sane thought since—ah—"

She'd closed her fingers around his erection through his trousers, and then it was a race—his mouth—damp suction, fevered plea—her fingers moving, more firmly than she would have thought he'd like—except he did like it, she knew that now, knew the pitch and gritted gasp of his culmination—

"Let me," he muttered, and yanked at her skirts, his forehead pressed to her collarbone. "Let me do this for you. Can't spend in my trousers—"

"My mouth, then?"

"Ruby," he groaned and licked the inner curve of her breast. "I'd think I'd died, except God knows I'm not headed for this sort of paradise." He had his hand beneath her skirts now, but he'd stopped at the level of her garter, his thumb rubbing hot circles into her skin, pressing, seeking. "So pretty," he murmured, "so luscious. You taste of sugar and liquor—of sun—God, the sweetness of you—"

"Mm," she said—wordless affirmation—and felt her thighs

go slack. The pins in her hair rubbed against the brick behind her head, little points of almost-pain, and she heard one clink to the ground, and then she heard—

"If you approach me with that devil-spawned article one more time, I will cover you in the grease from a pig and let Zenobia eat you while you still live."

Ruby's eyes flew open. "Malcolm," she hissed, "let me go!"

He was already breaking apart from her, his eyes all hot blue desire, his voice a raspy laugh. "I thought you were keeping the watch."

"You distracted me!" Good heavens, her friends had returned sooner than she'd anticipated. She didn't even have her gloves on, and the buttons on her frock still felt impossibly small. Perhaps—perhaps she could clamp her straw hat over her décolletage—if only she could *find* her hat, which he'd evidently flung to the ground somewhere in between licking her neck and—and—what *had* he done to her stocking?

He bent, presumably to tie her garter back on.

"Stand up," she hissed. She still had four more buttons to do up, and neither the buttons nor her fingers would cooperate. "You can't be under my skirts if they stroll out the back door!"

"I was rather thinking I could hide under there." His dimples flashed, gorgeous, irrepressible. "Stay all afternoon."

"You are dreadful," she said, and thought, *I could live the whole of my life on that smile.*

The back door eased open, and Alice put her head out. "Ruby?"

He sobered rather quickly at the sight of Alice. He reversed their positions, setting Ruby between himself and the shop, an action that rather puzzled her until she felt the startling brush of his erect member against her bum.

"Help," he muttered into her ear, and heaven save her—

She laughed.

"There you are," Alice said. Her gaze remained fixed squarely on Ruby's face, and she did not acknowledge Ruby's deshabille, except if one counted the smothered sound of her voice. Unlike Tamsin, Alice had not thrown herself into ruthless teasing the first time she'd noticed all the little bites on Ruby's throat. "Might you perhaps return to the shop? I fear there's some— there's some—"

She broke off beneath the sound of crashing and barking and a screech like a whistle that Ruby was confident had not come from Tamsin.

Ruby gave up on her hat and her right stocking. "To be sure. How were the rest of the errands?"

"Ah," Alice said, "well. Vigorous?"

Back inside the shop, Tamsin had hustled Princess Serafina into a corner. The princess, her waist-length black hair pinned up in a crown of shining braids, was glowering at Tamsin. Her arms were locked around Zenobia, who had been doused in some sort of dark, mysterious liquid. The whole room smelled powerfully of whiskey and licorice.

"This place is a threat to the public good," Serafina was saying, a shout-whisper plainly audible even at the back of the store. "It is not Zenobia's fault that the glass is placed so precariously to spill the tincture."

"*You* are the threat," Tamsin growled back.

The princess gasped. "Never—never in Mon—"

"How many times?" Tamsin pitched her voice higher, either to drown out the princess's next words or because she could not help herself. "How many times must we remind you that you are meant to be concealed? Not drawing attention to yourself in every store, in every possible fashion—"

"I cannot help that I draw attention!" Serafina hissed. "I am the princess of—"

"If you say the word 'princess' again," Tamsin growled under her breath, "I will *give* you to your enemies, gift-wrapped with a bow around your neck, and I shall *like* it—"

Ruby stepped forward. Her stocking collapsed down from her knee and puddled around her right ankle. "Your Highness," she whispered. "Tam. Perhaps we might recommence this discussion when we return to the house?"

The princess stuck her nose in the air and wheeled away from Tamsin. She waved a hand dismissively. "I had no intention of remaining here until I was set upon."

"You tried to leave," Tamsin said, "without paying. Your bloody horrible dog—"

"Do not speak Zenobia's name!"

"I didn't. I wouldn't. I—"

Archer smiled blindingly at all and sundry and interrupted Tamsin's rising crest of outrage. "Not to worry. I shall pay for the— What *was* that?"

"Fudding's Elixir," put in the apothecary, a round fellow in a fragrant apron who'd been watching the proceedings with avarice-tinted fascination. "Seventeen bottles of it. All in from London just this week."

"I'll pay for the Fudding's," Archer said. His voice sounded very deep and sweet and the faintest bit reckless. "And any other breakage this party is responsible for. Send the bill to Pomeroy House. We'll take care of it all."

Princess Serafina's mouth pinched, looking distinctly less

charmed than Ruby felt. "This means that I shall pay for it, I presume. Since I am the—"

"Yes," Archer said loudly. "Indeed. You are the . . . purser. Of Pomeroy House. Come along, Madame Purser, and tell me precisely what budgetary wrongs have been done in your name."

He attempted to take her arm, was greeted by a low snarl from Zenobia, and sidled slightly away instead. He smiled wider, proffered his elbow, and then visibly stifled a laugh when the princess disdained to acknowledge it as she strode out the door and into the sun.

He followed after her, and as he did, he looked over his shoulder and winked at Ruby.

Her cheeks warmed at the sight of him—incorrigible, sunlit, hair still tousled from her own hand.

Oh saints. She was in such terrible trouble.

"She is a plague," Tamsin muttered as she bent to gather crushed lavender and paper packets of dried valerian. "A torment. A devil."

"Zenobia?" Ruby asked. "Or the princess?"

Tamsin gave a sort of guttural moan. "She made no effort to conceal herself whatsoever, despite promising to do so. She wanted to wear a scarlet morning robe, and then when I told her no, she proposed a bathing costume instead. She nearly caused a riot in the churchyard because she attempted to run off with a marble headstone, and I believe there is still a small stampede ongoing because she somehow terrorized a bull."

"Do you know," Ruby said, "I *thought* you were talking about the princess, but I found myself less and less certain the more you spoke."

Tamsin threw up her hands in a shower of fragrant herbs and stalked after Archer and Princess Serafina.

Inside the shop, Alice took Ruby's arm. "Not to worry," she said to the apothecary. "We can be relied upon to make recompense for . . . all of this." Her black lashes fluttered as she looked down at Ruby. "Can't we?"

"Yes," Ruby said stoutly, and made for the door.

They had only just begun to follow in the wake of their straggling parade of companions when Alice tightened her grip on Ruby's arm. "Oh! I almost forgot. The mail coach delivered a letter for you straight into our hands. Well, my hands—Tamsin was busy hauling the princess out of a tavern fight." She removed a slightly battered envelope from her reticule and passed it to Ruby. "Here. I think it's a reply from your father."

Ruby froze in the middle of the street.

It was her father's handwriting, to be sure. She recognized the careful precision of his downward strokes; he cut his quills perfectly; his pens never broke or spattered.

She flipped the letter over and found his seal pressed into the smooth circle of crimson wax. Her fingers trembled as she broke it.

He had written back already. Had he discovered with whom Verdura had schemed? Did he have some superior notion in mind for the protection of the princess?

She thought of her father and Cassandra in Rome, hot coffee and rose-petal jam—of Liverpool and the drapes on fire. She thought of the *Royal Archaeological Journal*, crisp black print on cream paper, laid next to her father's plate at the breakfast table.

Her chest squeezed tight, and she pictured her father's elegant, lean hands set to pen and ink, and she hoped—she *hoped*—

And then, instead of hoping, she read his letter.

Chapter 21

Ruby did not come down to supper.

Archer had watched her enter Pomeroy House just behind him. He'd waited for her to look his way, but she hadn't. Her head had been bent with Alice's, and she had not acknowledged the pack of dogs that greeted her, only pressed her palm against her breastbone and hurried up the stairs.

He'd watched her ascend until even her trim little boots were out of sight and told himself to be patient, to wait for her, to stop being such an outrageous fool.

He wanted to hold fast to her ribbons and keep her beside him. He wanted to smile at her and have her smile back, a thousand times, *every* time.

He did not pretend, even for a heartbeat, that he was not watching her place at the table, waiting for her to come.

But she didn't. They'd all taken to eating in the kitchen, even the princess, who was as fond of Wall's cooking as she was disdainful of the sailors' table manners. Archer's eyes lingered on the braided straw chair, left empty for Ruby, plain and silent.

He didn't make it to Wall's dessert course. He pushed back from the table with an abrupt scrape and strode for the door.

Something was wrong. He knew it was.

She wasn't anywhere on the ground floor: not the blue parlor or the library or the chamber for the hounds. She wasn't in the tower—despite the 197 steps he climbed to search for her, and then another 197 back down to keep looking. She wasn't in her own chamber. Nor Archer's.

He found her, finally, in a small, disused room at the back of the house—the conservatory, he supposed, though little was kept and tended inside its glass-and-iron walls. Before Ruby had come, it had been dusty and vacant, the windows thick with salt spray.

She sat on a settee with her knees drawn up, her chin in her hand, and her eyes fixed upon the glass, looking out at the sea.

"Ruby."

She looked up. Her face was drawn, the blue in her eyes drowned out by gray. "Malcolm."

"I've been looking for you." It was absurd, probably, the way he'd chased her down. Transparent. He couldn't bring himself to care.

"Oh." She glanced down at the settee, a thick flutter of curly lashes, and then back up to meet his gaze. "Have I missed supper? I . . . was not attending to the time."

It was growing dark; the sky was a thousand shades of purple in the dusk. She had to have known she'd missed the evening meal.

"What's the matter?"

She shook her head. Her mouth made a tight line, holding

something in. "Nothing. I've—" Her voice cracked, and her lips clamped down harder, her eyes going back to the sea.

He was at her side before he could stop himself, and if she did not want this—didn't want his arms and his mouth and his shameless abandon—then she could bloody well order him to stop.

"Tell me," he said and put his arms around her, resting his palm on her knee.

She took a quick breath and did not look at him. "I've had a letter from my father. An answer to mine."

Archer's heart pitched. Dropped.

He hadn't—thought it would come so soon. That was all. This parting. His arms tightened around her: stupid, foolish, as though he might keep her. As though, if he held on hard enough, he could tear her out of the fabric of her world.

He made himself ask. "He has a plan then? For the princess?"

"He does not believe me."

He couldn't parse her words, although they'd come out steady. As though she'd said them again and again in her mind.

"What?" he demanded

Her breath hitched, her chest rising in a tight jerk beneath his hands. "Of all the things I imagined he might say, I must admit that this did not suggest itself. He says—he says I am to go back to Bridestowe before I make a spectacle of myself, and if I do not go, he will have me sent to our country seat with a chaperone of his choosing. He says that the Princess of Monfalcone is safe at home, that she has no plans to visit England, and that if I spread this wild tale beyond our family, he will be forced to take more drastic measures to ensure the sobriety of my mind."

Archer felt like he was choking. He did not know what to do

with the ire throttling his throat, the clumsy outrage that made his fingers numb. "Ruby," he said thickly.

She flung up her chin, fast enough to nearly knock his nose with the back of her head. "I'm not going to Bridestowe. I'm not giving up on any of this. On the house, on the princess."

On you.

He almost heard her say it—or else wished he had.

"I know," he said. "It's not in you to give up."

"It's only that I—that I—" She flung herself out of the circle of his arms to stand, crossing to the window, her whole body vibrating with tension. "I don't know. I don't know how to feel."

He had some suggestions. Anger. Stupefaction. Scarcely checked and distinctly murderous rage. He could run Hangleton through for the way the man kept on betraying her.

"I was prepared for criticism," she said. Her voice shook as she looked out at the ocean. "Of how I had handled the situation. For some action I had taken or failed to take, for some standard of perfection I did not meet. But this—" She stopped abruptly and turned to look at Archer, blue-gray eyes brilliant, sun on seawater. "He let me down."

He moved to stand beside her, feeling helpless, afraid to take her hands. "He did."

"He disappointed me."

"He was wrong," Archer murmured. "Over and over. He's been wrong about you."

"I know," she said, and now the tears that had threatened her voice spilled through her lashes and glittered like gemstones on her cheeks. "I know that he does not value me. That he does not appreciate what I've done for our family. But I thought—" She reached up and swiped at her face, and the naked anguish in her eyes cut Archer off at the knees. "I always believed that if I truly needed him, he would be there."

He set his hands to her shoulders, caressing the seam of her dress with his thumbs. "Ruby."

"Even now—" She broke off and looked back at the window. The deepening dusk had turned the glass to a mirror; Archer could see the ghost silhouettes of their bodies, standing close enough to form a single whole. "Even now, I keep thinking it must be some mistake. That perhaps—if only I write to him again. Explain myself better. Perhaps then I can make him—"

"Stop." He gripped her shoulders harder. Too hard. He would leave bruises there to match the ones he'd put on her throat, on her belly. "Stop it, Ruby."

She looked back at him, all damp, wounded eyes. "Is it so ridiculous? To think that I could somehow make him change?"

"You don't have to change his mind," Archer said. "You don't need him."

And even as he said the words, he meant them another way, a dozen different ways.

Let him go; let him roast in the pit of Hell; don't let pleasing him matter to you any longer.

Let me do this for you instead.

Let me.

She lifted her hand to his shirtfront for half a beat, and then she let her palm drop. "I do. This was our plan. Our best hope of securing the princess's safety."

He swallowed. It had been swirling in his head for almost a fortnight, this mad, foolish notion. He'd thought of it as he'd pressed his hand to hers in the cove; when he'd held her in the night, his palm fitted to the curve of her lower back.

This didn't have to end.

"I can do it," he said. "I have another scheme in mind."

Her lips parted. Her lashes flickered. "I beg your pardon?"

His throat was tight, his whole body held close with tension. But the words were there, the way they always were, even if it was a struggle to set them free. "I have a ship."

"You—what?"

"The *Delphinium*. She's in the harbor at St. Petroc's. She's slow and ancient, and I don't advertise that she's mine. But we could do it—Wall and Eugénie and Gerry and Lamentation. And me."

He had pictured it all, these last weeks. Cast it aside, then considered it again, refining, imagining. Feeling afraid.

"There's a fellow I can talk to—my old warrant officer from the *Swallow*. A captain now, with his own ship in the Mediterranean. I'd trust him with my life. If we can smuggle the princess to Genoa, there are people who could help us get her the rest of the way home."

He felt torn in two as he spoke the words. Even as he wanted to press the vision into her skin—this was how they could protect the princess, this was the path forward, they did not require her father's intervention—he also wanted to claw the words right out of the air.

He let me down, she had said, and she'd meant the words for her father, but he'd heard them for himself.

He had hurt her already. More than once. He'd kept his secrets and he'd lied to her, just as he was lying to his crew. If he promised her this—this gamble, this venture hazarded—and then failed, he did not know if he could stand it.

"You would do that?" she said. "Risk your ship? Your crew?"

His chest ached as he gazed down at her. She looked delicate, her skin almost translucent in the pale illumination of moonlight and a single candle. But she was not fragile. She was guts and iron; stubborn will and a mortar knife taken to a cracked and forgotten wall.

It was not the risk to his ship he feared. He loved the *Delphinium*, but it was only wood and canvas, wax and salt water and his knuckles nicked to the bone.

And the risk to his crew—God, the danger to them was no greater than it had always been, ever since they'd chosen to stay by his side.

No. The true risk—what he feared most of all—was here. Was in this room, in Ruby's eyes: that he would try to be more than what he was, more than a scoundrel and a smuggler and a liar. And he would fail.

"I would do it," he said, "for you."

Her breath hitched. "I don't understand."

"I'd do this for you. To show you that you do not need your father's assistance or approval. To show you"—*that I can be something, that I can be worthy of you*—"that it's possible to carve a new path."

He was so close to her. She smelled of crushed herbs from the apothecary shop; her frock was still unbuttoned at the top, baring the notch between her collarbones. He wanted to press his face into her skin, whisper promises he didn't know if he could keep.

When he spoke again, his voice was very low. "You have no idea, Ruby Ballimore, what I would do for you."

"Malcolm." Her brows had drawn together, and as he watched, her mouth worked, trying to hold something back. And then she gave in, a torrent of agonized speech. "Why?" she demanded.

"Why would you say that? You could have anyone you wanted. You smile and the whole world falls at your feet, and meanwhile—"

"Ruby—"

"And meanwhile," she said again, her voice thick, her eyes wet and gray, "no one has *ever* chosen me."

He stared at her. Everything inside him felt churned-up, boiling and icy cold at the same time. He could not tamp down his want and his fear; his emotions felt as though they might burst through the paper-thin barrier of his skin.

He was still holding her shoulders, and so it was easy to spin her around. To make her face not the window but the inside of the conservatory. "Look," he said, and it was an order, an officer's command. "Look at this room."

"I don't—"

"Look around," he snapped, "and tell me what you see."

"Glass. Plants. Some—pots." Her voice shook.

"You." He shook her, just a little, because he could not be easy or gentle right now. He was furious with her father, and guilty and desperate, and he wanted and he *hoped*, and wanting and hoping hurt too. "You, Ruby. That's what I see when I look around this room. When I look around every inch of this house. When I look—bloody fucking Christ, when I look at myself in the mirror. It's all you."

"I only—"

"No. You didn't 'only' anything. You scrubbed these goddamned windows by hand. I saw you. You clipped the plants and made Gerry haul up better soil, and you painted every single one of these blasted pots with some pretty pattern that only you know the name of—"

"Rectilinear meander," she said in a smothered voice.

"Right. The rectilinear meander. Of course." He stared down at her: her blond curls escaping from her pins, her dress crumpled, her eyes devouring him as if to discern whether or not he spoke the truth.

"Damn it, Ruby," he muttered. "It's not just here. It's everywhere." He pushed her toward the threshold, where they could see out into the corridor, the library, the yellow parlor. "Every inch of this house bears your stamp. And it's not only that you made everything beautiful, though by God, you did. You made it whole. You made it *home*. You made this place—where we were merely existing, merely scrabbling for another day—into something good and generous and safe." His hand was on her waist, and he caught his thumb beneath the ribbon there and held on. "You think I don't see how much your Alice has changed since you came here? She says the things she truly means now, not whatever nonsense she most imagines will please. Do you think—"

He broke off. He was breathing hard, and so was she, and he caught her chin with his hand. "Do you think I don't see how you have changed?"

She moistened her lips. He felt the cool intake of her breath over his fingers. Slowly—so slowly—he moved behind her, angling her by the waist so that they both faced the window once more.

It was full dark now. He could see their reflections clearly. His own form, a head taller, his expression desperate and grave. And Ruby in front, her body a bounty of soft heat, every inch of her clad in white: an iced cake, waiting to be devoured.

He pressed his palm to her chest. The tip of his finger caught in the place where her top button was unfastened, and he let it linger there, a tiny stroke that he felt in the uneven rise and fall of her breath.

"Not here," he said. "You haven't changed where it matters. Not in your heart nor your head." He lifted his other hand, dragged it up her throat, and watched in their reflection as his thumb coasted over her parted lips. "Here. Here is where you've changed."

God. He had not meant this for seduction. But the position was almost painfully erotic: one palm on her chest, the other across the vulnerable column of her throat. He watched her, watched himself—felt almost out of his own body as his finger worked another button free.

Helplessly, he drank in the small revelation of her skin. The shadowed indentation where his thumb pressed into her lips. The heat of her body.

"You smile more," he said. His voice was rough. "More freely. You no longer look as though someone might steal it back."

"Steal what back?" she whispered. Her mouth moved against his fingers, and he felt the damp heat of her breath.

His cock had hardened as they stood before the glass, and he resisted—sweet, agonizing restraint—the urge to press himself into her body. He stood an inch behind her, smelling amber and herbs, spicy licorice and her skin.

He rubbed his thumb across her mouth and ached.

"Your joy," he said very softly. "It's yours. You aren't asking for permission or waiting for someone else to give it to you. I've spent all my life playing a dozen different roles, and I have never— not once—been as true to myself as you are every single day, and I . . . God, Ruby. I think you are extraordinary."

He had the words ready. He'd shaped them in his mouth, sometimes, just for the pleasure of it. He meant every one.

"I have never in my life," he murmured, "felt as happy as I do when you smile back at me."

She trembled beneath his touch. Her eyes were locked with his in their reflection, and she stood very still for a long moment.

And then she reached up and unfastened the buttons of her bodice.

His palm shifted as if of its own volition to press against her newly bared skin. In the window, he watched her lips part. Felt the movement beneath his hand. He watched himself slide his fingertips beneath the soft white fabric of her chemise.

"Malcolm," she said. The tip of her tongue brushed his fingers.

He shuddered at the feeling, and at the sound of his name in her mouth. It had been the better part of a lifetime since someone had used his name the way she did: simple and true and devastating.

When he spoke, his voice came out scratchy and deep. "Ruby."

"I'm not asking for someone else's approval. I'm not waiting." Her breath had quickened. Her cheeks were flushed. She felt like a flame in his arms as she put her hand atop his at the level of her chest and then, slowly, guided his fingers down.

His fingers—hers—they tangled, touched, stroked the edge of her areola, and then cupped her breast and lifted it from her stays. All of it felt heady, dizzying: their fingers locked together, the unbearable softness of her skin, the weight of her breast overflowing his palm.

And then, as he watched, her other hand moved too, peeling his free hand from her throat and moving it to her abdomen. Her fingers covered his, pressing his palm hard into her lower belly. He made a hoarse sound; his fingers twitched against the embroidered fabric. His cock throbbed. His mind went blurred with memories of how she felt, wet and pulsing on his hand.

His eyes came back to her face. In the glass, her lips were parted, a damp, vulnerable pink that almost hurt to look at.

"I want you to touch me," she said. "And I want to watch."

Chapter 22

He stepped away from her, and Ruby felt a cold wash of disappointment. She had thought—oh God, she had been so certain—

But he was only moving to lock the door.

"Tell me this has a latch," he said, a trifle breathlessly. "I swear to you, Ruby Ballimore, if it doesn't, I'm having you anyway. Up against the door maybe. Don't care if this whole bleeding house gets an eyeful. It'll teach them to stay away."

She laughed, an unsteady sound. Her heart leapt in her chest. "Perhaps you could push the settee in front of it."

He picked an immense blue-and-white pot instead and made a rather impressive show, his muscles flexing beneath his thin shirt, as he shoved. "Every door," he muttered. "Let's make your next project locks on every bloody door in this house. The larder. The wine cellar. That one shed with all the garden tools."

"I had no idea your imagination was so exhaustive."

He was back now, behind her again, spinning her to face the window, palming her belly and mumbling into her hair.

"Comprehensive. Extravagantly so, when it comes to you and the places I have pictured taking your clothes off."

"The garden shed, though? Among the spades and trowels?"

He pulled her tight against him and lowered his mouth to her ear. "Poor pet. Let me show you the rake your life's been missing."

She laughed again.

He raised one hand to graze her lips, and in their reflection, his dimples emerged, retreated, emerged again. "I like that sound so much. I don't suppose I could ever get enough of it."

She trembled, just a little, in his arms.

It was almost too intense: his beautiful mouth, the clutch of his hands, the words he'd said so fiercely as he'd locked his gaze with hers.

He wanted her. He *saw* her, and still he wanted her.

Some part of her wanted to shy back, to run away. She believed him—believed every word, could look at his mobile face and *know* that he meant what he said. But part of her felt so uncertain too. He meant it now. But for how long?

But she steadied herself. She pressed her palms atop his and held him against her body. She was not asking for approval, nor waiting, nor pretending she did not want something because she was afraid she could not have it.

She would not waste a moment. Not now. Not with him.

He touched the loosed buttons of her bodice, caressing the tiny shimmering disks. There was something arousing about the sight: his long, tapered fingers circling the mother-of-pearl, sliding above and beneath. Her belly went hot, and she shifted, just a bit, to press back into his body.

He was aroused too. His body jerked into hers, and she felt the heavy weight of his sex against her lower back.

He made a rough sound. "Let me take this off you," he said. "Can I? God, Ruby, I want to see you so badly."

"I want to see you too."

She did—she *did* want to see him. But more than that—she did not want to be alone. She felt strangely revealed already. She had not undressed, but she had spoken her desires aloud: to watch as he brought her pleasure. It was what she imagined in the darkest part of the night, Malcolm a floor away and her body hot with wanting.

He smiled as he looked at her, and—merciful heavens, the man had such a talent for joy.

"As her ladyship commands," he murmured, and peeled off his shirt.

In answer, she twitched her shoulders, and her flounced white frock fell to her elbows. She tugged it off the rest of the way, letting it puddle on the ground at her feet, and then stood in her chemise and stays and stockings, and met his eyes in the glass.

His hungry gaze dipped down to the décolletage revealed now above her chemise, to the place where her stays lifted her breasts, pushing them up and out. And then his eyes dropped farther: her hips, her legs, the shadowed place between her thighs.

She could feel the slow path of his eyes like a fingertip, tracing over her flushed, sensitive skin. She shivered, and her chemise brushed her nipples. She felt restless—already wanting.

He set his hands on her hips to hold her still. "Let me look at you," he said thickly. "I could stand right here until the sun comes up and not grow tired of the sight." His palms tangled in her chemise, easing the fabric up.

Her breath came quickly, her chest rising and falling unsteadily, and she watched him in the window—watched the flex of his forearms, the pale high curve of his shoulder, the slow path of his gaze.

Her chemise was above her knees. His hands worked; the thin cotton rose higher, brushing her heated skin, and her hips shifted back, seeking him.

"Impatient?" he murmured.

She covered his hands with hers, traced the lines between his fingers. "I told you," she said. "I told you what I wanted."

"You did." He gave a breathy, uneven laugh. "God, you did, and I liked it so much. I don't know why it pleases me to draw it out. To make you wait."

"Because you wish to torment me?"

His left hand gripped the fabric taut, pulling it across her belly. His right hand slipped between her legs. She gasped, and he did too, grittily, groaning as he cupped her with his palm.

"Not torment you," he rasped, and his hand shifted, his thumb sliding through her wetness to circle her clitoris, and then retreat. "Well. Perhaps a little."

She felt dizzy. She felt her whole body cant down into his hand, tipping toward the place where he cupped her. The sight— ah—she could look down and watch his forearm ripple, his elegant fingers flex and move—and then she could look into the glass and see the ferocious focus on his beautiful face.

Her thighs went taut around his hand. Arousal built and built in her belly—she had learned, these past days, how quickly he could bring her to her culmination.

But this time, he stopped before she reached her peak, slipping his fingers free to clutch her hip.

She took a gasping breath, and he reached up and put his palm to her chest again. "Breathe. Yes. God, you feel good. Yes, breathe just like that."

She clutched his arm. Her breasts pushed up into his hand as she inhaled, and she felt his body grow harder where he pressed into her back.

"Torture," she got out. "I recognize it."

"No," he murmured, and palmed her breast with a little moan. "Can I take your stays off?"

"If you remove your trousers."

Now he laughed too, and pressed his mouth briefly to her neck, her cheek, and then her lips. "Done," he whispered against her mouth, and had himself out of his shoes and trousers in a heartbeat.

He was bare as the day he was born, and she could not help but chart the contours of his body while he worked her stays. His shoulders were broad; the muscles of his abdomen flexed. She had traced the scars on his biceps muscle with her tongue.

His phallus resembled no classical statue she had ever seen. Perhaps the Greeks had been loath to show off.

He had her stays off now, and then her chemise too, and then he was cupping her breasts, molding them, pressing them together and staring, staring at her in the glass, shamelessly grinding himself against her back as he devoured her body with his eyes.

She had never had strong feelings about her own form. Plumpness was generally considered a pleasing attribute, and she dressed in such a way to take advantage of her shape. But her breasts had always been cumbersome; when slim sweeping gowns had been in fashion, Ruby's bountiful bosom had made such straight lines impossible.

But now, as she watched Malcolm watch her, she could spare

no feelings for her own body except delight. She made him feel this way; her body brought him to a fever pitch of wanting. She felt a strange, vertiginous flush beneath her skin at the thought of her own power, a hot melting sensation in her lower belly.

He rolled her nipples, and she gasped. Desire felt like a seam deep inside her, pulled tighter and tighter, poised to split apart.

He slipped his hand between her legs again. "Breathe," he murmured. "Watch."

It was impossible to get enough air. She came up on her toes and then lowered herself back down, helplessly, against his hand. He refused to push his fingers inside her, even as she rocked against him, even as she made a little sobbing plea.

He pulled back, stroked the wetness that had slicked the top of her thighs. "I think," he said unsteadily, "it pleases me so much because it means you trust me. You do trust me, don't you, darling?"

She scarcely understood what he meant. Her mind felt thick, mazy, as though she'd slipped into a clouded dream. But she knew the answer—knew it as well as she knew the shape of his smile. "I trust you."

He shuddered against her. "I can't— Ah God, Ruby. I want it so much." His fingers were back between her legs, touching, teasing, and his other hand rubbed across her mouth. "You know that I'll take care of you?"

"Yes," she managed. She ground herself against his hand, and this time he obliged, pressing two fingers inside her in a slick, deep thrust.

"You trust me enough to wait for me?" he said hoarsely. "As long as it takes?"

"Yes," she said again. "Malcolm, please—"

"Watch," he murmured. "Watch us together. See how good we are."

She hadn't realized her eyes had closed. She forced her lids open, her body shaking, her mind a bright blaze of sensation. She watched his face and the flex of his arm—watched the way he watched her, so carefully, as she came apart.

She couldn't help herself. Her eyes closed again. Her body was alight, a desperate animal thing. Pleasure flooded her, crested— broke like a wave and left her gasping.

When she stopped shaking, he gathered her close, skin pressed to skin, and brought her down atop him on the settee. She still felt muzzy-headed, her thoughts slow and syrupy, her body washed clean in the aftermath of her pleasure. She skated her palms up his abdomen and then back down, marveling at the ridges of muscle, the dip of his navel, the dark hair that thickened as she approached his sex.

He made a rough, wordless sound as she touched him. His hips jerked.

It was extraordinary how much she liked that. Dizzying: this sense of her own power.

Slowly, she pushed herself up on one palm. He was splayed loosely beneath her—somehow vulnerable and potent at once, naked and confident in his skin. She wrapped her fingers around his length, firmly, as he liked, and his hips jerked again.

"Giving me—a little torment back, pet?" he gasped.

"No," she said. "No. I like to look at you too, you know. It's a mortal sin that you should be forced to hide all of this under your clothes."

His throat bobbed. She watched the muscles of his belly

tighten as her hand moved down to touch him lower. "I'm not certain you and the church agree on the nature of sinning."

"Probably not." Her gaze slid up to his face. "I know I'm right. I know beauty when I see it, Malcolm. Every inch of you."

She felt his length swell beneath her hand as she said the words. Watched the shape of his mouth grow almost pained.

"Do you like that?" she asked. "If I tell you that you are pleasing to look upon?"

He breathed a laugh and pushed up into her hand. "I suppose I do. Only because I know you can't lie to save your own skin."

"You please me," she murmured. Her hand moved a little faster, and she watched his eyes flutter closed and then open again. His thigh was pressed between her legs, and she felt the beat of her own pulse there, a quick throb. "You please me so much. Sometimes at night I close my eyes and imagine the way that you touch me, and I want you so much I can almost feel your hands on me."

"God," he said thickly. "Ruby."

It made sense to her, suddenly, that he should like to hear her praise. That was what he wanted: for her to see him, to know him for a good and decent man. He kept on telling her so; she only needed to listen.

"I ache for you," she said, and ah—she couldn't help herself. She pushed herself into the hot muscle of his leg.

He gave a deep, torn-off groan.

"I always want you," she whispered. "I think constantly of having you inside me."

"Enough," he rasped, and caught her thighs in his hands. "I can't— I want—"

He couldn't seem to put it into words. He mumbled

something—some nonsensical words of praise and yearning—and dragged her atop him, sliding his cock between her folds.

She gasped.

"Take your pleasure," he gritted out. "Make yourself come."

He showed her what he meant, sliding her against the granite length of him, a slow drugging rhythm. He pressed not inside her, but against her, stroking her clitoris with his erection. Her body felt full of sparks, burning, spinning, flickering behind her eyes.

"Set the pace," he said raggedly. "I need to—"

His hands left her thighs to cup her breasts, and his movements were shaky, uncontrolled. He gripped her hard, clutching at her, and it felt desperately good, and it made her ache—all of her felt hungry and aching and *empty*.

She shifted, angling her body so that his cock pressed against her entrance.

He froze.

Her mind was full of longing: for him, for this. For weeks, she had wanted this—wanted something irrevocable.

She said: "Please."

He took a single gasping breath. "Ah—God. Ruby. Don't—don't move."

She couldn't help herself. Her body jerked against him, a small, instinctive movement. She was flushed with desire, drunk on it, fevered. "Please," she said again. "I need you. I need—"

"Oh Jesus. Ruby." He moved; she felt an infinitesimal pressure, nowhere near relief. The muscles of his abdomen flexed. "You have no idea how hard I'm trying to give you what you need."

"I need *you*. I need this."

Shuddering waves raced up his body, again and again. His

gaze, fierce, urgent blue, fixed on her face. "I don't—want to hurt you."

Her body was already sinking down onto him, so slick that the accommodation was easy. She wanted him to drive inside her. Wanted to be filled. "You won't hurt me."

"I don't—mean it like that. I can't— I'm—" His jaw tightened; all his body shook with the effort not to move. He reached up to her face and brushed her hair back, pushing the damp strands away from her cheek and mouth. "Can't think. Ruby. You truly want this?"

She did not need to consider. She did not hesitate. "Yes."

"Jesus," he said. "All right. All right." He set his hand between them, touching her intimately, and as he did, he pressed up, tiny uneven strokes. "I'll withdraw. I promise—ah God, pet, I swear I'll withdraw. I won't—I'm not going to let you regret this."

She didn't know if the words were for her or for himself. Gradually, thrust by thrust, he pushed deeper; the slow stretch was more pleasure than pain. She felt herself tighten around him, as if to draw him in.

The pressure built inside her—almost too much. Unthinkingly, she shifted down, a clumsy pulse of her hips to take more of him.

The sensation was bright and raw: a lightning strike. She gasped; he groaned.

"Malcolm," she whispered.

He gripped her hips and bucked up, his breathing labored. He was, she thought, at the limit of his endurance. "Fuck," he said hoarsely. "This is what you want?"

Her hands were on his chest, heated and sweat-damp. "Yes."

He thrust again. He was fully seated in her now, the pleasure deep, almost too much to withstand. Her breasts jostled, and his gaze dropped from her face to her body as his pace quickened. She felt almost helpless, absorbing the pleasure of his body and the rhythmic movement of his fingers, and when he gave a choked moan, her climax bore down upon her like a storm. She trembled as it broke, and sobbed out his name.

She was still shaking when he withdrew. "Sorry," he gasped. "Ruby. Going to come."

"I want you to."

He brought her down to him—trapped his cock between their bellies and groaned as he spent himself. She felt the slow waves that shook his body, felt the hot sensation of his seed on her skin. Held him hard, his heart beating against hers.

They lay tangled up together for a very long time. And when he lifted his head, it was only to find her mouth with his.

"You make me so happy," she whispered against his lips.

At her words, he pulled back. His eyes were dazed and heavy-lidded, and she could see the faintest suggestion of his smile in the dark.

When he spoke, his voice was hoarse. "I thought I might die just now, you know. My brain went all white."

She laughed a little.

He dimpled back at her, but his eyes—dark blue in the shadows—looked serious. "Do you know what I thought, Ruby-love? On the point of death?"

"Tell me."

He let his head fall back. His lashes dropped. "I thought it would be a good death." His arm stretched across her body, holding her against him. "A good life. Because you existed in the world, and I got to see it."

Gently, he stroked the damp expanse of her back. She turned her cheek to press against his heartbeat. She was trembling, she realized. Not from fear, precisely, but from longing. She wanted what she had when she'd taken him into her body: a joining that could not be undone.

For as long as she dared, she let herself believe that she could have this. That this moment—this dark sweet pleasure, this night of slow fire and stars—need never end. That his hand on her back could shelter her from the rest of the world.

Eventually, she slept. They both did, holding fast to each other, until dawn broke the horizon and lightened the sky behind the glass.

They woke to discover that the princess was missing.

Chapter 23

They had assembled in the kitchen: Ruby and Archer, Alice, Signor Neri, Gerry and Lamentation, Eugénie and Wall.

No Princess Serafina. No Zenobia. And no Tamsin.

"They went back down to St. Petroc's," Alice said. Her voice was shaking, and she held Vanessa against her chest despite the way the puppy's nails raked across her muslin morning dress. "Last night. After supper. And they did not come back."

"I was not aware that she had gone." Neri was wringing his hands. His face was drawn, his thin mouth stiff with misery. "She did not tell me that she meant to go."

"I was outside with Vanessa. It was dark—I heard them arguing behind the kitchen. The princess was ordering Tamsin back inside, and Tamsin kept telling her not to, erm, be so stupid. And then Zenobia started to bark and they set off together." Alice's blue-green eyes seemed huge beneath the black fringe of her lashes. "I should have waited up for them. I assumed they would be back—I never dreamed—"

Ruby touched Alice's shoulder. "It's all right. It's not your fault."

"It is," Alice said miserably. "I should have told someone right away that they'd gone, only I didn't wish to anger them. I was afraid that if . . . that if I told anyone, they would see it as a betrayal."

"Alice," Ruby murmured.

But before she could say anything else, Archer cut in. "You raised the alarm as soon as you realized they hadn't returned. You've done well. We'll find them."

Alice lifted her lashes to fix upon him, and Ruby realized that she had done so as well. All of them had.

If he said he could turn the ocean into wine, Ruby thought, everyone here would believe him. And not because of his charm or his assurance in himself or his exquisite smile. But because he had proven, again and again, that he was a man worthy of their trust.

"What do we do, Cap?" Lamentation asked.

Archer took a breath. He looked like a pirate in truth: his face dark with his morning whiskers, his jacket thrown over a shirt open at the neck. His chest gleamed gold beneath the white cotton—gold but for the places touched with white scars. "First," he said, "we go down to the village and see what we can learn."

They went to the apothecary, the milliner, the colorman's stall: all the shops the princess had frequented. They divided their forces and looked in alleys and carts, checked the harbor, talked to everyone they could find. Ruby found it almost impossibly difficult to engage strangers in conversation that way—to interrogate them without explicitly mentioning the Monfalcone princess.

They reunited in Floss Enys's public room. Neri was too fretful to eat or drink; he merely paced in circles around their table, polishing his spectacles and straightening his velvet cuffs.

"I'm sorry," Floss said. "I've been asking around for you all day—quiet-like. Subtle, as you said." She broke off, and her eyes darted to the edge of the room. "Benji!" she shouted. "Don't you let that cat eat from your plate again—*curse* you, Benji Woon, to the pits of hell—"

She strode over, her apron flapping at her legs.

Benji laughed. "Flossie, my love, grant mercy."

"Mercy!" She plucked the kitten from Benji's lap and set it on the ground, where it immediately sank its claws into his trousers and started to climb back up. "Not likely. You're not the one left chasing this poultry-mad she-devil off your pillow every night. Listening to her wail near to dawn this morning because of that damned barking dog!"

Ruby tensed.

At her side, Archer came to attention—easily, gracefully, the way he did everything. "What dog, Floss?" he asked. His voice was casual.

"I don't know. Some mad thing down in the harbor. Barking and barking to raise the dead."

"I heard it too," Benji said. "Went down to check if it was trapped somewhere, but I couldn't find hide nor hair of it. Must've been on one of the ships. Wanted free, poor lamb."

Ruby's heart beat hard.

A dog trapped on one of the ships? Could it have been Zenobia?

"When did the barking stop?" she asked breathlessly. "Is the ship still there?"

She was betraying her urgency, she realized. Everyone in the room would know that this was important to her—that she cared far more than she ought about a little dog. If whoever had tried to assassinate the princess had watchers in the tavern, their gaze would inevitably turn to Ruby.

But Archer did not seem to mind her outburst. His fingers brushed her hand beneath the table, drawing her to her feet, bringing her with him as he moved toward Benji.

"Before dawn, I think," Floss said. Her eyes met Ruby's. "A few hours before dawn."

"Strange," Archer said. "You don't often hear a dog on a ship. Cats, maybe."

"I heard it too," put in another man, a stout fellow in a neat suit who blushed when he spoke. "Down in the harbor near midnight."

"Oh, did you now?" said Benji, laughing again. "And what were you doing down by the docks at midnight, Mr. Polkinghorne?" He glanced conspiratorially at Archer. "'Tis always the quiet ones who surprise you."

"Don't tease the reverend, Benji," Floss said stoutly. Her eyes softened as she turned to the blushing vicar. "Did you discern the ship, Mr. Polkinghorne?"

"That bore the dog? To be sure. A big black sloop by the name of *Vulcano*."

The rest of their party had crowded up behind them, and at this, Signor Neri drew in a sharp breath.

Archer turned. "You know it?"

"Madonna mia," the signore said. He swallowed. Pressed his hands together and murmured, "I know the name, yes. Verdura's ship."

Ruby felt a pulse of terror, stronger than anything that had come before.

She had believed the princess's story of pirates and assassins, and yet it had seemed distant. The princess had been whole and safe; she had not troubled to hide herself unduly, with her fine frocks and her air of command. The Duca di Verdura had seemed a distant, ghostly almost-threat, while the princess had been flesh and blood and vivid life.

But this—this was confirmation beyond all doubt. Verdura had taken the princess. Had taken, somehow, Tamsin as well.

What desperation was this? To attack the princess on her ship and then—when that failed—steal her straight off the docks?

He had taken Princess Serafina. He had taken Tam.

Ruby was at the door before she realized she had moved. She turned back in sudden hesitation, but Archer was already beside her, letting her lead, tossing a parting mention of bills to be paid to Floss as he kept pace with Ruby.

"Go," Floss said. "I know you're good for it."

They raced down to the wharf. Ruby's heart was in her throat as they scanned the ships, hoping even as she knew it was useless. *A few hours before dawn*, Floss had said, but it was full afternoon now. The sun had long since burned off the mist that rose over the water, and there was no black sloop in the harbor.

They trod the docks, and Ruby's eyes devoured every ship, every name.

No *Vulcano*. Tamsin and Serafina were gone.

They were all breathing hard by the time they reached the farthest edge of the small harbor. Signor Neri twisted his fingers together, and Alice put a delicate hand over his, a silent gesture of reassurance.

"What do we do?" Ruby asked. Her face felt sun-flushed; she was thirsty and hot and desperate to move, to *act*. "We'll need to track the ship, but I don't—" She looked helplessly up at Archer. "I don't know how to track a ship, for heaven's sake! It leaves no trace."

His throat worked as he looked down at her.

"The captain will know what to do," Gerry said. His voice was so deep that it vibrated, despite how softly he'd spoken. "He always does."

The words seemed to take Archer in the chest. He flinched a little; his gaze flicked from Ruby to Gerry and then out to the sea. He swallowed again.

"Aye," he said finally. "I know what to do." He fixed his gaze on the assembled company. "Wall, come with me. I want to make the *Delphinium* ready. Lamentation, I'll need you too, and Eugénie. And"—he hesitated, his voice dragging across the words like a rasp—"Gerry. Will you take the ladies back to the house?"

Ruby's mouth came open, words tumbling free before she could stop them. "Back to the house? You cannot . . . Surely you don't mean to leave without me."

He looked down at her. His eyes burned terribly blue in the afternoon light. "I'll come back to the house. I won't—go. Without speaking to you."

She reached up and touched his chest. Her gloves and his shirt made a thin, distinct barrier between their bodies, but the gesture was clear. Her hand lay over his heart.

"All right," she said. *I trust you.*

Archer had thought about lying. Even as he'd made the vow to Ruby, he'd considered breaking it.

It was a reflex. A habit. Lying would be easier—lying might keep her safe. It would be to her own benefit as well as his.

He had sent Wall, Eugénie, and Lamentation off to ready the *Delphinium* while he hastily secured provisions and called in favors. He needed someone to carry messages, to ride ahead on the mail coach to the ports he meant to search for the *Vulcano*. He needed, if it came down to it, to storm Verdura's town house and search for Princess Serafina there himself—which meant he needed someone to find out for him where the hell Verdura lived.

He'd tracked down Gill Oliphant, sipping ale in the warm dusk, and had only just related the first of his many requirements to the old smuggler when he'd noticed Alfie Enys wiping the same table over and over, eavesdropping shamelessly.

"Here now," he said, "Alfie, don't—"

But Alfie had taken off, and within ten minutes, more Enys boys had appeared, and then Benji Woon's equally mischievous sister Deborah, and then the apothecary's assistant, and the hawk-nosed shipwright, and even Mr. Polkinghorne, the vicar.

Ready with maps and ropes and tinctures, with cousins in Portsmouth and ships in Southampton, with advice and provisions and stout hearts.

All of them ready to help.

They had not come for Princess Serafina, Archer realized with a swoop of shock and giddy, fearful guilt.

They'd come for him.

It seemed that somehow these last years, while he'd been living at Pomeroy House and protecting his crew and scrabbling to keep them all fed and housed, he'd developed a kind of rootedness. A connection to St. Petroc's that felt, dizzyingly, like home.

They believed in him. They thought that he could lead them. He'd told them in all confidence that he knew what to do, and somehow, through sheer force of will, he had to mold that prediction of success into hard reality.

He felt sick with gratitude and terror together. It was as if he'd convinced them they could walk upon water, and now he had to watch them all try.

His mind turned, again and again, upon the direction he planned to take his crew as they searched the ports along the coast for the *Vulcano* and the princess. Closer to London—closer to where he'd failed last time, as Quenby.

If he did not bring Ruby with them, there was no chance they might come face-to-face with her father. If he left her here, he could keep her safe. Keep all of them safe.

Keep his secrets from his crew.

If he fled now, he would not have to face Ruby's disappointment. He could rescue the princess and come home in a shower of glory and pretend he'd never broken his vow to Ruby. Make believe he had not let her down.

He composed a note in his mind to excuse his flight. An apology. And as he did, the motto of House di Sangro came back to him, a shameful twist of truth.

Astra inclinant, sed non obligant.

The circumstances of his life—his own choices, for better and for worse—had set him on a path that seemed, at times, irrevocable. But he did not have to follow it. He could choose differently.

Since he'd been sent down from the *Swallow* and come to Pomeroy House, he had changed. He knew he had. He'd kept his crew together. He'd dug his hands into the earth and planted bulbs, and he'd hung on long enough to watch them bloom.

He'd become the type of man who wanted to stay.

And in the end, he found himself back at Pomeroy House.

Gerry met him at the door, two compact bags already packed: one for Archer and one for himself.

Archer's gaze went to the bags and then to Gerry's face. Gerry looked calm and steady; he was taller than Archer now by a head. Archer could see him in some strange double vision: the man he was now and the child he'd been. The thin angry face, seawater and tears on his cheeks.

Of course Archer had lied to protect his crew. Wasn't that what adults did? Embroidered a fantasy and made it seem real, because life was fragile and fearsome, and it was better—far better—to keep the people you loved from the worst of it.

"I thought it best to be prepared either way," Gerry said. "I'd like to go with you. But I'll stay if you think it right, Cap. If you want me to remain with the ladies."

"I do," Archer said, "want you with the ladies." Somehow he'd reached out to clasp Gerry's shoulder. To squeeze tight. "There's no one I trust the way I trust you. There's not another soul on this earth I would charge with the task of keeping them safe."

Gerry's throat worked. He had to look down, just a bit, to look into Archer's face, and the movement made the water in his eyes threaten to spill over.

Is this what it's like? Archer wondered, a little wildly. Was this what his own father had missed? The heart-shattering pride, the buzz of terror: The boy he'd once had a hand in raising was a man grown, honest and good, and Archer could no more keep him safe than he could capture the sea in his fist.

Behind Gerry, Ruby stepped into the parlor. Archer let Gerry go and had to blink hard to clear his own vision. Swallow against the ache in his throat.

"Ruby," he said roughly.

She didn't let him say anything more. She strode forward, clutching an overflowing valise before her like a beribboned shield. "No," she said, in a tone of some command.

Ah God. His stubborn, plainspoken pirate queen. He almost wanted to laugh. "No? All I said was 'Ruby.' Have you been re-christened in my absence?"

"My disagreement was preemptive."

"Oh well. Excellent to know that the cushion I had embroidered with your name is still useful."

She scowled at him. "Be serious, Malcolm."

"I am. In point of fact, I seem to be the only one thinking of the seamstress who'd have to unpick all that thread if you'd transformed yourself into . . . Myrtle, say. Or Jane."

She strode forward and stuffed her valise into his arms. "Do not dimple at me. I am immune."

"Are you?"

"And don't cavil either." She pursed her lips and lifted her chin as she stared him down, all ruthless gray. "We are going to your ship—together—to search for the princess and Tamsin. I will brook no disagreement."

He felt his grin soften into something crooked as he looked at her. Something more anxious—more true. "Are you the captain now?" he murmured.

She reached out and put a hand on his biceps muscle, flexed from holding her shockingly heavy valise. "I don't know much of seafaring. I might even get in your way. I realize that." Her voice firmed, and her pointed chin went up even higher. "But I do know London society. As the Earl of Hangleton's daughter, I can call upon people who know Verdura personally. If we cannot find him on the coast via ship, I can help us locate him another way."

It made sense. It made too much sense; he wondered if he believed her logic or if he merely wanted to, so he could keep her by his side.

She pushed her hand up to his shoulder, and then to the side of his face. "Let me stay with you," she said softly. "Wherever you go. I can't wish to waste a moment that we could be together."

He shifted the valise to his right arm and used his left to draw her close. He pressed his face into her hair and smelled amber and cedar, the fresh scent of starch, the memory of his *Delphinium*. "It would be safer if you stayed."

But he already knew he was lost. He'd given in the moment he'd seen her—the very instant he'd turned his gaze back to Pomeroy House.

"I'll be safe with you," she said fiercely.

His heart thudded against his ribs, a double beat of exhilaration and despair. She trusted him. Like all the rest, she trusted him, and he desired and feared it in equal measure.

He tightened his grip on her waist, his fingers biting into her flesh, but she only nestled closer, more secure. He clenched his jaw so hard his teeth ached and thought: *Ruby. My love. My own heart.*

She would be safe with him. Always. He could not let her down.

He looked up at Gerry over her head. "Hell," he said. "Looks like we're all going. Go tell the signore to pack."

Chapter 24

The princess was a breath away from screaming again.

Tamsin could tell. She had the sight memorized by now—the gulp of air, the flash of teeth. The way Serafina's mouth parted on a howl.

With a groan, Tamsin put her head back against the elm behind her. "Please," she muttered. "Don't."

The princess released her breath of air on an exasperated huff—*not* a scream, thank God—and whirled to face Tamsin.

Tamsin winced and closed her eyes, because looking at the princess was like staring at a small, evil sun.

"I am trying," the princess said, in the patient tones one used with a child, "to find Zenobia."

"I am aware of that."

"Or, failing that, some assistance." Tamsin couldn't see her, but she could *feel* the princess put her petite elegant hands on her petite elegant hips. "Perhaps it is not apparent to you that we are in some danger."

Tamsin was pretty damned cognizant of that fact, yes. Her face was sunburned, and she hadn't had a drink of water in some time, and she had a *broken fucking leg*. They were being hunted by mysterious sinister assassins, and she, Tamsin, could not, at this particular juncture, walk. Or move at all.

It had been five days since she, Princess Serafina, and Zenobia had been snatched right out of the harbor in St. Petroc's. Tamsin had been whacked across the face with something hard and blunt—by the splinters near the enormous goose egg on her forehead, she suspected it had been a wooden plank—and she'd been bleary and confused for half a day thereafter. She had only faint recollections of a dank ship's hold, her mouth dry and her head aching. Some blissful cool sensation against her bound wrists.

Just as she'd got her wits about her again, she and Serafina had been plucked off the ship and tossed into a miserable, filthy closed coach. Zenobia had not been permitted to enter the carriage, and the sound of her furious barking had trailed them for nearly an hour.

It was at this point that the princess had started screaming. *I will kill you all!* she'd shrieked. *I will tear your flesh from your bones with my teeth and redden my nails with your blood!*

Their captors—Verdura's henchmen, Tamsin supposed—were far gentler with Serafina than they were with Tamsin. *Serafina* had not been knocked over the head, despite doing everything in her power to tempt such a fate. When the driver banged on the carriage box and entreated the princess to keep silent, she'd refused to comply, only screamed until she and Tamsin both had been gagged.

It had added a pleasant little soupçon of imminent suffocation to their general torment.

Honestly. The woman was a nightmare.

They'd been in the coach for the better part of a day when Tamsin had managed to get her hands free. She'd yanked off her gag and the princess's too—despite her reservations about the prudence of such an action—and had had the mediocre pleasure of watching the princess's mouth work reluctantly around the words *thank* and *you*.

They had argued, in hushed, furious whispers, about the wisdom of leaping from the moving carriage.

Tamsin had been against it. They weren't, so far as she could tell, in immediate danger. Had assassination been their captors' goal, it could have been accomplished that first night in St. Petroc's with an ease that made Tamsin sick to think of. She'd made a very practical and reasonable case for waiting until the carriage stopped and mounting their getaway then.

The princess had been all for leaping. "Why," she had hissed, "would I stay with Verdura's thugs a second longer than I must?"

"Because we don't know where we are? And we're in a moving vehicle? And if they see us leap out, they're going to bloody well stop and throw us right back in?"

Serafina's extremely regal and cogent rebuttal had been to break open the door and hurl herself out of it.

Tamsin had gritted her teeth and launched herself after the princess.

They hadn't been seen. The coach had trundled on, unaware its captives had fled.

It would have been a fairly successful escape attempt, except for the fact that Tamsin had broken her leg when she'd landed.

At least, she thought it was broken. She'd swooned—a terrible and embarrassing experience that she hoped never to repeat—and had woken beneath the elm tree to a pain in her right ankle she couldn't wrap her mind around.

Luckily, it had stopped hurting an hour or so ago. Unfortunately, she'd also started shivering, and she couldn't hear very well, and her vision kept getting odd and gray as she looked at the princess's tiny, irate form. None of it boded well.

"You should go," Tamsin said. Her voice came out raspy, and her eyes were still closed. She didn't feel particularly inclined to lift her lids.

"I beg your pardon?"

For all the words were polite, Serafina still somehow sounded as though her tongue were made of acid.

Tamsin forced herself to open her eyes. The princess was standing halfway between the elm and the road. Her waist-length black hair was sweaty and snarled, and for the first time it occurred to Tamsin that the woman must have dragged her to this shaded spot.

"You should go," Tamsin said again. "As soon as they realize we've gone, they'll be back this way searching for us."

A muscle flexed in the princess's angular jaw. "I await Zenobia."

"Oh, for God's sake." Tamsin dropped her head back against the tree, which seemed more comfortable by the moment. "You mean to get yourself killed over a bloody dog?"

"Do not speak her name."

"I *didn't*." She gritted her teeth and tried to keep her eyes open.

The princess stepped closer. Her olive skin was sun-flushed. In the last rays of daylight, her hair looked like shimmering onyx.

Tam suspected she was succumbing to some brain fever, no doubt occasioned by whatever had happened to her right ankle.

"I'll watch," she got out. "You go hide yourself. Find a hayloft or a pub or something. Don't—tell them who you are. I'll wait here for Zenobia."

"Oh yes. A perfect plan. Then you will give Zenobia the direction of my hayloft, and when the men with guns return, you will subdue them single-handedly."

"Single . . . leggedly. Perhaps."

The princess did not laugh, because fiends possessed no sense of humor. She said: "I am not leaving."

Tamsin groaned. Her eyelids seemed impossibly heavy, and she let them fall with some relief. "Fine. Have it your way. Come along, assassins. We've put out a welcome sign for you, right here under this goddamned tree."

But the princess was not done. She was, somehow, at Tamsin's side. Her small hands wrapped around Tamsin's biceps, and she leaned in.

She smelled of rose water and caraway, Tam thought dizzily. Which was absurd. She ought to smell of brimstone.

"I am not leaving you," Serafina hissed into Tamsin's ear. "Brace yourself. This is going to hurt."

It did. It hurt spectacularly, extravagantly. As the princess dragged Tamsin deeper into the woods, Tamsin's ankle transformed itself into a molten iron bar made of piercing agony.

But the pain was short-lived. Tamsin took a gulping breath, looked up into the princess's face, and then—to her intense and everlasting regret—swooned again.

Chapter 25

Ruby stood on the deck of the *Delphinium*. The little ship had dropped anchor just outside of Southampton, and it rolled gently beneath her feet, forward and back. The spray stung her cheeks, soaking through her dress as she stared out into the starless dark.

They had been searching for Verdura's *Vulcano* for nearly a week—all of Archer's crew except Wall, who had remained at Pomeroy House to care for the dogs. They'd stopped at Plymouth, at Torquay, at Exmouth—every harbor large enough that a black sloop with an Italian name might hope to escape notice. Archer had produced as if from nowhere a whole network of old friends, and shipmates, and cousins of friends, and wives of shipmates, passing word of their search all along the coast. They'd heard rumors of the *Vulcano* but nothing tangible.

Nothing—until it had been sighted in Southampton.

The information, according to Archer, was ironclad. They'd broken anchor within an hour of receiving the express, which had been posted by Mr. Polkinghorne's spinster sister. The winds had been favorable, and they had made excellent time—so good, in fact, that Ruby had been astonished when Archer had ordered his crew to do something with the sails that made the ship slow abruptly and then dropped the *Delphinium*'s anchor before they drew close enough to discern the *Vulcano*.

As it turned out, he did not intend to let Ruby within striking distance of the people who'd abducted Tamsin and Princess Serafina. He had waited until night fell, and then he and Gerry and Lamentation, armed to the teeth, had made for the *Delphinium*'s dinghy.

Preparing, it seemed, to row themselves to the *Vulcano* and mount a surprise attack.

"No," Ruby had said stubbornly. "You've brought me this far. Let me go with you."

Archer had stepped close to her. Pushed her wind-tangled hair back from her face and then cupped her cheek in his hand. "Ruby," he'd murmured. "I need you to stay here. I know how hard it is to wait for word and not to act. But I can't—" He'd broken off, his hand tightening on her jaw. "I can't do what must be done if my only thoughts are of you."

"And how am I to do what must be done?" she'd whispered. "Do you think it's any easier for me?"

He'd bent and kissed her hard. "I'll be back." When he drew away, he was smiling at her—a flash of steely confidence, of charm so sweet it singed her skin. "You own me, Ruby Ballimore. My body. My soul. Don't think I won't come back for it."

She'd watched as the three men had rowed away, watched until they'd vanished into the dark. She had not moved from the deck—would not, she vowed, until they returned.

The night seemed to stretch interminably as she waited on the deck, her fingers tangled with Alice's. She thought of Tamsin and the princess, missing a week now. She thought of Malcolm: a brace of pistols strapped across his chest, a sword at his hip, a knife in his boot. Smiling at her.

She waited and hoped and prayed—nonsense prayers, all bargain and plea—and when she finally saw the rowboat in the distance, she almost thought she was imagining the sight.

But she wasn't. She freed her hand from Alice's to clutch at the ship's low rail, leaning out as far as she dared. Together, they strained to see what soon became plain, even in the clouded dark.

It was only Archer, Gerry, and Lamentation in the dinghy. No Princess Serafina. No Tamsin.

The men's faces were grim as they hauled themselves back onto the deck of the *Delphinium*.

"What happened?" Ruby asked breathlessly. The rest of the crew crowded forward, Signor Neri at the front.

Archer shoved his fingers through his spray-damp hair, and oh, she longed to run her hands across his face, his chest—anything to reassure herself that he was safe and whole.

But she didn't. He stood a handful of feet away, self-contained, radiating unhappiness like cold phosphorescence. He had something clutched in his fist—some white glitter in the night.

"They weren't there," he said shortly. "No one was."

"The *Vulcano* was empty?" Neri demanded.

"Stripped bare. The cabins, the lockers—there's no one and nothing left aboard."

Ruby's heart lurched. *Tamsin.* "Are you certain? Did you check the cargo hold? Could they have been trapped somewhere?"

He exhaled hard and met her gaze. The sapphire blue of his

eyes looked shadowed. Dark. "I'm a smuggler, Ruby. I know where to look." He opened his hand, and in it she saw a thin jeweled collar she recognized from Zenobia's delicate neck. "I found this, shoved between two planks in the companionway. They *were* there. But not anymore."

Ruby felt sick. Helpless. The *Vulcano* had been their only tangible connection to Serafina and Tamsin, and she couldn't seem to force herself to let it go. She tried to make herself quit demanding, for heaven's sake, but she couldn't stop herself. "Perhaps some false wall or—or casks with secret compartments, or—"

"He shouted," Lamentation said.

She broke Archer's gaze and turned to his former bosun. Lamentation's exquisite face was strained, and his palm twisted helplessly along the hilt at his side.

"He shouted," Lamentation said again, "even when Gerry and I told him to keep quiet. He shouted for them as soon as we were aboard, before we even knew that the crew was gone."

"I knew," Malcolm said roughly. "The ship felt empty."

"What would you have done?" Lamentation said. His voice rose. "If the ship had been manned? If they'd started firing at you before you could even draw your first pistol?"

"I knew it wasn't manned." Archer sounded confident and steady, all certainty. *Everything was under control*, his voice seemed to say. *You were safe with me*. "There might have been one or two sleeping sailors, but I could have fought my way past two men. I wanted—" He broke off. Looked to Ruby. Tried again. "I wanted them to know we were there. Tamsin and the princess. If they were on board, I wanted them to know we'd come for them."

Her heart felt like a live thing, the way it twisted at his words. Her whole chest ached as though she'd taken a blow.

He'd wanted them to know. He'd risked himself—his own life—so that they would know someone had come.

It was what his own crew had done, she thought. Gerry and Lamentation, Wall and Eugénie. When Malcolm had been sent down from the navy, the four of them had given up everything they had so that he need not be alone.

"Thank you," she said. Her voice wobbled. "Thank you for trying."

He'd been fretting over the ropes that held the dinghy, checking and rechecking his knots, but at her words, his hands stilled. He looked up, and the brilliant forced smile on his face was a hundred times worse than naked anguish for the way it stabbed between her ribs.

"A delay," he said. "Nothing but a delay. I'll find them, Ruby. I'll turn over a thousand rocks to see what crawls out. I'll—" His smile wavered, a candle almost blown out, and then recovered. "I won't let you down."

"Malcolm." She touched her fingers to his, still frozen on the rough knots. "You're not. You couldn't."

His smile faded as he looked at her—dimmed into something less brilliant. More true. "I could," he said.

Gerry was standing behind Lamentation, his hand on Lamentation's shoulder. "We can set the sails, Cap. What's our heading?"

Archer looked from Ruby to his crew. There was some struggle on his face; his throat worked. "London," he said. "I want to talk to Admiral Penney."

Gerry nodded and made to turn, but Lamentation gave a stiff jerk, as though he'd been struck. "Penney?" he said. "Why?"

"He's a baronet now. Well-connected. He may know something of Verdura's whereabouts. He . . . owes me a favor."

"He owes you a hell of a lot more than a favor," Lamentation said. His voice scratched on the words, and he looked suddenly, terribly young. "He owes you his career. He owes you that god-damned baronetcy for the way you saved his neck."

"Enough." Archer's voice was quiet, his eyes steady on Lamentation's face. "You've made your opinions on the matter known."

"It seems I haven't. You wouldn't consider going to him if you'd heard a thing I'd said since we lost the goddamned *Swallow*!"

"I have heard. I heard you then, and still I made my choice, Lamentation. Even if it's not the one you would have made."

Lamentation took a breath, shakily, and he angled his chin up as if to hold back whatever emotion had tangled in his throat. "I don't understand why you'd turn to Penney after what he did. I don't understand why we can't do it on our own, Cap! Why we're not—enough."

Archer's face was pale and carved beneath the clouded moon. "We need help."

"Not from *him*."

Ruby's eyes burned as she watched them. In truth, she felt the same as Lamentation did. Penney had put his hand in the net of Archer's life and twisted—in some places pulling him free, and in other places warping him so that he could not see himself clearly.

Penney was no hero. Archer was. But Archer had made his decision, and he had chosen loyalty. Ruby could understand that, just as she could understand the painful self-consciousness written on Lamentation's face.

I don't understand, he'd said, *why we're not enough.*

"We should go to London," she said abruptly. "But not for Penney." Eight pairs of eyes came to rest on her, and she swallowed hard. Hoped this was not a mistake. "I think we should go to my father."

Above them, the moon broke through the stand of clouds, washing the deck in cool translucent blue.

"I know he has not supported our efforts in the past," she said quickly. Almost desperately. "But I believe I know how to make him aid us. We're more than halfway back to London now. It would not take so long for us to get there if—if the wind is right."

She hesitated on the words as she looked up into Archer's face. *Please*, she thought. *Please let this be the right thing to do.*

"My father can get us into Verdura's town house," she said. "He could procure an invitation through diplomatic means, use his connections to help broaden the search for Tamsin and the princess. This time, I know I can persuade him."

Her father had let her down before. But she *knew* that he cared about Monfalcone, if nothing else. This time he would not think her story false. They had Zenobia's collar to convince him. They had Signor Neri.

Archer shook his head. Opened his mouth to speak.

But Ruby cut him off. She fisted her hands at her sides, trying to project confidence the way that Archer always did. Trying to persuade him through sheer force of her own hope that everything would be all right.

"I know you're worried that my father might recognize you as Quenby," she said. The words had come out as almost a whisper, and she made her voice louder, carrying, so that he would know she meant it. "But he won't. He saw you only once, and he was paying far more attention to my debacle than to your face. I will tell him who you are and swear upon my life that I never met you before Pomeroy House."

Archer's eyes were locked on hers, his fingers knotted around the rope. He swallowed. She watched the bob of his throat, pale in the moonlight.

And then Lamentation spoke.

"I'm sorry?" he said. "What? You—knew the captain? Before Pomeroy House?"

Ruby turned to him, hastening to explain. "I did not know him. Not in truth. I only saw him at a dinner party, posing as Professor Quenby. And—and my father saw him too, but he looked so unlike himself. I don't believe my father would draw the same conclusion I did. I think—"

She stumbled to a halt. Lamentation's face had gone stricken, his cheekbones growing tauter and sharper with every word she spoke, and somehow—

Somehow she was doing this. Somehow she was making it worse.

Lamentation's gaze shifted from her to Archer. "She knew?" he demanded. "She knew all this time? And you didn't tell us?"

A muscle in Archer's jaw leapt. His legs were braced apart, and he was still as a stone despite the pitch and yaw of the deck. "She knew," he repeated. "And I didn't tell you."

Archer felt torn straight down the middle as he watched them. Lamentation stood still, stunned—as though he'd been shot. He looked the way he had the day after the *Swallow*, when Archer had told him he was leaving the navy. Not by choice.

He looked as though Archer had betrayed him.

And Ruby—

Ah God. Ruby. Her clear gray eyes flicked from him to Lamentation and back again, and he could tell by her face that she didn't know what had happened. He could see—in the tiny curl of her shoulders, in the way her face tipped down—that she thought Lamentation's shock and anger were her own fault.

But the fault was his. It had been from the very beginning.

Anguish was a fishhook in his guts. He couldn't find any words, didn't know how to tell Lamentation the truth. He *had* to keep lying to his crew, because he needed them to believe he had the situation under control.

But he didn't.

The *Vulcano* was empty. He had a brace of pistols on his chest and a dog's diamond collar in his hand and nothing on his lips but false assurances.

The truth was he didn't know how to find the princess. He didn't know what came next.

"I didn't want you to know," he said to Lamentation. "I wanted you to think that the risk from the Quenby scheme was over. I wanted you to believe that you were safe."

"But we weren't!" Lamentation's voice cracked on the words. "We weren't safe. You knew we weren't."

"I thought I could resolve the situation before you came to any harm. I thought—"

Ruby broke in. "There was no danger to any of you. Not from us. The three of us agreed we would not reveal what we knew."

Lamentation drew back, as though her interjection stung. His throat worked as he looked at her and then looked back at Archer. "But you didn't know that," he said. The words were low, fractured—the rhythm of his voice broken, like a clock out of time. "When she came to the door and you recognized her face, you had no idea what she would do. Who she would report to. And still you let her in our house and told us nothing of the risk."

Archer felt like his chest was caving in, a solid sucking gravity inside him, drawing his bones and organs tighter and tighter.

He had wanted to protect them. He didn't want them to be afraid.

He'd wanted them to believe that he was strong enough and competent enough to keep them safe. That he was more than a convict or a disgraced sailor, more than an alley dog with too-sharp teeth and no future beyond bread and irons. More than what he'd been.

But as he looked at Lamentation, he felt nauseous, almost fevered.

He could tell himself all he wanted that he'd had the best of intentions. That he'd done it for *them*.

But that too was a lie. It had not all been selfless. He'd wanted them to believe in him so that he could believe it too.

"What would have happened to us," Lamentation demanded, "if Ruby had written to her father that very day and told him you were Quenby—if they'd carted you off to jail? What would have happened to Gerry and me if you left and never came back?"

Archer swallowed back the hot agony in his throat. "They wouldn't . . . Ruby wouldn't have done that." His voice was hoarse.

Lamentation looked hurt now, which was far worse than furious. "It's not about *Ruby*," he said. "It's about you, keeping your secrets *again*. Lying to us—for our own good, was it?"

"It wasn't like that," he tried to say, but he couldn't make sense of anything just now. He didn't know what it had been like. He could not remember anything beyond his own vast need and fear and shame.

It didn't matter anyway. Lamentation pushed his hair off his damp forehead and jerked his chin up. "I'll set the goddamned sails. But I'm not going with you after that. To the ambassador's house. Or to Penney."

Lamentation spun and stormed away. His boots slapped solidly against the slippery deck, and Archer could see him as he'd been a decade ago: wiry and mischievous as he clambered up the mast, blond curls whipping in the wind. A boy. A sailor. His.

Gerry stood alone on the deck. His gaze followed Lamentation and then, slowly, came back to Archer. "I understand why you did it," he said. "But you needn't have."

"I—"

"Don't apologize," Gerry said. "And don't lie." He broke off. Looked to Ruby and then back to Archer. "He thinks you chose Lady Ruby over him. Over us. The same way you chose Penney."

The words stung—scored his skin like a rope racing hot through his palm.

He hadn't. Or else . . . God. He hadn't meant to.

He couldn't find his bearings. Memories seemed to batter him, a brutal cascade of waves.

The *Victorious* plunging toward them, his orders raw in his throat, shouted, pointless. They were going to be hit, there was no time to turn—

Gerry in the sea, eyes dark above the water, and Archer's weightless terror as he'd leapt from the deck—

The room he'd lived in with his mother, the ice in her cup, her hand atop his—

When he'd been released from prison, he'd rushed straight home, ignoring his own dizzy hunger, heedless of the raw marks the irons had left on his wrists. He'd burst into their room and then hesitated, confused. Disbelieving.

Someone else had been inside. Some other woman. He couldn't

recall what she'd looked like, nor even what she'd said. Somehow, the stranger must have told him that his mother had died, but he couldn't remember the words. The blue delphiniums his mother had kept at the window had been gone and so had her books, and he kept on having to reach out to find the wall behind him. The world had rearranged itself: beneath and above and around him.

She'd died. And he hadn't been there.

He couldn't keep doing this. He couldn't keep pretending that safety was almost within his grasp. That he was one fancy step away from having everything under control.

He wasn't.

He watched Gerry go after Lamentation, following the curve of the hull until he vanished from sight. And then he looked at Ruby. She was standing very still, her fingers locked together, her lips parted as she looked at him.

"Wait," he said abruptly. He caught her by the shoulders, pulled her close, and pressed his palm to her back. "Wait. Will you wait? I need to—" He gestured at the dinghy, helpless and wordless. "I'll be right back. I'll be—"

He couldn't lie. But neither could he tell her what he meant to do—not until he knew for certain he could bring it into being.

"Wait for me," he said. "Please."

She took him in. Her gaze was clear and sharp, and he thought she could see the vicious storm within him, the jagged rocks beneath.

"I'll wait," she said very softly, "as long as you need."

Chapter 26

He did not come right back. Ruby waited all night—waited in the captain's cabin with Alice at her side, her heart shivering with dread as she tried to imagine where he could be.

He hadn't run. She could not believe that he had abandoned them all—that he had told her to wait and then meant never to return. He'd stood on the deck with his legs spread and taken Lamentation's words like a cannon blast to the ribs. He'd looked stricken, his face gone blue-pale in the moonlight, his jaw clenched tight.

He had made no excuses. And he had not told her where he meant to go.

It was well past dawn when someone knocked.

Ruby was across the tiny cabin in an instant. She pulled open the door, her heart in her throat—but it wasn't Malcolm in the companionway. It was Eugénie.

Ruby's lips parted in surprise. Eugénie wore an immense oilcloth jacket draped over her slight body, and her slim brown hand on the door was scarcely visible beneath the garment's heavy sleeve.

"Is he . . ." The words faltered, and Ruby moistened her lips and tried again. "He's not back? The captain?"

"He's not back. He sent a message. He wants me to fetch you. Both of you."

"He— What? Fetch us where?"

The corner of Eugénie's mouth curved down, a small anxious crimp. "Come," she said. "Put your wrappers on. It's going to be wet."

They listened. She and Alice scrambled into pelisses, and Eugénie led them up the hatch to the deck and then into the dinghy. Gerry helped lower the little rowboat into the water, and then Eugénie, her face set, pointed them toward the harbor.

"You won't tell us?" Ruby ventured finally. "Where we're going?"

Eugénie's slender arms flexed in a steady rhythm as she rowed. "I'm not sure I fully know. The captain—he—" She broke off and leveled a gaze at Ruby. The oars feathered in the air, then dipped back into the water. "There's something he wants to do before we venture back to London. Some assurance he feels he must make. And you . . ."

Ruby clutched her hands together in her lap. She was damp from sea spray, and in her haste, she'd forgotten her gloves. Her fingers were cold. "What about me?"

"You mean to bring him there?" Eugénie asked. "To London? To your father—your world?"

Ruby did not quite know what to say. "I think it is our best choice, yes. You don't have to worry about Malcolm. I won't let my father hurt him."

Eugénie's mouth was still tipped down, a crooked, unhappy arc. "It is not your father who concerns me. It seems to me that *you* are the greater risk."

"I?" Ruby leaned back in the dinghy, as shocked as if the other woman had reached out and slapped her face. "Why would I— I would never—"

Eugénie did not let her finish. "I was the wife of a pirate once," she said. "Before Wall. I thought the ship would be our great, grand adventure, and I wanted more of . . . everything. More than the life I had led up until then. I was so hungry for the world that I was sick with it." She shook her head. Her mouth was grim, and her eyes were fixed on the sea beyond Ruby's shoulder. "I was wrong. All of it was a fantasy. I knew nothing about life aboard ship, about maggots and sailcloth and the catgut thread I'd use to sew up bullet holes."

"I don't understand what you're trying to tell me."

Eugénie's voice was low. Her eyes came to settle on Ruby's face. "That's what this summer has been for you. A fantasy, snatched out of time. But what happens when you bring the captain to your house, to your father? What happens when you try to fit him into your world, and you find out that he does not belong?"

"Malcolm belongs wherever he wants to be," Ruby snapped. If that was by her side, then she would have him, and gladly. "There is no place I would forbear to take him. Nothing he does not deserve. He's all heart. He would tear himself to pieces for any one of you, and I—"

She halted, her voice fracturing.

Deliberately, Alice laid her hand over Ruby's. Alice's fingers too felt like ice, but her grip was firm. "Ruby. Dearest. What if your father disapproves?"

"Let him, then." Ruby jerked up her chin. "I don't care what he thinks any longer."

Alice regarded her for a long moment before she spoke. "Do you mean that? You would defy your father—for the captain?"

Ruby hesitated. She looked at Alice's wide cerulean eyes, Eugénie's steady hands on the oars. The words had leapt from her lips without deliberation, and yet . . .

Yes, she realized. She meant it.

She remembered her father's devastation after her mother's death. He had loved his wife—in her heart, Ruby believed that he cared for her and Cassandra as well. But when Ruby had not performed the role he'd expected of her, his affection had been a weak thing. He had neither the patience nor the desire to accept the daughter he had, rather than the one he wished for. And Ruby was no longer willing to settle for a love like that.

Love, she had learned, wasn't a cage. It was a key.

Alice spoke again, very softly. "I know how hard it is, dearest. To want so very much to make the people you love happy."

Ruby turned her hand to grasp Alice's fingers back.

It was true. She *had* wanted to make her father happy, for so long, for so many agonizing years. She had tried and tried—had dressed Cass up like a little doll because their father wished it, smiled at him across the breakfast table in Rome because she knew he'd smile back. They had traveled together to Venice and Athens and the Levant, and she'd taken his notes and read his books, and sometimes she didn't even know if she cared at all about classical art except for the fact that it was something they could talk about together.

But not anymore. She had been rearranged this summer. And she thought it had been for the better.

"I would defy the whole world for Malcolm," she said finally. "My father will be the easy part."

They were almost to the wharf now. Ruby watched the vibrant quilt of ships and sails come into focus. The seabirds' cries made a noisy tangle in her ears, almost as loud as the throb of her pulse.

Eugénie angled them carefully toward the low docks, and there was a long silence before she spoke again. "Did you know he grows the flowers at the house? The captain, I mean. Planted the bulbs himself when we first came. Thins them in the spring."

Ruby thought of the barrels of flowers on the side of the house facing over the sea: the irises, the alliums. The delphiniums. "I suspected as much."

"He's not all flash and dazzle," Eugénie said, "no matter what he might want you to think. He's the staying kind."

"I know." When Ruby closed her eyes, she could picture his hands in the soil: the slow patient work of bulbs and seasons. The house with all the dogs. Four hammocks in a line. His long-beloved crew, and all that steadfast loyalty. "I know him."

"Good," Eugénie said quietly. "I wanted to be certain before I brought you all this way."

The sun was fully up now, and it beat hot on Ruby's unbound hair as Eugénie tied them off at the docks. Ruby's wrapper was still damp from sea spray, her hem four inches wet, and she and Alice followed Eugénie all the way up the street and into the cool shade of a half-ruined church.

"This is it," Eugénie said. "He's inside."

Ruby blinked. "He's— What?"

Eugénie yanked open the heavy door and nudged Ruby and Alice through. "He's inside. He'll explain." She gave Ruby a small, rueful smile. "He'll try to explain. He may require some sorting out."

Carefully, Eugénie closed the door between them.

The dusty air was cool on Ruby's face as she peered into the tumbledown nave. Her eyes were slow to adjust to the dim interior. Little bars of sunlight spilled through the cracked entablature, and everything else was dark and quiet.

And then, suddenly, he was there, emerging into a shaft of golden light like a desperate, disheveled prince.

"Ruby." His voice sounded rough; his face was shadowed with whiskers and lack of sleep. "I thought you weren't coming. I thought—Bloody Christ, what took you so long? It's been—" He glanced at the window behind him as if for confirmation of the time.

A bass voice at the front of the church, emanating from a sun-splashed set of crimson robes, interrupted. "If you mean for me to marry you in the House of God, my son, I suggest you recall the sanctity of His name."

Ruby's lips parted. No sound emerged.

At her side, Alice's eyes went very wide. She swallowed hard. And then she waved them off and headed for the nave. "I'll handle this part. You two . . ." She waved her hand again. "Talk. Quickly."

"Shit," Malcolm said. And then, "Sorry. So sorry. Let me just—" He grabbed Ruby's arm, towed her into a shadowed corner, and dropped his voice. "*Shit.*"

Ruby thought her ears might be ringing. Perhaps she'd gone deaf. "Malcolm," she hissed, "what's going on? Who is that man?"

"That's the Bishop of Winchester."

Her lips parted. "*What?*"

"Oh God." Malcolm pushed her hair back from her face, cupping her cheek, brushing her mouth with his thumb. "God," he said again, lower. "Ruby. I don't— I can't— I wanted to do this all differently. I had a whole scheme—I was going to go to the

Archbishop of Canterbury after we rescued the princess. I sold the deed to the *Delphinium* before we even left St. Petroc's so I could afford the special license—"

"You *what*?"

"Because you can marry anywhere with a special license—I thought maybe—at Pomeroy House—after we returned I could . . ." He trailed off. His palm was against her neck, and his thumb seemed to search out the thundering beat of her pulse. "But after what Lamentation said on the deck, I realized I couldn't wait any longer. Only—Jesus, Ruby, did you know you have to wait seven days for a bishop's license? And it must be in the parish where you reside? I spent three times the cost of a special license bribing this fellow to falsify the register."

"I don't—Malcolm, I don't understand what you're talking about."

His eyes were hot sapphires in the shards of sunlight. "What if—God. Ruby. I keep thinking—what if you're with child? What if I bloody well *died* on this journey and left you alone? What if"—his voice cracked—"I got thrown back in jail, and you didn't even have the protection of my name?"

"Malcolm—"

"Marry me," he said. "Now. Today. This minute."

From this proximity, she could see the dark sweep of his lashes, the tiny shadows they cast along the cut-glass precision of his cheekbones. She could see the individual motes of dust in the air between them, floating in impossible refutation of gravity's pull.

He wanted to marry her? He had sold the *Delphinium*—for her?

She felt as if she were somewhere near the ceiling, nothing

beneath her feet but empty space. "I don't—understand," she said jerkily.

"I wanted to wait," he said hoarsely. "I wanted to prove to you that I could be"—he gestured, a wide, familiar arc that took in the dilapidated church and the usurious bishop and a parish register spotted with falsehoods—"better. But it turns out I'm exactly the same as I've always been."

Somehow, from inside his coat, he produced a pair of rings—plain gold, unadorned.

Worth, perhaps, the price of his own *Delphinium*.

"I know it isn't much," he said. "But I will give you everything I have. Everything I am. I will never let you go."

She reached out and closed her fingers over his, clasping the rings between their hands. She felt the press of his callused palm, the small endless circles hard against her skin.

"Yes," she said.

He looked less relieved than she might have expected. More terrified. Rather as though she'd stabbed him between the ribs and his lifeblood was slowly trickling out onto the stone floor.

"Are you certain?" he rasped. His face was growing whiter and whiter, and if he fainted, she was going to have the very devil of a time holding him up. "Because the bishop is right behind us, and if you come to your senses later on today, it's going to be awfully hard to undo, and I—"

"Yes," she said. "Malcolm. Yes."

He leaned very slowly toward her, until his forehead pressed against hers. "Oh God," he said. "Ruby. I hope like hell you don't regret it."

"I heard that," rumbled the Bishop of Winchester. "Mr. Archer, you have raised me from my bed at the devil's own hour, and I grow both hungry and impatient. Are you planning to make this woman your wife, or aren't you?"

Malcolm dragged himself back to his full height. He smiled at her—the ghosts of his dimples flashing—and towed her unsteadily down the aisle to where the bishop and Alice waited.

Tamsin's absence was an ache in Ruby's chest. But Alice's lips curved up, gentle and reassuring, and, hesitantly, Ruby let herself smile back.

And as she pledged herself to Malcolm Archer—as he slid the too-big gold ring past her knuckle—Ruby thought of what Alice had asked her in the dinghy. Would she defy her father for Malcolm's sake?

Yes. To do so flew in the face of all the choices of her life before this, and yet she had done it.

When he found out, the earl was going to be furious. His elder daughter, married in haste to a disgraced naval captain—a smuggler—a confidence artist. It was nothing like what he would have chosen for her, nor even what, in her lonely childhood dreams, she had imagined for herself. It seemed possible that, when he discovered the truth, her father would never see her again.

And still, knowing that, she had made her choice. She had chosen Malcolm.

The bishop spoke the words of their joining in a sonorous voice, and as he did, she looked up into Malcolm's pale, set face. She thought of the *Delphinium*—scarred and lopsided and slow and precious. Her ring slipped against his where he gripped her hand.

If there was a cost to this decision, she would pay it. With her own heart's blood, she would pay—as he had.

Chapter 27

He felt the veriest fool as he knocked on his own cabin door that night.

He was a mooncalf. A block. As nervous as a new-married virgin or—hell—a choirboy at a brothel, something he most certainly had never been.

His wife was inside his cabin. His *wife*.

He'd had mad dreams. Vivid fancies, as he lay in his bed at Pomeroy House and thought of her, as they crept closer to London on the *Delphinium*. He would win his way back to the navy. He'd rescue the Princess of Monfalcone. He would be heaped in glory, and he'd pile all the honors at Ruby's feet, and she could reach out and take his hand, and never be ashamed to say that she was Malcolm Archer's wife. Not ever.

But when Lamentation had confronted him on the deck, he'd felt cracked open.

What would have happened to the rest of us if they'd carted you off to jail? Lamentation had demanded. *What would have happened to Gerry and me if you left and never came back?*

It was no fearful fantasy, no unreal nightmare vision. It had happened before, with his mother. It could happen again. There was never any certainty to his future. No matter how he lied or dissembled, he could never make them all safe enough.

And when he thought of Ruby facing her father at his house, he kept on thinking that he did not want her to be alone. He refused to let her feel dishonored by their intimacy or abandoned by his failure to act. He wanted—

Christ. He felt afraid and guilty and desperately hungry for her. He felt ashamed. He'd meant every word that he'd said to her, there in the ruined church in front of the bishop. He would never leave her, not if he could help it.

But still, when he pictured bringing his wife to her father's house, he kept thinking: *Now, at least, she cannot change her mind.*

He'd meant to sail straight for London that very night, with Ruby defiant and ready at his side. But the winds had been unfavorable. A huge gusty storm had blown up from Dieppe, driving them westward until he'd given in and ordered the sails reefed. Everyone was belowdecks except a sodden Alfie Enys and Gerry, who'd wiped water from his eyes with the back of his hand and said, "Go on, Cap. We'll do fine on our own."

It had felt like chastisement and benediction at once.

It had felt, he thought, like a sentence. His wife was belowdecks. Alone. She was in their cabin, waiting for him, and it was— God help him—their wedding night.

And what would happen if he let her down?

At the sound of his knock, Ruby pulled open the door, caught his hand in hers, and dragged him inside.

"Ruby," he got out, and then she was on her toes, pushing his back to the door and sliding her warm, lush body against his.

He couldn't help himself. He caught her. He cupped her buttocks in his hands and groaned into her mouth as she kissed him hard. He wanted to say—something—but her lips were parted, her tongue touching the corner of his mouth, and his mind slid blessedly clean of thought in the pure euphoric sensation of her breasts, her tongue, her hair tickling his cheek.

He slid his palm up, relishing the plush swell of her hip, the delicate dip of her lower back. He could smell her—cedar and warm amber, fruit in brandy. Beneath the coarse fabric she wore, he could discern each perfect knob of her spine.

He pulled back. Jesus, his head was swimming already, and not for the first time that day, he had the distinct sensation that he was a single heartbeat from pitching face-first onto the floor, because . . . because . . .

Bloody *Christ*. She was wearing his own third-best shirt, the one that he'd ruined with walnut oil and blue paint. She must have laundered it somehow, but it still bore faint iridescent-blue splotches in various eye-catching locations, along with patches of damp from where she'd pressed herself up against his wet form. The hem hung nearly to her knees, but the shirt was open at the neck and stretched indecently across her breasts. He could see the dark shadowed valley there, and the pale-pink edges of her areolae, and suddenly he could feel his own blood beating in his cock because she was his *wife* and she was wearing his *shirt*, and he could have her—just like this, every day, for the rest of his life, he could have her.

The notion felt impossible. He didn't know how to let himself trust it.

She was gazing at him with an expression of faint concern in her blue-gray eyes. "Malcolm? Are you quite all right?"

"No," he said honestly, and pulled her by the hand back up against him. He might have worried she'd be cold from all his wet things, except he was fairly certain he was steaming. Pressed up against his body seemed the safest place for her to be. "I think I've had an apoplexy."

"Oh." She put her lips to his left pectoral muscle, and her mouth moved against wet linen, a sensation that made him shudder. "That sounds dire."

"I plan to recover."

"Excellent news."

"But you'll have to minister to me in my hour of need." He slid his hands from her back down to the hem of his shirt, and then up under it, where—sweet heavenly Mary—she had absolutely nothing between the rough-woven linen and her skin. "You can start by wearing this shirt every night for the rest of our natural lives."

"I suspect I can manage it," she said, "but—"

Hell. This woman and her damned attentiveness. She'd paused, pulling back. She'd felt the way his heart had tripped over itself at the words. She'd read it right there in his pulse.

"What's wrong?"

"Oh hell," he said, and put his hand to her cheek. "Pet. It's not you. It's only that—for the rest of our lives." He tried to make himself laugh, as though the words hadn't gutted him. But he couldn't—it sounded perilously like weeping instead. "Are you certain you want that? Because I can't promise you that I'll fill your life with honor and riches. I can't even give you a name you can be proud of."

She shook her head—silly, stubborn pirate queen—and held his gaze. "I am proud," she said. "I'm already proud. You don't have to prove anything to me, Malcolm. You have already proven yourself. At the inn, with your hammocks, and at the house, with your crew and your dogs and your pots of flowers. And here on your ship—" Her voice cracked, and suddenly her eyes were full of tears. "Oh, Malcolm. Tell me you didn't sell the *Delphinium* for me?"

"Only to Oliphant." His voice was rough. "He let me borrow it for the journey—and for that matter, if we wreck, pet, we'll be in a hell of a lot of trouble."

"Malcolm," she whispered. "You shouldn't have."

Very lightly, he caught her chin in his hand, cradling her face. "I don't know how many times I have to tell you, Ruby Ballimore. There's nothing I wouldn't do for you."

There were tears on her cheeks. God—he had not thought to make her weep.

"I want you to stay," she said. "That's all I want. Wherever we go, whatever happens next—I want you by my side."

The ship rose and fell beneath their feet and, carefully, he brushed his thumb across her mouth. Slid his palm down her throat and rested it between her collarbones. "You can still change your mind."

Her mouth quirked as she regarded him. "I'm not certain that's true."

"You can," he said. "It's not official yet. We haven't—" He looked, absurdly, at the hammock behind her, though he certainly wasn't about to lay his wife for the first time in a tangle of swinging rope.

Her brows arched. "We have, rather."

He winced. He supposed they had.

"Malcolm," she said, and she reached up and wrapped her fingers around his. "I don't want to change my mind."

"Ah God," he said, and he couldn't help himself. He tightened his grip on her hand to pull her closer. "All right. All right, pet. I'm trying to believe you."

Slowly—almost cautiously, as though she might break in half—he set his mouth to hers. He kissed her carefully, thoroughly. Greedily. And as she pressed herself against him, all luxurious warmth, it struck him that it was not Ruby he believed to be fragile.

It was himself. If he went wrong in this—tonight, the next night—how could he bear it? What would be left of him, if he lost her stouthearted loyalty?

What would he be, if he did not deserve it?

But it was hard to think when she arched up into him. Harder still when the ship's slow heave pressed her breasts into his chest. He groaned a little against her mouth—Christ, he could slip his thumb right into the gaping neck of that shirt and feel the unbearable hot silk of her skin.

He stroked the edge of her areola, the tight point of her nipple—*felt* her shaky gasp as he rolled the tip. His blood beat hot at the sound, and he did it again, again, and still he did not take his mouth from hers. He wanted to drown in her.

He kissed her until she was twisting restlessly against him, her hips lifting, her breasts arching into his palms. He kissed her until he thought he'd go mad with it: the slick suction, the brandied taste of her mouth. The tiny cry she made when he passed his thumbs over her nipples, one at a time and then both together.

It was Ruby who pulled away first. "Malcolm," she gasped, "I want you."

He brought his hand to her knee, sliding it up beneath the hem of her shirt until his thumb found the slick arousal on her inner thigh.

He felt dizzy again, and not just from the movement of the *Delphinium*. He was unmoored by his desire for her—for every part of her body and her heart.

He cupped her sex—oh *Jesus* she was searingly hot and wet— and brought his mouth back to hers. "Let me take care of you," he said roughly.

She fisted his wet shirt at the small of his back and drew him closer. Her lashes fluttered as she squirmed against his hand, pressing feverishly down, all need and lust-drunk demand. But—

"No," she said. "No, I want—I want you. I want everything. I'm not going to change my mind."

It was his turn to pull back. His breathing was shallow and uneven—as though he'd been striving toward some impossible height. And Ruby—

How he wanted her. Her chest rose and fell rapidly as she stared up at him, and he had to make himself look away from the Renaissance masterpiece that was his shirt stretched over her tits.

Nothing about this was as he'd imagined. In his fantasies, as he'd sold the *Delphinium* and counted his coin, he'd thought to wed her someplace beautiful. He'd envisioned a bed that would fit both of them, a cloud tower of soft cotton and down. He'd imagined iced wine and ginger cream, pictured himself licking things off various parts of her body until she was sobbing with need.

But he had this: a cramped cabin at the back of his ship, lifted in slow rolling waves by the sea. Ruby's skin beneath his mouth. His heart, delicate as a soap bubble, resting in her palm.

"I want it too," he said hoarsely. "God, I do. But the cabin—there's only this godforsaken hammock—and I want this to be good for you, Ruby. I want it to be perfect."

She was still gripping the back of his shirt, and her ocean eyes were fixed on his face. "I'm certain," she said, "that between the two of us, we can think of something."

He looked down at her: flushed and heavenly, soft-spilling flesh and kiss-damp lips.

His *wife*.

"Oh fuck," he said. "Ruby. Yes."

He spun her away from him. He nudged her forward to the small table at the center of the cabin and pressed her down across it.

She caught his meaning. She grasped the wooden edge and leaned forward. Her breasts crushed against the table, and as she bent, he pushed the hem of his shirt up to reveal the tops of her thighs, her buttocks, her sex.

Touching her felt like an impossible extravagance. Some holy luxury he'd never done anything to earn. He stroked her until she was whimpering, and then he knelt and put his mouth to her slick seam. He licked, caressed—used hands and tongue as her hips jerked against him and his body throbbed with need.

He felt the sobbed-out rhythm of her climax with a sense of wonder, with agonizing, tooth-grinding lust. His heart battered his ribs. His cock was so hard he could feel it twitch with every heartbeat, pressing against the waistband of his trousers.

She twisted to look back at him. "Malcolm," she gasped, "please."

"Yes," he said. "God. Whatever you want. Anything."

He kept on touching her, but he used his free hand to unfasten his fall. He gripped himself—Christ, *Christ*, this was going to be quick if he did not take care.

He got to his feet, dazed by the sight of her before him, pleasured, pink-flushed. He filled his palms with her buttocks, then reached beneath the shirt to find her waist, her back, the side of her breast. And then he pressed the head of his cock against her sex and did not let himself move.

She gasped a little. "Malcolm. What are you—"

"Wait," he murmured. "Wait."

He drew the tip of his finger along the outer curve of her breast and watched her tremble. And then the slow roll of the waves lifted the deck beneath them—canted his body into hers, pressing the head of his cock a bare half inch inside her.

And then the ship fell again, pulling him free.

She made a soft sound. Desperate.

His brain had gone white with need. Every muscle in his body felt clenched and aching, and bloody Christ, it was nearly impossible not to thrust into her.

But he wanted to wait more than he wanted to plunge ahead. He wanted to be certain, to be *sure*. He wanted forever, and he wanted it to begin like this: a slow, patient tide that came for them both.

He put his fingers to his mouth, wetting them, then slid them between her body and the table. She went up on her toes to give him room, and he moved his fingers to her clitoris, listening to the sounds she made because he could not see her face. He stroked her in little circles as the next wave came, and then the next, pressing him deeper, slow and slippery and searing, bare half inches at a time.

Oh God—it was bliss and agony to hold himself still. To fight the impulse of his body.

"Malcolm," she gasped. "I want—" She whimpered, hips lifting as she sought to take him in. "I want—"

"I know," he said thickly. "Oh fuck. Sweetheart. I know."

It took a dozen waves before he was fully seated inside her. Another two before he felt her thighs tremble and knew she was lost. Her body seemed to clutch at him, to hold him inside, clenching down again and again with her culmination. He heard himself groan, and he might not have moved even then, except she turned her head to where his hand had come to rest beside her cheek and sucked the tip of his finger into her mouth.

His head spun. His pulse was pounding in his ears, in his prick, and he caught her hip in his free hand, clutched her tight, and thrust hard.

"Is that what you want?" he said raggedly.

"Yes," she gasped. Her hips lifted higher as he slammed into her again. "Oh God. Yes."

He took her harder—because she wanted it, and because there was nothing he would not do for her. Nothing he would fail to give. He drove himself into her again and again, and only when he knew himself a heartbeat from his own climax did he withdraw. He pressed her thighs together and emptied himself there, in the slick channel made by her arousal and his seed.

And when they both were spent, he brushed her sweat-darkened hair off her face. He leaned down across her so that he might press his mouth to the nape of her neck.

"I'm yours now," he said quietly. "Body and soul."

Please, he thought. *Don't regret it.*

Chapter 28

Two days later, outside the Earl of Hangleton's town house with most of his crew behind him, Archer held Ruby's hand and perseverated briefly on shrubbery.

The home was surrounded by hedges, clipped in neat, precise rows. The leaves shone in the sun, as though they'd been polished individually by some gardener's gloved hand. Perhaps they had. The brick exterior was spotless; the windows gleamed; not even a pebble had dared to roll out of place as their carriage trundled up in front of the house.

And in front of all that perfect greenery stood Captain Malcolm Archer: dressed in his one unstained shirt, smelling of tar from the *Delphinium*, and holding for dear life on to the hand of Hangleton's elder daughter.

Whom he had made his wife.

There had been considerable wrangling over their plan of action as they'd made for the London Docks. Ruby had proposed to take Signor Neri to meet with her father, but Neri had had some alternative scheme in mind. He had insisted upon making his way to his own residence once they arrived in the city.

Archer had worried over that for some time. He suspected—he feared—that Neri did not trust the ambassador. And he did not know how to say such a thing to Ruby.

Lamentation had gone with the signore. He'd done his duty aboard the ship with a rigid, unfamiliar expression on his face, and when the opportunity to break from the rest of the crew had come, he'd taken it. Gerry had been speechless with distress, and Archer could scarcely recall ever in his life having felt so torn apart.

He looked at the tiny neat lines where the shrubs had been clipped—recently, he could still smell the grassy scent—and felt lightheaded.

This was a mistake. He should have forced the issue—should have gone to Penney instead. Penney knew where he'd come from. And standing here, in front of the fine glazed windows and the pristine shrubs, it had never seemed so clear to Archer that Ruby did not. He was a convict. Brig trash. He was as out of place here as a fly crushed bloody against stained glass.

Perhaps he could persuade her to lie to Hangleton a little longer. Perhaps he could leave this fancy square and try to find the princess some other way, let Ruby tackle the problem from the high-society end while he came at it from the bottom. Perhaps—

Ruby squeezed his hand and looked up into his face. Her lips had gone pale, and as he gripped her hand, he realized he was not the only one holding on a little too hard.

"Are you ready?" she asked. "It might be . . . unpleasant, at first."

He gritted his teeth. He squeezed her fingers between his own and then, helplessly, lifted her hand to his mouth.

He had to believe—he *did* believe—that he could do some good if he stayed right here, by her side.

He could talk. He was good at talking. He could persuade Hangleton to listen to his daughter; he would convince the ambassador that Ruby was the greatest thing that had ever happened to House di Sangro and the earl's political career. He could do it.

He made himself smile. "Hope you've still got that bayonet under your skirts," he murmured.

And, faintly, almost imperceptibly, her mouth twitched up. "Dash it," she said. "I forgot. I've brought the Elgin Marbles, though. Should they prove useful."

"I'm certain that, between the two of us, we can think of something."

She swallowed hard. And then she pasted on a smile and—bravely, as she did everything—knocked on the door.

It came open in seconds, and obviously Archer was an execrable butler, because he'd never opened a door so fast in his life.

The stern, bewigged fellow inside unbent slightly when he recognized Ruby, though he cast a doubtful glance at their crew and Ruby's hand entwined with Archer's. "Lady Ruby," he said, "welcome home. We were not expecting you. Shall I tell the earl that you're—"

"It's Mrs. Archer now," she said calmly, and Archer nearly swallowed his tongue.

Right. Well. Evidently there was to be no deception about the nature of their relationship, and no easing into things either.

It made him . . . proud. Idiotic, besotted fool that he was, it made him want to weep.

"You may alert my father, yes," she said, "and show my guests into the east sitting room, please, Finch—"

But before anyone could move, the Earl of Hangleton came around the corner and into view.

Archer recalled the man from Gravesmuir's cursed dinner party. Hangleton was tall, fine-boned, dressed with a ferocious elegance that called to mind the exacting shape of the shrubs outside. His hair was a sandy gray, and his cravat was starched to a level that Archer had heretofore never seen or imagined.

"Ruby," Hangleton said reflexively. "What in—"

His gaze flicked from Ruby to Archer to the small crowd behind them: Eugénie and Gerry and Alice and the Enys boys, all fresh off the *Delphinium* and in various states of dishevelment and disrepair. Sidney Enys, for some reason, had on two different shoes.

"What is the meaning of this?" Hangleton snapped.

"Father," Ruby said. "This—"

Hangleton didn't let her finish. "What could you possibly be thinking?" He strode to the door and peered out, looking left and right over Ruby's shoulder. "My God, anyone could see you like this. Anyone could see *them*—a gang of criminals, at my doorstep—"

"No," Ruby tried again, "they're not—" She stumbled on the obvious lie and tried valiantly to go on. "If you'll allow me to explain—"

Hangleton caught Ruby's elbow and towed her inside, and Archer, by virtue of still having hold of her hand, was dragged into the house as well.

"Oh, you will certainly explain," Hangleton said icily. "In my study. Alone."

"My companions—"

"Can take themselves off." He cast a frigid glance at the

ragtag crew, still arrayed before the door. "I'd advise you not to remain in this square, unless you'd like to have the magistrates brought down upon your heads."

Ruby looked miserably out at their companions. "You can . . . wait in the mews," she said. "I'm—I'm so sorry."

There was a crack in her voice as she spoke, and it cracked something inside Archer too. Fierce, bright anger rose in him: at Hangleton's hand on Ruby's arm, at the expression on the earl's face as he'd looked out at their crew.

But Archer thrust it back. He took every scrap of outrage and humiliation and shoved it into a ball, pressing it down beneath his breastbone. He could not afford anger right now. He had to be calm and pleasant and sure of himself. He had to secure Hangleton's assistance so that they might find the princess, and he *was not* going to let Ruby down.

So he sent his crew a bolstering smile and followed Ruby and her father down the hall to Hangleton's study.

Inside, Ruby sat down in front of the earl's desk and burst once again into hasty speech. "Father. I know that our arrival was unexpected. But if you'll only permit me to explain—"

"Unexpected?" Hangleton echoed. "That's putting it mildly. I distinctly recall telling you to go back to Bridestowe and stay there."

"I couldn't. Papa, I need you to listen to me. The Princess of Monfalcone—"

Hangleton, who'd half lowered himself into his chair, rose at Ruby's words. "This again? By God, Ruby—"

Ruby's face had gone pink. She looked wretched and embarrassed. "I know you told me not to interfere in the princess's affairs," she said thinly, "but I had no choice. She—"

"Not to interfere?" Hangleton gave a derisive little laugh. "When have you ever in your life listened to me when I told you to keep yourself out of situations where you do not belong? Let us simply add this to the long list of public embarrassments your actions have engendered."

Archer's pulse beat hard in his ears.

He looked at Ruby. Her eyes had gone to her lap, and her shoulders curved down, as if to make herself smaller in her chair.

His jaw tightened. His teeth ached. Words leapt to his mind, to his mouth—but he strangled them in his throat.

"Please, Papa," Ruby said. "If you'll only let me explain—"

"I'm sick of listening to your excuses. I cannot think why I imagined that a few months at Bridestowe might do you some good. You are once again entangled in a mess of your own making."

Ruby's face had gone from pink to white. She looked—

Not just hurt. Resigned. As though she'd expected this. As though she'd been braced for such a blow.

"I have long despaired," Hangleton went on silkily, "of your ever learning to behave differently. But now I begin to think that you are incapable of—"

Archer found himself on his feet.

"That's enough," he said, very low.

And—shit. Bloody fucking hell. He had not meant to say it. This was not how he'd intended for this meeting to go. He was meant to help, to *charm*. Not hurl himself into a confrontation that might ruin their chances of securing Hangleton's help. He had not, under any circumstances, meant to give in to the siren call of honesty.

But Ruby—

Ah God. Her transparent face was utterly stiff, and her blue-gray eyes looked faraway. Fogged over, as though she could not see clear.

And he couldn't bear it. He could not sit and watch, not even if he ruined his best chance of finding the princess. Not even if, later, Ruby blamed him for intervening. He could not stand idly by and, through his own inaction, fail her when she needed him most.

He would not let her father make her feel ashamed.

"What's that?" Hangleton snapped.

"That's enough," Archer said again. "Sit down."

Hangleton's gaze focused on Archer for the first time, and he treated Archer to a slow up-and-down perusal. "Sit down, is it? I beg your pardon. Who the devil are you to tell me what to do in my own house?"

Archer couldn't help himself. He looked back at Hangleton and smiled very slowly. "No one of import," he said. "Only your son-in-law."

Hangleton goggled. "You—" His face went mottled, then scarlet. "You are—"

"Cheers," Archer said blandly.

Hangleton turned to Ruby, his expression transfigured by fury. "I should have known. I should have suspected that you would run off and get yourself into some ghastly, humiliating—"

Archer cut in, his voice so soft that Hangleton, despite himself, went quiet. "Perhaps you did not hear me," he murmured. "I said, *sit down*. And do not speak another word until you've listened to what your daughter has to say."

He was a good two decades younger than Hangleton and no doubt outweighed him by several stone, but it wasn't the threat of physical violence that brought Hangleton's words to a halt. It was Archer's tone—the low assurance, the lethal command he'd honed a thousand thousand times aboard his ship.

This was what he did—spoke in such a way that people believed him. That people looked into his face and saw the truth.

And this time, he meant every word.

"You," he said softly, "do not deserve to breathe the same air as Ruby. You haven't got a hundredth part of her cleverness or courage, and she is good and brilliant and goddamned heroic *in spite* of you. In spite of your very best attempts to stifle her."

He broke Hangleton's gaze to look at Ruby. Her lips were parted, and he couldn't read the expression on her face.

But her eyes were clear as she looked at him; the strange distant despair he'd seen there had faded.

He had her back. And he wasn't letting her go.

He turned to Hangleton. "Listen to your daughter," he said again. "She is trying to save your skin along with the Monfalcone royal family, and I assure you, Hangleton, it is in your best interest to close your mouth and think very, very hard before you open it again."

The earl sat back down. He was still looking at Archer, and when he spoke, his voice was measured. "I know you," he said. "I've seen you before."

Fear moved through Archer's body. A shifting uncertainty, like sand pulled out from beneath his feet by the tide.

But before he could reply, Ruby intervened. "He is my husband." She lifted her chin and looked at her father straight on. "Before you accuse him of anything else, Papa, remember this: His name is connected to yours now. Forever."

Hangleton sat back. His eyes shifted from Archer to his daughter, and he didn't say anything else.

And very slowly, Archer lowered himself into his chair as well. "Your turn now," he said to Ruby. "Tell him what he needs to know."

Chapter 29

Ruby managed to get through her explanation of the princess's arrival at Pomeroy House and subsequent abduction without crumbling, weeping, or flinging herself at Archer and tearing his clothes off—all of which seemed roughly equal in terms of their likelihood.

When her father had started in on her list of flaws and failures, she'd felt more raw and exposed than she could ever remember feeling in her life. It was worse—much worse—than the catastrophe with the drapes or her faux pas in Gravesmuir's ballroom. This time, it was not a roomful of strangers watching her, but her husband.

She had been afraid to look at him. She could not bear to see how he had taken her father's words.

But when he had risen to his feet—when he had spoken up for her and trammeled her father into silence . . .

She'd felt undone. She had felt as though the world were a brilliant parti-colored kaleidoscope, whirling and then settling into a new shape she could not quite make sense of.

Though she had resolved not to care about her father's opinions any longer, when he'd closed the door on their crew, she had been forced to confront the fact that some little, impossible-to-quash part of her had hoped for a reconciliation. The same foolish corner of her heart that had placed the *Royal Archaeological Journal* by his plate. The same part of her that, when she thought of her family, wanted to recall nothing but sunny mornings in Rome, rose-petal jam, and Cassandra's small hand tucked into her own.

But when Archer had put her father back on his heels with swift, ruthless, and frankly arousing efficiency, she'd found that all those foolish dreams had fractured into shards. Had, when she was not attending, coalesced into something new.

He devastated her. Curled her toes and rent her heart to pieces. He had faced down her father and defended her like he meant to keep speaking until he ran out of breath. And then he had looked at her, all stubborn blue earnestness—as though she were worth every word.

He was a *hero*. And he was hers.

As quickly and succinctly as she could, she finished her story of the abduction and their thus-far-unsuccessful efforts to recover Tamsin and Princess Serafina. She described their search of Verdura's empty ship and then bit her lip, hesitating on her next words.

She did not quite know how to speak to her father anymore.

But she thought of how Archer had faced him—how *her father* had quailed under Archer's implacable authority—and she lifted her chin.

"I understand that you were skeptical of my association with the princess in the past," she said. "But the evidence is clear. I have with me the diamond collar we recovered from the *Vulcano* and a letter from Signor Neri. We have come to you because the princess is in danger, and because we believe that you can help us find her."

She reached into her reticule to pull out the collar, but her father waved a hand in dismissal. He'd calmed as she'd told her story, and his expression had gone sharp, all calculating politician. "I don't need to see it. I don't doubt your tale, Ruby, wild as it seems."

Ruby paused. She did not trust the hope that wanted to rise up inside her. Cautiously, she set her reticule back down in her lap and crossed her hands atop it. "So . . . you will help us?"

Her father leaned back in his chair. His eyes roamed Ruby's face and then Archer's. "Verdura is not in London. There is nothing to be done except to wait and see what happens."

Ruby gritted her teeth. "I can't believe that. You know the Duca di Verdura. You can find out where he is. You could use your connections to uncover his associates."

"I could," the earl allowed, "if I thought it wise."

"What do you—"

"Ruby." Her father's voice sharpened, and he leaned forward in his chair. "This is how it works, child. We don't burst into situations unprepared, like a bull trampling a field. We exercise patience. We wait until we know for certain which way the die has been cast."

Ruby felt Archer grow tense at her side, and she looked to him, trying to make sense of the ice that had chilled his expression. "I don't understand. What do you mean, *wait*? The princess and Tamsin could be killed if we dally."

"He means," Archer said, very low, "that he already knew about Verdura."

Her lips parted. She looked to her father. "What?"

"I did not know," her father said coolly. "But when I received your outlandish letter, I suspected."

He seemed blurry, suddenly. Everything felt muffled, her blood rushing in her ears. "You suspected . . ." She tried to swallow, but her mouth was too dry. "But you told me you did not believe my story. You told me to wait in Cornwall. You—"

"You are precipitate," the earl said. "Naive. You plunge into situations without grasping their ramifications."

"I don't understand," she got out.

But she did. Her perception of the past rearranged itself—slow and devastating.

When she had received her father's letter in St. Petroc's, she had supposed that he had merely underestimated her. She had thought that he was, once again, letting her down.

But he had not truly disbelieved her. All those words of criticism—all that terrible, wrenching betrayal—had been purposeful. He had meant to keep her quiet.

"Did you—work with Verdura?" It was difficult to get the words out past the thick constriction of her throat. "Did you plot with him?"

"Of course not." Her father laid a hand on his desk, palm up. "But I have heard rumor of the duke's intrigues for years now. We must wait to see how this gambit plays out."

"It's not a *game*, Papa." Her voice broke. "We can't sit back and let the princess—let *Tamsin*—"

But her father cut her off. "Verdura is a powerful man, Ruby. If we cross him and he does take the throne in Monfalcone, our family will have made a dangerous enemy. It is far safer to bide our time."

She looked at her father. The familiar arc of his cheekbones, the straight blade of his nose.

Safety, he preached. *Restraint*. But it was not concern for their family that motivated his actions. It was wealth and influence he wanted: proximity to power. She could see him clearly—the motivation that he tried to burnish over with delicate, politicking words. If he allowed both sides to think him loyal, he could retain his position no matter who took control of the throne.

Her father let his voice drop, soft and suggestive. He looked her in the eye. "Come home, Ruby. We can cover up your mésalliance. Find some way to undo it. If we allow Verdura to believe us an ally, who knows how we might be rewarded—not only me, but my family as well. We can find you a position at my side."

There was a slow, brittle silence as Ruby held his gaze. As she considered his words.

Come home, Ruby.

My family.

At my side.

It was, she supposed, what she had always wanted.

She thought of delphiniums. Of years of devotion, of the patient, necessary work of hands.

There was no choice to make. She had already chosen. A thousand times, over and over, since the first time she'd seen Captain Malcolm Archer at Pomeroy House. She reached out and took her husband's hand.

"I'm sorry," she said to her father. "I'm very sorry that you have made this decision."

"I have made no decision," her father said. "I have simply chosen not to involve myself."

But complicity was as much a decision as any other. She knew that. And so did her father. "We must go," she said. "We will trouble you no longer."

"Ruby," her father said sharply. "Do not involve yourself further in this matter. I should think you'd know by now that your actions reflect back on me. Don't forget whose name you bear."

Her nose was burning, and her eyes, but her face was dry. "I shan't forget."

She did not think her father registered the import of her words. His face did not change as she rose. But Malcolm's did. He gave her one glance—a flash of blue, almost stricken—and gripped her fingers tight as they made their way to the door. Her ring pressed hard against her bone.

She thought of the name she had been born to. And then—with a hot surge of pride and pleasure—a different name. The one she had chosen to take.

She took him out to the mews, where their crew waited. In the stable's dim interior, the familiar scent of hay and horses filled her nose. As her eyes adjusted to the light, she picked out Gerry and Eugénie seated on a bench. The Enys boys were arguing noisily, and one of her father's grooms leaned against a wall.

And Alice stood very close beside—

Ruby blinked. Squeezed her eyes closed, then opened them again.

She said: "Cassandra?"

Her sister looked up. She was dressed neatly and fashionably in a silver-embroidered, high-collared riding habit. A tiny hat was perched atop her buttery hair, and her gloved hands were twisted together.

She looked like the daughter of an earl and the wife of a viscount, and still, somehow, she looked like Ruby's baby sister.

"I went for her," Alice said softly. "I told her everything. I hope you don't mind, Ruby. I feared . . . your father . . ." She stumbled over the words. Tried again. "I suppose I thought we might need some help. And I thought—it was what Tam would do. If she were here."

Ruby felt a painful rush of tenderness for Alice, who might well have been turned away at Cassandra's door. Alice's father's reputation had blackened their family name so thoroughly that Alice could never be certain of her reception.

And yet she'd gone for help anyway.

Beside Alice, Cassandra took a step forward and searched Ruby's face. "I came," she said. "Lady Alice told me you might need me, and so I came."

"Cass—" Ruby started to say, but her voice wobbled. She closed her mouth.

Her sister was linking and unlinking her fingers, a familiar little gesture that called up a lifetime of memories: Cassandra seated before the pianoforte; Cass at her court presentation, sick with nerves; Cassandra with the fledgling bird their father hadn't let her keep.

She hadn't protested when her father made her put the bird back outside. Ruby had, vigorously and vociferously, and when they'd been forced to set it back beneath the hedge anyway, Cass hadn't cried either. Only blinked very hard and gripped her own hands for comfort, exactly as she was doing now.

"I want to help," Cassandra said. "It's—difficult. For me. To go against Papa. But I would do it if you needed me to. The truth is, Ruby, I've been trying very hard these last years to be more like you."

She stood very straight, Cass did. Her shoulders made a perfect line, and her chin nearly topped Ruby's head.

Ruby had to look up to meet her sister's eyes, and somehow, she couldn't remember when that had happened. "Me?"

"You," Cassandra said. "You were always yourself. No one could dim your light, Ruby. Not even Papa."

Ruby had the kaleidoscope feeling again—the sense of reality swirling and settling around her in new, fantastic shapes. She had left her father behind. She had forged a new path.

She had done that.

It wasn't over. She still had Tamsin and the princess to find, a hundred impossible hurdles to cross. But she didn't have to cross them alone. She had Malcolm and Alice, the *Delphinium* and all its crew. She had Cassandra, and her sister wanted to help.

"Please," she said unevenly. "Yes. We need you, Cassie. We could use your aid."

"Anything," Cassandra said. "Tell me what I can do."

Malcolm had his arm around Ruby's shoulders, and he pressed his chin against her hair. "Your father says Verdura has fled London. I think our next best bet is to get to Penney. Find out if he knows where Verdura has gone." A muscle in his jaw flexed as he looked at his assembled crew—as he thought, Ruby suspected, of the absent Lamentation and the words Lamentation had hurled at him on the deck of the *Delphinium*.

But he steeled himself and turned his gaze back to Cassandra. "Rear Admiral Lord John Penney, I mean. Can you get me to his house?"

Cassandra regarded him steadily. "Of course," she said. She raised her chin—looked, suddenly, like the viscountess she was. "Leave everything to me."

Ruby glanced up at Malcolm. He was holding her very tightly, his face grave and intent. But a shadow of his dimples emerged around his mouth as he met her eyes—an expression he meant to be reassuring, she knew, and that looked only halfway forced.

He leaned down and kissed her forehead. "Penney will help us. We're going to find them, Ruby. I promise."

Chapter 30

Without Ruby's sister, Penney's butler would never have let them in. Archer had given his name, his former rank, his long association with Penney, and still the man had only looked bored and dismissive. Archer's chest had gone tight with anxious dread.

But Cassandra—the Viscountess Dearne—had slipped the butler her card, and the man's expression had gone dubious. When she'd tipped her head toward her crested carriage, he'd consented to go and see if Rear Admiral Lord Penney was receiving.

Cassandra had grinned and stepped back to rejoin their waiting crew.

Ruby had taken Archer's hand and looked up into his face. "Are you certain you wish for me to go in with you?" she'd whispered. "You could take Cass instead. I do not . . . excel. At these sorts of things."

He cupped her cheek, then leaned in very close so she could see him clearly. So she would know he meant what he said. "I want you with me," he murmured. "All the time. If I had to lead a ship into battle, Ruby Ballimore, I would want you at my back. Armed, I hope, with your mortar knife."

Her lips curved crookedly up. "Archer," she whispered.

"Yes?"

"No, I meant—" She broke off to put her hand over his, finding the lines between his fingers, brushing lightly against his ring. "Not Ballimore. Archer."

He was just on the point of kissing her witless when Penney himself came around the corner.

Penney's gaze almost passed over them—then paused, abruptly caught on Archer's face. Archer watched his expression transform with shock and recognition. And then he watched Penney smile.

"Archer!" Penney was nearing fifty now, but his face was still boyish, his thick chestnut hair barely touched by gray. He reached out and took Archer's hand in his. "I thought you well settled in Cornwall, my boy. What are you doing here?"

It was impossible to look at Penney and not remember . . . everything. Maps and cannons, sailcloth rippling in the sun. An inn with a fiddle. A cliffside chase. The rending of a ship.

"I am settled in Cornwall," Archer said. "I'd like to be." He touched Ruby's shoulder. "Jack—this is Lady Ruby. My wife."

Penney's brows shot up. "Your— Good God, son. Felicitations!" He took Ruby's hand in his. "*Lady* Ruby?"

Ruby let him press a kiss to her knuckles before she spoke. "My father is Earl of Hangleton and ambassador to Monfalcone."

Penney glanced from Ruby to Archer and back again. "Hangleton's daughter?" He clapped a hand on Archer's shoulder, then turned the embrace into a pivot as he led them both away from the front door. "You *have* come up in the world. I told you—didn't I always tell you that you'd make good?" He laughed a little, warm and unvarnished, and then swept a hand toward the corridor. "Come. Come with me to my office. We'll sit down, have some Madeira for old time's sake. And you can tell me exactly what's brought you here."

Swept by the tide of Penney's bluff enthusiasm, they went.

Presently, they found themselves seated across from Penney in a small, lavish study. The evening was warm, and Penney did not pause to stoke the coals in the grate before settling himself behind a large rosewood desk. Behind his head, the wall was lined with books and decorative plasterwork; the sconce in the wall shone with gaslight.

"Archer," Penney said again, turning a pleased smile on them both. "What a sight for sore eyes. And now Mrs. Archer too." He put his hands on the arms of his chair as he leaned toward them—a gesture so familiar it made Archer's eyes burn. "Tell me everything that's happened since I got you that job at the end of the world. How's the Cornish holiday house?"

Archer reached out and caught Ruby's hand in his. The kidskin leather of her gloves was butter-soft. He wished, painfully, for the warmth of her skin.

He took a breath and told Penney everything. He recounted the story of Signor Neri's arrival at Pomeroy House and the princess's attempted assassination. He told Penney about the kidnapping of Tamsin and Serafina, their discovery of Verdura's ship, their recent marriage.

And when he was done, he hesitated.

He felt helpless—an awful, unbearable emotion. He'd spent the last eighteen years trying never to feel that way again.

They needed Penney. Archer did not know where else to turn. And if Penney rebuffed them—if Archer could not accomplish what he'd promised Ruby—he had no defenses left to shield himself.

His gaze flicked to Ruby and then back to Penney's face. "I'm hoping you can aid us," he said. "You know the Monfalcone royal family—and that includes Verdura. Hangleton says Verdura has fled London, but we're not willing to give up yet. We want to track the duke down."

He paused a long moment, not certain how hard to press. But it was Penney—and Penney knew what Archer had done for him.

"Please," he said finally. "We need your help."

Penney sat back in his chair. "My God," he said. "Of course I'll help. Only let me think what to do."

Relief blossomed inside Archer's chest, so fast and hard his head spun.

It was going to be all right. He clutched at Ruby's hand, harder than he meant, and he tried to make himself stop, only—

Penney was going to help them. Archer thought of the *Swallow* and the cold regret on Penney's face. He thought, painfully, helplessly: *I did the right thing.*

Penney was going to aid them. Archer had not thrown his life away for nothing.

"Do you know anyone who might be able to tell us where Verdura's gone?" Ruby asked. "My father suggested the duke had fled, but did not know his destination."

Penney drummed his fingers on the arm of his chair. "I believe I can put my connections to use to track Verdura, yes." He looked sharply at Ruby. "What else did your father tell you? Anything we can use to our purposes?"

She shook her head. "Very little."

"Anything of Verdura's coconspirators? Any persons who might have had a hand in the attack?"

"Nothing of the kind." Ruby's lips compressed. "I wish he had."

"That's all right," Penney said. "We'll figure this out." He turned to Archer. "You still have your little sloop at the docks?"

"For now," he said, "yes."

"Good." Penney leaned forward again. "If I can work out where the duke's headed, I can send some of my men—my sailors—with you. I assume you want to track him yourself?"

"Yes," Archer said instantly. "Of course. I'll go anywhere."

But Ruby was shaking her head. "Wait," she said. "Do you not think that overhasty? Ought we not investigate Verdura's London residence before we fly off to heaven knows where?"

Penney smiled approvingly at Ruby. "Yes," he said, "you're right. I knew my boy would pick a clever woman when he settled down. Of course we should investigate the town house. You two prepare Archer's old tub, and I'll go there myself."

"To Verdura's house?" Ruby asked.

"That's right." Penney grinned at Archer, a familiar lopsided flash of mischief. "This damned name of mine ought to be worth something after all these years. I suspect I can persuade the duke's butler to let me in."

"Thank you," Archer said. Relief was still shuddering through him. He'd known. He'd *known* Penney would not let them down.

"And you'll tell us?" Ruby pressed. "If you find anything? You'll send word before we go?"

"Of course," Penney said. "With any luck, I'll turn up your princess and your friend and even that absurd little dog before the two of you break anchor."

There was a hiccup of silence as Archer's brain caught on what Penney had just said. Read it back, as if engraved in ink.

With any luck, I'll turn up your princess and your friend and even that absurd little dog before the two of you break anchor.

Only Archer had not, at any point in his recital, mentioned Zenobia.

Archer made his lips curve up. He schooled his expression in neutrality. It was easy. It was the habit of a lifetime. But his mind galloped ahead, spun, and then raced back again.

What else did your father tell you? Penney had asked. *Anything of Verdura's coconspirators?*

Archer had taken the words on their face. He had thought Penney meant what he'd said—meant only to help them. But Penney had no reason to know that Zenobia had been taken too.

His head spun. Was it possible that *Penney* had some involvement in this scheme? His mind—his stupid, foolish heart—wanted to shy away from the notion, and yet—

Penney had got Archer the job at Pomeroy House in the first place. Penney *knew* the Monfalcone royals. When confronted with news of Verdura's scheme and their determination to track the duke down, Penney's first thought had been to send them out of the country.

Penney had not even told them where he wanted them to go, and Archer had leapt to do his bidding.

There was some thin panic fluttering in his chest. Some desperate desire not to see—to turn away, to pretend he had not caught the import of Penney's words.

He tried to find something to say. Something easy, something that did not reveal his nauseous, mounting suspicion.

But Ruby spoke before he could. "The—dog?" she said unsteadily. "How do you know about the dog?"

Archer's whole body went cold, as though he'd plunged into an ice-choked sea. Ruby—ah God, Ruby, who could not lie to save her own skin. Who had no defense against the truth.

Penney sat back in his chair. "Oh, my dear," he murmured. "I had hoped you would not notice."

Ruby's voice pitched up. "You hoped I would not *notice*? What are you trying to say? You already knew that they were missing? Do—do you know where they are?"

Her eyes blazed. Archer could see her with a mortar knife in her hand; he could see her, blunt and fierce and heartbreakingly loyal as she protected him from her own father.

"Archer," Penney said softly, "tell her it's all right."

Archer looked at Ruby. And then he looked at Penney. His throat felt tight. His hands were numb. "I—" His voice jerked. Stumbled to a halt. "I don't . . ."

"You know you can trust me," Penney said. The words came out low. Persuasive. "You know I care for you, don't you, son? I got you a ship when no one else in the navy would touch you. I got you the position at Pomeroy House when you had nothing left."

"Don't," Ruby snapped. "Don't you speak to him that way."

But Penney wasn't looking at Ruby. He was looking at Archer with an expression of cool intensity. "I'm trying to help you," he said. "I put you there at Pomeroy House because I knew we might be in this spot one day. That there was a chance Verdura might rise to the throne, and we could position ourselves in such a way as to assist him. I made you an officer once, didn't I, my boy? Only think what I can make you with a king on our side."

The revelation was hot and cold at once. Searing.

Penney had got him the position at Pomeroy House not because Archer deserved the job or because Penney regretted what had happened to the *Swallow*.

He had done it because he knew he would someday need Archer to look the other way. He believed that Archer would turn a blind eye to his misdeeds, and he had *reason* to think so. Archer had done exactly that already.

He couldn't—hear clearly. There was the sound of water in his ears, rushing, screaming, stinging his skin.

"You think Verdura will reward you for helping him?" Ruby demanded, her eyes fixed on Penney's face. "Don't be a fool. He's made you his sacrificial lamb. He's fled the city—you are the one remaining here to take the fall if the princess is found dead." She leaned forward, her expression ferocious and defiant. "Were those your sailors who attacked the princess's ship? Whom we spotted prowling the cliffs? We *saw* them—and the princess did too. Do you truly believe House di Sangro will not uncover the truth?"

Penney's jaw flexed. "Princess Serafina does not concern me. Verdura will be the future of Monfalcone."

"Well, she ought to! *We* ought to concern you. We—" Ruby broke off. She sent Archer a glance of agonized confusion, and he knew it was because he was still sitting—frozen, motionless. Silent.

Penney too turned back to Archer. "I know I can trust you to do the right thing," he said evenly. "How many years did I keep you at my side? How many years did I invest in you—raised you up from brig trash to the sailor you became? I made you a man worthy of an earl's daughter, Archer. You know I did. Tell your wife I would not lead you astray."

Still—helplessly—Archer wanted to believe him.

He had chosen Penney once. More than once. He had been alone and afraid, and Penney had given him a way out. Penney had *made* him. Penney had looked at a cocky loudmouthed little convict and seen . . . something worthy. Someone who might, someday, be a good and honorable man.

If Penney did not deserve his loyalty, then what did that say about *him*?

He had the sense of water in his ears, in his mouth. An old terror rose in him: He was lost; he was vulnerable; he was going to drown, abandoned under the waves.

And then he looked at Ruby, her hair falling down around her shoulders, her gloved hands locked together in her lap. Her eyes— clear and blue and steady on his face.

He had thought to prove himself to her by charming her father. By finding the princess and restoring his good name. By showing her that his loyalty to Penney had not been in error.

And Christ—again and again he had failed.

But she was looking at him now, and she trusted him, and this—*this* was the moment of decision. This was the test he could not fail.

He had chosen wrongly before. But he could choose differently this time. He could change.

"No," he said hoarsely. "No, Jack. Not again."

"Son," Penney said, and it . . .

Hurt. That word.

"I don't want to do this," Penney said. "I hope you know that."

For just a moment, Archer didn't know what he meant.

And then he did. Penney had eased open the drawer at his

desk, and something glimmered there, a tiny refraction of light, like stars on water. Like metal glittering under gaslight.

Somehow Archer was on his feet. "Jack," he said. "Don't."

Penney closed his hand over the pistol.

For the space of a heartbeat, Archer thought of Ruby. Her eyes, her laugh, the thin gold band on the fourth finger of her left hand.

And then he threw himself across the desk.

He heard the gunshot—loud, close—and felt heat blister the side of his face.

Wait, he thought. *Ruby—*

Chapter 31

The darkness seemed to suck at Archer's brain, towing him back down when he wanted to wake. His chest hurt. His head. When he forced his lids up, everything still seemed black.

He blinked. Lifted his hand to his face and rubbed at his eyes, which—ah fuck, that hurt too, everything hurt—where *was* he—

Memory struck him like a cannon blast. Panic.

He sat bolt upright. "Ruby," he tried to say. His voice was a soundless rasp, and the room revolved around him, a slow nauseous spin.

He threw himself to his feet. He was—Christ, he hadn't been blinded, he was merely trapped in some tar-black enclosure. Was it a brig? A cell? There was almost no light, and his feet slipped against stone as he hurled himself forward.

He remembered the gun. He remembered Penney's hands raising the pistol, the heat searing his cheek. But somehow . . . somehow he was alive.

Had Penney missed? Or—

His heart clutched. Fear drove into his bones like a spike.

Had Penney's gunshot found *Ruby*?

The room came into vague focus around him as his eyes adjusted to the dark, though black spots still floated in his vision. His gaze landed on a door, and before he could think, he hurled himself at it. He yanked at the handle fruitlessly, then pounded at the rough wooden surface.

He was going to kill Penney. He would break down the door in his dumb animal terror, he would tear his fingers to shreds, he would die for her a hundred times, a thousand times, he had to get *out*—

"Penney!" he howled. "Jack Penney! Where the fuck is my wife?" He slammed his fist against the door, and it rattled beneath his hand. "If you've touched her—if you've hurt her—I'll fucking kill you, do you hear me? You think this door can stop me? A goddamned *grave* couldn't stop me!"

"Malcolm."

It was Ruby's voice. Low and familiar and soothing, and he—he couldn't hear properly—he didn't know where she was. He spun wildly toward the sound.

"For heaven's sake," she said, "calm down. I'm right here."

He plunged through the dim interior, tripping over God knew what, half blinded by tears of pain and relief, until he had her in his arms.

"Oh God," he mumbled into her hair. "Oh fuck. Ruby."

There was a terrible sawed-off sound, a jagged breath, and he thought it was Ruby, weeping into his chest.

But no, he realized. He was the one who wept.

She held him hard, stroking his hair, and he gritted his teeth until he got himself under control. "You're all right?" he rasped. "Penney's shot went wide?"

"Yes—yes. I'm fine." Her voice, muffled against his chest, shook. "He missed us both. And then his wretched batman came, and he—"

"Did he touch you?" he demanded. He couldn't bring himself to pull away to check, so he ran his hand up her back, finding the bare skin of her neck.

"You absolute madman—*you* are the one the batman beat senseless, not me!"

Archer supposed that explained the agony in every muscle of his body. "But you're all right?" he said. He was still swinging dizzily from rage to relief and back again. "If he hurt you, Ruby, I swear to God, he's not going to survive the day. I'll tear his heart out of his chest. I'll—"

"I'm fine," she said. She reached up and caught his throbbing face in her hands. "Malcolm. Listen to me. I'm perfectly well. No one hurt me."

"Oh God," he said. His vision dimmed once more. The room whirled.

It seemed prudent to sit down very hard on the stone floor and pull Ruby into his lap.

He held her for a long moment in the dark, breathing in her warm scent. Her cheek was wet where it pressed into his neck, and her fingers shook where she clutched at his shirt. *She's all right*, he told himself. *She's all right. Calm down.*

But he—

God. He couldn't. His heart was still pounding with terror and fury, and he loosened his hold on her because he feared, suddenly, that he would hurt her.

But even as he relaxed his grip, she fisted her hand in his shirt and dragged him closer. "Malcolm," she said. "You idiot. You—you—What were you thinking, to throw yourself at him so?"

His battered shoulders protested the ferocity of her grip, but he didn't care. He relished it. "He had a pistol, Ruby. He could have—"

"I know what he could have done, Malcolm! I watched it happen. I think some—some chunk of plaster must have struck your face—your cheek was *bleeding*, all down your neck and your shirt, and I did not even know if you—if he—"

He pushed back her hair and made small soothing sounds against the tangled curls. "I'm fine. Everything's all right."

"Don't lie." Her voice broke. "Don't lie to me, Malcolm. There's still dried blood on your neck. I couldn't get it all off."

"Darling. Ruby-love. I'm not lying." He tipped her face up and let himself indulge in the creaturely miracle of kissing her mouth. "I've the devil of a headache, but I'm fine. I'm right here. And . . . you're all right. That's what matters. That's all that matters."

"If you throw yourself in front of a firearm like that again," she whispered, "I will kill you myself."

"Pet." He kissed her again, helplessly. "I can't make any promises. I would throw myself in front of a bullet a thousand times to keep you safe."

"That's not—"

"I told you." He caught her palm, pressed it against his chest. Felt the tiny indentation of her ring through his shirt. "There's nothing I wouldn't do for you."

"Malcolm," she whispered.

He held her hand against his heart. He wanted some gilded

declaration, wanted words like a liturgy. Wanted to spool out promises like golden thread. But instead, when he opened his mouth, his voice came out hoarse. Abrupt. Unsteady.

"I love you," he said.

In the shadowed dark, he watched her lips part.

"I love you," he said again. "I can't— God, Ruby. I keep thinking I'll get it right. I'll do everything perfectly and *prove* to you that I can be more than what I've always been. But I—" He broke off. He wrapped his fingers around her hand and kept it pressed against his chest. Holding on. Powerless to let her go. "But the truth is, Ruby-love, this *is* who I am."

"I like who you are," she said softly.

"Sweetheart." He gripped her fingers and fought the hot burn at the backs of his eyes. "I kept telling myself that I wouldn't importune you until I'd proven myself. That I wouldn't ask you to be with me, to take my name, until my name meant something. And then—oh hell. Ruby. And then somehow I was leaping across a goddamned desk at Penney, and all I could think was, *I'd die for her, and I still haven't told her that I love her.*"

She was closer now—so close he almost spoke the words against her mouth.

"I love you, Ruby Ballimore," he said. "Of course I'd take a bullet for you. I'd take it and be goddamned grateful for the chance. There is no world for me if you're not in it. No sunrise—no *sun*—without you."

She put her fingers to his lips, silencing him.

"*Archer*," she said. "Not Ballimore."

And then she moved her hand to his hair and pulled him down to her mouth.

He closed his eyes and drank in the taste of her: sweet and cool and safe.

Still here. Still his own.

He kissed her for a long time, there in the dark. He kissed her until his pulse calmed, until he'd touched and soothed every inch of her he could reach. Until his body seemed, finally, to believe that she was safe.

When she pulled back, it still didn't feel like enough.

She stroked his hair off his brow. "I love you too," she said. "I told you about a hundred times when you were unconscious on the floor with your head in my lap. But in case you don't remember—" The low ferocious intent in her voice went directly to his heart. "I love you, Malcolm. I chose to be your wife *because* I know who you are. Not in spite of it."

He swallowed hard.

She did know him. She had always seen him clear—even from the first.

"I have made enough mistakes to fill an ocean," he said. "But I'm going to keep trying. I'm not going to fail you. I could be a week-dead corpse, Ruby-love, and I'd climb out of the ground to keep you safe."

"That," she said, "sounds horrifying."

Very slowly, like a tree toppling, he leaned against her. He pressed his forehead to hers, and then he laughed until tears came to his eyes.

He loved her. He loved her so much.

She held him, all sturdy patience, until he got hold of himself again. After a long moment, he pulled back to stroke her cheek. He couldn't see the precise color of her eyes in the dim interior, but it didn't matter. He knew it even in the dark.

"I'm getting you out of here," he said. "I'll claw the door down with my nails if I have to." His head still wanted to spin when he moved too quickly, but he tried to ignore that pertinent fact. "Do you, erm, know where we are?"

"Penney's wine cellar, I think."

"Jesus." He winced, a small movement which still somehow hurt like hell. "I don't understand why we're still alive. Why didn't Penney kill us when he had the chance?"

"Ah," his wife said primly. "Well." She looked up at him from under her lashes. "I lied."

"You—lied?"

"To Penney. I told him that my father knew precisely where we had gone, and if we did not reappear from Penney's house, my father would know exactly whom to blame." Her mouth tipped up. "It seems my father was useful for something after all."

"Ruby." He kissed her again—his brilliant, quick-thinking pirate queen. "Thank Christ for your brain."

She kissed him back, hard, then pulled away. "We're not precisely out of the sauce. Penney tossed us both down here and went, I presume, to make some alternative arrangement for our untimely demise. I was growing a trifle concerned, I must admit, that I would not be able to rouse you in time to escape."

"Right." He heaved himself to his feet, closing his eyes against the wave of dizziness. "Let's get out of here, pet, before the admiral realizes how clever you are."

She stood as well and dusted off her skirts. "As to that," she said, "if you're up to some exertion, Malcolm . . ." She bit her lip, considering, then met his gaze straight on. "I believe I have an idea."

Chapter 32

It was just past dawn when they got the door open. Ruby felt faint with relief and exhaustion together.

From the moment they had entered Penney's house, she'd noted its elaborate millwork. The decoration had reminded her of *The Polychromatic Ornament of Italy*, except more colorful and *far* more ostentatious: Penney, it appeared, had dreadful taste. The cornices did not match the architraves, and the faux Grecian plinths were far too large for the doors they framed.

Which meant, she'd realized, that the doors did not fit properly in their jambs. From deep inside the cellar's Stygian blackness, with Malcolm's head in her lap, it had dawned on her that there was a gap around the door fully large enough to put a crowbar in.

They didn't have a crowbar. They had, however, managed to pry two iron staves off a barrel of port, and that had been enough.

When they had the door forced open—fragments of cheap, ugly molding scattered across the floor—she put her hand to her husband's upper arm, holding him back before he plunged through. As her eyes adjusted to the light, she could make out the dried blood dotting his shirt, mingling with stains left by a minor flood of tawny port.

It occurred to her that she hated Jack Penney with every fiber of her being.

"Jesus," he growled as he looked down at her. He appeared to be having some revelations of his own. "Your face."

She put a hand to her cheek. "What's wrong?"

"You have a black eye, for Christ's sake. Your cheek is purple. I couldn't see it in the dark."

"I do?" She had not been treated delicately as she'd been thrown into the wine cellar behind Malcolm's unconscious body. She supposed her face *had* connected rather firmly with a shelf of wine bottles.

"I'm going to enjoy killing the admiral," he said. His voice sounded pleasant and terrifying.

"Ah." She blinked. "About that. Do we have . . . some sort of plan?"

"I don't need a plan." His teeth flashed, an expression more a snarl than a smile. His face was bruised black. "I have a very large piece of metal."

"Well," she said, "I'm sure that's an excellent beginning. Perhaps—"

She broke off abruptly as a crash resounded from deep inside the house. She froze, her hand still on his arm. In the distance, something shattered.

Her eyes flew up to lock with his.

"I suppose I can't convince you to stay here?" he rasped.

"Not by any means short of insensibility."

"All right," he muttered. "Get the other stave. And stay behind me."

She snatched up the stave and followed him in the direction of the clamor.

It seemed to be coming from the kitchen. Outside the door, he paused and put a finger to his lips for silence. She nodded, and then, cautiously, he eased open the door, stave at the ready.

Inside the kitchen, amid a tumbled array of crockery and flatware, Ruby beheld—

She blinked hard. Twice.

"Alice?" she said.

It *was* Alice. She looked beautiful and ferocious in an ebony frock, a carving knife in her hand. She brandished it threateningly in the direction of Penney's batman, who was bound hand and foot to a kitchen chair.

Alice's gaze flew toward them, then just as quickly darted back to the batman. "Good Lord!" she exclaimed. "They've found you already?"

"Alice," Ruby repeated incredulously. "What in heaven's name is going on?"

"Cap?"

Ruby and Archer spun away from Alice and toward the voice that had emerged from the corridor behind them.

It was Gerry—and Eugénie and the Enys boys.

And, in front of them, prodded forward by the barrel of a rifle, was Jack Penney.

"Cap!" Gerry said again. "Thank—Christ—" His voice cracked.

"Gerry—" Malcolm broke off, staring in stupefaction at his crew. "What the devil are you—"

Gerry's deep voice stuttered over the words. "He said—he said he'd *killed* you. He said—" Speechless, his words overcome by the depth of his emotions, Gerry jabbed Penney in the back with the rifle's barrel instead.

Ruby was so thunderstruck by the appearance of their crew that she almost did not see it happen. In one graceful motion, Penney spun, tore the rifle out of Gerry's hand, and lifted it to point at Archer.

Or at least, he would have lifted it. He was halfway through the motion when Archer stepped forward and slammed his fist into Penney's face.

Penney dropped like a stone. Archer yanked the rifle out of his grip, leaned down, and smashed it deliberately across Penney's windpipe.

"That," he said, very low, "is for my wife."

Penney didn't even struggle. He blinked once up at Archer, his face going purple and then, slowly, white. Archer held the rifle's barrel across the admiral's throat for a long, long moment, until Penney's supine body relaxed into unconsciousness.

And then he held it there awhile longer.

"Good heavens," Alice said finally from the kitchen. "Do you need a knife as well?"

Archer cleared his throat. His eyes found Ruby, lingered on her cheek, then shifted back to Alice. Carefully, he set the rifle and his stave beside Penney's limp figure. "Don't tempt me."

As if his words had lifted whatever force had kept them still, Gerry and Eugénie rushed into action. They hastily bound the admiral hand and foot and tossed him unceremoniously into the kitchen beside his batman.

And Ruby, seeing that her husband's hands were free, seized the opportunity to throw herself headlong in his direction.

He caught her. He wrapped his arms around her and held on.

His heart beat loud and steady beneath her ear. His shirt was dotted with bloodstains, and her cheek ached where she pressed against him, and she didn't care—only gripped him tighter.

"You didn't have to do that," she murmured.

"Pet," he said. He reached down to catch her chin, turning her face up to his battered one. "You've no idea what I would do for you."

He looked like he'd been three days in drink. His left eye had a starburst of blood in it, and they both smelled horribly of port, and her knuckles were raw, she realized, where her hand was fisted in his shirtfront.

It didn't matter. He was *safe*. Somehow, despite the admiral's very best efforts, Malcolm was here, in her arms, and he was all right.

She went up on her toes and kissed his mouth.

He kissed her back for an endless moment, until, belatedly, he seemed to remember their circumstances.

His arms still wrapped around her waist, he lifted his head and addressed his crew. "Eugénie," he said, "is there anyone else in this house who might be poised to sneak up on us with a weapon?"

"The house is safe," Eugénie said firmly. "There were a handful of servants, but they didn't seem particularly loyal—they all fled around the time Lady Alice started brandishing cutlery."

Alice blushed charmingly and waved the carving knife.

"Good," he said. "That's very good. And now if you'll forgive me for asking—what the devil are all of you doing here?"

It was Gerry who answered his captain—quiet, steadfast Gerry. "We waited. You two never came back out. Surely you didn't think we'd leave you here alone."

When Archer spoke, his voice was uneven. "No," he said hoarsely. "I never did."

Ruby was pondering whether she could use her port-soaked frock as a handkerchief when a polite knock sounded at Rear Admiral Lord Penney's back door.

She froze. Her eyes went to Archer. Who could it be, here at Penney's house at dawn? Could it possibly be Verdura?

Very slowly, with his eyes still resting on the unconscious admiral, Archer moved to answer the knock. His crew turned as one to guard his back; Ruby located her stave and held it carefully at the level of her chest.

But the stave, it turned out, was not required.

At the back door stood Cassandra, Signor Neri, and Lamentation. And in Lamentation's arms was a filthy, flower-dotted, snarling Zenobia.

With a bark of pure canine glee, Zenobia wriggled out of Lamentation's arms and hurled herself at Gerry.

Chapter 33

It was Alice, in the end, who found Tamsin and the princess.

When Signor Neri had broken from their crew, his clandestine tasks had included the hunt for one dreadful Italian greyhound. He had done it—he and Lamentation and half a dozen other Monfalcone representatives in London had scoured the city until they'd located Zenobia, barking furiously at the London Docks near where the *Delphinium* floated at anchor.

They had taken the dog to the ambassador, in search of Ruby and Archer—and, outside Ruby's former home, they'd come face-to-face with Cassandra instead.

It was Cass who'd brought them to Penney's town house. And it was Alice, cautiously petting Zenobia where she nestled in Gerry's arms, who had figured out where to go next.

Very slowly, Alice had lifted her hand from Zenobia's muddy coat. She'd gazed incredulously at her fingers and blinked two or three times in quick succession.

And then she'd looked up. She'd turned the force of her

immense cerulean eyes on Ruby and Archer and said, very deliberately: "Surrey."

"Surrey?" Ruby repeated.

"Yes," Alice said. "They're in Surrey. I know they are."

Ruby had stared at Alice in astonishment. And Cassandra had said instantly: "I'll bring the carriage round."

They piled hastily into the viscountess's barouche—excepting the Enys boys, who gleefully elected to remain with Penney and ensure his continued state of insensibility. Alice had, with some reluctance, relinquished her carving knife.

The moment they set off, Ruby leaned forward. "Alice," she demanded, "what do you mean, 'They're in Surrey'? How do you know?"

Alice looked somehow both modest and enormously pleased with herself. "Well," she said, "it was not so difficult to figure out. It was the eggs, you see."

Ruby wondered if she'd run mad. "The eggs?"

"The butterfly eggs," Alice clarified. "On Zenobia's coat. They were Camberwell Beauty eggs. I recognized them." She looked proudly around the carriage and then deflated slightly at their looks of befuddled consternation. "The Camberwell Beauty does not lay its eggs in England," she explained. "It's not native to our shores. They arrive sometimes on ships in the harbor, but they cannot lay in this climate except under very specific conditions."

They stared at her.

"Conditions," Alice said, "that have been re-created at the Aurelian Society's butterfly house in Surrey."

There was a general silence in the carriage.

Alice regarded them calmly. And then, very slowly, her mouth curled into a grin.

"You three," Gerry said fervently, "are the *best* ladies-in-waiting."

Ruby's heart was in her throat the whole of the carriage ride down to Surrey. It wasn't far from the docks where they'd found Zenobia—it seemed possible that a determined and vindictive little dog could have made the trip on her own.

They'd been in the carriage perhaps a quarter of an hour before Lamentation spoke. "Cap," he said, "I'm so sorry."

Archer shook his head. His arms were wrapped around Ruby, who'd been forced by virtue of the crowded coach to nestle in his lap. "There's nothing to apologize for. You were right about the admiral. All this time, you were right."

Regret carved itself in little lines around Lamentation's mouth. "I was right about the admiral," he acknowledged. "But—Cap—" He looked at Gerry beside him, and then back to Archer. "I was wrong about you."

"You weren't wrong." Archer's voice went rough, and his grip on Ruby's waist tightened. "I should never have lied to you. To any of you. I'm sorry, Lamentation."

Lamentation's throat bobbed as he swallowed. Gerry's arm had come to rest across his shoulders, and Lamentation's body fit against his beloved's as though he belonged there. "You shouldn't have lied," he agreed. "But Penney—and your wife—it's not the same. The two situations were never alike, and I shouldn't have pretended they were. It was only that I was angry, Cap, and hurt. And—scared, I think. Of losing you."

"I know," Archer said thickly. "I understand. But Lamentation, the fault—" His voice cracked. "The fault was in me, all this time. Not in you. Not ever."

Lamentation lifted his chin and looked his captain in the eyes. "I shouldn't have left," he said. "I should have had your back. I would follow you straight into Hell, Cap. You know I would."

"Oh God." Archer laughed—a hoarse torn-off breath, very like a sob. "I can't think what I've done to deserve that kind of faith."

Gerry made a deep wordless sound in his chest. His eyes said more of devotion and restraint than any speech Ruby had ever heard. "We know you'd bring us back out," he said. "You never let us go, Cap. That's what matters."

Ruby pressed her palm to Archer's knee, and he covered her hand with his own. She suspected he was on the verge of weeping. She wanted, if she could, to give him something to hold fast to.

There was, after that, a long stretch of quiet. And when they arrived at the Aurelian Society's Surrey estate, the first to make a sound was Zenobia.

The greyhound put her front paws to the barouche's window, barking furiously. As the vehicle rolled to a halt, Zenobia threw herself at the door, a wriggling dynamo that snarled and growled until the door came open and she sprang free.

When she was on the ground, she ran. Her small body made a gray blur against the leaf-littered ground.

The rest of them ran after her. They chased Zenobia past the main building, the conservatory, the orchid-strewn glasshouse where the butterflies were kept. They followed her down a slope and through a pasture and, finally, into a tumbledown dairy barn.

Zenobia's frantic barking had drawn out a petite black-haired woman. At the sight of Zenobia, the woman's lips parted. She stepped forward and opened her arms to the little dog.

Zenobia launched herself into the air.

Serafina Fiammetta Paxe Maria, Princess of Monfalcone, caught the dog to her chest. She went down on her knees.

And for the first time since she'd stepped foot on English shores, the princess buried her face in Zenobia's mud-covered flank and wept.

Within moments, they had all converged upon the dairy barn. Signor Neri, who appeared to have lost the power of speech, arrived first. He dabbed at the princess's face with his handkerchief and stroked Zenobia's enormous ears with outright abandon. His wig had fallen down over his left ear.

"Tam," Ruby said breathlessly. "Where's Tamsin?"

"Inside." The princess gestured to the stone dairy. "She's there—she's well—"

And indeed, when Ruby and Alice hurled themselves across the threshold, Tamsin was upright and waiting for them. Her face was pale, her copper hair streaked with dirt. She leaned heavily against the low stone wall, balanced precariously on one leg.

"Oh, thank Christ," she said when she saw Ruby and Alice. "One more day alone with the princess, and I'd have assassinated her myself."

The princess, who'd turned to watch the reunion, only looked smug. She held Zenobia against her chest. "I told you. Did I not predict this? Zenobia is a little heroine."

"Zenobia," Tamsin said, "is a hellhound."

What followed was a not inconsiderable clamor, particularly when the head of the Aurelian Society noticed Cassandra's carriage and came down to the dairy barn to investigate.

It took a very long time to die down.

Upon interrogation, Tamsin revealed that she and the princess had been hidden in the dairy barn for roughly forty-eight hours. After an abortive escape from Verdura's thugs halfway between Southampton and London, they had reunited with Zenobia on the road and then made their slow and painful way to a nearby farm. A day later, they'd escaped via hay wain and begun a meandering trek toward London. They had stopped at the dairy barn for a night's rest when Zenobia had suddenly vanished without a trace.

"Her Highness insisted on remaining," Tamsin explained through white lips. The head of the Aurelian Society, a natural philosopher by training, was applying a splint to her ankle, and Tamsin's face had taken on a greenish cast.

"For Zenobia," the princess explained. "I paused merely to await her return. *Not* because you travel so poorly and require so very much assistance."

"I have," Tamsin growled, "a *broken leg.*"

The head of the Aurelian Society patted her freckled knee. "Ankle, my duck. But it's healing very well."

Signor Neri stepped forward. He had restored his wig, though he still looked rather overset. "Captain Archer," he said formally, "the royal family thanks you for your service. House di Sangro will not forget the aid you have rendered its eldest daughter."

Archer blinked. He looked at Neri, and then at Ruby and Alice and Tamsin and Lamentation. "To be honest," he said, "I'm not certain I did anything."

From her place atop the dairy's low stone wall, which she'd perched upon as though it were a throne, Princess Serafina gestured for Neri to attend her. They bent their heads together, whispering in hasty Italian, for several minutes. Ruby could make out only a handful of words—*Verdura* and *alive* and *escape.*

No one, as far as she had been able to work out, had any idea where Verdura had fled to. He was still alive. Still, Ruby feared, a threat to the princess.

His attempts on my life grow increasingly bold, Serafina had told them. *This was not his first attack.*

And perhaps not the last either.

Finally, the conversation between Neri and the princess seemed to come to some conclusion. Serafina had a sour expression on her face, and she flung her hand out in a sweeping arc. "Give it to him," she said in English.

Neri nodded. He turned to Archer and began to unfasten his satin waistcoat.

"Sorry," Archer said. "Give me what?"

A frown line had appeared between the princess's winged black brows. "When he arrived in London, Neri went to his residence to retrieve a large fortune in gold coins, in the event a ransom was required to secure my freedom." She glanced briefly at Tamsin and then back to Archer. "Thanks to you and your companions, such a stratagem was not required."

"Ah," Archer said. "Right. What?"

"I intend to give it to you," the princess said. "And in return, you will hunt down Verdura."

Archer made a choking sound.

"I would like to hire you," she clarified, "as my personal pirate."

Archer's mouth opened, then closed again. He blinked and seemed to sway slightly on his feet. It occurred to Ruby that they had not slept in some days.

Finally, he managed to summon words.

"No," he said. "Thank you."

Lamentation gave a deflated sort of sigh. Princess Serafina opened her mouth to argue.

"Not that I'm not honored by your offer," Archer said hastily. "In fact, I know someone with a small armada who'll be your privateer with pleasure."

The princess gave him a peevish look. "I presume you want only the ransom, then?"

Archer laughed, a warm breath that ruffled Ruby's hair. He slung an arm across her shoulders; his hand spread warm at the base of her throat. "I'm probably going to regret saying this, but—no. Keep your gold. What I'd like . . . What I truly wish for . . ."

He paused. He looked down at Ruby. His eyes were sun-streaked blue. His dimples made tiny joyful arcs beneath the blood and bruises on his face.

And then he looked back up at the princess. "What I'd truly like, Your Highness," he said, "is a job."

Epilogue

ONE YEAR LATER

Sidney Enys was panting slightly when he burst through the door to the Pomeroy House library.

"Mail!" he gasped. "Here's your mail. All of it. Just delivered."

The beetle Alice had been sketching toppled off the end of his stick and landed upside down, legs waving in mild dismay. She righted him, placed him carefully in his nest of leaves, and then looked up to where Tamsin had already risen from the sofa to greet Sidney.

"I'll take the letters," Tamsin said.

Sidney didn't seem to hear her. He crossed to Alice's desk, blanched at the sight of the large iridescent green beetle, and then deposited the letters as far from Alice's glass enclosure as possible. "Here you go, Lady Alice."

"Thank you, Sidney," she said. "You don't have to come all the way up to the house, you know. We can retrieve our correspondence in the village."

"I know," he said enthusiastically. "I don't mind, though."

"Well." She smiled at him. "Thank you, then."

He blushed scarlet, then stood motionless for several long moments until Tamsin cleared her throat. He jumped, spun back toward the door, and departed with a final parting wave over his shoulder to Alice.

"Dearest," Tamsin said as she crossed to retrieve the letters from Alice, "that boy is one extended glance away from dropping to his knees and proposing."

"Tam! He's only fifteen."

"I believe he's asked Eugénie to forge his birth records on the off chance you'll have him."

Alice laughed, though her heart wasn't in it. She'd finished flipping hastily through the letters and had set them back down unopened.

"No reply?" Tam asked gently.

Alice bit her lip and shook her head, then reached down and ruffled Vanessa's velvety ears.

Alice had once been the first female member of the Aurelian Society. But as a woman, her place in the group had always been tenuous; after her father's disgrace, she'd been cast out.

When they'd visited the Aurelian Society's estate in Surrey, she'd spoken to Professor Joyce about her possible readmission, now that the scandal around her father had mostly died down. He'd told her he'd bring the matter before the society's leadership, and she—perhaps foolishly—had nursed a small and futile hope that she might be one of them again.

She'd written to Professor Joyce three times in the last year. He'd yet to respond.

Tamsin picked up the letters and frowned down at them.

"Fools," she muttered. "I hate them, Alice. Start your own bloody bug association."

She gave Tamsin a grateful smile, then picked up her beetle and delicately placed him back on his twig. She thought this one was a male—as a general rule, the male musk beetle grew longer antennae than did the female—though she had not yet witnessed the creature's mating posture to be certain.

Tam settled herself back down and began to sort through the correspondence. Vanessa jumped up beside her—she was almost the size of the entire sofa now—and placed her black head in Tamsin's lap.

After Captain Archer had told Princess Serafina the truth of his and his crew's circumstances, the princess had agreed to hire Archer, Wall, Eugénie, Gerry, and Lamentation in a permanent capacity. They had no need to smuggle any longer, a fact that seemed to both relieve and alarm Captain Archer. He'd been forced to devise increasingly onerous household tasks for Lamentation in particular, lest the young man grow bored and invent more fictional sea monsters.

Alice and Tamsin had found themselves somewhat at loose ends. The princess had been rather pleased and amused by the prospect of maintaining a trio of court ladies in Cornwall, but the notion had been deferred when she'd returned to Monfalcone shortly after her testimony at Jack Penney's court-martial.

Her departure had left Tamsin gloomy and irritable for weeks—a fact that Tamsin would have denied vigorously had Alice been imprudent enough to point it out.

They'd spent some time visiting Tamsin's Aunt Frankie at her estate, and then, to their mutual satisfaction, they'd received word from Ruby that their presence was once more required at Pomeroy House.

Ruby, it seemed, had concocted a new scheme—and she needed their help. At her request, Captain Archer had put her into contact with the Dorset sculptor who'd produced Gravesmuir's fake marbles. Ruby had enthusiastically taught the woman a far better technique for mimicking aging on the sculptures' stone surface.

And then Ruby had had the notion of selling them.

"Not as the real thing," she'd explained, looking earnestly at Alice and Tamsin as she outlined her proposition. "As replicas. As *excellent* replicas. They're all the rage, you know. You recall Penney's house. The more decoration the better, some seem to think."

"I should like to point out," Tamsin had said, "that I do not, in fact, recall Penney's house. Because I was trapped in a hayrick with an Italian hell-demon."

Alice had patted her ankle. "We were very worried about you, though."

"Yes, I'm sure. So worried that you planned an entire *wedding* in my absence."

"I would not say 'planned,'" Ruby had protested, and Tam had laughed.

Over the next several months, Ruby, Alice, and Tamsin had crafted a strategy to anonymously transact the sale of the replicas. They'd filled an auction house on Bond Street with the statues, put notices in every paper, and then arranged for Ruby's sister—and a number of Monfalcone loyalists hand-selected by Signor Neri—to buy the marbles in a frenzy of heated bidding.

Within a handful of weeks, the replicas were all the rage in Mayfair. The Earl of Hangleton, who had no notion of his elder daughter's involvement in the scheme, had bought almost two dozen.

Now Ruby managed the replica production. Tamsin arranged the logistical details with their London man of business. And Alice . . .

Well. Once, she would have endorsed the fashionable statues in every ballroom in London, but that time had long since passed. She tried very hard not to miss it.

The musk beetle, who'd once again reached the end of his twig, plummeted off for a second time.

Male, Alice thought. *Most assuredly.*

Tamsin's voice broke into Alice's entomological reverie. "This is an interesting letter."

Alice rescued the beetle again, then looked across the desk at Tamsin. "What does it say?"

Tamsin was gazing down at the ink-covered sheet, her left hand absently stroking Vanessa's ear. "It's from a group of painters. The Baring Brotherhood of Naturists. It says they've received a special dispensation from Princess Serafina to spend the summer here at Pomeroy House. It says they are 'in search of pacific vistas of rural splendor to instantiate a Platonic union of reason and soul.'"

Alice pondered the current state of Pomeroy House, which was home to eight dogs, seventy-nine captive beetles, and approximately five hundred faux Greek sculptures in various stages of completion. "I would not describe the conditions as pacific, exactly."

"I fear they're in for something of a shock when they arrive in"—Tamsin squinted at the narrow handwriting—"about forty-four hours, apparently. Have you ever heard of the Baring Brotherhood of Naturists?"

"I can't say that I have." She gazed at Tamsin. "Are you . . . entirely certain they're painters?"

Tamsin's brows drew together. "It does sound rather . . ." She glanced back down at the letter. "Perhaps I've misread."

"Maybe Ruby will have heard of them."

Tamsin folded the sheet of paper and attempted to find somewhere on the sofa to place it that wasn't occupied by Vanessa. "Let us hope. Have you seen Ruby this afternoon?"

Alice considered Ruby: her oldest, dearest friend, so radiantly happy these days that Alice's heart squeezed to think of her.

"I believe," she said, "that Captain and Mrs. Archer are spending the afternoon in their cove."

There was sand all over them: their entangled legs, their arms, their clothes. Somehow, there was a smear of the stuff directly across Ruby's cheek, and Archer pondered whether there was any chance he could brush it away without leaving an even larger trail in its wake.

No, he decided. *Not a chance.*

He wrapped his arms around her waist instead and pulled her even closer, rubbing his chin against the top of her head. He breathed her in: amber and cedar, brandied fruit and a fortune of gold.

"This," she murmured, "is my favorite place."

He grinned. "This cove?"

The view *was* superlative—the sun was setting, and the sea was the exact blue-gray of Ruby's eyes. From here, he could just see the harbor at St. Petroc's; if he squinted, he thought perhaps he could make out the *Delphinium*.

It was a miracle beyond anything he could ever have dreamed of: to travel to London together in his ship, Ruby's replicas lovingly crated on the decks and Gerry and Lamentation manning the sails.

He had told Princess Serafina the truth about himself and his crew right there in Surrey. It had been difficult, that raw vulnerability. It went against the habit of a lifetime to put himself—his people—in someone else's power.

But it had been the right thing to do. And with Ruby at his side, nothing felt impossible. Not anymore.

The princess had taken in his revelations with a slow, cool nod. And when Archer had ended by asking for posts at Pomeroy House for all five of them, the princess had granted his request with a wave of her small hand.

Signor Neri had followed later with the paperwork.

The princess had been considerably more pleased by Gill Oliphant's mercenary enthusiasm as her personal pirate. As promised, House di Sangro had given Oliphant a minor fortune to hunt down Verdura, though Oliphant had not thus far proven successful. The duke, it seemed, was devilishly slippery, on top of being a murderous, grasping coward. Archer suspected that Oliphant might have a very long future ahead of him as a Monfalcone privateer.

And while Archer had not taken any of the princess's ransom money, he had willingly accepted a go-between fee from Oliphant, in exchange for putting Oliphant up for the job.

Archer's choice of payment had been the return of his own *Delphinium.*

The notion had been Ruby's. His wife, he thought smugly, had considerable promise as a pirate queen.

"Not the cove," she said. She leaned up and planted a kiss along his throat, then made a little humming noise as she rubbed her nose against his unshaven jaw. "Though I like that too. But no, I meant"—she wriggled in demonstration—"here. In your embrace."

"Keep squirming like that," he muttered, "and you'll be in for something else."

She grinned, and his heart leapt. It always did when she smiled at him like that. "Heavens," she murmured. "Threats from the captain. Shall I be forced to walk the plank?"

"Bound to the mainmast, more like."

"Goodness. Immobilized by a column of erected wood." Her cheeks were pink with sunset, and her mouth was all mischief. "You sailors are positively depraved."

He rolled her over in one swift move, and she laughed and pushed her fingers into his hair.

He kissed her hard and thoroughly, though it was difficult—no matter how much he wanted her—to make himself stop smiling.

When he finally came up for air, Ruby's face was a trifle more flushed than it had been. Her breath came quickly, and her skirts were rucked up high enough that he had a hand on her bare thigh.

She was so delicious—so warm and edible and *pretty*, all painted with sunset oranges and lavenders—that he lost his breath for a moment looking at her.

There was something about the sight of her here in the cove that never failed to make his blood run hot. It had been in the cove that he'd told her he'd got the *Delphinium* back—and here too that she'd broken the news that her replicas had been featured in the *Royal Archaeological Journal* for their exceptional attention to historical detail.

He kept the memory of Ruby's expression that day like an engraving in his heart: all stunned gratification and slow-blossoming smile. He thought of it whenever they were parted and resolved to make her smile like that again—always—for the rest of his life.

He was startled from his daydream by Ruby's squeak of alarm.

"What?" he demanded. "What is it?"

He rolled off Ruby, ready to throw himself to his feet at any indication of the missing Verdura or marauding seals. When he landed, however, he was promptly made aware of what had caused Ruby's surprise as his arse met half an inch of frigid ocean water.

"I believe," Ruby said, rather primly for someone whose skirts were soaked and sandy, "that the tide is coming in."

"Do you know," he said, "I think you might be right."

She was laughing again as he pulled her up to standing, as he dragged her deep into the shadows of the cove where he'd once stripped off her gloves and kissed her senseless.

He did it again. He kissed her until she was breathless, until the sun dipped below the horizon and the water splashed around their ankles.

"We should go back," she murmured against his lips. "A few more minutes and we'll be cut off from the house."

He wrapped his arms tight around her. His heart was full of her too—overflowing with sweet, raw tenderness. She was the ocean and the tides, the moon and all the comets.

There was, in the end, one star that bound him fast—that held him steady at the wheel.

His Ruby. His true north.

"Good," he said. "Let the tide come. Everything I want is here."

Author's Note

This is the part where I tell you that many of my wild flights of fancy in this book are inspired by historical reality. And so I am pleased to report that the autonomous principality of Monfalcone is . . .

Not even a little bit real. Sorry! I firmly believe that everyone should get a princess-from-a-fictional-principality story at some point in their lives, and this one's mine. Monfalcone and its royal family were inspired by Laura Kinsale's Monteverde and Meg Cabot's Genovia, among others—as well as the stories I heard growing up from the original Nonna Vasti, who was born in Italy and lived there until she was in her twenties.

The Duca di Verdura is also not real—and yes, as you no doubt noticed at the end of the book, he remains at large in 1818. Will he get his just deserts? Or is someone else behind the plot to eliminate our terrible princess? Only time (and the next two books in the series) will tell.

Pomeroy House is very loosely based on St. Michael's Mount

(in Cornish, Karrek Loos yn Koos), a tidal island featuring a castle perched atop a cliff, accessible by footpath only when the tide is low. Happily, the castle on St. Michael's Mount is in much better repair than Pomeroy House.

I chose the post–Napoleonic Wars setting for this series in part because it was a period known for its superior smuggling. While earlier eras were characterized by violence, smugglers after 1815 were famous for their craftiness and ingenuity as they invented new ways to sneakily transport their goods. In *The Three Cutters* (1836), Frederick Marryat explains: "Smugglers do not arm now—the service is too dangerous; they effect their purpose by cunning, not by force."

It's also worth noting that smuggling was a major industry in the seventeenth, eighteenth, and early nineteenth centuries due to actions taken by powerful aristocrats in the British government. Though many urban and rural populations suffered from extreme privation, the government imposed increasingly punitive tariffs on imported goods. These tariffs, like the Corn Laws that Alice mentions, artificially inflated prices on both necessary and luxury items. The rich got richer, smugglers got increasingly creative, and immense popular criticism eventually led to the tariffs' repeal in the middle of the nineteenth century.

Ruby and Archer repeatedly mention the Elgin Marbles, an extraordinarily hot topic of debate in the Regency. Between 1801 and 1812, Thomas Bruce, 7th Earl of Elgin and ambassador to the Ottoman Empire, removed numerous sculptures from Greece and had them shipped to England, including half the sculptures on the Parthenon itself. He then promptly sold these sculptures to the British government. This act was enormously controversial at the time, and though Elgin claimed he had acquired the statues legally, many local reports contradicted his assertions. Lord Byron bitterly opposed Elgin's actions and wrote repeatedly in protest of Elgin's "plunder." (And yes: Ruby's dad, earl and ambassador, is very loosely based on Elgin.) Contemporary readers should note that though Greece has requested the return of the statues for decades, the British government still refuses to let them go. (I am hopeful that someday this note will be out of date!)

At the beginning of the novel, Ruby festoons her favorite book, Thomas Hope's *Household Furniture and Interior Decoration*, with colorful foodstuffs. (In my head, she has several copies of this book—the food-painted one is going to be weird after a few days.) I chose this book for Ruby's first, small defiance because Thomas Hope was such a fascinating and complicated figure. The first to coin the term *interior design*, Hope was also an enormously wealthy banker who patronized numerous artists. One of my favorite Hope facts is that every bedroom in his house was outfitted with a personal, multilingual library for each of his guests.

In 1810, Hope fell in love with a sexy Greek sailor named Aide and, to the horror of his entire family, promptly and unsuccessfully attempted to launch the young man into British high society.

You can see why Ruby likes him so much.

Acknowledgments

First: Thank you to *you*, for joining me on this rollicking Cornish romp, which marks the start of a brand-new series! Whether this is your first adventure with me or you've been in the Vasti-verse since the beginning, I'm so grateful you're here.

Immense thanks, again and always, to my wonderful agent, Jessica Alvarez, as well as my fantastic editor, Christina Lopez. Can't wait to keep making more books together!

Thank you to my darling angels Kejana Ayala and Angela Tabor, who are the BEST team, as well as everyone else at St. Martin's Griffin who had a hand in making this book, including Joy Gannon, Melanie Sanders, Chrisinda Lynch, Olga Grlic, and Laura Jorstad.

Thank you to Meghan Deist for the cover of my dreams—you had no idea you'd just met your biggest fan that one time you came to book club and I told you that you were really good at coloring!

Speaking of book club: My infinite gratitude to Blue Cypress Books, my second home, my favorite place in the world. I love you, Jodi and LeeAnna and Elizabeth and Percy and Georgia and Mattie and Rayna (and if anyone else gets hired between when I wrote these acknowledgments and when this book comes out, I'm sure I love you too). Thank you to all the wonderful booksellers who've supported my career with such joy and generosity, especially Rachel at Tropes & Trifles; Lucy at Blinking Owl; Becca at Meet Cute; Jonlyn at A Novel Romance; Katie at Dog-Eared; Angela, Jackie, Isabella, Valentina, Mandy, Charlotte, Sami, and so many more!

Thank you to the many authors who have so generously given their time in writing blurbs and doing events and chatting and hanging out and generally being the best. Big, giant hugs to Laura Piper Lee, Naina Kumar, Ellie Palmer, Jill Tew, and Danica Nava. My endless devotion to Colleen Kelly and Raisa Rexer and Kathryn VanArendonk. Huge thanks to my brilliant and thoughtful critique partners Jane Maguire, Bella Barnes, Leigh Donnelly, Kate Lane, and Marianne Marston. Thank you, Felicity Niven, my darling friend. Thank you to Ali Hazelwood for the Italian in the book! (Prepare yourself: There are two more coming.)

To Matt and the little Vastis, my forever heroes and heroines— thanks for coming to Cornwall with me in real life!! I promise we can go back soon.

About the Author

Alexandra Vasti is a British literature professor by day and *USA Today* bestselling romance writer by night. After finishing her PhD at Columbia University, she moved to New Orleans with her family. Her books have received starred reviews from *Library Journal*, *Kirkus Reviews*, *Booklist*, *BookPage*, and *Publishers Weekly* and have been featured in *The New York Times*, NPR, *Entertainment Weekly*, *People*, and elsewhere.

Need more Regency romance?

'A captivating Regency romance'
Buzz on *Earl Crush*

'Steamy and witty'
Red on *Ne'er Duke Well*

Available in paperback and e-book

"What a joy! Cat and Georgiana's tale makes for an absolute treat of a book: full of banter, yearning, combustible chemistry, and a healthy amount of gothic spookiness and murder. A near-perfect addition to the sapphic hist-rom genre."

—Freya Marske, *USA Today* bestselling author of *Swordcrossed*

"*Ladies in Hating* is the gay gothic rom-com of my dreams, suffused with Vasti's usual, sincere affection: for her characters, and for her readers."

—Alix E. Harrow, *New York Times* bestselling author of *The Everlasting*

EARL CRUSH

"*Bridgerton* at its sexiest . . . *Crush*? Ha. I'm in love with the earl!"

—Eloisa James, *New York Times* bestselling author of *Viscount in Love*

"Wildly delightful! With *Earl Crush*, Alexandra Vasti has crafted a marvelously funny and sexy read featuring a brawny Scottish earl, zebras, and a feminist heroine ahead of her time. This belongs on every romance reader's keeper shelf!"

—Joanna Shupe, *USA Today* bestselling author of *The Duke Gets Even*

"Sexy, kind, and full of adventure . . . Alexandra Vasti is an immense talent, and I look forward to reading everything she writes until the end of time!"

—Naina Kumar, *USA Today* bestselling author of *Say You'll Be My Jaan*

"With her deft hand for writing witty banter, endearing characters, and smoking-hot chemistry, Alexandra Vasti's *Earl Crush* will enchant readers and establish her as a breakout star of historical romance!"

—Liana De la Rosa, USA Today bestselling author
of Isabel and the Rogue

"This historical spy caper has plenty of sexy fun and terrific banter, all in a fast-moving plot."

—Booklist (starred review)

NE'ER DUKE WELL

"All hail a new (and most welcome) voice in the historical romance space . . . Vasti writes with a warm, whimsical voice, underscoring her hysterical interludes and cutting asides with a deep well of emotions."

—Entertainment Weekly

"A gem of a Regency, with dazzling banter and more than the usual amount of charm."

—Olivia Waite, The New York Times Book Review

"The kind of romance you want to wrap around yourself like a blanket."

—NPR

"As hot as it is heartfelt, this will have historical romance fans hooked."

—Publishers Weekly (starred review)

"*Ne'er Duke Well* is a delightful, quicksilver romp with unforgettable characters that readers will be rooting for from start to finish."

—Deanna Raybourn, *New York Times* bestselling author of the Veronica Speedwell series

"An irresistible delight from a remarkable new talent . . . Vasti has quickly earned her place on my list of favorite writers."

—India Holton, *USA Today* bestselling author of *The Ornithologist's Field Guide to Love*

THE HALIFAX HELLIONS SERIES

"This sexy Regency with dual narration and endearing characters will make Vasti fans swoon and thrill readers of historical romances with prominent feminist overtones."

—*Library Journal* (starred review)

"These stories are hot, smart, funny, and charming as hell—much like the Hellions themselves. I've read them each twice."

—Alix E. Harrow, *New York Times* bestselling author of *The Everlasting*

"Delightful, truly scrumptious—like if Lisa Kleypas and Tessa Dare had a sexy baby. Alexandra Vasti is my favorite writer, full stop."

—Mazey Eddings, *USA Today* bestselling author of *Late Bloomer*

"I'm forever in awe of Alexandra Vasti's talent."

—Sarah Adler, *USA Today* bestselling author of *Happy Medium*